THE
SLOWEST
BURN

THE
SLOWEST
BURN

a novel

SARAH CHAMBERLAIN

ST. MARTIN'S GRIFFIN
NEW YORK

First published in the United States by St. Martin's Griffin, an imprint of
St. Martin's Publishing Group

THE SLOWEST BURN. Copyright © 2024 by Sarah Chamberlain. All rights reserved.
Printed in the United States of America. For information, address St. Martin's
Publishing Group, 120 Broadway, New York, NY 10271.

www.stmartins.com

The Library of Congress Cataloging-in-Publication Data is available upon request.

ISBN 978-1-250-89472-4 (trade paperback)
ISBN 978-1-250-89473-1 (ebook)

Our books may be purchased in bulk for promotional, educational, or business
use. Please contact your local bookseller or the Macmillan Corporate and
Premium Sales Department at 1-800-221-7945, extension 5442, or by email at
MacmillanSpecialMarkets@macmillan.com.

First Edition: 2024

10 9 8 7 6 5 4 3 2 1

For Craig,
who taught me so much about cooking,
found family, and unconditional love,

and

for Tom,
my favorite person to cook for

Cooking, and the people who love you: the two greatest and most practical miracles of all.

—Ella Risbridger, *The Year of Miracles*

THE
SLOWEST
BURN

CHAPTER ONE

Ellie

"This is all a celebrity chef needs to get a cookbook deal? A two-line email from his agent and a ridiculous nickname?" I waved the offending printout at my best friend, unable to keep the exasperation out of my voice.

Nicole stretched elegantly in the conference room chair, like a cat soaking up the weak January sun. "Tobias Paul represents anyone who's anyone in food, and the Happy Pirate Leprechaun is a great nickname."

"For the mascot on a box of marshmallow cereal," I grumbled. "Happy New Year to me."

Most days, ghostwriting cookbooks was my dream job. Publishers paid me both to cook and write, which would be my hobbies anyway. In addition to capturing my subject's voice like every ghostwriter had to, I was also a translator, taking the huge quantities and multiple subrecipes of restaurant dishes and turning them into straightforward instructions an ordinary person could follow in their home kitchen. But I was a guide, too, a companion, helping chefs and home cooks connect to each other so everyone could eat delicious food.

To ghostwrite a cookbook successfully, I had to be rock solid: methodical, precise, great at managing money and time, and, above all, patient with people's foibles. But the lack of information on this project left me feeling like I was balancing on an office chair, the wheels on the verge of going out from under me.

It didn't help that Kieran O'Neill was late.

The local chef's victory on the reality TV show *Fire on High* had triggered a six-way bidding war to publish his first cookbook. Alchemy Press's editor Tad Winthrop had won the auction by promising him a ridiculous amount of money and the services of his most diligent ghostwriter. I would write recipes and stories in Kieran's voice, and Nicole would shoot the accompanying pictures. Today, we were all meeting for the first time to discuss our plans for the next several months of work.

I read the email aloud, hoping that more words would magically appear. "'Kieran O'Neill wants to write a cookbook about having fun in the kitchen. Call me.' Having fun? Great, thanks, that tells me everything I need to know."

Nicole checked the ends of her long black hair. "*Fire on High* is the competition show of the decade. I know you only watch historical British people falling in constipated love, but even you've absorbed that by osmosis."

I shook my head. "Not just osmosis. I did watch the whole season, also known as fifteen hours of my life I could have spent learning to knit or finally reading *A Suitable Boy*." Or if we were being honest, five historical romance novels.

She dropped the strands. "How could you not like it? Like *him*? He goes on a *journey*." She waved her hands. "Underdog made good! Figuring out his voice!"

I folded my arms and sighed. "Your jazz hands are super cute, but you know I only watched it because I had to. I'm not trying to yuck anybody's yum. It's just not for me."

I went to the floor-to-ceiling window, soaking in the peacefulness of the view. The Golden Gate Bridge was an elegant red line in the distance, and Marin's hills rolled out like deep emerald velvet in the early afternoon light.

Nicole leaned on the glass next to me, but she wasn't looking at the view.

"I know you believe it's not what cooking *is*," she said, the humor turned to concern. "That it shouldn't be about showing off and gimmicks. It should be about caring for people and making them happy. But a lot of people like the performance. The *Banquet* YouTube channel wouldn't have billions of hits if they didn't."

"But it's so *fake*."

"OK, fine, you're never going to watch goofy cooking videos with me. So did you just watch the show through your fingers? Or do you actually know what his deal is?"

I rested my hand on my chest, fake-offended. "How dare you doubt my search engine prowess? I know his full name is Kieran Michael O'Neill, and he's twenty-seven. He was born on December eighteenth."

Nicole smiled. "Of course, he's such a classic Sagittarius."

My eyes rolled to the ceiling. "Yes, if you think an individual's entire personality is determined by where the stars are in the sky at a random date and time."

"Spoken like a true Virgo," she tutted.

"*Anyway*. He's from Ojai in Ventura County, graduated from Nordhoff High School and then from Santa Barbara City College with a Culinary Arts certificate. He worked at the Pacific Hotel in Montecito for two years, then Steve Yuan brought him to Qui in San Francisco. He went from intern to sous in under four years."

"How did he get his nickname?"

"Pirate because of the black bandanna he wears. Leprechaun because he clicked his heels at one of the judging panels and became a meme. Also because he's short and redheaded." Not that he could help either of those things.

"Favorite ingredient?"

Which he'd been asked in every interview. "Citrus. He likes how it 'wakes up food.'"

Nicole threw up her hands. "OK, you know a bunch of facts. But you don't know what he's *like*."

"I guess I'll figure that out once I meet him. If he ever gets here."

She growled. "I don't get it. This project is so not your bag.

Why did you say yes this time? Before you give me a ridiculously complicated answer, I need sustenance." She turned around and plucked one of the wan supermarket croissants from the plastic tray in the middle of the table, leaving a greasy silhouette behind. "Want one?"

I shook my head. "Sad pastry."

"Sad pastry is better than no pastry."

I eyed the drooping croissant in her hand. "I beg to differ."

"So picky."

"I prefer 'discerning.' One, I said yes because Tad asked me especially. He said he needed his most reliable person." I prided myself on never making promises I couldn't keep and on always delivering with a smile.

"The world won't end if you say no to him occasionally," she said with the tiredness of having had this conversation many times before. "You don't always have to be available."

I ignored the niggling edge of her comment. Being available wasn't an issue when I didn't have anywhere else to be. "I owe him for being so good about Max."

She softened a little. "You owed him two and a half years ago. And it wasn't like you were behind on the La Estufa cookbook for no reason. Your husband *died*. And you've been amazing since then. You're beyond even."

"Maybe." Tad had told me to take all the time I needed, no questions asked. He'd sent ready-made food to stock my freezer and a book of Auden poems he loved, and checked in with me every week until I was ready to work.

"Not maybe, but whatever. So I know what Tad wants. But what do *you* want, Ellie?"

I watched a little boat scoot toward the Emeryville Marina, silently cheering for it to make it home.

I knew what I wanted.

Certainty.

After spending a decade holding everything together for my

younger brother while our dad was nowhere and our mom may as well have been, Max and the Wasserman family had been the safest of harbors. I learned that when I visited them, his father Ben would always kiss both my cheeks with a smack, then pour me a beer and ask what I'd thought of the latest Warriors basketball game. That his mother Diane would pull me into the kitchen to taste a sauce and debate whether it needed more salt or lemon, then press her new favorite novel into my hands.

After Max and I got married and he'd been hired at UC Davis, I'd known that every time he came home from a long day teaching Flaubert and Balzac in French to undergraduates, he'd tell me how much he loved seeing my smile. That he would bring me red roses every Wednesday. That every Friday afternoon we'd drive back to Berkeley for Shabbos dinner.

I'd known too that once he'd won tenure, we'd buy one of the old-fashioned clapboard houses near the university, and we'd have a baby. A sweet baby with Max's dark eyes, who'd grow up in a home full of love and warmth. Who'd know in their bones they were wanted.

All of those certainties dissolved in a late-night phone call from Paris two and a half years ago. No more Max, no more home, no more sweet, dark-eyed baby.

"Seriously, though. Why not go out with someone who's, like, Max's opposite?" Nicole asked through the haze of memory.

I blinked awake. "Why on earth would I do that? He'd drive me up the wall."

"I know Max decided you were his soul mate on day one, but for most people the first date is supposed to be *fun*. Why not go out with someone just for fun?" She pointed to the printout. "Are you against fun?"

"Oh, for Pete's sake, I am *not* against fun!"

Two male voices got louder and louder outside, and Nicole tapped my arm. "Then prove it. Here he comes."

Before he walked into the room, I'd thought I'd known what

Kieran O'Neill looked like. But Nicole was right—there were facts, and there was experience.

On-screen, he was handsome in a fey kind of way, pale-skinned and wiry and high-cheekboned. But in person, with his wide mouth smiling and his eyes crinkled in laughter? He was mischievous Puck from *A Midsummer Night's Dream*, with hair like an autumn bonfire hanging down to his jaw and silvery green eyes. All he needed was a crown of leaves, and to be bare chested instead of wearing a holey old band T-shirt. Its neckline had split away, his jeans had rips to match, and his Chuck Taylors were so old that the black canvas had faded to dark brown.

Maybe you weren't supposed to notice the scruffiness once you saw his face, but his face wasn't going to help me buy the home I'd always wanted.

"Let me introduce you all," Tad said, like we were at a cocktail party and not in a room that smelled like lunchtime pizza. "Kieran, this is Nicole Salazar, who'll be shooting your book."

Kieran grinned. "Nice to meet you, Nicole. Steve told me all about you."

She chuckled. "I'm surprised. Your boss still owes me twenty bucks from when I beat him at Ping-Pong."

He flailed his arms in pretend shock. "But no one's *ever* beaten him."

She blew on her fingernails. "I'm just that good."

I just barely repressed my eye roll at their banter.

Tad finally turned to me. "And this is Ellie Wasserman, your ghostwriter."

When we shook hands, his was rough in the right places for someone who'd worked with knives and fire for a long time. His grip was strong, too. Though I didn't know why chefs insisted on having knives tattooed on their arms. It wasn't like they were going to forget what they did for a living.

"Pleased to meet you, Kieran," I said. His skin was warm, and when he smiled back at me with all his teeth, it stretched the tiny scar below his lower lip. I blinked a few times, but that delicate little line still pulled my attention.

"The mysterious Ellie Wasserman," his lips said, smiling wide. "But I guess that's a ghostwriter's job, to be all spooky."

He waved his fingers in the universal sign for "spooky," and my distraction went up in smoke. Just what I needed, someone who didn't take my job seriously. I narrowed my eyes at him, and his big smile shrank.

"Let's get started," Tad said, turning to the table.

Once we'd sat down, I laid out my planner and my notebook, lining up my black Pilot pen next to them. Nicole pulled out her reporter's notepad and opened a new voice memo on her phone.

Across from me, Kieran took out nothing and jammed his hands into his armpits.

His eyes darted around the room, over my shoulder, looking anywhere but at Tad, who was describing the publishing process. Finally, Kieran picked up one of the cheap Alchemy ballpoint pens. Maybe he'd write something on his hand? No, he just clicked the pen open and shut. Open and shut. Open and shut, open and . . .

Pop!

The pen exploded, and a spring shot across the table and landed on my notebook. Tad stopped speaking. I carefully pinched the spring between my thumb and index finger and put it to the side.

"Shall I carry on?" Tad asked.

Kieran said, "Of course, my bad."

He smiled and mouthed *Sorry*, at me. I shook my head. It was obvious why I was getting double my fee. I'd have to earn it.

Kieran

Cookie, I thought when I looked at Ellie.

Not that I wanted to eat her. I wasn't a cannibal or anything.

But she reminded me of the cookies my mother baked when her bridge group came to our house. The smell of them in the oven was all rich vanilla and spice, oh-so-sweet.

Ellie was a little shorter than me, with endless curves that swooped and dipped, creamy skin sprinkled with cinnamon freckles up and down her arms and across her round cheeks. Her short hair fell in soft honey-colored curls, and her big blue eyes . . . well, that's where the whole cookie idea fell down, but they made me think of my favorite pair of worn-out jeans.

But back to those cookies. Every time, I'd tiptoe to the cooling rack and reach for one perfectly round, warm cookie when I thought Mom wasn't looking. And every time, out of nowhere, she'd slap my grubby hand away, snapping, "Not for you."

Ellie may have looked warm and round, but she had "not for you" written all over her. It was in her extremely professional handshake, just the right amount of grip. The old-fashioned, belted, button-up black dress with no wrinkles, the matching ballet shoes with no scuffs. The only hint of color was a thin gold necklace that caught the sunlight where it threaded under her collar. Everything plain and boring and tidy.

She was going to hate me. She'd already cringed at my stupid ghost joke. Why did I always run my mouth around pretty women?

"Kieran?" my editor Tad said.

Damn it, not *again*. "I'm listening, sorry." I'd forgotten my stress ball at home, so I tapped on my leg instead, hoping that'd be enough to keep me present.

"We're aiming for publication on March seventeenth next year," he continued.

"Saint Patrick's Day," Ellie said with a calm nod as she wrote something in her planner. Her handwriting was all elegant curves and slashes. "You want to lean into the leprechaun persona?"

"Exactly."

I tried not to wince. I knew I was the most Irish-looking person alive, but I'd thought the Happy Pirate Leprechaun joke would die eventually. Instead, it kept going and going. "Sounds great," I lied.

The nickname had happened in the big episode 5 challenge, meat and potatoes. I'd come in second-to-last in the previous two major challenges by being overambitious and running out of time, and Edna, the head judge, had told me she would lose patience soon if I didn't stop trying to show off. I'd been nervous, and I'd fucked up. I'd parboiled potatoes for too long and wrecked my plan to roast them and serve them alongside prime rib. But I'd thought fast, crushing the potatoes and frying them into little cakes topped with sour cream and salmon roe, then scattering everything with fresh dill. Hart, the front-runner, had crashed and burned with a tough, gristly piece of beef shank, and I'd *won* for the first time ever. I was so happy that I'd jumped in the air and clicked my heels like a little kid.

Now I was stuck with this dumbass name. But Tobias had told me that I needed to lean into it. Everyone would know who I was, and that meant my restaurant would get more press and that I might be successful enough that my parents would think I'd made a good life choice for once.

"The manuscript deadline will be August eleventh," Tad continued.

Over seven months from now? Plenty of time. It was just a few recipes and some random stories that I wouldn't even write.

"Which I know is a tight turnaround," he said.

Wait, what?

"But, Ellie, I'm confident you can keep the project on track."

"You bet," Ellie said, as if that didn't sound ridiculous. "Has there been any further correspondence about the book since you forwarded me Tobias's message?" She held up a printout with a few lines on it.

"I'm afraid not," Tad said, not meeting her eyes.

She was kind of cute when she looked miffed. *No, Kieran,* down.

"But I'm sure Kieran can fill us in on his vision," he said quickly.

"That would be helpful," Ellie said. She leaned forward, and

I needed to look at her face, not at her chest, because I wasn't a horny teenager. Even though it was fantastic. Crap.

"I'd love to know what you mean by 'fun,'" she said, clearly not impressed.

"Exciting, I guess? So much of home cooking is doing the same thing day in, day out. I want people to mix it up."

My mom cooked the same six dinners every week: London broil, steak hash, pork roast, pork hash. Salmon on Fridays, spaghetti on Saturdays. I'd learned early on to eat because I was hungry, not because anything tasted amazing.

"And how would you do that?" Ellie asked coolly.

Warmth crept up my neck. "I don't know yet," I tried to answer calmly.

"I'm sure Ellie will help you figure that out," Tad interrupted.

"Sure," she said, her eyes narrowing. "Who's your audience for this book?"

It was like having a nightmare where I was simultaneously falling from the sky naked and taking a test I hadn't studied for. "Everyone?" I tried.

Ellie rubbed her temple, like I was giving her a headache. "Can you be more specific?"

I felt myself digging into defensive mode. "How?"

"Well," she said slowly, "do you have any authors that you like? Someone who you'd want to be compared to? You'd be targeting similar readers to them."

I shrank in my chair, hearing my teachers' disappointment and my parents' anger for the first time in a decade. "Nope," I muttered. "I don't use cookbooks."

My failing grade was written all over her face. "You want to write a cookbook, even though you don't use them or know why someone would?"

Shame and anger flared hot and bright, and I opened my mouth, but Tad said loudly, "OK! You two will have a lot to discuss. Kieran, why don't you go away and think a little more about what you might want and then ask Ellie to schedule a one-on-one meeting. I'm sure you'll work it out."

Ellie looked like she would rather schedule a meeting with a bathtub full of banana slugs, but she just smiled tightly and said, "I look forward to hearing from you, Kieran."

"Good!" Tad said.

I don't know how he was so chirpy as the meeting wrapped up. Who was I kidding? I'd made a lot of progress in becoming a functional human, but this project demanded things I straight up struggled with. I had a career that didn't involve reading or writing for a reason.

Maybe Tad was oblivious to what a bad idea this was, but Ellie Wasserman was looking at me like I was a plate of dog food she had to choke down. As for me, I wasn't sure whether my sudden stomachache was an incoming ulcer or just a sense of doom. Probably both.

CHAPTER TWO

Ellie

*I*t was Thursday afternoon, and for once my inbox was empty. Soft winter rain pattered on the roof of my cottage, and everything was cozy and warm and conducive to getting some work done. If I had work to get done.

I refreshed my emails again. Nothing.

Two weeks had passed since the meeting with Kieran O'Neill, and I had cleared the decks so I could give all my focus to the project. And the waiting hadn't been a total waste of time: my budget spreadsheets and my kitchen were equally immaculate, and I'd even filed my taxes three months early. But I was *supposed* to be working on Kieran's book.

I punched the button again, and for a second my hope flew up. But no. Just an email from the library reminding me that my copy of *The Highlander's Hellion* was due in three days.

Why the hell hadn't Kieran emailed me? August eleventh may have seemed ages away to him, but when a cookbook was made of 150 recipes that had to be tested multiple times and introduced by quirky anecdotes, every day of work counted. He could afford to be cavalier, but I'd never had that luxury. I needed to *work*, damn it. Otherwise, all my plans fell apart.

But that wasn't helpful. I closed my eyes and breathed, thought about tamping down the fire in my chest. I'd learned young that hot frustration wouldn't remind my mother to give me the week's grocery money or help me forge her signature on Hank's health forms for school.

I wrapped my arms around my torso and squeezed, but it didn't help. I missed Max's bear hugs. In the before times, when a pitch for work would fall through or my mother would be even more self-absorbed than usual, he'd whisper, "Relax, kitten. It doesn't matter," and I would sink into his broad chest and rub my cheek against his sweater. He'd rest his chin on my head and squeeze me oh-so-tight, and my stress would float away.

I couldn't have a Max hug, but at least I could write to Tad and ask him to chase Kieran's agent. I could talk to Hank, if my little brother remembered that we were supposed to catch up today.

Speaking of my younger brother's forgetfulness, his birthday had been two days ago, and I hadn't heard any response to my presents or voice mail.

I opened up our text thread. I wrote mini obituaries whenever the absent-minded future professor hadn't called me in more than two weeks. He'd been run over by a bicycle while writing code in his head, crashed his car going the wrong way down a one-way street . . .

Now I typed, "Henry David Scott, RIP. Doctoral candidate in computer science at the California Institute of Technology and be-loved not-so-little brother of Eleanor Ruth Wasserman, died age twenty-four, crushed under a mountain of dirty laundry."

Thirty seconds later, I smiled when my phone rang and his name flashed up on my screen. "Sorry, sis," he said when I picked up. "I just got distracted."

"I know you," I said warmly. "Don't worry. I'm running out of causes of death, though. Did you like your birthday presents?"

His happy voice filled the room with sunshine. "Oh, yeah, the pretzel blondies were amazing, and the Warriors T-shirt is really cool. Thank you, Ellie. I'm sorry I didn't call you when I got them. Sam and Josh took me to a party in Silverlake and it ended up be-ing an all-night thing."

"That's all right. Did you do anything nice with Malia, too?"

He swallowed. "Things are a little weird with her right now."

Shit. I liked this girlfriend. We'd met when she and Hank had flown up from Pasadena last year. She was a calm and grounded presence, and she seemed to forgive him when he was focusing too much on research. "Oh no, what's wrong?"

"Nothing. She's just spending a lot of time getting ready for the bar exam. She's not home much."

"Kind of a ships-in-the-night situation for you guys?" I asked, crossing my fingers. "It'll pass, right?"

"I guess. But when she's here she gets mad that the bathroom's a little messy and the dishes aren't done and cleans instead of hanging out."

The words shot out of my mouth before I could stop them. "Well, you could just wash the dishes yourself."

"I thought you were on my side," he said, his voice small.

I rubbed my forehead. "I am. You can always count on me."

He sighed. "I know. Anyway, thanks for the presents. I'm glad *you* remembered my birthday."

Uh-oh. "Didn't Mom send you something?"

A long pause.

"Oh, for crying out loud," I groaned. According to Instagram, my mother had been driving through Mount Zion National Park three days ago, and if she'd had enough signal to post about her new boyfriend Rocky, she could have at least called my brother.

"Why does she suck so hard at being a mom?" he asked.

I knew it was a rhetorical question, but the placating words came anyway. "She could be worse. She never hit us, and she wasn't an addict or anything."

"Yeah, but she's this selfish hippie woman we see when she feels like it, and then she drives off with whoever her latest guy is. Hashtag vanlife. Hashtag blessed."

"I know, Stretch," I said, trying to calm him with his old nickname. He'd been taller than me by the time he was nine, and by eighteen he'd grown to six foot four. "But she is the way she is, and you've got me, no matter what."

He sighed. "I know I do. I love you, Shrimp."

I smiled at my phone. "I love you, too." I glanced up at the clock. "But I have to start dinner."

"You're still doing Shabbos for Ben and Diane?" he asked.

"Yeah. I like doing it."

"I'm jealous." A second of quiet. Then, "I'll call again soon, Ellie. I promise."

I wouldn't hold my breath, but he meant well. He always did.

• • •

ONCE I'D LAID out all the dinner ingredients in my in-laws' kitchen, I began the weekly ritual. One can of smoked sardines cracked open and drained of their oil. One big handful of wheat crackers on a little plate. One small swirl of yellow mustard squeezed out. One bottle of lager poured into a worn blue plastic beer mug.

One father-in-law appeared in the kitchen a minute later. Ben bent down and kissed both my cheeks. "Good Shabbos, sweetheart."

"Good Shabbos, Aba."

"What's for dinner?"

"Your chicken and carrots, of course." I'd tried marinating the bird in buttermilk, coating the skin in butter fragrant with garam masala and saffron. But all Ben wanted was a plain chicken rubbed with salt and pepper and roasted hot and fast, with vegetables under it to soak up the schmaltz. "Roasted potatoes with whole garlic cloves and rosemary, fennel and orange salad, and mocha cheesecake for dessert."

He said in his still-thick Long Island accent, "Beautiful. Diane will love that cheesecake with her sweet tooth." We both knew it'd be most of the calories she'd eat today.

I waited for him to ask me how my day was, but he seemed preoccupied.

"How was the office?" I asked. Ben was mostly retired, but he still saw a few teenagers at his family medicine practice.

"The kids are all right." He rubbed his forehead. "But Diane has had a rough week."

I bit down my dismay. Some days she came back from her office at Cal more cheerful, when she'd had a fruitful discussion with one of her doctoral students or the undergrads had been paying more attention than usual in her Dickens lecture. Other days, it was clear she'd spent the day playing bridge online and looking at Max's Facebook memorial.

Ben settled in at the end of the kitchen island with his crossword puzzle. For a little while, the only sounds were the bite of my knife through carrots and fennel, the scratch of his ballpoint pen, and the crunch as he ate his mini sardine sandwiches.

"Fourteen down," he suddenly said. "Cooking preparations *en français*, three words. Four, two, five."

"*Mise en place*," I answered.

"*Très bien*," he said. "Your accent is still excellent. Did you ever find that conversation partner like I suggested?"

"I've been too busy with work. And I can keep practicing French with you, right?"

He smiled. "Of course. But I'm old and forgetful, you know. You need someone young and sharp."

As he said the words, the front door opened and shut firmly. I put my knife down and Ben capped his pen.

"Good Shabbos!" my mother-in-law said as she bustled into the kitchen.

At the cheer in her voice, Ben's eyes found mine and widened like we'd seen a burst of sunshine after a week of rain. Was the old Diane back, the one who'd been queen of the kitchen, the life of every department party? "Good Shabbos, Ema," I said, trying not to sound surprised. "How was the faculty meeting today?"

"It was wonderful, sweetheart. Couldn't have been better." She held up a burgundy paper bag to Ben. "I got those pistachio éclairs you like for dessert, Benny."

My tentative smile got more genuine. I'd already made the cheesecake, but I wasn't going to look her good day in the mouth. "That's great," I said, taking the bag from her. "Do you want to set the table?"

For the last month she'd been hiding in her room and only came down to dinner reluctantly, but she chirped, "Sure! Let's get the good china out."

That should have been our warning. I thought we were just celebrating for the sake of celebrating. I wasn't expecting Diane to raise her glass of chardonnay halfway through dinner and say, "I'm retiring at the end of the semester."

She said it like it was just another sentence instead of a screeching left turn. "Retiring?" I asked carefully. She was sixty-seven, so it wasn't a crazy idea. But all the relief I'd felt turned into more familiar worry.

"Yes," she said after a big sip of wine. "I told everyone at the meeting that this year would be my last. I've given too much of my life to Berkeley. Grinding out publications. Teaching ungrateful students."

"You never said you were so unhappy, my love," Ben said slowly. His confusion mirrored mine. Before Max died, the two things Diane had loved most were cooking and teaching. She'd always had her little flock of undergrads who followed her around worshipfully, and her grad students came to the house every semester for lavish dinner parties that lasted until two in the morning. Her fairy godchildren, she'd always called her advisees.

I'd taken over the cooking two years ago when she hadn't been able to get out of bed, and she still seemed content for me to feed her and Ben. But without her teaching, what was left?

"What would you like to do instead?" I asked hesitantly.

Her eyes ducked mine. "I haven't decided. I just couldn't take it anymore, and it felt so good to say no to something for once."

The slow sinking in my stomach turned into a free fall.

"Maybe we could travel, like we always talked about," Ben said, the optimism in his voice shaky. "We haven't been back to London for a decade. And I've always wanted to go to Japan, remember?"

Diane looked down at her plate, her effervescent mood suddenly flat. "I thought you two would be happier for me." She pushed it away. "I'm finished. You can have the éclairs."

Later that night, I settled in with my latest romance novel, knowing I wouldn't have long. My in-law cottage in Ben and Diane's backyard was cozy and quiet. When I'd first moved in, it'd been spartan, furnished and decorated for guests staying for a day or two. I'd made it as nice as I could: with Ben's help I'd painted the walls a soft, leafy green, built cheap pine bookcases and filled them with cookbooks, and bought jewel-colored blankets and pillows to liven up the basic gray furniture.

But someday I'd have someplace where I'd picked everything out myself. Eighteen months ago, I'd read a blog about an English cookbook author who wrote, tested, and shot her books all in her living room and kitchen. I started pinning photos of combined working and living spaces that same day and opened a new spreadsheet to track how much money I could save week by week for a down payment. I already didn't pay rent, but now I cut coupons for groceries, stopped buying new clothes, borrowed books and movies from the library.

Someday I'd have a double oven again and a dishwasher. I'd have a huge wooden table that would be both a place for big, crowded dinners and a set for taking pictures. I'd collect beautiful old glassware and dishes for props and hire the space out to photographers and food stylists for when they wanted a homey backdrop.

Best of all, I would *own* it. I wouldn't have to move because my mother thought her latest boyfriend was getting clingy or because my husband had died and my landlord's idea of condolences was doubling the rent.

Max hadn't wanted to think about buying a place until he'd gotten tenure. When I'd showed him real estate listings, he'd kissed me and promised that we had time. "You're my home, kitten. We could be living in a treehouse or on a submarine, as long as I knew when I came through the door, you'd be waiting."

And he'd been right. After he died, our rickety apartment in Davis wasn't home anymore, even before I'd been effectively evicted. It'd been cold, empty, airless. When Ben had called me and asked me if I wanted to move in with them, I'd said yes before he could change his mind.

The cottage wasn't what I really wanted, but it had kept me safe when I'd needed it and given me a purpose. Ben and Diane had given me so much, loved me so much, it was only right that I repay them.

A questioning meow snapped me out of my memories. "Aren't you nice?" I murmured to the feline emperor on my lap as I petted him.

Floyd yawned and stretched out so that his huge striped head rested on my knee and his tufted white paws waved off my thighs. The vet had said there must have been some Maine Coon in my cat to explain his quantities of fur and ridiculous size.

The therapist I'd seen for a few months after Max died had suggested I adopt a pet, for companionship and to give structure to my days. At the shelter, most of the cats had been flat against the backs of their cages, but this enormous animal had strutted out and collapsed onto my feet. I'd known something about love at first sight, and I'd signed the adoption papers then and there. Floyd had been a swaggering vagabond in his previous life, and along the way he'd picked up the feline immunodeficiency virus. He couldn't go outside because of his compromised immune system, but that didn't stop him from sitting and yowling at the front door every morning until I lured him away with breakfast and cuddles.

But this late at night, he was content to be my lap warmer. I stroked the long crescent of his spine and he rewarded me with a loud purr. "That's it, we're good, aren't we? Just the two of us all curled up together."

I turned back to my book. A big stoic Scotsman was saving a stubborn English damsel in distress. It wasn't going to win a Pulitzer, but after tonight's dinner, all I wanted was a few hours of believing in happily ever after.

The hero and heroine finally got down to business on a windswept mountainside, and I thought that maybe I'd be able to get to bed undisturbed for the first time in a while, when I heard a timid tap. Diane's shadow floated outside the curtain.

When I opened the door, she said, her voice as fragile as her too-thin body, "I saw your lights were still on and I thought I'd say hello."

"Of course," I said, keeping my voice warm and steady. Did Diane's visits make me more of an insomniac, or did the fact that sleep was capricious make her appear on my doorstep?

She held out her hand. "I wanted to bring you your Yahrzeit candle, too."

The anniversary of Max's death wasn't until July, and it was still January. But from the way her eyes blinked and her lip wobbled, I could only say, "Thank you. Would you like anything to drink? Peppermint tea, maybe?"

"That sounds nice." She wandered in, and I put the candle down and busied myself with the teakettle, ignoring how exhaustion settled on my shoulders. She'd been visiting me like this for over a year. Sometimes once a week. Sometimes night after night.

She wandered over to my bookshelves and picked up the picture of Max and me in its silver frame. "Such a beautiful couple, like something from Old Hollywood," she told it. "You two had a love affair for the ages."

Diane had taken the picture at Max's doctoral graduation. Twenty-four-year-old me was wearing a light-blue dress, a burst of clear sky next to his black-and-navy velvet-trimmed gown. I smiled with my eyes closed, my hand resting over the heart that my husband promised beat just for me, while he bent to press a kiss on my crown.

I smiled a little. "He always made me feel special."

"You both were. We were so happy," Diane whispered, a tear slipping down her cheek.

Three years later, Max had flown to Paris for an academic conference. He'd begged me to go with him, but Tad had given me my first big ghostwriting job. I didn't want to blow it, even for the promise of a hot night in a five-star hotel after Max was done listening to papers and networking. The day before he was supposed to return to me, he'd gone to sleep and never woken up. He hadn't suffered, the police officer told me. But it was exactly the kind of white lie I would have told a woman who'd been widowed at twenty-seven, one who could barely speak through her sobs.

I don't know how I didn't turn into a dried-out husk that first year, with how much I cried for him. In my cold bed, I wished for one last night wrapped in his strong arms, one last night of feeling cherished and protected.

But now I was thirty. Thirty-one in August. Next year, I'd be older than Max had ever been. I'd had therapy, and did yoga badly, and cared for Floyd, and cooked. It wasn't perfect, but it was enough to get me out of bed every morning.

I still wished for someone to love me at the end of the day, when I was clean out of sweetness and light. But that hope was vague and formless, while Diane's hurt now was concrete and sharp-edged.

My husband had been her precious gift, born after years of hopes built up and dashed month after month. Ben had had to hold her up at the funeral, and her animal howls when dirt struck plain pine still echoed in my head on bad nights. We'd both been holding her up ever since.

Diane sniffed hard. "The students said in their evaluations for last semester that I was distracted. That I just didn't care about them. Of course I'm distracted. We're allowed to be distracted when the best person dies out of nowhere, aren't we? Aren't we allowed to miss him?"

"Of course we're allowed to miss him." But a small, traitorous voice inside me asked, *This much? For this long?*

She ran her palm over my head and gave me a watery smile. "He loved you so much, you know? You were his sweet little kitten.

"The day he ran into my office," Diane said, still remembering, "I was so surprised. He'd seen girls at Harvard but never brought anyone home, and now he wanted to get married after one date? And you only just nineteen. But he was right. You were his bashert, and he was yours. Meant to be."

"Yeah, I remember." I had been a wide-eyed freshman in my first French literature class at Berkeley, and he'd been the boy wonder grad student, a young Gregory Peck with intellectual swagger for days. I'd been dragged to a weekly French conversation group at a bar on Telegraph, and Max had presided over the scratched-up table like a king with his court. His eyes had found mine, and without a word he'd stood and pulled up a chair right next to him. When I sat down, he'd leaned in and whispered in French, "Do you know what a *coup de foudre* is?" and that had been us for the next eight years.

Now I could hear Diane's crescendo of grief coming. I'd occasionally pet her hand and make soothing noises, but she wouldn't hear me until after the pain had peaked.

"I miss how things used to be. The way he cherished you, the way you worshipped him. Everything's different, and I hate it. *I hate it.*"

"I know." I wasn't a therapist, but something told me that repeating the same words several times a week for years wasn't the healthiest thing.

I'd tried to tell Ben about the late-night visits right after they'd started. But when I'd said, "Diane's struggling," he'd replied, "Please know I appreciate everything you're doing. She needs someone to talk to whom she's not married to. It's a mitzvah." What could I say after that?

"Thank you so much, sweetheart," she finally said now. "It feels so good to get that off my chest." She reached out and petted my hair again. "You still look wonderful with short hair, by the way.

I'm glad you took my advice to cut it all those years ago, and to stop wearing those awful baggy jeans."

"Thanks, Ema." Going to Diane's hairdresser had been a perfumed, luxurious universe away from trimming my split ends in front of the bathroom mirror. And Diane's fulsome compliments when I put on a dress for the first time had made the daylong march around Union Square's department stores worth it.

Diane had cared about me, and I tried to give that caring back.

But out of nowhere, Kieran's wolfish smile and light green eyes flashed across my memory from two weeks ago. The ease with which he sauntered in and out of that room, like he knew that someone else would clean up his messes, while I knew I'd always be the person doing the cleaning, forever and ever.

But that was OK, right? I'd always been good at making things better for everyone else.

I blinked away a wave of envy.

She squeezed my hand. "You're a good girl, Ellie. Max would be so proud if he saw you now."

I wasn't sure about that. I didn't know if Max would recognize this part of me, the sharp, sour bite of resentment I felt at Kieran's fecklessness. "Thanks, Ema," I said quickly. "That means a lot."

"And you'll make his dinner again this year? It'll be good to get all his friends around the table."

"Of course." I cooked a memorial dinner of all of Max's favorite dishes every July. Again, six months away. But Diane's sense of time was different from mine. She woke up every morning feeling like Max had died yesterday.

When she left, sleep was miles away. When I picked my book up again, I was jealous of my happily shagging Highlander, too. He only had to deal with warring clans and freezing castles without indoor plumbing.

CHAPTER THREE

Kieran

What the hell was I doing, looking at my emails in the locker room? I could hear the soft hum of Qui's kitchen coming to life behind the gray swinging doors across from me. I should have been in there, laying out my knives and gathering my *mise en place* for the day. But instead of putting my phone in my backpack, I turned away and sat down on the bench in front of my locker, thumbed the screen one more time.

Looking at two messages in particular was like poking my tongue against an aching tooth. It didn't feel good, but I couldn't resist nudging it again and again.

The newer one was a save-the-date for my parents' thirty-fifth wedding anniversary. The green-and-pink image didn't work with my text-to-voice software, so I mouthed my way through it again. June third, at five thirty, at their house in Ojai. Cocktail attire, whatever the fuck that meant. No gifts except my presence.

Since when was my presence a gift to them?

I shook my head. Other people's parents invited them to their wedding anniversary parties, no big deal. Though other people's parents communicated with them besides sending a birthday card with nothing written in it, the way Mom and Dad had for the past decade.

I scrolled down to the email from Ellie Wasserman studded with the red exclamation point for Important Messages.

The robot reading the email aloud would make Shakespeare sound flat, but Ellie's words asking about my plans for the book had been blander than unseasoned oatmeal. Bland but bitchy. I snorted thinking about bitchy oatmeal.

"Please reply at your earliest convenience to arrange a time to meet." The words repeated in my head in her low, bone-dry voice. So smart and so cool, and hot embarrassment shot up my neck again.

It wasn't that I didn't have conveniences. I could find the time, if I really needed to. What was inconvenient was coming up with an idea for a cookbook. And by *inconvenient* I meant that I had no ideas. Zero.

"Not good enough, Kieran," I heard my dad say, heavy with dismissal. "We expected better," my mom added.

The back of my head tapped against my locker as a surge of uncertainty bubbled in my chest. I took a deep breath to push it down, to shove back the past so I wouldn't spin out. I knew I hadn't been a disaster for years. I was sober, I kept myself fed and clothed, I had good friends, and I was really fucking good at my job. I just had to go and *do it*.

Phone in backpack, backpack in locker. Chucks and jeans shucked off, checked chef pants and steel-toed boots yanked on. White jacket buttoned over Joy Division T-shirt, navy apron tied over jacket. Black bandanna folded and tied to keep my hair out of my eyes.

Now, deep breaths. Cool and calm, like the leader I needed to be. I pushed smoothly into the kitchen.

"Morning, Chef!" everyone called.

"Morning." My shoulders came down, and my hands unclenched. My basement studio in the Mission with dirty mustard walls and a mattress on the floor was where I slept. This place was home.

It was like a cross between the engine room and the hospital on a twenty-fourth-century spaceship. Shiny and clean didn't even begin to describe it. Ranges ran along one wall, pots and pans already sizzling on a dozen gas flames. My colleagues lined up along the central steel island, heads down over chopping boards. One commis chef, Jesus, minced a huge pile of mushrooms, while his best friend, Manny, stripped leaves from thyme branches. At the far end of the room, Sasha the pastry chef stretched buttery dough over a marble table while her assistant Valentin dipped strips of candied grapefruit peel in chocolate.

Things would speed up later during service, when every second counted. But the quiet right now still buzzed with purpose.

"Chef, why are you still here?" Jesus called, the same way he'd done every Wednesday since I'd won *Fire on High*.

"Yeah, man, why don't you have your own place already?" Manny chimed in. "You got that sweet-ass prize money."

Two hundred and fifty thousand dollars. That money could be rent, salaries, ingredients. It could be a softly lit dining room, handmade plates, glowing reviews and handfuls of stars. An open door to what most chefs would only ever dream of. But I couldn't see where I would go once I walked through it. I knew Qui, I knew my life now. I *liked* my life now, and so many restaurants crashed and burned in their first year.

I shook my head, blushing. "Yeah, yeah. I can't open my restaurant until I find a team as hilarious as all you smartasses."

They were smartasses, but they were the fucking best, too. The day after the final episode aired, I came in to find all the walls covered with printed-out pictures of my goofy face when the judges had told me I'd won, and bottles of sparkling cider popping open all over the place. Sasha had made me a glossy strawberry tart decorated with little pastry crowns, and the whole team had gone in together on a beautiful handmade santoku knife, with ripples in the Damascus steel like waves in the ocean. But Mrs. Hutton had sent me the best present: the name of her investment advisor, with an address and a meeting time. Instead of shoving the prize under a virtual mattress, I had my own little money machine churning away for whenever I was ready to build my own place.

I would be ready. Someday.

"How're those sunchokes?" I asked Amitai as I made my way to my station.

The Kiwi intern flicked a glance toward the endless pile he had to peel. "Good, Chef."

"Sweet. Keep it up." More power to the nineteen-year-old for not rolling his eyes or sighing. He'd learned fast that whining wouldn't get him out of the most boring tasks, the same way I'd learned five years ago.

I got to my station and laid out my knives and sketchbook. Maybe Steve was upstairs talking to Austin and the other front-of-house people. Maybe I'd gotten away with my lateness and could join the workflow.

"*O'Neill*," he said behind me.

Wow, he hadn't used my last name in four years. I only got called O'Neill when I was completely spacing out.

I tried to smile my way out of it. "Morning, Chef."

But he was already walking away. "My office, now."

I squeezed in the door and leaned back to close it as Steve slid behind his desk, his face stern. The wedding picture on the metal shelf behind him showed the smiley version I was more familiar with, and I asked, "How's Katrine?"

"My wife is happily plotting new ways to make the world a better place with robots, thank you for asking," he said, tapping together a stack of papers on the tiny desk's greenish metal surface.

"Could she make a robot do my laundry?"

"I'm sure she could."

Shuffle. Tap. Shuffle.

"You guys going to see her folks in Copenhagen for Christmas this year?" I asked, my tone a little higher than I wanted it to be.

His eyebrows went up. "We haven't decided yet, because in case you didn't notice, O'Neill, it's still January."

"That's a good point," I said faintly.

"Are you done trying to distract me? Because I can't do a long pep talk today. The boss's accountant's coming, and I'm getting the terrible, terrible reminder of how much I suck at this stuff." He held up one of the stacks. "Because this is what running a restaurant really is. Supplier invoices and payroll and fucking spreadsheets."

I tried to keep my shudder on the inside. "But you said Mrs. Hutton hires people to take care of that."

"Yeah, but her people can't do their job if I just hand them a bunch of receipts. I have to be organized, too."

The *o*-word. I'd heard it yelled at me so many times by my parents and my teachers. The question "Why can't you be . . ." also ended with "focused" and "still" and my dad's all-time favorite, "*quiet,* for fuck's sake?"

I could be all of those things now. The meds helped, and so did little things like alerts on my phone and deep breaths and long runs. My *mise en place* was always on point, and I kept my knives sharp. But there wasn't a little thing that could keep my family's words out of my head. That required a big act of will every single day.

"Kieran?"

I pushed my dad's voice away. "What?"

"I can tell something's bothering you. You usually bounce around like you're on springs, but you've had a gray cloud over your head for a while."

I shifted on my feet. I didn't know how to tell him about the sticky, muddy feeling that there were so many things I should be doing, the emails that I hadn't answered and the notifications piling up on social media, now that everyone knew who I was. The anxiety paralyzed me, and I was getting annoyed with myself for being stuck, which made the paralysis worse. "We haven't had any complaints, have we?" I said instead. "I didn't choke or poison anybody?"

"No, the customers are happy. But you're just keeping your head down at your station, not checking in so much with what the rest of the team is doing." He paused. "Do you need to go to a meeting?" he asked quietly.

I shook my head hard. "No way. I know booze doesn't solve anything."

When I was twenty-two, Steve had sat me down at the end of my two-week internship. He'd said he wanted to make me a commis chef and thought I could be much more than that. But he'd only hire me full-time if I agreed to meet once with his psychiatrist, Dr. Meyer.

"I have to go to a shrink for this job?" I'd asked.

"I think you have ADHD, like me. And I think you're self-medicating, like I used to," he'd said.

"Doesn't everyone self-medicate?" Every chef looked for ways to decompress after hours of service, and the booze was right there.

He'd leaned back and said, "Dr. Meyer told me once that neurotypical people use because they want to escape reality. Neurodivergent people use so they can tolerate it."

"Neurotypical? Neurodivergent? What textbook did you swallow?" I'd said loudly, trying to get away from the sore spot his words touched.

"Do you drink to escape? Or do you drink so that you feel like you can function?"

"Is that a trick question?"

He'd sighed. "Just give him an hour."

Three days later, when I'd been downing way too many shots of tequila with the dishwashers after another judgy phone call with Mom, I'd realized that he might be right.

Getting sober had felt like climbing up a fraying rope, but I'd learned from Dr. Meyer that living with ADHD was hard enough without adding other chemicals to my dopamine-starved brain. I hadn't had a drink since.

"And your meds are up to date?" Steve asked me now.

"Whoever set up subscription delivery was a genius," I said.

He *hmm*ed. "You don't have relationship trouble, as far as I know."

I shrugged easily. "Nope." I was too focused on cooking to be anyone's boyfriend. "You told me to simplify my life. Besides, do you really want me mooning over someone when I'm at the stove?"

He shook his head. "No, but the last time I checked, I'm running a restaurant, not a monastery."

I snorted. "You think I'm a monk?"

He grinned. "We both know you'd make a lousy monk."

He wasn't wrong. If what you wanted were laughs and orgasms, I was your guy. Everybody came, everybody went home and slept in their own beds.

Now he looked genuinely concerned. "Seriously, man. What's going on?"

I sighed. "You know that meeting I had at the publisher?"

He snapped his fingers, "Oh yeah. You were going to meet my friend Nicole Salazar, and Ellie Wasserman."

"You were right about Nicole—she seems cool."

"Yeah, she's a riot. Never play Ping-Pong with her, though. What about Ellie? She keeps to herself over in Berkeley, but I know Khaled and Laila loved working with her on the Herat book. They said she was really sweet, and a good listener."

"Sweet? Seriously? She's ridiculously uptight. It's like her hobbies are straightening picture frames and ironing." She must iron that black dress of hers to drive the wrinkles out. It had looked impossibly smooth.

An evil smile spread across Steve's face. "I think you met a woman who isn't going to let you get away with anything. This is going to be *great*."

I shook my head. "Everything's fine. I'm not worried about her at all. Stop rubbing your hands together like you're Mr. Burns taking over Springfield."

Steve stood up and scooted around the desk. "That was totally convincing. I hope you've got more conviction when Anh's here later."

Another woman with nice clothes and sharp eyes who made

me feel two inches tall. "She's just dropping by?" I wished out loud as I got out of the chair.

He slapped my shoulder. "She said specifically that she wants to see you."

"In the middle of service? Seriously?"

His shrug was a little helpless, a lot resigned. "I know, I know. But what she wants . . ."

I exhaled, giving in to the inevitable. "She gets."

Once I was back at my station, the world went quiet. I could lose myself in the flow of the kitchen, lean into making beautiful and delicious things. I'd racked up days off over the years, and I could be sitting on a beach or on top of a mountain somewhere, but why would I want to go anywhere else?

Amitai went by with a crate of Belgian endives. Right, I needed to pay more attention to what was happening around me. "What's for family meal?" I asked.

"José made a bunch of baked pasta with the vegetables and cheese we didn't use yesterday. There's salad and bread, too."

"Carbs for everyone!" I said, and it was good to see him laugh.

Thirty seconds after I grabbed my plate, a bunch of front-of-house people came downstairs from the dining room, my best friend, Jay, leading the pack. Once she had her food, she raised her eyebrows, and I grinned and scooted over so she could push her chair in next to mine. I nudged her shoulder, scooped up the cauliflower I'd separated out of the pasta, and put it on her plate. She put her finger up to tell me to wait a second, then gave me her Kalamata olives.

"You two are doing your freaky twin telepathy thing again," her boss, Austin, said as he sat down. "Kieran, maybe you should come be a floor manager with Jay. The tips would be ginormous."

Jay shook her head, smiling, and I said, "Nah, man, I'd just distract everybody with my hot bod."

Austin laughed. "It's been five years and I still don't understand how you two are so different and yet so close."

I mean, he was right. I was a straight, short-ass ginger man who'd needed two tries to graduate from community college, and Jay was a model-tall queer Black woman who'd studied for her MBA from USF while she worked at Qui. But we'd started on the same day, me as an intern and she as a host, and that coincidence had turned into awkward small talk about restaurants we liked, and the awkward small talk had turned into remembering each other's coffee orders, and cappuccinos had turned into long runs in Golden Gate Park when our days off lined up, and running had turned into having each other's backs no matter what.

"Heads-up," Steve said, and all the chefs and servers piped down. "We've got a big day ahead. First, something about VIPs tonight, Austin?"

"Yup." The manager grinned at us. "The newest James Bond is shooting in SoMa, so we've got some really big names coming for dinner . . ."

Once we finished obsessing about the new star, Steve talked us through what was new on the menu, then said, "Kieran, you're expediting."

For the first hour and a half that night, I stood by the pass and checked every plate before it went upstairs to the dining room, making sure each one matched the sketches I'd drawn from Steve's verbal descriptions. I took the incoming orders, calling them out so that the kitchen knew the pace of the meals playing out in the dining room, speeding things up or slowing them down.

On a podcast I'd heard a poker player talk about how he could play multiple hands of Texas Hold 'Em at once, making fast decision after fast decision, for hours at a time. Expediting was the same kind of high.

"Two scallops, one lamb, one quail," I said as loud as I could without yelling.

"Yes, Chef!" the kitchen responded.

"Fire two venison."

"Yes, Chef!"

"Two sole, no mushrooms for both." I felt terrible for people who'd had bad experiences with soggy, rubbery mushrooms. The wild ones we used were like eating a forest, in the best kind of way.

"Kieran?" Steve appeared right next to me. "It's time."

I waved to Manny to take over. When I reached to untie my bandanna so I could tidy my hair, Steve said, "Leave it. They'll want you to be like you were on TV."

Oh, OK. As long as they didn't make me click my heels, it'd be fine.

The kitchen wasn't noisy, but the dining room made it look like a rave. Mrs. Hutton's designers had created a hideaway from the outside world, servers gliding around the oyster-gray room like silent swans as they took care of our guests' every desire.

"Here they are," Mrs. Hutton said as we walked up to her table. "Brooke, Dorie, this is Steve Yuan, Qui's executive chef, and our young champion, Kieran O'Neill."

I was five foot seven on a good day, but I towered over Anh Hutton when she stood up so I could kiss both her powdery cheeks. She had black hair in a neat bun and wore a light-gray wool suit and pearls. She may have looked like a tiny harmless grandma, but she ran six high-end restaurants, three with Michelin stars, and knew every little thing that happened inside them.

"Is there a Mrs. O'Neill?" Dorie asked me, fluttering eyelashes that looked like spiders.

"That's my mom. She'll be thrilled you asked after her," I lied.

"Oh, aren't you just the cutest thing," Brooke said. "I want to put you in my pocket and take you home with me."

This was why I'd spent a year as a kid praying I'd grow another six inches. At least she hadn't pinched my cheek. "Thank you very much," I said instead, and they cooed again.

They asked me what it was like to be in front of cameras during *Fire on High*, what the host Mark Delacroix was like in person, whether anyone had actually eaten the whole suckling pig I'd roasted for the medieval challenge in episode 7. While I answered them, my brain tapped its foot and checked its watch.

Steve nudged me and mouthed, *Chill.*

My fingers were rubbing my forearm tattoo, my anxiety tell. I put my hands behind my back instead.

"Kieran," Mrs. Hutton finally said.

"Yes?" I tried not to say too loudly.

Her eyes may as well have been lasers. "You're going to write a book."

"Yes." I swore I knew other words.

She laced her fingers together, like we were in a business meeting. "That's a big project for you to take on. A lot of moving parts. Will you be able to focus? Take it seriously?"

Forearm again, shit. She'd had this effect on me the few times we'd met before, but I guessed that's why she was the big boss. "Yes?"

Her voice was calm as she appraised me. "I'd like you to plan a ticketed dinner here for two weeks from Monday. Given your victory, I think we'd get a lot of interest, and it would be something different from the usual Valentine's Day dinners in town."

All of a sudden, I was buzzing like I'd just eaten a whole bag of Skittles in five seconds. "That's awesome. I'd love that."

"I'm intrigued to see what kind of menu you'd create on your own," she continued.

She raised her eyebrows, and I gulped. This wasn't just a dinner. This was an audition. "Wow, sure. Thank you, Mrs. Hutton."

Finally, she smiled. "If you do this well, and give your book the attention it deserves, perhaps we'll be on a first-name basis soon."

I'm sure I was doing a good impression of the cod on the menu, because Steve nudged me again. "Awesome," I yelped. I barely heard Steve say we needed to get back to the kitchen, I was so excited.

﹒﹒﹒

THAT NIGHT I couldn't sleep, even though I hadn't gotten home until after midnight. I woke up already feeling a little hyped, my excitement getting an edge of anxiety, and after I showered and made a trip to Mr. Gonzalez's bodega to get breakfast, I tried to remember the adulting I had to do.

My grocery situation would be fine later today. I'd ordered enough bread, peanut butter, and protein bars for a week.

But laundry, shit. I needed to do that. No matter how boring it was to sit in Señor Burbujas's for hours.

I could go to the gym. I could lift enough heavy things that my brain would settle down and I'd be sore and exhausted instead. Then I could do laundry and listen to the *Banquet* podcast about fermenting vegetables.

My phone found its way into my hand, and I flipped around all my usual apps.

I bit my lip as I stared at the notifications on my Instagram. Tobias had said it would be good to engage with a few fans. But could I be the Happy Pirate Leprechaun right now? It wasn't like he was a separate person. He was just me at my most impulsive, bouncy, motormouthed. But for today, I wished I could just be quiet.

But being myself wouldn't answer all those exclamation-pointed emails from Ellie. What could I tell her, anyway? That cooking made me feel settled? That combining the sound of smashing and peeling garlic, the sappy, sharp smell of rosemary, and the sour sunshine taste of oranges made sense to me in a way that random rules and expectations never did?

I didn't use cookbooks, but even I knew that you couldn't write a book about how cooking made sense. I could just see Ellie's rolling eyes when she got that message.

A flash of feeding her a segment of ripe orange filled my head. Pressing my thumb against her full lower lip until she opened her mouth. Her ocean eyes closing slowly, her stern expression softening just for a second. I'd be quiet, and she'd be quiet.

I blinked the soft-edged image away, leaving me with Ellie's crisp words on my phone screen. I definitely couldn't tell her I wanted to feed her and take a picture of her blissed-out face.

My agent's name flashed up on my phone midthought.

"Hi, Tobias," I answered quickly.

"Kieran! Were you taking a nap or something?" His deep voice boomed across the room.

I rubbed my face to get rid of any more Ellie thoughts. "No, I was just thinking about this dinner I'm making at Qui." I told him about Mrs. Hutton's offer.

"That's fantastic. Do you have someone handling social on the day? Your fans will eat that up."

"Absolutely." Or I would, once I asked someone to do it. If I remembered.

"Awesome, awesome," he drawled. "Listen, I heard from your editor. Tad's not happy with you, man."

"Why?" I asked, even though I could guess the answer.

"Dude, you need to talk to your ghostwriter. She told him you're not cooperating."

First the snotty emails, and then she tattles on me? Fucking great. "We've been slammed at the restaurant. Doesn't she have enough from *Fire on High* to write something that sounds like me?"

"You don't want her to write random shit. It's not going to help your career if there's a bad book out there with your name on it."

"I guess."

A deep sigh came down the line. "Do you really want this?"

"Yes," I half-lied. I wanted to hold up the published book and show that I could achieve something concrete, something that my parents might even look at someday. But everything that led up to that? I hadn't typed anything longer than a text since I graduated from community college.

"You're only going to be a big deal for so long, dude. A book will keep the Happy Pirate Leprechaun on people's minds long after they've forgotten the other people on the show."

I didn't really want to be remembered as a cartoon character, but it was better than not being remembered at all. "OK. I'll reply to her now."

"And tell me first if there are any more problems. We're supposed to be business partners, man. Kieran O'Neill Incorporated, remember? Ciao for now."

I closed the call and punched open a new voice-to-text message. I couldn't keep the sneer out of my voice as I said, "Dear Mrs. Wasserman: As per your communication of last Tuesday, I have been so busy with my actual career that I have been unable to think of any brilliant revelations . . ."

No, Kieran, you can't be that big of a dick. Even if she tattled on you. Delete.

Wait. Maybe I was on the right track with wanting to feed her instead of write to her. New draft.

"Dear Ellie, I would like to invite you to my dinner at Qui on February fourteenth," I said more politely. "It'll give you a better idea of how I think about food. The Phoenix Group PR will follow up with more details. See you there."

Short and sweet and sent. Done.

With a sigh of relief, I opened a voice note. I had to put together the most grown-up, classy menu I could think of.

When I'd been on *Fire on High,* my MO had been SoCal high-end comfort food, because who didn't like all the seafood and avocado everything? But now I really needed to show off.

"Ideas for a big fancy dinner," I told my phone. "I wonder how much caviar I could convince Steve to buy? And can I get truffles?" I smiled to myself. "Ellie Wasserman, I'm going to blow your mind."

CHAPTER FOUR

Ellie

Qui's dining room made me think of the heart of a forest on a winter day. I ran my hand across a tablecloth as pristine as a first snow, ironed on the tables so there wasn't a hint of crease. A tiny architectural arrangement of mosses and driftwood sat in the middle of Nicole's and my table, shades of green and brown and gray that echoed the storm-colored walls and mahogany floors. Every seat was full for Kieran's dinner, and most of the guests had their phones either tilted up for selfies or pointed out for pictures of the dining room. A few had sleek professional cameras.

I wasn't even close to fancy enough to be here. But Kieran had specifically requested my presence, and I'd stuffed down my discomfort. Maybe he finally knew what he wanted.

"One donut says someone stands on a chair for the Gram before the night's out," I offered Nicole.

She checked her camera's light settings. "No bet."

I slumped in my chair. "You're no fun."

"No, babe, too easy. Two donuts say someone brought a stepstool."

"You're on."

She scanned the room, then discreetly pointed at a thirty-something couple in the far corner who were *both* standing on stools, conducting an entire photoshoot around their centerpiece.

"Oh, for crying out loud." I noted the donut IOU in my phone as Nicole ceremoniously blew on her nails.

The room gave off a low hum of excitement that I associated

more with visits to the opera with Ben and Diane than going out for dinner. "It's like a luxury bubble," I wondered aloud.

"The outside world disappears for a little while in a place like this," Nicole said.

"But any restaurant can achieve that. When I went to Locatelli's with Max, it was just us with some candles, big plates of pasta, and decent wine. We didn't need tiny, overtweezed towers of fancy." He'd lean across the white tablecloth and regale me with stories from grad student life, making me giggle into my glass of chianti, the adoring audience for his stand-up routine.

Nicole put the camera down. "If you could turn off the Statler and Waldorf act for at least the first hour, it'll be a better experience for all of us. Try and make the most of being out in a hot dress."

"I wasn't trying to be hot," I muttered. It was just a boring black wrap dress from the back of my closet. At least I'd hunted down a pair of Campari-red flats on clearance at Target, and resin hoop earrings and lipstick to match them.

My friend studied me like I was a museum display. "The dress is plain, but your boobs definitely aren't."

I yanked my neckline up, to basically no avail. "Thank you so much for that."

She sniggered. "Hey, if I had them, I'd flaunt them."

A server in a crisp black jacket interrupted my retort with menu cards printed on rough brown paper.

"Wait, that's how many courses?" I asked as I read, and read.

Nicole tapped the page. "Sixteen, and that's what's written down. The normal Qui menu has random treats thrown in too, so I wouldn't be surprised if he does the same."

"Oh, God." My fingers went to my phone for one last check.

"Diane won't bother you, will she?"

I grimaced. "She knows I'm here."

She patted my shoulder. "If you turn on Do Not Disturb, I'll share the wine pairing with you."

"I was going to do it anyway, but sure. Why is the menu just names of ingredients in equations? Like I'm supposed to know what 'duck + blood orange breakfast textures' are?"

She cracked up. "Come on, girl, you're supposed to let him sweep you away on a sensory journey."

"You're kidding me." I groaned.

"That's what the press release said. Shush, it's starting."

Servers swept across the floor as if they could hear invisible music to oohs and aahs from all the tables. Ours presented us with a palm-sized white plate with two teensy golden choux pastry puffs.

"Foie gras spheres with Sauternes jelly," he proclaimed.

The sweet-savory cloud dissolved on my palate, and I couldn't help but hum. "Holy crap, can I have fifty of those and call it a day?" I said. "That's fantastic."

Nicole nudged me with a grin. "Told you."

After the puffs came neatly squared smoked eel sandwiches, the fish's smoky richness bitten off by sharp horseradish. They were delicious, and fairy-sized. So were the next two dishes.

I trailed my finger down the menu, wondering when we'd get some kind of main course. "None of the stuff I read said he was into miniature food. Am I missing something?"

The lines across Nicole's forehead deepened. "No. This is all different from what he did on the show."

I studied the tables around us. There were plenty of enjoyment noises, but there were also a lot of faces like Nicole's. Uncertain. Confused. Like they'd gone to a Taylor Swift concert and Yo-Yo Ma was playing instead. Equal caliber, but totally different styles.

By course seven, I was getting worried and hungry. By course nine, I was ravenous and, even worse, annoyed. "Is he going to serve an actual meal at some point? Or is his artistic statement making an entire meal out of canapés?"

Nicole snapped our shot glasses of lobster meat and saffron gelée. The layered white, pink, and yellow looked like little sunsets.

She cocked her head. "It tastes amazing, though. Maybe he wants to go in a much more luxury direction?" she thought out loud.

If she didn't want me to be afraid, she should have been more confident. "It does, but I can't translate this to a home kitchen. This bears no relation to how people normally cook."

"It's haute cuisine, though. Like haute couture. It's art, not practical."

"Prada and Valentino don't expect a civilian to break out their sewing machine and replicate their designs."

"That . . . damn. That's a good point."

The room was getting a little louder, as we got deeper into the wine pairings. I could pick out occasional exclamations from the other tables like "Genius!" and "Masterpiece!" But it was like they were trying to convince themselves of something.

Was I just not getting what Kieran was trying to say? Or was there nothing to hear?

After course 10, a single quail drumstick, I rested my chin on my fist. "I think there's a big problem. There's no story behind any of this. No big idea."

Nicole flipped through images on her camera. "Just the fanciest ingredients he could get his hands on."

"Excuse me?" A tall athletic woman in a navy pantsuit hovered. "Ellie Wasserman and Nicole Salazar? I'm sorry it's taken me so long to come and speak to you two. I'm Jay Poole, the manager for tonight. Are you enjoying the dinner?" Her box braids were twisted into a neat bun on top of her head. I wasn't even an artist and her queenly bone structure made me want to sketch her face on my notebook. But while Jay's face made me think about art on a wall, Nicole was clearly thinking about bodies in bed.

"Yes, we are, thank you so much," Nicole purred as she openly ogled her. "You're all doing such a fabulous job." She leaned forward. "You know, I noticed you earlier and I'm dying to take your photograph."

I buried my head in my hands. "Please don't use your powers on unsuspecting mortals when we're trying to work."

But Jay's professional smile had shifted into something a lot more bashful. "Really?"

Nicole grinned up at her. "Of course. Your high cheekbones, your deep brown eyes. The camera would love you."

The perfectly composed, elegant woman giggled.

"Come on, tell me I can take your picture. Pretty please?"

"Yes?" Jay sounded like a balloon leaking air.

"Good." Nicole pulled out her phone. "Give me your number."

They texted each other, and Jay said with a dreamy look on her face, "Wow. Cool. I guess I'll see you soon."

"Wait. Can I talk to Kieran?" I said before she could leave. "It's important."

"I mean, he's a little busy right now," she said uncertainly. "We have several more courses to go. Is everything OK?"

I exhaled. I didn't want to lie, but I had to be polite, too. "That depends on him."

Nicole reached for Jay's hand and stroked the back of it with her thumb. "I'm sure he can find a second for his ghostwriter, right?"

My friend smiled big and Jay melted. "I'll see what I can do," she said.

As she floated away, I said, "Dude, really?"

Nicole said, "Just because you haven't gotten laid in over two years doesn't mean you can spoil my fun." She watched Jay make her way back across the room and down the steps to what must have been the kitchen.

"Inside voice. And it's not as easy for me." It was also worse than that. I hadn't slept with someone who wasn't Max in *eleven* years.

She raised her eyebrows. "Step one, walk into a bar wearing that dress. Step two, say yes. What about this is hard, exactly?"

"Not hard. Intimidating." Sex had been wonderful, but what if I'd lost the knack? Or had only had it with my husband? "Well, now

that you're done with your seduction, we can get back to the food."
What there was of it, anyway.

Kieran

"Chef?"

Steve and I both looked up from our stations. "Which one?"
he asked.

Jay looked like she'd just sprinted a mile. "Ah, Kieran."

"How's it going?" I had my sketch by my elbow and twenty
plates lined up in front of me, each with two piles of thinly sliced
rare duck breast and shredded duck confit, squeezing and spooning
dots of blood orange hollandaise sauce and homemade marmalade
around them.

"Um, it's all right."

My hand jerked and a drop of sauce splattered onto the rim
of the plate. "Just all right?" I asked as I wiped it away. I'd seen the
scraped-clean plates and bowls coming back. I knew it was better
than all right.

"It's Ellie Wasserman. She wants to talk to you. She looks concerned."

Shit, that wasn't the look I was going for.

Steve put his knife down. "What does she have to be concerned
about?" he asked me. "You've been talking to her, right?"

Dot of hollandaise at nine o'clock and three o'clock. Crescent of
marmalade at ten and two.

"*Kieran.*"

For fuck's sake. "I've been really busy getting ready for this dinner." And wasn't my food telling her enough about me? That I was
super classy?

Steve grumbled something, then said to Jay, "Is she having a
nice time, at least?"

Jay said, "I honestly don't know. When I looked over earlier, she was taking a lot of notes."

He turned to me. "You need to go up there and make nice. You may be busy, but she has a job, too."

"Kind of in the middle of something here." If I broke my flow now, the odds were good it'd be impossible to get back. It was a totally valid excuse.

But he wasn't buying. "I'll take over. Don't be rude."

"Fine. She's come all this way, may as well make it worth her while." I grabbed one of the finished plates and jogged up the kitchen stairs.

I'd just taken a few steps into the dining room when I realized that, for the millionth time in my life, I hadn't thought things through.

The room exploded with flashes.

"There he is!"

"Kieran!"

"Pirate!"

"Leprechaun!"

Jesus, they were clapping, and I probably looked terrible. I'd barely slept because I was so wired for tonight, and I'd been working in a hot kitchen all day. I made a few joking bows, and my audience cheered. But I didn't think the person I had to talk to would be taking my picture. I wouldn't run up to her like a scared kid, though. Selfie after selfie, big smile after big smile. Even one or two phone numbers shoved in my pocket. Let her see how much people liked me.

I could see the two of them out of the corner of my eye, an island of calm focus in the noise around them. As Nicole spoke, pointing at something on the table, Ellie scrawled something with her left hand, blond curls hiding her eyes when she nodded.

With one last scribble on someone's menu, I couldn't avoid it anymore. I tried for extra charm when I swaggered up. "Good evening, you two. Thank you for coming to try my food. I thought I'd bring you the next course myself, since it's my favorite." I put the duck right where it caught the light, and the marmalade gleamed like a jewel.

Ellie just kept writing. Nicole raised an eyebrow at me. "What's up, Kieran?"

"Everything's fantastic, thank you, Nicole. You wanted to talk to me, Ellie?"

No answer.

"I've been told it's polite to look someone in the eye when they speak to you," I finally said.

She underlined something with a hard black slash and looked up. And I forgot to breathe, because the light overhead sparked her curly hair with gold and made her eyes mountain-lake blue. They popped against the bright red of her mouth and the cream of her skin.

"It's also polite to reply to professional emails promptly," she said, and my dream bubble popped.

I rubbed the back of my neck, embarrassed. "I've been super busy." I was starting to hate the sound of that word in my mouth.

"Doing what? Because I'd like to be busy, too." I could hear the current of annoyance flowing under her icy voice. "You have your salary here, and the money you won, but if I don't get this done, I can't buy groceries or feed my cat."

Of course she had a cat.

"So if you could please humor me for a moment," she said, "I'd like to ask you about your choices tonight."

I hadn't heard that tired, disappointed tone from anyone in a decade. I gave a huge teenage shrug. "I'm all yours."

She hummed tunelessly as she flipped page after page of neatly bulleted notes. "It's interesting, what you did with the saffron in the lobster dish. Turning it into both a foam and a gelée."

"Interesting good, or interesting bad?"

Her nose wrinkled. "Just interesting. What inspired you?"

I tapped on my tattoo. "I think it's a beautiful color. There's no other shade of yellow like it."

"Why do you think it's beautiful?"

What was it with her asking "why" all the damn time? I dug the toe of my work boot into the wooden floor. "Can't I just appreciate it for what it is?"

"If you're going to ask a home cook to buy the most expensive spice in the world, you'd better have a good reason. Similarly, the use of caviar with the mackerel and truffles with the venison."

"It's aspirational."

"Aspiring to what?" she asked. "Besides cleaning out someone's bank account?"

Fuck. I could feel the eyes in the room on my back while I talked to her stony shoulders. She was making me look like an asshole just because I couldn't answer her questions. My voice came out sharp when I said, "If you're just going to argue, I'll go back to the kitchen."

Her pen stopped. "This isn't an argument, Kieran. We're not having a difference of opinion. I'm asking questions and you're stonewalling me for no reason."

I felt trapped in the hole I'd dug, but Ellie's judgmental look and big words just made me want to keep shoveling.

Ellie

On a scale of one to ten of terrible ideas, this whole escapade clocked in at twenty-three. I had crammed myself into shapewear, crossed the Bay, sat through course after course of overworked "art," and I still didn't know how I'd write as Kieran. He was like a hyper little kid who'd grabbed whatever he wanted in the candy store.

I should have just stayed home and made something up. Half-assed it.

But who was I kidding? I wasn't physically capable of half-assing it. I had to use my whole ass, all the time, because no one would ever care as much as I did. I cared whether Hank had clean clothes and hot meals to eat, I cared that Diane found some solace from our late-night talks. I cared because that was love, to me. Paying attention. Being responsible.

Now I was tangled up with this guy, who wouldn't know responsibility if it bit him in *his* ass.

"I thought I would be able to collect material for the book if I saw you in action. Get an idea of who you actually are as a cook. More fool me," I said, trying to control the shake in my voice.

He blinked. "You hate the food."

"No, I don't hate it. See?" I took a bite of the so-called breakfast textures. Sweet and sour and fatty flavors shot across my palate. It was really good, but it coated my tongue and throat with richness without offering any comfort.

"Everything is technically perfect," I said once I swallowed. "But it's shallow. Superficial. It doesn't tell me anything about *you*."

He flushed. "You're calling me shallow? So you know so much about this, huh? Which restaurants have you worked in?" He held his hands out. "Where are your scars?"

I stiffened. I shouldn't have to pour out any of my pain for him to take me seriously. "I don't have to have worked in a restaurant to know what makes cooking really good," I snapped.

He folded his arms like a sulky fourteen-year-old. "Then educate me."

That clearly wasn't an invitation, but screw it. I stood up and planted my hands on the table. "*Caring*. I don't mean for the details. I mean caring for the person who's going to eat it. Giving them a little piece of what you love the most." I jabbed my finger at my plate. "All of these dishes, they're just about showing off."

He rubbed his forearm hard, his face stony. "But I won *Fire on High*. I'm kind of a big deal, in case you didn't know. I think it's OK for me to show off."

I held up a finger. "You won *one* competition," I said slowly, contempt sneaking into my voice. "This year. Can you name the person who won two years ago? Three? Unless you take this seriously, your book will gather dust in a remainder pile somewhere, a historical record of a leprechaun in a stupid bandanna who was famous for a hot second."

The stone in his expression crumbled away. Bright green eyes flashed, hands clenched. His mouth opened and closed, and finally he hissed, "Who the fuck are you to tell me that? You're nobody. You can't even get your own name on a book. Who gives a shit what you think?"

My voice shot high with anger. "I'm the woman who has to clean up your mess, you entitled, arrogant *brat*."

It was quiet. Not the silence of people eating delicious food. It was post-atomic-bomb-explosion quiet.

"Holy hell," Nicole whispered.

There were people holding up phones. Lots of phones. Shit, how long had they been filming?

A petite Asian woman in an impeccable Chanel suit and pearls materialized at Kieran's side. Nicole kicked my calf and mouthed, *Anh Hutton*! Double shit.

"Who's this, Kieran?" she asked.

My face hurt from the force of my blush. "I'm Ellie Wasserman, Mrs. Hutton. It's lovely to meet you."

"Mmm," she nonanswered. "I wish we could have met under less noisy circumstances. Since you're not enjoying yourself, perhaps you and Ms. Salazar would like to leave?"

"That's probably wise." Kieran was glaring at me, and I said to Nicole, "In-N-Out sound good to you? I'm starving."

Bull's-eye. Kieran opened his mouth, but Mrs. Hutton clamped her hand onto his forearm.

Nicole grabbed her camera and shoved my purse at me. "A Double-Double Animal Style sounds awesome. I'll get a Lyft."

I kept my head high as we walked out, the adrenaline of my

anger making me move fast. I felt weightless from saying exactly what I felt the moment I felt it. Like I could take flight, coast through the air burdened by nothing. But for all the exhilaration, I knew this moment would be fleeting—it always was for me.

Who knew if I'd still have a job when I hit the ground?

Kieran

Somehow, I survived the rest of the service, smiled and accepted everyone's congratulations, when all I wanted to do was curl up in a ball.

But now all the plates were washed, all the stained tablecloths gone to the special laundry, my uniform put away, and I was out back, letting the cold from the concrete steps seep through my jeans. My arms were wrapped around my knees, my head resting on top. I wanted to make myself as small as I felt.

I knew the hurt I was feeling was mostly my ADHD talking. My brain made embarrassment and shame feel a million times bigger, but knowing that didn't make it burn any less.

The outside door opened and closed. "Hey," Jay said softly.

I jammed my hands into my armpits. "Hey."

She nudged my knee with her foot, and I shuffled over so she could ease down next to me.

I leaned into her and she wrapped her arm around my shoulders. "You did good," she said.

I scoffed. "No, I didn't."

"A lot of people loved it," she said encouragingly. "Talked about how whimsical it was. You're going to get some great blog write-ups."

I shook my head, tasting orange-pith bitterness. "Whimsical? That's a cute way to say I didn't know what the fuck I was doing."

She squeezed me. "Is this the thing that happens sometimes, where I talk, but you're so upset you can't hear the good parts?"

"Pretty much." I sighed, exhausted.

We sat together, quiet, Jay's warmth making me feel a little bit less shitty.

"This is about her. Ellie," she finally said.

"She hated it."

"That's not true."

I tugged on a loose thread inside my sleeve. "Well, she definitely hates *me* now."

Silence. Jay messed with one of her braids, and I let her think.

"Maybe you shouldn't do this book," she said. "You're making yourself miserable, and making other people miserable, too."

I shook my head hard. "No, I need to. I'm not a teenage dropout anymore. I'm a grown-up and I need to see a project through from start to finish."

"You don't have to prove to anyone you're an adult. You can just, you know, be one."

Which I was, most of the time. But writing this book would be like throwing off the last boulder that had been weighing me down.

"OK," Jay said slowly in response to my silence. "Maybe you could tell Ellie how worried you are and she can help you?"

"She wouldn't get it. She has an answer for everything."

She snorted. "That can't be true. Everyone has their soft spot. Also, she's just trying to do her job, bud."

"Well, I guess her job is making me feel like an idiot."

She shook her head as she stood up. "You know what? You made this big dinner that a lot of people liked, and I got a really hot woman's number, so we're going to El Molino and getting burritos to celebrate."

I looked up. "What hot woman's number?"

She grinned. "I won't tell you unless you blow your pity party."

"Fine, you win." I knew carnitas, guacamole, and a massive cup of melon agua fresca wouldn't solve my problem, but at least it would push it away for a little while. The same way I could push away how Ellie's eyes flashed as bright as gas flames when she was angry.

CHAPTER FIVE

Kieran

"*P*lease don't break another pen," Ellie said as we waited in the Alchemy conference room for Tad.

Her face and voice were dull, the opposite of the red-mouthed, burning-bright woman in the restaurant a few days ago. I guessed she wasn't excited to be called in for an emergency meeting, either.

I spun the Alchemy-branded ballpoint, then threw it in the air and caught it. "They won't miss it. It's a cheap piece of crap. They probably have thousands of them in a supply closet somewhere."

She smoothed a wrinkle on the skirt of her charcoal-gray dress. "That's not the point."

I tossed the pen again. "What *is* the point?"

She paused, her eyes flaring, then swallowed. "Never mind," she said quietly, clasping her hands in her lap. "It doesn't matter."

That's right. What mattered was that we'd been dragged into the principal's office because she couldn't wait for me to figure my shit out.

"Sorry I'm late," Tad said as he bustled in. "A call from the publisher. Sy is very excited about your book, Kieran."

"Thanks," I said.

"Gosh, it's dim in here." Ellie's hand came up in front of her eyes when he raised a shade and blasted us with afternoon sunshine.

Now Tad was looking at his monitor. "Ellie Wasserman: Feminist Icon." He clicked. "Ellie Wasserman: Every Smart Woman Who's Had to Deal with a Mediocre Man." Click. "Ellie Wasserman: Raging Man-Hating Rhymes-with-Witch."

"But that's so wrong," Ellie said indignantly. "I'm not a misandrist. I was just trying to get my work done. Isn't that what you pay me for?"

Tad pressed his forehead into his palms. "I take your point, Ellie, but the last time I checked, having a public temper tantrum wasn't in your job description. I'm surprised, and I'm disappointed."

The last word was like a needle, and Ellie instantly deflated. "I'm so sorry, Tad," she told her lap. "I shouldn't have drawn attention to myself."

I watched her make herself small in her chair, and something inside me kicked hard. I'd spent the first two-thirds of my life getting blamed for anything that went wrong within a mile of me, but she hadn't had a screaming fight by herself.

Tad sat forward. "Well, I wasn't expecting to get attention for the book this early in the process, but it's not all bad. Alisha in publicity says most of what she's picking up on socials is positive. People are even more excited for Kieran's book."

Ellie looked up, eyes wary. "You're not going to fire me?"

"Not at all, but I do want an explanation for your behavior. What exactly happened?"

Ellie took a deep breath. "He invited Nicole and me to the dinner," she said slowly, eyeing me as she spoke in flat tones. "I asked him what his thinking was behind the menu, and I found his answers evasive and unhelpful. I should have let it go, tried some other time, but I was pretty emotional at that point, and I snapped at him. And then he said something that hurt my feelings, so I said something rash back."

"Kieran?" Tad asked. "Do you agree with Ellie's account?"

"Yeah." I recognized everything she was saying. Neither of us looked good. But Ellie didn't have a public-facing job, and I did. She wasn't hoping to have her own restaurant, and I was. The anger climbed back up my chest and I said, "But did you really have to scream at me in front of everybody, including my boss? Why couldn't you just chill the fuck out?"

Ellie threw up her hands. "If you're not writing anything, and you won't answer my questions, and your cooking style changes by the week, what am I supposed to do?" Those last words were almost begging, like she was bewildered, lost.

"I was going to do it eventually." I hated the childish whine in my voice, but her exasperation reminded me too much of my parents' sighs and growls. "I have a lot of other stuff going on besides this book. Why don't you get that?"

All of a sudden, her face fell. "Is it me? Do you dislike me?"

My jaw dropped a little at how brave she was. I couldn't give her direct question a direct answer, though. It wasn't her fault that I had a history of everyone getting annoyed at me for being myself, but it didn't make her attitude bug me any less.

It didn't help that if I'd met her anywhere else, I would've wanted in her bed.

Ellie looked at Tad after I'd stayed quiet. "Maybe you need a different ghostwriter."

"Let's not be hasty here," Tad replied. The phone rang, and he lifted the receiver and punched a button. "Hello, Tobias, thank you for joining us."

"Tad, let's get this done fast," my agent's deep, drawling voice said. "Kieran, bro, you need to listen to Tad. The ghostwriter gets paid to make this happen for you. You have to let her do her job."

"I have a name," Ellie grumbled quietly.

"The book is going to be a big part of your brand," Tobias continued, not hearing her. "It's critical for future projects, understand? Now, are you going to be a good leprechaun and go make us a pot of gold?"

I tried not to flinch at the nickname. It wasn't just about the money, though that definitely helped. I had to prove I could achieve something on my own. "Fine," I said shortly.

"Great. Talk to you later. Toodles, Tad." And he was gone.

"But Tad," Ellie blurted, cheeks flushed.

"What?" Tad said impatiently.

Ellie winced, but kept going. "We're not compatible."

I mean, we were compatible in the sense that a tiny part of me wanted to know what she tasted like. But the rest of me wanted to break a whole box of cheap pens.

Tad shook his head. "No, Ellie. It has to be you." He dragged his fingers through his light gray hair. "I haven't had to do this before, but I think it's time for extreme measures."

"Extreme?" Ellie said.

"I'm sending you both to my cottage in Sonoma. You'll stay there for a week, and when we meet again at the beginning of March, you should have a list of recipes and a broad structure for the book."

What the hell? He couldn't ground us like we were twelve years old. "But I have *work*!" I said.

"So do I!" Ellie snapped.

We glared at each other until Tad said my name. I turned back to him and he said, "I spoke with Anh Hutton and Steve Yuan, and they're willing to release you for a week." He looked at Ellie. "And, Ellie, I know you haven't left town in over two years."

"How did you . . ."

"Instagram doesn't lie. And it's been far too easy to book you."

For a split second, the stern boss disappeared and something gentler and sadder took its place. Ellie closed her eyes and exhaled like an invisible burden had dropped onto her shoulders.

When she opened them, she said quietly but firmly, "If you need me to go, I'll go. Please tell me there's more than one bed in this place."

He stared at her for a second. "I'm not a monster. There's a king-sized bed in the primary and a futon in the office. You'll have to flip for it."

I couldn't keep the confusion off my face. We were adults here, no one had to share a bed with anybody if they didn't want to, and I absolutely, positively did not want to go to bed with her.

Be in bed. I didn't want to *be* in bed with her.

Ellie

"*C*an you wait a moment?" Tad said to me.

After we'd hashed out the dates for our imprisonment, Kieran had oh-so-casually ambled out the door, while I'd paused to re-organize my beat-up old purse. It had looked like a professional black leather tote two years ago, but now the cheap vinyl was splitting around the straps from all the stuff I carried. Maybe if I had any money left over from a down payment, I'd buy something sturdier.

"Are you all right? You look ill," he said.

"Didn't sleep last night." Diane had knocked on my door at ten and talked at me about Max and how terrible everything was for two hours. After consoling her, I was too depressed to sleep.

He exhaled and settled back in his desk chair. "OK. I wanted to talk about you and Kieran."

"What about us?" Not that we'd ever be an "us" in a million years. Empires would rise and fall and he'd be pestering me in the ruins.

He tented his fingers, studying me. "He needs someone to keep him on task."

"The last time I checked, the job description for ghostwriters didn't include babysitting."

"Not babysitting. Just some supervision. He doesn't have your discipline."

"Every Smart Woman Who's Had to Deal with a Mediocre Man" went through my head. Though Kieran wasn't mediocre. He was talented. Handsome. And really, really annoying.

I tried to stifle my impatience when I asked, "Why aren't you telling *him* to be responsible for his own behavior? He's a grown man."

"A lot is riding on this book." Tad took off his glasses and rubbed his forehead. He had so much more gray in his light blond hair than when we'd met over a decade ago. When had that happened?

"What are you not telling me?" I asked.

"The editorial board isn't happy with the results from my last few projects."

"But the Jamaican book Roland Campbell wrote is seminal. People in the field will be talking about it decades from now. And that patisserie book from the place in LA was stunning. And award-winning."

"Sy says seminal and stunning aren't selling." He exhaled. "Alchemy needs Kieran and his fanbase. And I really need you to ensure that this process is as smooth as possible. You've never missed a deadline, and you've never been over budget."

He'd stood by me when I'd needed him to. I couldn't bear to disappoint him. "I'll get it done."

He reached out and patted my hand. "I know you will," he said with a tired smile. "You're so dependable."

I smiled back weakly. Forget no rest for the wicked; the truth was that there was no rest for the good.

My phone buzzed.

Ben: How about *The Thin Man* tonight? We'd love your company.

I'd wished for an evening of Floyd in my lap and a romance novel in my hand, but that was OK. Diane had been the one to introduce me to the fizzy joy of black-and-white movies. Watching one with them would be a little taste of the before times.

When I came out of the office, Kieran stood up from one of the lobby chairs. At least he'd made a minuscule amount of effort for the emergency meeting. His blue-and-green flannel shirt only had a few big wrinkles in it. I ignored how beautifully the colors contrasted with his hair, how they made his eyes look like ice.

"What are you still doing here?" I asked incredulously.

He shoved his hands in his jeans' frayed pockets and bounced a little bit. "I figured it'd be better if we talked about the trip face-to-face."

He couldn't have brought this up in the office? "I'll just send you an email. It'll be faster."

He snorted. "And risk you coming to the restaurant and yelling at me again? No thanks."

I felt like I'd done more eye-rolling in the month since I'd met him than I'd done in the past decade. If anyone came up with an eye-roll jar, Kieran would bankrupt me in a week. "Well, I'll meet you up there, obviously."

He shrugged. "Not so obviously, I don't own a car."

I blinked. How did he even survive? Public transport in the Bay Area was haphazard at the best of times. I wouldn't dare rely on it. "You're a Californian adult and you don't own a car?"

He raised an eyebrow. "No, I'm a bunch of Muppets in a trench coat. I don't know how it took you so long to figure that out."

That wasn't that funny. But my mouth curled involuntarily.

"Have you tried looking for a parking space in the Mission every single day?" he said. "Zero out of ten, would not recommend. I bike everywhere. Or run."

"I suppose if you're in good enough shape, you could ride your bike to Sonoma," I thought aloud.

He laughed. "Yeah, no. I'm not one of those Lycra guys. I'll get a Lyft up."

I was already visualizing the hit on the expenses spreadsheet. "No, I'll drive us up."

"Suit yourself. I live at Twenty-Third and Bryant in the Mission."

I scoffed. "If you think I'm driving in and out of the City during rush hour, you've got another think coming."

He tilted his head and mused. "I always thought it was 'thing coming.'"

I didn't have time for his deep thoughts on word usage. "It's not." My phone buzzed again, probably Diane doubling up on Ben's message. "I need to head out. Meet me at my house on Thursday at four. I'll email you the address—please don't ignore it. Bring your knife roll, too."

He put his hands up. "Has anyone ever told you how bossy you are?"

I paused. A string of adjectives that Max had used for me popped into my head. *Shy. Quiet. Soft.* "No," I said, unable to keep the surprise out of my voice. "Never."

His green eyes held mine, reflecting back my shock. Like we'd accidentally done a magic trick.

"What?" I said eloquently.

"Well. You are. So there." As if that third-grade phrase won the argument. He waved a hand in the air to dismiss the spell we'd cast over each other. "See you Thursday."

"Fine," I said, snapping myself out of it. "Thursday."

CHAPTER SIX

Kieran

*D*id Ellie Wasserman live in a fairy house? The Berkeley Crafts-man's wooden siding was chocolate brown, the trim was a cheer-ful poppy red, and tangled green vines ran along the eaves and surrounded the front door. The only greenery on my block was a sickly maple that was a toilet for dogs, and sometimes for humans.

But she'd told me her place was around the back. Gravel crunched under my feet as I walked up the driveway, around a little red sedan and past a fire pit with a few dingy plastic chairs around it. The whole backyard was full of California winter colors: highlighter-pink and cream camellias, a dark green Meyer lemon tree loaded with saffron-yellow fruit. I picked one off the tree and scratched the peel that smelled like sunlight.

The guesthouse in the corner of the yard was a tiny, rickety-looking version of the main building. But that was life in the Bay Area. You found a little bit of space where you could and paid rent that would make people cry-laugh anywhere else. At least she got more natural light and fresh air than I did.

I tapped my knuckles on the green door. Quiet greeted me. Maybe she was in the middle of something?

Ten seconds later, I knocked again. Then I twisted the knob. It wasn't locked, so I stuck my head around the door. "Ellie?"

"DON'T!" she yelled at the top of her lungs as a blur shot by my feet.

The lemon went flying. "What the fuck?" I yelped.

But Ellie wasn't looking at me when she ran up to the door. "Floyd, no!" She shouldered me to the side and lunged down to the ground. She came up with a squirming cat that let off an angry meow.

"I'm so sorry, sweet boy," she said softly as she carried the huge tabby back inside. Her voice was like I'd never heard it before, warm and soothing like the first sip of hot chocolate on a cold day. "I know you wanted to go do catty crimes. But you can't be the terror of the neighborhood anymore." She rubbed her nose against his fluffy cheek when he yowled again. "You have to let me look after you."

My finger found the collar of my sweatshirt and heat flooded my skin. Maybe I wouldn't have gotten into as much trouble as a kid if someone had hugged me and talked to me like that when I broke something or flunked another test, instead of lecturing me over and over again about how I was letting everyone down.

"Could you close the door, please?" Ellie said.

I inhaled, then breathed the memory out. Business Ellie was talking to me now. "Good afternoon, Kieran. Good to see you, Kieran," I said as I pushed the door shut behind me.

She closed her eyes for a second, then put the cat down. "I'm sorry. Kieran, good afternoon. As you saw, I was a little distracted."

Could I get her to use that gentle, cozy voice again? I liked that better. "Why can't the cat with the awesome name go outside? Isn't that what they're supposed to do?"

"He has FIV."

"FIV?"

"Like HIV, but for cats. He doesn't have an immune system, so if he went out and got into it with another cat, he could both get really sick and pass the virus on." She shook her head, a little smile curling her full mouth. "And he absolutely would, because he's a fuzzy little hooligan."

What was someone as careful as her doing with a bruiser as a pet?

She said, "I'm going to need ten more minutes, since you're early."

A surprised laugh burst out of me. "I was early? That must be some kind of record. Can you write that down somewhere?"

She didn't laugh back. "I have to speak to someone before we go. Have a seat"—she pointed at a little gray couch—"and please don't mess with my stuff."

"Yes, ma'am." Could we take the cat with us? He definitely made her more human.

She dove through the door and crossed the yard to where an older woman had come out onto the back deck of the big house. She was Ellie's opposite, tall and way too thin, with gray hair cut super close to her head. Couldn't have been her mom. Or maybe she looked like her dad? Was she adopted? I didn't really know anything about her.

A minute went by. Two. I took out my keys and spun them, dropped them. Picked them up, spun them again, dropped them again.

Looking wasn't messing, right?

I shoved my keys in my pocket, got up, and wandered over to the little kitchen. Frying pans hung from hooks on the ceiling, and a magnetic strip on the green wall held a few knives. A big orange cast-iron pot sat on the back burner of the stove, with enough black marks on the bottom to show it wasn't just decoration. A "Packing List for Sonoma" was stuck to the fridge.

A peek around the green-and-gold folding screen at the other end of the room and I found a tightly made double bed, paperbacks piled on the nightstand next to it. Floyd was sprawled on his butt in the middle of the mattress, licking where his balls used to be. He glared at me when he caught me staring.

"Nice, cat. Real classy."

I left him alone and went to Ellie's wall of books. I recognized a few from Steve's office, big technical manuals full of diagrams. But there were a lot of things I hadn't seen before, in French and

Spanish as well as English. Post-its in pink and yellow stuck out from over the top of the pages, and when I pulled out one book, its spine cracked open to a page titled "Cassoulet" covered with greasy brown dots and blue scribbles.

Maybe she hadn't worked in a restaurant, but anyone who made their cookbooks look like that must have known something.

I flipped through a few others. Thai salads, meringue-topped cakes, Carolina barbecue. Then on the bottom shelves, I found a row of cheap black-and-white speckled notebooks. They didn't fit the grown-up vibe of the rest of the room. Everyone has a soft spot, Jay had said. I reached for one.

"Cooking Notes," it said in sparkly green pen on the cover. The handwriting was rounder. A kid's.

"October 25," I read slowly, trailing my finger along the page.

Fish sticks. Cook at 400F for two minutes longer than the box
says. Hank likes one tablespoon ketchup and one tablespoon
yellow mustard mixed together. Mom likes one tablespoon
mayonnaise with juice of a quarter of a lemon and one teaspoon
Tabasco.

Hank's waffles. Toast Eggos on medium, put on butter and
maple syrup, then microwave for ten seconds to melt everything
together.

I flicked through a year of little Ellie's cooking. A lot of it was her trying to dress up convenience food—pancakes, ramen. Toward the end of the notebook, she'd started to try random scratch recipes. Ground Turkey Tacos had lots of stars and fireworks drawn around it, while another for zucchini omelets only had "Yuck."

"Ellie!" a man's voice called outside. A huge bear of a guy with bushy white hair and black eyebrows came out of the house and put his arm around the older woman's shoulders.

He looked familiar. As I put Ellie's notebook back, I saw his younger clone smiling in a picture frame. He was wearing a fancy graduation gown and kissing a younger, blonder Ellie on top of her head, her closed eyes and soft smile all contentment.

"I'll text as soon as I get there," Ellie said loudly. She jerked her thumb back at the cottage, and the man nodded. They all hugged, and he bent to kiss Ellie's cheeks, like a blessing.

I'd gotten used to my parents not being big on physical affection, but I still felt like an alien watching strange human rituals whenever I saw families hugging.

Ellie turned to walk back to the cottage, and I realized that I was still holding her old happiness.

"What were you doing?" she said as she came in, a split second after I'd put the picture down like it scorched me.

"Not touching anything," I said.

Her mouth opened, and I recognized the annoyance on her face from Qui. But her mouth closed and she shook her head. "Sure. Let's hit the road."

"You live with your boyfriend's parents?" I asked as she led me to the red car. But wait, that didn't make sense. I hadn't seen any guy's sneakers, or a jacket, or anything that said a man lived with her.

"Ben and Diane are my parents-in-law," she said, popping the trunk.

"You're *married*?"

"Nope. Bag goes in there."

My brain flailed while I shoved my duffel between a suitcase and packed paper grocery bags. "You're divorced and you live with your in-laws? That's rough. But then why would you have a picture of your ex?"

"Still wrong," she said distractedly.

"Then *what*?" I said, my voice high with confusion.

She sighed like I'd dumped a bag of cement on her shoulders. "I'm a widow."

But widows were old, and wore black, and sat crying at home

in the dark. They weren't pretty blond girls with cheeks dotted with freckles. But what the hell did I know about the inside of Ellie's head? Or heart? "How?" I asked, still uncertain.

She rubbed the gold chain around her neck. "The usual way. We were married, then he died. Please get in the car."

While Ellie navigated through city streets, I was busy trying to make sense of this huge new piece of her story. Maybe she'd been fun once, to get someone to marry her. The guy in the picture looked like he'd been happy. Until he'd *died*. Fuck.

"I've never heard anyone think so loudly," she said.

I sat up. "Huh?"

"Though I guess that's because you're fidgeting."

I tried to sit still for a whole three seconds. "I was just thinking that I'd never met a young widow before."

"I am a statistical outlier, yes." Her voice was drier than a desert in August.

She was right; I needed to keep my awkward thoughts on the inside. Had her husband been old? No, idiot, that wasn't an old picture, and his parents looked like they were in their late sixties, maybe? But people could die of lots of things. Oh my God, did she *kill* him? No, that's really stupid. Why would she live with his parents if she'd killed him? Unless she had some kind of creepy serial-killer plans to take over the house?

"How old are you, anyway?" I asked. She was so cautious and serious, I'd bet she was in at least her late thirties. Or forty?

"I'm thirty."

And this is why I didn't bet with actual money. "You're about my age."

"Three years older. Today is just full of astonishing revelations for you."

Her hands gripped the wheel tighter and tighter, and I knew I was prying, but I couldn't help myself. "How old were you when your husband died?" I tried to ask gently.

"Twenty-seven. Now, are you done asking historical questions?

Because I need to focus." She turned up her music and merged onto the chaos of the freeway, her body straight, almost stiff as she watched the traffic.

By the time she was my age, she'd met someone, loved him enough to promise him forever, then lost him. No wonder I thought she was older. It was like she'd lived her life on fast-forward, while I'd been doing it in slo-mo. I couldn't imagine how I would have coped if someone I cared about died.

"Is that *opera*?" I said to distract myself, pointing at the speaker.

"Yeah," she said, rightfully a little confused at the sudden change of subject. "*The Marriage of Figaro*."

"It's awful."

A surprised laugh burst out of her. "It's *Mozart*."

I liked that sound. It meant she wasn't sad. "So it's old *and* awful," I said, hamming it up a little.

She batted my hand away from the dial. "Driver picks the music."

I fake-sulked. "You actually like this? It's just strung-out vowels."

"If you think about it, all singing is vowels. We don't vocalize consonants," she said in her teacher voice.

There was the bossiness I recognized. "OK, fine, but she's torturing them to death. Cats having sex sounds better than that," I joked.

A small smile. "You are, of course, entitled to your opinion."

I snorted at the jab. "That's a very fancy way to tell someone you don't give a shit what they think."

"Whatever you say." She gestured toward the back seat. "By the way, I have a few books for you to look at. Some of the stuff you said at the first meeting made me think of Jamie Oliver, and I thought Emeril and Heston Blumenthal might speak to you, too. They're in the tote bag behind you."

My joking mood died instantly. She wanted to start work already? I liked it when we bickered better. When we poked at each other, I could give as good as I got. The thought of reading like a turtle in front of her made me imagine my parents' boredom and frustration. "You don't want me to look at those right now."

"Why not?"

"Because I'll puke all over your dash. I get carsick super easily." Which wasn't a lie. But I knew I was only buying myself a little time.

"OK. When we get there, then."

I sighed and stared out the window.

Against my will, I listened to the music drifting out of the speakers. The woman's voice fluttered like a bird's, and the background music sounded like spring rain. It had the warm crackle of an old recording, too, and I felt my body relax as the notes filled my brain. "What's she singing about?"

Ellie smiled. "She's playing a teenage boy who has a crush on an older woman. He's asking her how he'd know if he were in love."

"He doesn't sound very smart," I said dryly.

"Well, his hormones and his self-awareness are in inverse proportion to each other," she said, her voice amused.

The music was still pretty, but the big question was climbing up my throat and demanding to come out. "Ellie?"

"Kieran?" she answered back in the same fast way.

"How did your husband die?" I blurted.

She glanced in her mirrors, suddenly wary. "Why do you need to know?"

Way to go, Kieran. Open mouth, insert foot. "I'm sorry."

"Nothing to be sorry about," she said smoothly, though her back had stiffened again. "It's just irrelevant to the work."

"What do you mean, irrelevant?"

"For the next few months, I'm supposed to be you. Who I am isn't important."

Yes it is, I almost said. Like part of me wanted to shake her, tell her that she mattered. Since when did I want to give pep talks?

"But shouldn't we get to know each other?" I tried instead.

"Well, I certainly need to get to know you. Me not knowing

you is why we got in trouble in the first place," she said matter-of-factly.

"So I'm supposed to bare my soul and you get to sit there all tidy and perfect and not say anything at all?"

The car lost speed as we rolled through a toll lane. "I'm not perfect."

Her voice was low and quiet and lonely.

The same part of me that wanted to tell her she mattered whined like a sad puppy. "I'll answer one of your questions if you answer one of mine," I offered.

She shook her head, smiling a little again. "No thanks."

"Come on, Ellie, pretty please? This isn't fair." Out of nowhere, I wanted her to open up to me more than I'd ever wanted anything.

She snorted. "You're just going to have to live with unfairness like the rest of the grown-ups."

We sat in silence for a second, and I tried to think of any way in. Wait, I knew something else about her.

"Who's Hank?" I tried.

She knocked her crown against her headrest. "It's like the past five minutes of conversation never happened. Do you have some kind of time-turning charm?"

"You tell me who he is, and I'll tell you something about me," I coaxed.

"You should just tell me anyway," she coaxed back.

I kept my mouth shut.

"Hank is my younger brother," I finally said with a sigh. "What is your family like?"

"They're . . ." Argh. Why did I give her that opening? Not that Brian was bad. But talking about my parents was like DIY fingernail removal. "They're a lot."

It was going to kill me, but I stayed quiet.

"And?" she finally said.

I raised my eyebrows at her. "You first."

She studied me, like she was deciding something important.

"OK," she finally said, and I held back an exhale of relief. "Hank lives in Pasadena and he's studying for a doctorate in computer science at Caltech. He looks exactly like me, except he's a foot taller and fifty pounds lighter."

A scarecrow with wild blond hair and denim-blue eyes appeared in my head. "And he likes ketchup and mustard mixed together with his fish sticks."

One hand came off the wheel and slapped her forehead. "Seriously? I thought I asked you not to mess with anything? You're incorrigible."

I wasn't totally sure what that meant, but it couldn't have been too terrible if she was laughing when she said it. "I didn't break your old notebook, I swear. They're pretty cool, those recipes. Little Ellie figuring out how to make things taste good."

"I'm glad someone thinks nine-year-old me was cool," she said, like she didn't believe me.

All of a sudden, I really needed her to hear me. "I'm not being funny. I mean it. So, ketchup and mustard?"

"Hank likes ketchup and mustard mixed together with pretty much everything. Even french fries, the weirdo. But how did you learn how to cook? From your parents?"

"Hah. No. Mom would have kicked me out of the kitchen in thirty seconds." I also would've broken anything I touched.

"So how?"

"I started cooking at Coconut Pete's."

She smiled. "When I hear the name Coconut Pete's, I think of buckets of rum concoctions and various fried things to soak up the booze."

"Pretty much. Anyway, I was eighteen, washing dishes there when one of the cooks didn't show up for service. The boss yanked me out of the back and put me in front of a deep-fryer, and that's where I stayed. I went home every night smelling like cheap soybeans, but I'm awesome at deep-frying. I did a lot of experiments with candy bars on slow nights."

"What's the weirdest thing you ever deep-fried?"

I couldn't help but laugh. "Great question. Reese's Peanut Butter Cups. FYI, don't mess with perfection."

"So you enjoyed it? Even if it was just deep-frying?"

Marin's green-and-gold hills rolled past us like slow ocean waves. I leaned my head on my hand and watched them as I thought aloud: "I liked the flow I could get into, and I liked that I could sleep late." I didn't say that it was a job so easy that I could show up with a world-ending hangover and still get paid. But now it was my turn again. "Where are you from?"

Her fingers tapped on the steering wheel before she answered. "I'm from everywhere. Born in San Jose, then I lived in LA, San Diego, Palm Desert, Mendocino, Arcata, Truckee, Chico, and finally Stockton."

The way she recited that list of places all over California bugged me, like she was trying to make something fun when it wasn't. "Was your family military?"

"Nope. We just moved a lot."

Maybe moving that much as a kid could have been exciting. Or it could have felt like she was a balloon, with no one holding tight to her string.

"Why did you move so much?"

"My mom thought it was fun." Her mouth turned down for a second. Then she seemed to shake off the bad feeling. "What happened after Coconut Pete's?"

"I got a job doing prep at a hotel restaurant in Montecito, the Pacific. The chef de cuisine there, Ximena, she was big on tough love. I was a skinny little punk, but she thought I had something. She made me feel like going back to school wouldn't be a waste of time. I could get a better grounding in techniques, and she tied everything I was learning to what we were doing in the restaurant. Stuff made so much more sense to me when it was concrete, and I got so many new shiny toys to play with. Then she hooked me up with Steve when I wanted to do an internship at somewhere cutting edge."

Ellie nodded. "That's cool that you had someone like that, who thought you could do more."

A warm feeling curled up in my chest, but unlike all the other times with Ellie, it wasn't embarrassment. I felt recognized. "Yeah. I was lucky."

Ellie

Kieran squinted out the windshield as I pulled up to Tad's house. "I thought a cottage was a tiny place with a straw roof."

"Yeah, I don't think the Big Bad Wolf's going to blow that down anytime soon."

Of course, Tad was twenty years older than me and a lot further along in his career, and his husband, Bobby, had sold his software start-up and retired at thirty-eight. It wasn't like I lived in poverty now, either; Ben and Diane would make sure I was OK, and my emergency savings account was fat and happy. But there would always be a scrappy kid inside me digging through the racks at thrift stores and buying bulk cereal, and that kid's mind boggled at this so-called "cottage."

It was only a little smaller than my in-laws' house. Most of it was one big open room, with white paint and high-beamed ceilings that made it feel airy. There were woven hangings on the walls, rust-red and lapis-blue souvenirs from annual vacations to New Mexico. Big squashy tobacco leather couches and armchairs made two parentheses around a dark wooden chest that served as a coffee table.

I unfolded a list from my purse and stuck it to the enormous fridge with a rainbow-flag magnet. "You brought your knives, right?" I called to Kieran.

He held up the tidy canvas bundle, eyebrows raised. "I do listen sometimes when you tell me things."

I ignored his impatient tone and kept unpacking kitchen gear, and he wandered around the living room, picking things up and putting them down, and then looked down the short hallway opposite me. "Which of us gets the futon?" he called.

"Aren't you going to be chivalrous?" I called back.

He stroked his chin as he leaned against the archway. "You like your five-dollar words, don't you? I'm not sure I know what that means."

He was acting casual, but it was a little studied. It made me wonder how much of the rest of his behavior was a façade. But the traffic had been intense and I wasn't in the mood to dig into his brain anymore tonight. "Anyway. How about rock, paper, scissors for the real bed?"

He sauntered over. "Sure. I'm amazing at this game. Ready?"

I looked at him incredulously as I held out my hand. "No one is amazing at rock, paper, scissors. One, two, three . . . I didn't say go!"

He waved his scissors in the air. "You said three. Isn't three when normal people go?"

"I *am* normal. OK, one, two, *three.* Argh!" He did a victory dance that consisted mostly of hip thrusting. "Two out of three?" I asked, half laughing.

"Fine." His wide mouth crooked up, and my eyes stuck on it for a second before I got back to business.

"One, two, *three* . . . no!"

"I won, I won! That king-sized bed is mine." He jogged in a little circle like he'd just scored a goal in the World Cup final, and I felt a grin stretch across my face. He was just so *goofy,* and I couldn't help but be a little bit charmed.

But wait—this was what Tad had warned me about. "Yes," I said, forcing the smile out of my voice with cool professionalism. "All yours."

Kieran raised his arms and stretched, and I absolutely did not notice that his sweatshirt rode up. Except his happy trail was auburn. *Shut up, libido.* "So what's the plan for the rest of the night?" he asked.

"Checking Tad's supplies and then a quick trip to the supermarket. I have a standard list of ingredients we need for testing."

His head cocked. "You're not a 'buy what you feel like' kind of person, then?"

I gave his rhetorical question exactly the amount of attention it deserved. "Then we should do some planning. Start to think of things you want to try out and then write down some kind of outline. There's a farmers' market in Sonoma Plaza day after tomorrow, too. We should go raid it."

Out of nowhere, he looked uncertain. "Sounds like you've got it all figured out," he said with a lightness I didn't buy, his fingers rubbing his forearm.

"That's why Tad pays me the moderately sized bucks." I tilted my head. "Is that all OK with you?"

He shrugged. "Totally fine. You're in charge. If you want me, I'll be rolling around in my enormous bed." And with that, he wandered off.

So he was fine when he was playing, but as soon as we talked about work, he checked out? That wasn't a good sign.

A little part of me said that I'd liked playing too, once upon a time, but I ignored it. One of us had to stay on task, and it was clear it wouldn't be him.

CHAPTER SEVEN

Kieran

"*I STAY OUT TOO LATE!*"

My body shot out of bed, and half a second later my brain screamed back, *What the actual fuck!*

Taylor Swift, that was the actual fuck. "Shake It Off" was so loud it was like a force field, and by the time I dragged my exhausted carcass to the kitchen, my hands were over my ears. "Ellie!"

"*SHAKE IT OFF, SHAKE IT OFF,*" she sang off-key. Citrus oils sprayed into the air as she zested an orange.

I leaned across the island. "ELLIE!"

She reached over and tapped her phone screen, and the earthquake-causing music coming from the living room speakers dropped to Starbucks volume. "Thank you for joining me at the impossibly early hour of"—she checked her watch—"nine thirty."

"Haven't you heard of knocking on someone's door to wake them up?" I groaned.

"Hasn't anyone told you you're a ridiculously deep sleeper?" She tilted her chin and gave me a snarky little smile. "Cute boxers."

I stopped rubbing my eyes long enough to look down at the Wile E. Coyote and Road Runner print. "Thanks," my mouth said before my brain locked in. "Wait, no. Not thanks. I don't thank mean people who make Taylor Swift scream at me."

She massaged her temples like she was the one who'd been yanked out of bed way before she was ready. "You know what? Go ahead and think I'm mean. We have work to do." She grabbed her notebook and a crisp blank page snapped open under her fingertips.

"Since you haven't given me much yet, I started cooking with what I bought at the supermarket last night. I wanted to try that dish you did with blood orange and duck with the ridiculous name."

"Breakfast textures."

"That's the one. I went to three different grocery stores, but only one carried duck at all, and they were out. So I thought I'd try chicken, and we could make an orange sauce to go with it." She glanced up. "Of course, you would need to put on pants."

Surprise and offense woke me the hell up. I had sketched and played around for hours to get that dish right, and she was overhauling it just like that? "But orange usually goes with duck, not chicken. And it wasn't just a sauce. It was a marmalade and a hollandaise."

"We can't ask people to make their own marmalade," she said like it was totally obvious. "The last time anyone made marmalade at home regularly, married women were property."

Her cool, dry voice was too much for my tired brain. "Fine," I said flatly.

"More people can buy chicken," she said matter-of-factly. "And haven't you been to Panda Express?"

I looked up. "Chicken is boring, and Panda Express is terrible."

"You are, of course . . ."

"Entitled to my opinion," I said, and her round cheeks blushed. Which wasn't cute at all.

"Anyway," she said. "Let's try it with chicken. Once . . ." she waved her hand at my bottom half.

I groaned. "Pants. Right."

⚬ ⚬ ⚬

"TELL ME YOU didn't buy boneless, skinless chicken!" I yelled at the open fridge. "The bone and the skin's where the flavor is!"

She came up beside me. "The only bone-in chicken was from battery hens. Would you have preferred I buy that?" She was asking like she knew the answer already.

"No," I muttered, reluctant to prove her right. "I accept that an animal has to die for me to cook it, but what they do to those birds is abuse."

She sighed, and I suddenly saw the bags under her eyes, the stress in them. "I'm sorry, Kieran. Can you make it work with what we have?"

Her *sorry* dulled the edge of my irritation. A little bit. "At least they're thighs," I said to the package. "I'll do my best."

It turned out my best was not much today. Ellie interrupted me every three seconds to measure something or ask a question. Forget flow. I was swimming through concrete.

"Oh God," she groaned when she tasted the sauce with me. Not the good kind of groan.

I spat hard into the sink, chugged water, spat again. "Gross. So gross." I'd put in too much sugar, and the orange peel bullied the other flavors. It was like wood cleaner, and it would have been better on the floor than in my mouth.

When she finally stopped drinking from her water bottle, she said, "I was going to say foul."

I snorted. "Because we're cooking with chicken?"

"Ha!" shot out of her mouth before she clapped her palm over it.

My hands clapped. "Oh wow, a whole *ha*. Put one in the win column."

Did she smile for a split second? Nope, it was gone. She put the bottle down, rolled her shoulders and said, "Take two."

Three hours later, it was take five.

"I'm going to smell oranges in my sleep," she said.

"Can we do something else?" I asked hopefully.

She grunted. "No. I'm going to get this right, even if it kills me."

"Plenty of places for me to hide the body," I muttered.

It felt like we were a covered pot on high heat. Our sentences were getting shorter and shorter, our bodies more and more tense.

"Hold out your hand," she suddenly ordered.

"Why?" I snapped.

She pointed to my palm. "Because I need to measure that."

"You need to measure a pinch of salt?"

"That's not a pinch."

How bossy could one woman *be*? "Seriously, you're going to argue with me about what a pinch means now?"

She smoothed the front of her apron and took a deep breath. "No, listen. If you didn't put that salt in, or only put in a little of it, what would happen?"

"It would be underseasoned."

"But then how is the person reading the recipe supposed to know when the food is underseasoned or overseasoned?"

"By tasting it and guessing. Duh."

"But they can't just *guess*."

The stick up her butt must get bigger all the time. "Why the hell *not*?" exploded out of my mouth. "This isn't science. You can't rely on it to be exactly the same every time."

Ellie's composed mask slipped. "You *should*!" she said loudly. "That's the whole *point* of having a recipe!" Her eyes closed, and she looked for a second like she was in pain. When she spoke again, she wasn't yelling. She just sounded tired. "We can't waste time like this. Please give me the salt."

I dumped the salt into her open palm, she confirmed it was indeed a quarter teaspoon, then said, "I need the bathroom. Don't touch anything."

Five seconds later, my hands moved before my brain did and found a spice jar. A pinch in the pan, a quick taste, and there, that was better.

A second after Ellie came back, she popped a spoon in her mouth and her eyes widened. "What did you do?"

"I added a little ground fennel. Or was it five-spice powder?" I quickly tasted it again. "No, fennel this time. And pepper."

She closed her eyes. "How much is a little?"

"Uh, between a tiny bit and a lot?"

She closed her fists. "You . . . you . . ."

All at once, I wasn't in this Sonoma cottage anymore; I was fifteen years old, sitting across the kitchen table from my parents after they'd picked me up from the police station, my mother's face stony, my father's red as he spat cold, furious words about *his* humiliation, *his* shame that I'd been caught stealing a candy bar, of all the frivolous things. "Come on, Ellie, what am I?"

"Jerk!" she yelled.

The laugh exploded out of me. "Seriously? That's all you've got?"

"Aaaah!" She stormed out and slammed the door behind her.

Ellie

I paced the driveway and counted. And counted. And counted some more.

By the time I'd made it to ten fifteen times, my temper was still simmering, but no longer about to explode. But I wasn't supposed to have a temper at all. He was just so fucking *provoking*. Why didn't he *listen*?

The gravel crunched under my feet as I stomped back up to the house. I had to make this work. The chance to make my own home was too important to lose because of one ridiculous recipe.

"You're back," Kieran said, looking up from his phone. "You want to call it quits?"

I made a show of cracking my knuckles. "No. I'll wash the dishes, go buy more oranges and chicken, and then we'll try a sixth time."

He slapped his phone down. "What is *wrong* with you?"

I definitely wasn't feeling like myself, but this infuriating man didn't need to know that. "Nothing at all."

"You want to know what I think?" he said, leaning against the counter beside me while I grabbed a dirty frying pan.

"Not particularly," I said, scrubbing with a vengeance.

"You couldn't do what I did," he said matter-of-factly.

My sponge stopped. "Do what?"

"The challenges on *Fire on High*. Compete under time pressure, with people watching and all the restrictions. You're way too attached to rules."

I had no idea it was possible for someone to sound that patronizing. "I'm sure I could do it."

He shook his head mournfully. "Nope. You don't have what it takes. Don't feel bad," he said, clearly hoping I did.

I threw the sponge down in sheer pique. "I have what it takes. I *can* make things up."

He put his face to mine. "Prove it."

"*Fine.*"

He turned and dug around in the fridge and then the fruit bowl. Onto the kitchen island went two red-and-green apples, a head of broccoli, and a chunk of Parmesan. "OK. Combine these in one recipe. You have thirty minutes. Your time starts"—he flourished his phone—"now."

I grabbed a pot, filled it with water, and put it on a back burner on high. I knew it would take a while to boil. Kieran nodded, and I didn't feel a little spark at his approval.

I cut a tiny piece off one of the apples. Mostly sweet, a little tart. The broccoli was the opposite, green and bitter from chlorophyll. How could I get them to meet in the middle? The salt and funk of the Parmesan would highlight the differences between the broccoli and the apples and they'd fight with each other more. I needed to make the apples more like a vegetable or the broccoli more like a fruit.

Kieran slapped the counter. "Come on, Ellie."

"I'm thinking."

"Think less and do something."

"*Think less and do something,*" I mimicked in a nasal voice. Patronizing jerk. Fine. Pickles. I could quick-pickle the broccoli once

I'd blanched it and add a lot of sugar to the vinegar to make it sweet and tart. But how much sugar and how much vinegar?

Once I'd blanched the florets in the boiling water, I guessed, measured, and tasted. Augh, disgusting. It was candy-sweet. More vinegar, and I could toast some spices?

No, it was even worse once I'd added those. Maybe I was wrong about the vinegar. I'd start over and use lemon instead. I grabbed one from the fruit bowl, then fumbled it onto the floor and had to rinse it.

"How are you so slow?" Kieran said impatiently. "The knife is sharp; you can trust it."

I'd cut up a lemon a thousand times before, but not with adrenaline racing through my system. As I sliced, the juice squirted everywhere. A moment after I realized my guide hand was too close to the blade, the knife skipped and a flicker of pain streaked across my right thumb.

He leaned forward. "What did you do now?"

The inch-long white line on my skin turned into a row of deep red beads that swelled larger and larger. I swallowed slowly. My mouth was full of metal.

Kieran's "Ellie?" echoed in my head as black curtains pressed in.

Kieran

I hadn't known I could move that fast, but Ellie's white face and slumping body had me out of my seat in half a second.

Her hips, shoulders, and head slammed onto the wooden floor with a horrible thump. Shit, shit, shit. I kneeled and patted her cheek, trying to be gentle. "Ellie! Wake up. Please wake up."

After what felt like forever, she blinked. "Ow."

"No shit, *ow*," I yelled. My heart was flailing in my chest like a trapped bird. But me freaking out wouldn't help right now. I should be soothing. "You cut yourself and then you fainted," I said more quietly.

She sat up, and I put pressure on her shoulders so she wouldn't stand. "Wait. Tell me what day of the week it is."

Her eyes narrowed. "Friday. Who are you to tell me to wait, Mr. Don't Think, Just Do Something?" she mimicked again.

Good to know she wasn't a cool, sophisticated grown-up all the time. "The person who took a first-aid class at Qui, that's who. Who's the president?"

"I'm not concussed," she grumbled.

"I saw you hit your damn head. I had to check."

She rubbed her eyes. "Was I out long?"

"Ten seconds, maybe. Tell me how you're so casual right now, because that was fucking scary."

"Vasovagal syncope," she said, pronouncing every syllable.

"Vaso-what now?"

She took a deep breath and her cheeks got the smallest amount pinker. "I see blood and it's lights out."

I blinked. "Then how do you cook meat?"

She winced when she shook her head. "Not that kind of blood. Human blood, from an injury. I see it and everything goes funny."

Relief took over more real estate from panic, but my hands still wanted to flap. I needed to use them for something more helpful. "Yeah, not so funny for me. Don't look at your right hand and stay still."

She leaned her temple against the cabinets and closed her eyes. I wrapped a dish towel tightly around her hand, and saw a patch of pale shiny skin on her right wrist. "Did you burn that a while ago?"

"Yeah. Touched it against the top of the oven when I was fifteen." She opened one eye. "I know you have more scars than me, though."

"I'm glad you don't have as many as I do." Every scar would mean a time when she'd been lying on the floor like a broken doll. "I'm going to check your head. Keep holding still."

A tiny smile kicked at the corner of her mouth. "Do I look like I can do anything else?"

"Such a smartass," I said as I ran my fingers through her curls. I didn't feel anything wet, but she cringed when I moved them over a spot that was already starting to swell. Her hair was so silky, and up close I could see all the streaks of champagne and wheat and caramel that made it blond. It smelled like clean laundry and citrus. Not lemon, but something greener.

I cleared my throat. "You're going to have a fat knot there soon. Do you hurt anywhere else? Your shoulders, or your hips?"

"Nah, I have plenty of padding in both those places."

No, I would not think about how padded she was. "Then you need to lie on the sofa."

She shook her head for a split second before she winced in pain. "Why? I can keep going. How much time is left? Five minutes?"

"No." Since when did I growl? "Fainting means you rest and drink water and take ibuprofen."

"But I need to prove to you I can do it."

My hand found her upper arm before I could think about it. "No," I repeated. The firmness in my voice surprised me. "You don't have to prove anything to me."

Her eyes flicked down curiously to where my fingers were wrapped around her bicep, and I snatched them away. "Yeah," she said. "Right. Because you've been taking me seriously this whole time." She grabbed the counter and pulled herself up.

Worry surged up inside me. "Easy," I blurted.

"As you can see, I'm not made of porcelain." She tilted her head, and something in her eyes shifted. "Are *you* all right?"

"You're the one who fainted and you're asking if *I'm* OK?"

"You look freaked out."

I'd seen her collapse like someone had cut her strings. I'd have been freaked out if anyone did that.

Wouldn't I?

I pointed into the living room. "You. Sofa. Now."

She was still holding on to the counter, and her knuckles had gone as pale as her face. "Give me a second."

The tether I hadn't even known was there snapped. "For fuck's sake, put your arm around my shoulders."

Her forehead furrowed and her mouth opened wide. But nothing came out. And then, slowly, slowly, she reached for me. I stepped into her and put my arm around her waist, and she relaxed into me.

"Are you the Bossy Pirate Leprechaun now?" she said as I walked her to the sofa.

"Don't call me that," I said, easing her down until she was sitting.

"Pirate Leprechaun? Why not?"

Because for a second, caring for her, I'd felt big and brave, instead of small and ridiculous. "Just don't. Keep your arm up."

It was like lying down had made her realize what had happened to her, and she was quiet while I hunted down the first aid kit, bandaged her thumb, and tucked a blanket over her legs. I did get a little eye roll when I handed her pain pills and water and told her to drink it all, but no more snark.

"Can I help you clean up later?" she asked.

"Nope. Your job is to rest. You should take the bed tonight."

I went back into the kitchen, but when I reached for the cutting board covered with broccoli florets, she said softly, "Don't throw it away. Just put it in some dishes with plastic wrap. I'll finish the challenge later."

"You still want to do it?" Apologies were climbing up from my chest, sitting on my tongue.

"I'm not traumatized," she said, sounding sleepy. "I'll be more careful next time, that's all. You won the bed fair and square."

She turned her face into the corner of the couch and closed her eyes, and I grabbed the dirtiest, stickiest pot. As the grease and muck lifted away under the sponge, I focused on the ache in my arms, the sting of the too-hot water on my hands.

I'd been a real asshole, taunting her like I was sixteen and full of myself. I bit my lower lip. It wasn't pierced anymore, and I'd shaved the dyed black hair off my head, but the selfish, feckless dick I'd been back then still hung around, shoving in when I was exhausted, or stressed.

But when she fell, I wanted to scoop her into my arms and growl at the world at the same time.

I shook my head and got back to scrubbing. Protectiveness, what a load of bullshit. I was only good at looking after myself. I didn't have any business trying to take care of someone else.

CHAPTER EIGHT

Kieran

A grunt from the other side of the bedroom wall woke me up. Though after the Taylor Swift explosion yesterday and Ellie's getting hurt because of my bullshit, my sleep wasn't the deepest anyway.

"Come on, come on," Ellie said from far away.

I slid out of bed. Was she already testing?

I wandered into the living room, waiting for her to grumble at me for being late, even though it was early o'clock. Instead, I found her butt wriggling in the air in a small, tight pair of black shorts. She stretched her leg behind her and lowered to the floor in a deep lunge, then brought her other leg back until she was in the top of a plank. Her arms shook and she hissed her breath out.

Yoga, my brain finally said after going through all the sexy options. The woman on Ellie's laptop was going through the same string of poses.

I could've let her know I was there. But all the words I had were "Yes," and "That," and "Want."

Oh no. Hard no. She was grumpy and stubborn and as much fun as Mass on Good Friday. The fact that a low-down part of me wanted to pull those shorts down and take a bite of her was irrelevant.

Now you're thinking like her.

I needed to go, but the floor had turned into wet concrete.

She turned shakily into a side plank, and her eyes met mine. "Ack!" Her arm collapsed under her and I jerked forward, but she turned fast and eased into a sitting position. Her blue tank top cut low and tight across her chest. "Good morning."

"Morning," I definitely didn't say to her breasts. "Sorry. I'll go now."

Her eyebrows went up. "You've never seen a fat woman doing yoga badly before?"

"No." I shook my head hard. "I mean, should you do that after yesterday?"

"I'm fine." She tucked her legs to the side and tilted her head. "So you were staring because you were worried?"

There was no good answer to that question except to get out of here.

I'd go for a long run, that would help. Then I'd take an even longer shower. A cold one.

Ellie

When I'd come out of the shower, Kieran was gone, because of course he'd disappear without telling me.

I'd long finished my scrambled eggs and was updating the expenses spreadsheet when a key scratched in the front door lock.

"Where were you?" I asked impatiently when Kieran came in.

He picked up one foot and stretched out his quad. So elegant. Clearly, he'd be much better at yoga than me without even trying. "Running. You're not the only one who likes to exercise in the morning. It's really pretty out there. The hills are super lush and green."

A blurry splatter of pinkish-brown skin stretched across his knee. A burn scar? That must have been agony for him. I shook my head. "If you want to run for hours, please get up earlier. We . . ." Then my brain shorted out, because he'd pulled his T-shirt up to wipe sweat off his face.

"Something wrong?" he said as he dropped the fabric, giving me a shit-eating grin.

Not helpful. I kept my eyes on his scarred red eyebrow. Eyebrows weren't erotic.

He wasn't even my type, for crying out loud. Max had been six-two and played rugby for fun. He'd made me feel small and delicate, in a way that undermined all my feminist credentials but never failed to get me hot, especially when he tugged me close to whisper about all the filthy, delicious things he was going to do to me.

In comparison, Kieran was more jockey than rugby player. But jockeys still had abs. Defined ones.

"Please take a shower," I said to interrupt my thoughts. "I can smell you from here. And we need to get to the market before all the good produce disappears."

"I'm pretty sure they'll still have stuff in an hour. Can I at least have breakfast before we go?"

"I bought granola bars," I said, all business. "You can eat one in the car."

His eye roll could be seen from space, but he didn't argue with me for once.

Thirty minutes later, we could smell and hear the farmers' market before we saw it. A jazz band sent jaunty trumpet and sax notes bopping through the air, where they mixed with the aromas of rotisserie chicken, kettle corn, and just-picked vegetables. Green-and-white gazebos lined three sides of the square, and dogs and toddlers frolicked in the grass. Groups of people sat in circles under the soft winter sun, sharing the picnics they'd put together.

"Pickings aren't going to be amazing because it's February, but we'll definitely find some good citrus and bitter leaves," I thought aloud. "Maybe we'll get lucky and they'll have some super-early asparagus."

No response.

I turned around to see he'd stopped to talk to a young guy who was holding out a phone. "Uh, Kieran?"

"Kieran!" someone echoed.

"Kieran O'Neill!"

"Hey, Leprechaun!"

As more people crowded closer, holding up their phones, I stepped way back.

"Can I get a selfie?" an older woman said.

"You're the best, man," a man declared.

"Thank you very much," Kieran said, again and again. The words must have been meaningless after a while, but his warmth and ease never changed, his big smile never faltered. He *liked* this, I realized, sharing his enthusiasm with all these people.

"Where's your bandanna, man?" some smartass asked.

Kieran signed someone's arm and said cheerfully, "Left it at home!"

"Can I get a selfie?" someone interrupted. I lost count of the number of pictures he took.

"Who's she?" a woman asked him, suddenly looking directly at me. "She looks super familiar."

I had no desire for Tad to get annoyed with me again. When Kieran made eye contact with me, I gave him the tiniest headshake. He gave me a miniscule nod back.

"Don't know," he said, conspicuously turning his back to me, and I made myself scarce, ignoring the little spark of gratitude in my chest.

Kieran

*B*oy, being famous was nice sometimes. Everyone was acting like I made their day better just by showing up. All I had to do was grin, take a few selfies. And live with the ridiculous nickname. I hoped someday I could be just Kieran O'Neill, badass serious chef who happened to be short and ginger.

But after a while I was missing quiet. I was missing focus. I was missing calm. I couldn't see the person who was all those things.

"Thanks so much, everybody, but I need to get going. All this beautiful produce isn't going to cook itself." I repeated myself a few times before everyone took the hint, but finally I could look around for Ellie.

She'd found a bench a few hundred feet away and had stretched her arms across the back, face turned to the sun. Everything about her was still and relaxed. As I walked toward her, I let out the breath I didn't realize I'd been holding. "You all right?" I asked when I got to her.

"Just working on my tan," she said, eyes still closed. "How was everybody?"

Her slow, gentle voice made me want to sit next to her and lean on her shoulder, which would be totally professional. "Really good," I said fast to push the intimate image away. "Super excited about the book."

Her eyes opened and mouth turned up, and I wondered what her biggest smile would look like. "That's exactly what you want. I'm glad you have people who support you."

There was the big mystery of Ellie Wasserman. What did *she* want? What made her happy? Our first meeting had planted a seed, and now my curiosity was a tiny little plant, growing more and more every day.

I was about to ask when a high, sweet voice said, "Kieran?"

I turned to see a college-age girl, all straight black hair and long skinny-jean legs. "Would you be interested in some local honey?" she said, looking up from under her eyelashes, biting her glossy lip just a little.

Not really. But then Ellie said dryly, "Sure he would."

Just for that snark, I lied cheerfully, "I love honey. Please, lead the way."

Ten minutes later, I was full of sugar and regret. Ellie was tapping notes on her phone at my side, but the girl ignored her completely, giving me spoonful after spoonful.

Less note-taking, more rescuing, I thought at Ellie. Why didn't Vulcan mind-melding work in real life?

Instead, I took the next tiny spoon the girl offered me. "Delicious," I said as the tenth different honey coated my tongue. After this, I was going to need a gallon of water to rinse away the sticky sweetness.

"You said that about the first one." She pouted.

"Mmm. But this one is also delicious."

She bustled around the stall, looking for more things to torture me with. "You should tell your pastry chef to use honey in her desserts instead of sugar. Sugar's so bad for you."

"Uh-huh." The day I told Sasha how to bake was the day I decided I didn't need my balls anymore.

"Oh, and you have to try this," the girl said. "This is super new and special. We found an old recipe and started brewing our own mead. We're not selling it yet, but I think you'll love it." She took out a small pitcher from a cooler and poured the gold liquid into a taster cup.

I smelled it first and jerked my head back a little. "Um, how alcoholic is it?"

"Four percent. About the same as a Coors Light. My dad lets me drink it at home."

Shit. Even after five years of sobriety I hated announcing to total strangers, *Hey, I'm in recovery.* How could I make sure people knew I didn't judge them for drinking, just that it turned me into a walking, talking shitshow? I didn't want anyone's pity either.

Dr. Meyer and Steve had both told me to get over myself and be honest, but my mom demanding that we always look like a perfect family in spite of my dad's friendship with Jim Beam made some habits hard to break.

"Why aren't you tasting it? Is there something wrong with it?" she asked, confused.

"No, no. I'm just enjoying the fragrance." I took a great big sniff.

She shrugged. "I mean, it's not wine. It smells like honey. You should just drink it."

No new customers appeared, and my phone didn't ring.

"Dude, share the wealth." Ellie plucked the cup from my hand and chugged the contents.

I tried to act grumpy and not relieved. "Please, Kieran. Thank you, Kieran."

She ignored me and smiled with all her teeth at the girl. "That was excellent."

The girl blinked. "Good."

Ellie's voice turned into that low, soothing purr she'd used with her cat. "I'm so sorry, that was totally rude of me to interrupt. What's your name?"

"Hayden?"

"Nice to meet you, Hayden. Where did you get your top? That red's such a joyful color."

She plucked at the fabric. "Oh, thanks. I got it at the thrift store."

"You have great taste. Now, I just ran out of the acacia honey I've been using at home and I want to try something new. What would you recommend that's dark and rich?"

Five minutes of breezy small talk later, Ellie handed over her cash. "You've taught me so much, thank you. I'll have a small jar of that buckwheat one, I appreciate you being so helpful."

When we walked away, I waited for her to say *What the hell?* or *Why didn't you just drink the mead?* but she just put her sunglasses on and walked to the next stall.

"Don't you want to know?" I finally asked as she studied a farmer's pile of winter salad leaves.

"Why you were stalling?" she answered, distracted.

I felt like I had walked out onto a conversational tree branch that I wasn't sure would hold my weight. "Yeah."

She bit her lip, then said, "I saw she was trying to make you do something you didn't want to do. *Why* you didn't want to is irrelevant."

"But do *you* want to know?"

She lifted her sunglasses and her eyes gave me a flash of being on the beach in early September. Hot white-gold sand cushioning my feet, the silvery blue sea just waiting for me to dive in.

"You'll tell me when you're ready," she said quietly. "I can wait."

Before I could say thank you, she pulled out a piece of paper and Kind Ellie changed back into Business Ellie. "Come on, we still have to buy stuff."

"Let's split up," I suggested.

Her eyebrows went up, all skepticism.

"No, look. If I follow you around, I'll get bored and you'll get pissy. I've got cash. I'll meet you back here in half an hour."

She sighed and dug around in her huge purse. "OK. Here's a bag for you. Can you get receipts, even if it's just a piece of paper with a number on it? I need to add them to the spreadsheet so Tad can pay you back."

"Sure, sure," I said, already thinking of all the delicious things I could find. Farmers' markets had always been my happy place.

Ellie

𝓐s Kieran jogged off, I thought I knew what he might be hiding.

He'd looked at that sample cup like it was poison, and I knew that some chefs struggled with addiction. But Kieran was bright-eyed, clear-skinned, and had run for miles this morning. Whatever he was doing to stay sober was working.

He'd run off to look around the market like a kid let loose on the playground. Maybe that was the kind of positive energy that could move the whole project forward.

I had no idea what he'd get, so I stuck to basics. Speckled brown eggs that the farmer promised had been laid just that morning, two dark loaves of sourdough that crackled when I squeezed them gently. Meaty bacon from happy pigs, a chunk of salmon glowing coral and smelling like the sea. Little waxy potatoes firm to my touch, dirt-skinned onions, bouquets of fresh herbs. As I inhaled the scent of a bunch of rosemary, hot dusty summer captured in its needles, I felt my worries loosen their grip on me for a second, pleasure taking their place. When she'd taught me her recipes years ago, Diane had insisted I smell, taste, touch with every step, telling me to trust my senses.

Anxiety surged again. I hoped she was coping without me. I wasn't sure she could.

Thirty minutes later, I was ready and waiting on the bench. Fifteen minutes after that, Kieran ran up muttering, "Sorry, sorry, I lost track of time." My mouth opened, and he put his hand up. "And I know I should've looked at my phone. I forgot. I always forget. But I'm here now."

It was like he wasn't just talking to me, but also to the many, many people he'd had to explain or apologize to. "All right. What did you buy?"

His bag hit the bench with a heavy thunk. "Some really nice fennel with lots of fronds," he said, pulling out the vegetables as he went. "Some Belgian endive and radicchio from a hipster lumberjack guy, and some brand-new green garlic."

"Oh, I love that. The baby cloves are so tender and sweet."

He grinned. "Exactly. See, good things come from just looking around and picking whatever you want."

A tiny candle of an idea lit up in the back of my brain. But it wasn't bright enough just yet. I looked down into the bag and saw a pile of fruit. "How many oranges did you buy?"

"A bunch? This woman had these blood oranges that were just gorgeous. Here, I'll show you."

I glanced at my watch and saw it was past time to go back to the cottage. "Wait, you can show me later."

"Just chill a second," he chided. He dug his thumbnail into the blushing peel and pulled until the dark red fruit appeared, spraying citrus oil everywhere. As he pulled the fruit into its sections, it glowed like rubies. It made the fruit I'd bought at the supermarket for our ill-fated experiment look dry and stale in comparison.

"Why do you have to show me now?"

I stopped cold, because he'd grabbed my chin. His fingers were soft, insistent.

"Because I want to. Open," he said. He was smiling, but there was something in his eyes I hadn't seen before. Determination?

When I gaped at him, he popped the orange segment in my mouth.

I bit down, and my eyes fluttered shut. Sweet-sour fireworks exploded across my tongue, and I couldn't help but moan a little bit. I tasted orange, of course, but there were raspberries and a little bit of rose petal, too.

"That's incredible," I said once I'd swallowed. "Like eating a sunset."

When I opened my eyes, he was staring at my mouth. I felt fireworks again, this time in my stomach. But a second later, he smiled big and said, "I was going to say a party in my mouth, but I guess that's why you're the writer."

I tried to shake my head, but his hand was still on my jaw. "Were you going to feed me something else?"

He blinked, then jerked away like I'd singed him. "Sorry. I should have asked before I grabbed you."

"No, I get it." The tang of the orange, the roughness of his calluses on my skin—it was like I'd drunk a glass of champagne on an empty stomach. My voice was a little high and shaky when I said, "Thank you for sharing it with me. It was really special." I swallowed and said more normally, "Home time?"

He nodded, and as we walked to the car he kept up a string of chatter about the people he'd met. I nodded, and smiled, and kept my fingers from finding the place where he'd touched me.

CHAPTER NINE

Ellie

*T*o avoid a repeat of yesterday, this morning I did my yoga on the square of carpet in the office, only knocking into the futon frame two or three times.

Kieran's face when he'd caught me had been priceless. Though a small, unhelpful voice said that there had been something else in his expression besides surprise, something that looked a lot like hunger. I'd seen it when he'd fed me, too.

When I came back from my shower, his bedroom door was open, and the siren scent of frying bacon filled the air.

I wandered into the kitchen and leaned on the counter next to him. "What are you making?"

"Breakfast," he said, eyes locked on the pan.

I nudged him lightly so he'd look at me. "Specifics would be nice," I said encouragingly.

"Nothing special. Just hash with some bacon, potatoes, and greens." He pushed cubes of potato into the oil, and a crisp, earthy smell rose up from the pan. They spat and sizzled as he hit them with salt and pepper. "Watch out for the oil."

"Cuts make me faint, not burns. Hang on, I'll grab my phone."

"It's not much."

"Let me be the judge of that. Recipes can come from super-random places."

I typed notes and snapped some photos as he worked. The camera really loved him, all his angles and shadows. He was wearing tan cargo shorts and another old T-shirt, dark brown with "Franz

Ferdinand" written across it backward. He'd clearly put in time at the gym since he'd bought the shirt, and his biceps flexed as he shook the pan to flip the potatoes. And no, my fingers were not wondering what those muscles would feel like.

When he pivoted away from the stove, the scar on his knee stretched.

"Is that from Coconut Pete's?" I asked, pointing.

He looked down. "Yup." He sighed. "I was lazy and wore shorts one day, and then I got splashed with boiling oil."

The pain and shock he must have felt shot through me. "Jesus!"

A smile tightened his mouth. "That's what I said, but a lot fucking louder. The pain was bad, but to be honest, the shame was worse. When my mom got to the hospital, she was so freaked out. She kept asking me how I could do that to myself. Even when the nurse said it was an accident, Mom kept muttering to herself."

Guilt knotted my stomach. That was an awful thing his mother had done, but how much time had I spent thinking that Kieran was deliberately trying to frustrate me? That if he just did what I thought he should, everything would be fine? Maybe I'd been unfair. Maybe I was the one who needed to dig deeper.

"I love fried potatoes," I tried.

He stared at me. "Really?"

He was right to sound confused at that non sequitur. "Yeah. Always have. The reason no one's put me in charge of America's nuclear secrets is that I'd give them all away for a basket of french fries."

He looked skeptical. "You even feel that way about In-N-Out's?"

"Sure. Mediocre fries are still pretty good. But they're a distant second to the burgers, of course."

He folded his arms, which did delightful things to his shoulders. "What are the best fries you've ever had?"

I rubbed my neck. "Kind of a show-off answer."

"Still curious."

"I was in Lyon, studying abroad. There was this bistro near the university that did a ridiculously cheap prix fixe. The *frites* were always fresh, and they came with this garlicky herb mayonnaise that was just outrageous."

"Parlez vous français?"

I blinked at him. "Of course," I answered in surprised French. "I studied both French and English at Berkeley. How do you speak it?"

"I work at expensive restaurant in France in two . . . ," he answered in heavily accented French, then snorted. "Shit. I don't know big numbers," he said in English. "Or past tense. But I staged at a place called Néroli right before I became sous at Qui."

My jaw fell open. "You mean the three-star place near Cannes? Working there would be the experience of a lifetime."

He stopped. "That's one way to say it. The chef de cuisine made a drill sergeant look relaxed. But I learned a fuck ton, and I picked up a little French, even though the guys made so much fun of me every time I spoke."

"But you tried," I said earnestly. "You deserve some credit for that. Someone else might have run screaming out of that kitchen after ten minutes."

He flipped the hash with a flick of his wrist. "I guess. I'm definitely better at cooking than I am at languages, that's for sure. Anyway, this is done. I'll just fry some eggs. Sunny-side up cool with you?"

He was weirdly shy about compliments, but his blushing face and tense shoulders told me that disagreeing with him wouldn't get me anywhere right now. Maybe I was feeling a little shy, too. "Yeah, cool. I'll set the table."

Once my plate landed on the table, I couldn't help eating the hash like I was starving. He'd added a little sauteed garlic and parsley at the end, and the fragrance against the crispy potatoes made me hum with happiness.

I was about to pick up my plate and his to wash them when he said, "I could make amazing fries if you wanted."

I shook my head. "They wouldn't work for the book. People think deep-frying at home is incredibly messy, and the low-fat and low-carb lobbies finished the job."

He laced his fingers behind his head. "That's a shame. But I didn't mean for the book."

I stared at him. "You'd make fries just for me?"

His cheeks went a little pink. "You'd have to come to the restaurant. We had an intern who'd worked at a really fancy gastropub outside London, and she taught me how to make the best chips in the world."

"That's sweet of you." His blush got a little deeper, which wasn't adorable at all. "But wouldn't Steve and Mrs. Hutton throw a fit if you used their precious kitchen to make french fries?"

"You think they're a lot more uptight than they are."

"Are you telling me Mrs. Hutton wears Hawaiian shirts and listens to the Grateful Dead?"

He snorted. "OK, fine. Not Mrs. Hutton. But Steve saved my ass when he could have shown me the door."

This talented, energetic chef had been on the edge of being fired? "What do you mean?"

A beat. He squinted at his plate. "Never mind. I think I'll try different seasoning for the potatoes next time. A little paprika, maybe."

Fine. I'd said I could wait.

I thought he'd go mess around on his phone like he usually did when we had downtime, but instead he leaned on the counter next to me while I washed the dishes. But this time he wasn't goading me and I wasn't being a killjoy. "How did you start cooking anyway?" he asked. "Based on your relationship with knives, I'm guessing you didn't go to culinary school."

"No, I taught myself," I said. "Mom picked up extra shifts at the hospital after . . ."

"After what?"

"After we moved to San Diego." That was easier than saying,

After my parents' farce of a marriage finally went down in flames and I learned they'd never really wanted me.

"So she showed me how to do really basic meals for Hank," I said. "Boxed mac and cheese, ramen, frozen dinners. After a few months, I went to the library after school and asked if they had books about learning to cook. God bless that librarian, Mrs. Ferraro. She didn't think I was a precocious little dweeb. She ordered some kids' cookbooks for me, and put Post-its on the pages to mark things I should try first, and she wrote down some of her recipes for me before we moved again. I still make her Sunday gravy, and I can't improve her lasagna."

He tilted his head. "So the Ellie Wasserman Cookbook Library came later?"

I smiled. "Oh, yeah. But not by much. When I got my first paycheck from tutoring in high school, I went to Barnes and Noble and bought a brand-new cookbook."

He paused, then nodded. "So you *did* kind of go to school," he said thoughtfully. "You learned from all those writers how to do it."

I looked closely, but I didn't see any mockery on his face. He was genuinely hearing me, just as I was.

"Yeah," I said, feeling warm for a second as respect flowed down a new channel between us. "So I know how you got started cooking, but why did you keep going? You don't get to work at a Michelin-starred place just by falling into it."

He ran his hand through his hair. "It's hard to explain. Have you ever found something and it just made sense to you? Felt right?"

Hank's smile when I'd fed him brownies. Max's first kiss that had tasted like Guinness. It had been forever since I felt that way. "Yeah. When did that happen for you?"

"Two weeks into my job at the Pacific, we got these beautiful Page mandarins, and Ximena talked about how much possibility they had in them. You could make a vinaigrette with the juice, or marmalade with the peel, or preserve them in salt, or add sugar, eggs, and butter and turn them into custard for a tart. That's when I realized there wasn't only one right way to treat an ingredient; there were many. I'd spent my entire life never getting anything right, and now I could just follow my senses, my gut instincts, and make something delicious that people liked."

I'd listened to him tell stories about his cooking history, but now he sounded different. Less glib, more earnest. "That's why you like citrus so much," I realized aloud. "Not just because of how it wakes up food."

He grimaced. "Yeah. I said that too many times."

I put the last dish in the rack, turned off the tap, and grabbed a towel to dry my hands. "But where did the gut instincts come from? You don't just learn to cook from nothing."

He looked hard at the floor, and I let him formulate his thoughts. "Repetition, I guess," he said after a minute. "Especially with physical stuff like knife skills. But just cooking the same dish over and over would be boring as shit, and disrespectful to the ingredients. It's better to learn by starting in the same place, but then thinking about what produce looks good to you that day, what you're craving."

The candle that had lit in the back of my brain yesterday suddenly became a flaming torch. "You talk a lot about doing what you feel like when you pick ingredients and when you cook," I started.

Confusion furrowed his forehead. "Yeah?"

"Well, what if we made the book about that? Cooking based on feeling?"

"But you said we needed recipes."

"No, humor me a second. What do you like to eat when it's scorching hot outside?"

He looked up at the ceiling. "All the salad." When I circled my hands, he said, "If it's summer I want to eat watermelon. Peaches. Tomatoes, once they're in season. Lots of mint and parsley and cilantro."

"What about when you've had a really long day?"

A chuckle. "Pizza. Always pizza. I'm on a first-name basis with my local delivery person."

I scribbled that down on my notepad. "Cheese and carbs?"

"Cheese and carbs forever."

"And when you need a pick-me-up?"

He tapped on his scarred lip. "Something spicy. Like eggs with a lot of tomato and chili. Shakshuka, huevos rancheros, things like that."

"*Yes.*" I ripped out a page, and on the blank sheet I drew vertical lines, then scored another line across the top. In each box I wrote single words: *Comfort, Refresh, Awaken.* I thought for a second, then added *Treat* and *Seduce.*

He blinked as I scrawled. "What's going on?" he asked. "You look even more serious than usual."

"A lot of people wake up in the morning with no clue what they're going to make for dinner," I said, filing the dishes he'd mentioned into the columns. "And most cookbooks rely on you knowing that you want Mexican food, or chicken, or pasta. But what if your starting point was just how you felt, or how you wanted to feel?"

He glanced at the paper. "So if you wanted to be refreshed, or comforted, or . . . Jesus, seduced?"

I raised my eyebrows. "You've never cooked for someone you wanted to get into bed?"

"No," he said briefly, his skin turning pink.

That was interesting. He didn't seem like he'd never had a girlfriend. He was too objectively pretty for that. "Well, if you ever did, you could turn to that section and pick a recipe."

He thought for a second, then said, "So it'd be a seasonal book, but, like, personal seasons."

I smiled at that little bit of poetry. "That's a perfect way to say it."

His face lit up for a second, then dimmed. "That's a cool idea."

Why did he sound wary? "So," I continued tentatively, "we'd

just have to come up with a few other feelings, and then fifteen recipes for each of them."

"That's a lot of recipes," he said faintly, but I just kept scribbling.

"I'm sorry, this must be really boring, watching me write." I turned the page toward him. "Do you want to add anything?"

He pulled on his fingers. "Can't we just keep talking about it?"

"But it's not real unless you write it down."

"I'm sure it's fine. You're so smart it can't be wrong." His hands pressed into the table, and he looked like he was about to haul ass out the door. I remembered the afternoon I cut myself, how when I was vulnerable, he stepped up.

"Please," I begged quietly.

He froze.

"I need you, Kieran. I can't write the book by myself." I pushed the page toward him. "Just take a look. Maybe something will come to you."

He took a long deep breath and sat back down. "OK." He took my pen and started dragging it along the line, speaking each word silently.

And a formless something that had nagged at me whenever I'd watched him fidget and dart around over the past four days solidified.

One of the first people I'd tutored in high school had dyslexia. She'd mouthed as she read words. She couldn't spell for love or money, took extra time on essays and tests. And whenever I could, I'd take her out for walking conversations around the track instead of sitting together at a desk, because otherwise she'd get so distracted she could barely hear me.

Thirty seconds later, he finished reading the page that I would have grasped in five. He looked worn out. "OK. That looks fine to me. Anything else?"

"Kieran? Are you dyslexic?" I asked as gently as I could.

His fingers clamped on the table. "Yes," he answered tightly. "Why?"

I resisted the urge to bang my head on the table. I'd been wasting so much time being annoyed at him, when I should have been giving myself a talking-to. "Because we're supposed to be writing a book, and if you're dyslexic, I've been going about this all wrong."

"No, *you're* writing the book. I'm here to look pretty."

He was doing an excellent impression of my cat when he knew that he was going to the vet, hunkered down and ready to bolt.

"Hey," I said softly.

"What?" he snapped.

"What do you have to lose? I'm on your team, Kieran. Please."

CHAPTER TEN

Ellie

I was about to write us off when he said the magic words. "I'm scared. I'm so fucking scared of this, and I'm going to mess everything up, and I can't."

The force of his emotion hit me like a sucker punch, and it took me a moment to finally say, "Scared of what? I think you're immensely capable. You just have a different brain."

He shook his head hard. "No. I figured out a way to do only the things I'm good at. I have a job which is a lot of little tasks strung together, and where I don't have to write or read." He sighed. "I know I'm not a walking disaster anymore. I've been diagnosed with dyslexia and ADHD. I'm on meds. I got sober. I have a toolkit for adult life. But a whole book is big. Too big."

I felt like I'd dug through a layer of Kieran's thought process and now my shovel had hit rock. "What makes you think you couldn't be any good at this, even if you try?"

"Because I really sucked at it in the past. I almost flunked out of high school, Ellie. Actually flunked out of community college." He rubbed his face. "My parents couldn't deal with a kid who was anything other than an overachiever, and they'd get so angry with me." A bitter chuckle. "It didn't help that I was a little shit."

I swallowed down the surge of anger at his parents' selfishness and asked, "Are they still in your life?"

He stared at the table. "We're not officially estranged or anything. But I know they're bad for me, and I keep my distance. Brian, my brother, he sometimes tells me what they're doing." He rubbed his forehead. "This whole thing, it gives me flashbacks to being in school, before I was diagnosed."

I couldn't tell him that everything was fine, that he had nothing to worry about. It would infuriate me, if someone negated my feelings that way. "I hear you. That must be hard, and I'm sorry."

He rolled his eyes at me. "What do you know about it being hard? I don't think anything is hard for you."

I repressed a laugh. If only. "This is big for me, too. I haven't worked with anyone as famous as you. If this goes wrong, it's a huge hit to my career. And I've messed up a few times in the past, when I was first working on cookbooks. I wrote a pasta recipe which told the cook to add a tablespoon of salt to the sauce instead of a teaspoon. That book got ten one-star Amazon reviews because of my mistake."

A headshake. "That's not the same," he said quietly. "Tell me something you're really afraid of, Ellie."

I couldn't ignore the pleading note in his voice. I needed to meet his fear with mine, and for a second my mind let loose the anxieties that clawed at me: Diane and Ben turning their backs on me. Tad shaking his head sorrowfully as he said there wasn't any more work for me. Anything at all happening to Hank.

But I couldn't bear to tell him anything in present tense. I had to keep it together. "I was so afraid when my husband died," I finally said. "He'd been so strong, so vital, and he was gone, just like that."

Kieran paused, then asked quietly, "What happened?"

I sighed. "He had a congenital heart defect. One night he went to bed and just didn't wake up."

His mouth opened and shut. "Were you there?" he finally asked. "Did you find him?"

A hard squeeze on my heart. I got out, "No. He was in Paris, for a conference. He was supposed to come home, and I got a call from the police at two in the morning instead."

"That's really shitty. I'm so sorry," he said.

When other people heard about Max for the first time, their *sorry*s were laced with incredulousness, like they couldn't believe my bad luck. But Kieran seemed to believe it, and feel my pain as his own. "Thanks," I said, the courtesy not feeling empty for once. I could feel the tears in a hard, hot ball in my throat, and I shoved past them to say, "I felt like I'd been dumped onto a deserted beach. There was the ocean on one side and a dark forest on the other. No map to guide me, no radio for rescue. It was just me, alone, and I had to choose between drowning and walking into the unknown."

He shook his head. "You wouldn't have drowned."

I raised my eyebrows. "No?"

"You would have found a way to make some kind of machete and hacked your way through that forest no matter what. You're tough." He smiled a little. "It's what makes you such a pain in my ass."

I snorted at his crassness, and I felt another emotion sneaking in alongside my respect for his drive and his talent. Liking. I *liked* this man.

But we still had work to do. "Now, can we move forward? I need you to have faith that the two of us together can make this happen," I said firmly.

He grinned at me. "You and me against the world?" he asked.

I met his silver-green gaze, and I felt a tiny, delicate conspiracy forming between us. "You and me against this deadline," I said, trying to make my voice all business.

◆ ◆ ◆

I HADN'T REALIZED how tiring fighting with Kieran had been until we stopped. The rest of that day had gone by in a blur of brainstorming, and for the next four days, instead of waking up every morning thinking, *Oh God, what now?*, I'd think, *Let's go!* We still had skirmishes: I'd had to threaten to solder measuring spoons to his hand before he finally took me seriously about checking quantities. In return, I didn't interrupt him every ten seconds. It worked better to turn on the recorder and sit and listen as he cooked, only stopping him when I absolutely had to.

I'd heard the word "flow" before in terms of creation, but when Kieran was in it with cooking, it was like watching a musician composing at a piano, picking out a single riff, then expanding and expanding until it became a song. I'd always sneered at anyone who talked about cooking as an art. Art was something to be admired at a distance, not something for comfort and warmth.

But his art was effervescent and colorful and even a little goofy. One day we'd had leftover black olives and pearls of mozzarella from an eggplant pasta recipe we were trying for the "Comfort" section, and he made kitschy little penguins on toothpicks with carrots for their noses and feet.

I'd tried to keep my face straight. "Big kid's birthday energy."

"Yeah," he said cheerfully. "They *are* the cutest things you've ever seen."

One night, I stayed up listening to his chatter on headphones and transcribing. I started scribbling out more recipe ideas, annotating them, then crumpling them up and starting over again. It was a fine balance, trying to capture his humor and excitement while making sure the reader would know what to do.

Suddenly, there was a tap on the office door.

When I opened it, Kieran stood there scratching his head. In the soft light, his hair looked like rose gold. "Wow." He yawned. "You literally don't sleep."

I blinked at the computer's clock, its black numbers showing 6:00 AM. It'd been years since I'd pulled an all-nighter. "Guess I was too excited."

He smiled. "Don't do a me, here. You're supposed to be the sensible one."

I snorted as I stretched my shoulders. "That is the whole point, me doing a you."

The smile widened into an evil grin. "Get some rest, Ellie. I'll blast 'Take Me Out' at nine thirty if you need an alarm."

On our last day, we'd finished sketching a seafood stew laced with cream and a little saffron for the "Treat" section, and I was working away at the yellow stains on Tad's nicest pot when Kieran said, "I'm going to go for a run before it gets dark."

Exactly the opportunity I'd been waiting for. "Cool. I'll have something to show you when you get back."

He stopped, sneakers in hand. "You can't show it to me now?"

"Nope, it's a surprise. Merry very early Christmas."

He bounced on the balls of his feet. "Have I told you about the time I was six and I went into our living room at three in the morning and opened every single Christmas present? Including the ones that weren't mine?"

I cracked up. "Why do I find that extremely believable?" And really freaking adorable, but he didn't need to know that. "Go, run, now."

He grumbled good-naturedly as he closed the door behind him.

An hour later, I spread out the torn yellow sheets across the kitchen table. A cookbook production editor would have had a heart attack at my haphazard efforts, but I had the gist on paper. I'd drawn boxes with crude circles in them for photos and copied in outlines of the recipes we'd thought of in the past few days, with abbreviated lists of ingredients and one-line instructions that I thought captured his voice. Light and easygoing, but grounded in his culinary smarts.

The front door opened and closed, and a waft of clean man sweat pulled me into the present. "What's that?" he asked over my shoulder.

"Your book." I tapped my pen across each page, ignoring his rough breathing that did not make me think sexy thoughts. "I wanted you to see how much progress we've made."

For a solid minute, he was totally silent. He picked up each page and studied it, and now I was the one fiddling with my pen.

"We're making a cookbook?" he finally asked.

"We're making a cookbook."

His fingers tugged at his hair as he laughed in disbelief. "This must be some kind of fluke. I got a C minus in senior-year English, and I only got that because my mom pushed me through every essay. So the fact that I'm really going to have a book with my name on it blows my mind."

I smiled. "You did good, Kieran. I think we're going to make something great."

He tapped one of the introductory pages. "Can we change one thing, though? Can we not mention anything about pirates or leprechauns?"

I cocked my head at him. "Why? That's how people know you."

He groaned. "I get that, but it makes me feel ridiculous. I like to have fun in the kitchen, that's important to me, but I'm not goofing off. I feel like a dick saying this, but I am a serious chef."

I nodded. "Of course you are."

He blinked at me. "Of course?"

"No one gets to where you are flying by the seat of their pants. You're a lot of things, but you're not a cartoon character. I'll take the name out."

He closed his eyes, and was that relief all over his face? "Thank you," he said.

Kieran

She looked at me with her blue eyes, warm and sharp at the same time, and I felt good enough.

I wanted to bottle that feeling. And then I wanted to wrap it in bubble wrap, put it in a safe deposit box in the world's most secure bank, and visit it whenever I wanted, take it out and hold it up to the light.

She gathered the yellow papers up. "Kieran? You good?"

"Yeah," I said, my voice high from all the feelings pressing on my throat. I coughed to release some tension, then asked, "So what happens now?" I almost didn't want to go back to my cruddy studio, and protein bars, and being alone.

"Well, we could find a kitchen to rent so we can test together on your days off. There's a space in West Berkeley, and another in the Dogpatch, not far from you." She bit her lip, then said, "Or you could also come work at my house. I've had two people cooking there before. It's a tight fit but it's manageable. You'd just need to bring your knife roll. It might be good for you to replicate the experience of a home cook, anyway."

"That sounds nice," I said in a very Ellie-ish polite understatement. I'd gotten a little taste of what she was like when she let her guard down, and I wanted more of that warmth, that easy quiet. I wanted Ellie playing with her massive cat, Ellie stirring something in the big cast-iron pot on her stove, Ellie chewing her lip as she studied one of the bajillion cookbooks on her shelves. Ellie at home, relaxed and comfortable.

"Cool. So we're all set?" she asked.

I blinked my cozy dream away. "Yeah." When she smiled at me, it was like she'd taken the jumble of puzzle pieces inside me and laid them out in a clear picture. Everything was rearranged now.

CHAPTER ELEVEN

Kieran

*A*fter three months of recipe writing and testing, Ellie and I had warmed up to each other, and the weather followed our lead. Now it was the end of May, all long, hot, blue-sky days, with citrus and dark greens giving way to piles of strawberries, cherries, and raspberries at the farmers' market.

I knew my ghostwriter a lot better now. When she was in the middle of a task, she would make up these dorky little nonsense songs with no tune at all, telling asparagus it was delicious or ordering chicken to cook faster. A tortoise could still dice vegetables quicker than she could, and tortoises didn't even have thumbs. She'd read pretty much every book about food and cooking, and she remembered it all. If they could give out a degree in knowing about food, Ellie would have a PhD.

She also had a routine that she stuck to like superglue. When I came in the door in the mornings, the air would smell like freshly ground coffee and buttered sourdough toast from her breakfast, her hair would still be wet from showering after yoga, and someone would be singing old jazz songs on her speaker. She would have checked through her to-do list, washed all her dishes, and sharpened all her knives.

Every time I went to her, my shoulders relaxed as I walked the blocks from BART, knowing she'd greet me smiling and that a hot cup of coffee with extra sugar would be waiting for me. It helped that her place was about a thousand times cleaner and nicer than my apartment, and it was good to talk about food with someone who listened so closely to every word I said and who had interesting things to say back. Who had a smile that made me feel warm and toasty inside.

Maybe we could be close friends, the way that Jay and I were close. Even if I'd never dreamed about Jay's bare shoulder peeking over my comforter, begging for my kiss.

Jesus, fantasizing on public transportation was a new low.

My train had just pulled into Oakland's bright sunshine when my pocket buzzed. Brian. I couldn't let him ruin my good mood, but my thumb slipped and pressed the green button instead of the red one. Shit.

"Kieran? You there? Hello?" my brother said.

Too late. I leaned my head against the window and put the phone to my other ear. "Hi, Brian."

"At last, the Happy Pirate Leprechaun finally answers his telephone, to be sure."

I pressed my knuckles hard into the glass, hating his fake Irish accent with everything I had. "That's not fucking funny."

He said in his normal voice, "Speaking of not funny, you haven't returned any of Mom's calls. Are you too famous now?"

The sun was still out, but as far as I was concerned, the gray, miserable fog had rolled in. "If you want me to stay on the phone, a guilt trip isn't the way."

"OK, OK. I'm sorry," he said quickly. Unlike the rest of our family, he almost always backed off when I told him to.

"How's Houston?" I said, trying to keep my voice easy.

"Fine, as far as I know," he said without much enthusiasm. "I'm too busy to get out much, and I was on a project in Omaha last month."

"I guess they have software to troubleshoot in Nebraska, too."

"Yeah. Windowless offices are pretty much the same everywhere. Did you get Mom's emails about the anniversary party?"

Damn, I thought that might be why he'd called. I'd opened

them so that the red number wouldn't show up on my inbox, but I hadn't actually read them. "Uh-huh."

"So you're coming?"

"Nope."

"Kieran!"

"Don't say my name like I'm eight and broke your Nintendo again."

"But it's our family," he said firmly. "It's what we're supposed to do."

It was so easy for Brian to talk about what we were supposed to do when he could, you know, do it. He wasn't the one who'd been screamed at every damn day. "When have I ever done what I was supposed to do where our parents are concerned?"

"Ah, but then you doing it would go against their expectations. So you'd wrongfoot them anyway."

I couldn't hold a laugh back. "I see your reverse psychology and raise you 'I have billions of better things to do.'"

Suddenly Brian sounded serious. "Kieran. Listen to me. You *have* to come."

My back stiffened. "I'm twenty-seven years old. I don't *have* to do a damn thing."

"No, listen. It's supposed to be a surprise, but the party's for you."

I looked at the phone like it had turned into a guinea pig. "What?" I said, totally confused.

"I mean, not all for you. It's still their anniversary. But they want to celebrate you winning *Fire on High*, too."

I stared at my phone. Had I had this all wrong? Had they been trying to reach out to me and I'd been blind? "What's the catch?" I asked slowly.

"No catch. They think it's a big deal. They think you're a big deal."

I closed my eyes, trying to center myself. To save my sanity,

I'd closed every stupid childish wish I'd had about my parents in a box, then taped it shut and shoved it into the back of my mind's attic. But all of a sudden, something pushed its way out of the box. Something that looked a lot like hope, pale and shaky from no light or air. "They're proud of me?" I couldn't keep the question out of my voice.

"Why would they throw a party if they weren't?"

That was Brian, always optimistic when it came to our family.

This was too big a change to digest in ten seconds on a train. "I'll think about it," I finally said. "Honestly, I didn't know that we were on speaking terms again."

He sighed. "You're the one not speaking to them. Anyway, they're doing a fancy party at the house. You'll need a suit, and Mom said she wants us for breakfast the next morning."

I rubbed my neck, trying to get the tension out. "If it goes wrong, at least it'll make my next dentist appointment super fun in comparison."

"I assume you'll come on your own for this?"

God, he could be so patronizing sometimes. "I guess," I answered, my voice bratty.

But then I thought about being there by myself. I'd be surrounded by people who'd known me when I was a teenage dirtbag, Mom's librarian friends and Dad's golf buddies. My old teachers. Brian cared more about making them happy, so who knew how much help he'd be.

If things went south, I'd be all alone.

"Is Mom giving you shit about bringing someone, too?" I asked quickly to distract myself.

"Of course she is. She told me that no little O'Neills running around is unacceptable. It's like me turning thirty made her lose it."

"Bri?"

"Yeah?"

"Do you think you'll ever bring anyone home?" He'd never had a girlfriend, or a boyfriend. He'd lived at home during college and spent all his time on his computer, and even after he moved to Texas for work, he was always on the road fixing software.

His pause filled my ear, then he said, "I don't think so. But I don't know how to tell them that. You were hard enough for them to deal with as it is. But two strange sons?"

I jerked back in my seat. Brian could be bad at reading me, but that was below the belt. "Thanks a lot, asshole."

"Shit, Kieran, I'm sorry. I didn't mean it like that."

"North Berkeley," the announcer called.

"I need to go," I said, desperate to be outside, away, far away.

"OK." Brian sighed. "Just read your damn emails, please. Mom is relentless."

I was grateful for the walk from the station to Ellie's. I needed all that fresh air to get my balance back. When I knocked, she called warmly, "It's open."

I couldn't repress the sigh of relief at being back here. It was bright and tidy and smelled like oranges. Ellie stood at the sink wearing an old-fashioned sundress, navy blue with red roses, with a deep V that showed her upper back. Brown beauty spots dotted her creamy skin.

What would they taste like?

The grumpy voice I'd had in my head since Brian called lost the attitude and instead started to list reasons why kissing Ellie's neck would be amazing. The dip of her waist would be perfect to rest my hands in. She'd smell like Earl Grey and clean sheets, and taste like salt and citrus. She'd turn in my hold, rest her arms on my shoulders, and her soft blue eyes would flutter closed like they had when she'd tasted that blood orange at the farmers' market.

Reality smothered my fantasy. Even if she liked me that way, she wouldn't kiss me in a million years. We were coworkers, and Ellie was a professional.

"Good journey?" she asked over her shoulder, soaping up a mixing bowl.

"Yeah," I said, trying to remember to breathe. Breathing was definitely the first step to being a professional. "BART was quiet, and not in a creepy way."

She rinsed her hands and dried them on a cherry-printed kitchen towel. "Your timing's perfect. I just reran the duck and orange recipe. I'll make you a plate."

"What did you do this time?" Ellie had suggested a few weeks ago that we rework the "breakfast textures" duck-orange combination as a salad with raw oranges, and this was the second version she'd tested.

"I thought it needed something really bitter, so I tried arugula. I figured the hot duck would wilt some of it, and then the rest would be fresh for contrast. Like a salade lyonnaise. It's pretty, isn't it?"

She was right—the deep green of the leaves played well against the browns and oranges of meat and fruit. But when I took a bite, salt burned my tongue. "Where's the duck confit from?" I asked hoarsely.

She raised her eyebrows. "I bought it ready-made from a guy at the Grand Lake market. If you can get a Saturday morning off, I'll take you."

"Ah," I murmured after I chugged half a glass of water.

"Is it bad?" Her voice was suddenly small.

I swallowed. "He's using too much seasoning. It's a little like corned beef right now. Have you ever made duck confit yourself?"

"Nope," she said tightly.

"You just need to get past the whole poaching something in a fuck-ton of oil. And if we do it ourselves, the readers can replicate it exactly instead of hoping their duck tastes like what we bought." I took another bite. "One other thing. You didn't supreme the oranges. There's a lot of pith."

Her shoulders slumped a little. "I don't know how. As you probably noticed, I don't have your knife skills."

"It's not hard."

"I'm sure it's not. Are you going to eat the rest of that?"

I sat back. "I shouldn't. We're testing a bunch of other stuff today, right?"

"Yeah." Her back was straight and tense when she scraped the salad into the compost.

Another thing I'd learned? Ellie really hated getting things wrong. It was like she thought that overspiced duck and bitter oranges meant she was a bad person.

"Ellie, it's OK," I said gently. "We'll figure it out. Don't stress."

Her eyes didn't meet mine. "I shouldn't have tried to take a shortcut. Stupid of me."

For the next ten minutes, she banged around the kitchen and gave brittle one-word answers to any question. I didn't know how to soften her again.

But when she went to the bathroom, I saw the bunch of asparagus on the counter and had an idea.

Ellie

*W*hen I came out of the bathroom, trying and failing to push down my frustration at screwing up the recipe, Kieran was washing dishes and humming. It sounded weird. A little choked.

"Kieran?"

He turned around, and I slapped my hand over my mouth. Asparagus sprouted from behind his ears, and he'd shoved stalks in his bandanna, too. For the piece de resistance, he'd jammed an orange slice into his mouth so the peel filled the whole space.

"What on earth?" I said through my fingers.

The goofball wiggled his eyebrows at me. He was absurd. Ludicrous. And then he crossed his eyes, and that was me gone.

"What?" he half-said through the orange.

"You look, you look," I gasped with laughter, pointing at him, just barely holding myself up with a kitchen chair.

He spat the orange into the sink. "This is, like, a new style? Though some people say it has to be, like, *white* asparagus behind your ears?"

My giggles bent me in half, my stomach muscles tight. "Stop, stop, you're such a dork."

"I am awesome, thank you very much. You all right there?"

"Fine, fine, just dying. Oof. I didn't know I needed that." I wiped tears from my eyes. "How did you know I would laugh at that?"

He plucked out the spears from around his head. "I guessed from how you smirked when Hayden force-fed me honey. You can appreciate when a situation is totally ridiculous. Do you feel better?"

My frustration was gone. "I do." And why was I blushing now, at the focused way he looked at me? He'd just tried to cheer me up.

"Now I want to show you how to supreme an orange," he said. "Come on over."

I went around to his side of the counter, grabbing an orange from the fruit bowl on the way.

"So start the same way you prepped them. Cut the top and the bottom off, then follow the shape of the orange to take off the peel."

It was like a hand had turned the volume way down on the hum of anxiety that always buzzed in my head. He was all calm competence. He knew what to do, and he'd tell me how in that dark-brown-sugar voice, and I could just *be.*

I slowly followed his instructions. He leaned in and I got a whiff of white soap and pine forest. "Closer," he said softly. "Cut closer."

He could whisper in my ear, he was that near. His scarred lower lip so close to my skin. *Focus, Ellie.* "I don't want to lose half the orange," I murmured.

"Have a little faith," he murmured back.

I couldn't help but smile at his smartassery. "That's my line." But I did what he said.

"Now follow the divots to trim out the segments."

The tip of my tongue stuck out as I slid my blade into the fruit, millimeters from my fingers.

"Careful," he coaxed.

Any notion of knife skills evaporated out of my head as all the blood in my body rushed either to my cheeks or between my legs. I couldn't think, I could only want. I *wanted* him to coax me, to be so careful with me.

But we weren't in bed. We were at the kitchen counter, and I still had a sharp knife in my sweaty hand. "So I cut right to the middle?" I forced out.

He cleared his throat. "One second. May I?" He held out his hand.

I reached out to meet him. The juice had made my fingers sticky, and they clung to his just a little. "Sorry," I said, awareness of him shortening my breath. I gulped. "Messy."

"It's fine," he said quickly, pink coloring his white skin. "You just need more of an angle. Like this." He grabbed his paring knife and with two precise cuts, extracted a perfect crescent of fruit and dropped it on the board. "See?"

I tried to focus on anything but his soft voice. "Your tattoo," I said, staring at the delicate black outline on his forearm.

He glanced down, confusion on his face. "It's been there the whole time. Did you just notice?"

"No. That," I said, pointing to the knife he held, "is your tattoo. Most chefs have a huge knife on their arms. Or even a cleaver. Not their paring knives."

He twirled it slowly. "This was my first good knife. Ximena and the other senior chefs at the Pacific had rolls full of these beautiful blades, and I only had cheap-ass plastic-handled ones. I tried to keep them sharp, but I still mangled and wasted ingredients. So I ate a lot of ramen and canned beans, and on my day off I drove to this kitchen store in Chinatown in LA. When I picked up this tiny thing for the first time, it felt like I could do delicate stuff and get it right."

The way he said "delicate" made me think of him doing nonculinary things. Like kissing me. Like tracing his fingertips over my skin, whispering sweet words as he mapped me.

But Tad was depending on me. And kisses and touches wouldn't keep us on task. "You need to stop saying these things when I don't have my phone recording," I said as lightly as I could. "That's gold."

His mouth quirked. "You'll remember. You try, now."

"OK. Here goes." My first segment was more ragged than his.

"Good," he said softly. "Again."

I shivered.

"You cold?"

The opposite. I imagined taking an ice bath in a blizzard and said calmly, "I'm fine." I spun the fruit slowly, making neater and neater cuts, until the last segment was exactly right.

"Nice," he said approvingly. "That's how you supreme."

"That's not too bad to describe to a home cook, but doesn't that leave a lot of fruit behind?"

"Yeah, but watch." He held his hand out for the fruit's skeleton. When I gave it back, I didn't linger on how my skin stuck to his again.

But now he was still, and this was too much eye contact for coworkers. "Kieran?"

He shook his head hard and the link broke. "Sorry. Pass me that little bowl?" A trickle of red juice fell into the bowl when he squeezed as hard as he could. "See? No waste."

"That could be the start of the vinaigrette."

"Exactly. Though the blood orange is pretty sweet. It would need something really sharp to stand up to all the olive oil. Like . . ."

I tapped my lip. "Some sherry vinegar? Or mustard?"

"Definitely the first one. But we don't want a sweet mustard vinaigrette."

"Wouldn't be much. Only half a teaspoon. It'd help the dressing emulsify."

He shook his head. "It should come together without that."

"With a lot of practice, definitely, but it's good to give the cook a safety net. They're not going to get it right every time."

"So it's like making the recipe a little more forgiving?" he asked.

I nodded. "Exactly."

He thought for a second, then smiled. "We all need that sometimes. We'll do it your way."

"Thank you." His trust settled over me like a soft blanket. I let myself savor the breakthrough for a second, then called up my spreadsheet that tracked my tests of all the recipes in *Whatever You Want*. "OK. Buy duck legs and a lot of oil for next time. And I'll think about the proportions for the vinaigrette recipe. But right now we should rerun the asparagus salad for 'Refresh' and the pavlova for 'Treat.'"

I called out ingredients, and Kieran pulled more asparagus, eggs, and fruit out of the fridge. While I put a pot of water on for boiling and blanching, Kieran grabbed both our knives and ran the edges over a porcelain wand to sharpen them.

"Did you ever think about writing your own book?" he asked as he worked.

I carefully split one of the eggs and put the white into one bowl, the yolk into another. The bright orange yolk would become mayonnaise, and the white would make meringues that we'd top with whipped cream, raspberries, and roasted rhubarb. "I have a proposal, but it's never really gone anywhere."

He shook his head. "Well, that's their loss. I'm sure you wrote something awesome."

I grimaced at the bowls instead of looking at him. "No, like, I've never submitted it. I don't have an agent or anything."

"Why not?"

I bit my lip. "I was working on it before Max died, and it's probably old news by now. Three years is a long time in food."

He turned to the sink and quickly washed his hands. "I want to see it."

"I don't know—it's a mess. You'll probably cringe at it."

His eyebrows shot up as he grabbed a towel. "Come on, Ellie, why would you think that?"

Because Max would look briefly at recipes I'd worked on, but he was a lot more interested in eating the food. He would ask how I'd spent my days, then just nod at my answers. Over time I began to say, "Fine," instead of telling him details, and I'd ask him about his day instead. I hadn't had his knack for storytelling, anyway.

"I don't know." I lied now, pushing away the less-than-glowing memory.

"Please, pretty please, with a cherry on top?" Kieran said in the present, giving me puppy-dog eyes and a trembling lower lip.

But Kieran wasn't Max. He cooked too, and food had made us both, in different ways. Maybe he'd get it. "OK."

He clapped. "Yay, I get to see cool Ellie stuff."

What a sweet goof he was. I washed my hands, smiling, then opened the proposal and turned my laptop toward him. "Here you go."

I knew reading would take him a while, and there were always more dishes to wash when we were testing. I stood over the sink and let hot water and suds flow over my hands, but I couldn't help but listen to the tap of my keyboard as he scrolled through the pages, seeing Hank's fettuccine Alfredo with pops of green pea and scallion, Max's towering devil's food birthday cake, the roast lamb leg scented with herbs de Provence that Diane used to serve to guests' oohs and aahs. Seeing pictures of Nicole pretending to be the Spaghetti Monster, of Ben carving a chicken with a huge grin on his face, of little Hank with a fat streak of turquoise frosting through his light blond hair.

"Why are you calling it *Nourish*?" Kieran asked.

"I think feeding people goes deeper than just filling their bellies," I said. "I think it makes us feel connected. Safe. So it's not just about physical hunger."

He studied me. "Food is love, for you."

I blushed under his gaze. "Yeah," I said simply. "Always has been."

He looked back at the screen. "No wonder you take it so seriously," he said. "Max was a lucky guy."

I shook my head. "I was the lucky one. Max could have had anyone, and he picked me."

"But you could have had anyone, too."

The way he said that, with such calm certainty. I tried to rub the blush out of my cheeks. "Incorrect. I was fresh out of high school and hadn't been anywhere. Totally rough around the edges. Diane taught me how to dress and how to be." I'd had to get used to my new reflection in the mirror, but I'd liked the way my cheekbones looked sharper with short hair, how my skin warmed with wearing colors and prints instead of basic gray and navy. Max's wolf whistles hadn't hurt either.

A minute later, Kieran closed the laptop. "I like this a lot, but something's missing."

"What? A recipe?"

"No. There's not a lot of *you* in it. No pictures of you, no recipes you make for yourself."

I resisted the urge to shy away. "There aren't really any pictures of me as a child. And I like everything in that proposal. I wouldn't have put it in if I didn't." Which wasn't quite true. I liked the way cooking the recipes made me feel. I liked the satisfaction of watching someone else relish my food. I wouldn't choose to eat everything in there, but that wasn't the point.

"Seriously?" Kieran said. "My parents took thousands of pictures of us." His mouth turned down. "When we were little kids, anyway."

I tried to shrug. "My parents were super hands-off. My dad left for good when I was nine, and my mom worked a lot. When she wasn't working, she needed time to herself."

His mouth tightened. "They had you, but they didn't want to raise you? That's some bullshit."

I heard Hank's scorn in his voice, and I tried to lower the temperature. "Mom did the best she could." Which was terrible. "I don't blame her. She had me when she was twenty." She hadn't grown past that point, though. "I didn't know much of anything when I was that old, let alone how to care for a kid." But I'd known enough to marry a good, loving man with a solid career who'd actually wanted to be a dad someday.

Kieran's hand lifted and moved an inch toward mine, then stopped. "Thank you for trusting me with that," he finally said. His eyes on me were so soft, and for a second all I wanted was to bury my face in his neck.

"At least my parents were hands-on, even if it wasn't great for me," he said. He exhaled hard.

His tension stretched out between us. "What's the matter?"

He rested his head on his arms. "Brian called when I was on my way here. My mom has been bugging me to come down for this party in June, and I've been saying no. But now he says that it's not just for their anniversary. It's a party to celebrate me winning *Fire on High*."

"I mean, that's great." But he wasn't exactly brimming with excitement, so I toned mine down. "Do you think it's great?"

He sat up and rubbed the back of his neck, grimacing. "I don't know." He half-laughed. "I can't help hoping that they've changed a little. If they haven't, I would be alone with all their judginess, and that would suck."

"What would they judge you for?"

"I don't value the same things as them," he said with a shrug I didn't buy. "They're big on pretending. Smiling big even when things are shit, dressing up. My parents want me to wear a suit to this thing, and I really hate wearing fancy clothes."

Which was the surprise of the century, given that I'd only seen him in old jeans and worn-out concert T-shirts. "What's wrong with dressing up?"

He gestured to me. "I don't mean you. Your dresses always look comfortable and pretty . . ." He swallowed. "I mean, nice. Pretty nice. But suits are scratchy and too hot and I don't know which ass-hole invented ties, but they're torture, not clothing." As he spoke, he scratched his neck like he could feel the constriction.

I didn't want him to feel trapped. How could I let him out? "What if I could take you somewhere you could get a suit you loved? Something that would make you feel comfortable, not like you're being suffocated?"

He shrugged dismissively again. "Thanks, but that suit doesn't exist. I'll just go to T.J.Maxx and buy whatever. I won't waste my money."

But there was something under the dismissiveness. I remem-bered how for years I had dressed in plain baggy clothes to make myself invisible, and how Diane had shown me that cotton and jer-sey and silk could be a source of confidence instead. "Don't buy the suit for them, Kieran," I finally said. "Buy the suit for *you*. Because it makes *you* look like a million bucks."

He blinked. "A million bucks, huh?"

I nodded. "There's a tailor in North Beach my father-in-law goes to for super-special occasions. I could take you there on your next day off and he could measure you."

"You want to give me a makeover?"

I smiled. "Not a makeover." I waved my hand in his direction, "Just something to make you look on the outside the way you are on the inside."

He leaned forward on the counter and grinned widely. "How am I on the inside, Ellie?"

Smart. Talented. Funny. Dashing, to use an old-school word. But I couldn't tell him any of that. "Not a complete pain in my neck," I said lightly.

A little smile snuck across his lips, and I told myself it wasn't any more attractive than his huge Pirate Leprechaun grin that he handed out to everyone. "Fine. Take me to your magical tailor."

CHAPTER TWELVE

Kieran

The San Francisco fog had started to burn off, but it was trying to stay behind in the clothes of the people walking through North Beach. We were all dressed in blacks and grays against the chill. So much for May being spring.

But Ellie hadn't gotten the dark-colors memo. She leaned against a brick wall in a long wool coat the color of the jacaranda tree that bloomed outside my parents' house every year: bright, vivid, electric purple.

"I didn't know I had to dress up to visit a suit store," I said as I walked up to her. "T.J.Maxx only makes me wear a shirt and shoes."

She chuckled. "Sure, but you would have bought a suit that you hated every second it was on your body, then shoved into the back of your closet. Here you can get a suit that you'll want to wear as much as possible. Mr. Murphy's a genius."

She walked a few doors down an alley and then down a short staircase. Was this basement a store? More like a cave. The morning sunlight sparked the dust in the air. A few old mannequins were dressed in *Mad Men*–style suits, and black-and-white cardboard posters covered the walls. On the largest one, a skinny freckled guy straddled a Vespa, and a curvy woman with a blond beehive rode behind him.

"Is the tailor invisible?" I whispered. "Or are there a bunch of mice cutting fabric in the back?"

"Mr. Murphy?" she called. "It's Ellie Wasserman? We had an appointment?"

"Yes, with you in a mo," a distracted British voice replied from behind the counter. A tall, lanky man unfolded himself with a grunt. He had a cap of white hair with longish sideburns, and a few stray red hairs popped from his matching eyebrows.

A gentle smile grew on his face. "Max's Ellie, so good to meet you. I was so sorry to hear about his passing. I really enjoyed kitting him out for your wedding—never seen a man more excited to tie the knot."

I felt Ellie take a heavy breath next to me, and my hand moved a few inches toward her lower back before I shoved it in my pocket. I couldn't comfort her like that.

Mr. Murphy leaned across the counter. "So what brings you here today? Your father-in-law is my first and favorite customer, but I don't think one of my ladies' suits would do you justice."

I could see Ellie pushing the sadness down. "You're right—I'm a dress girl for sure," she said with a brave smile. She stepped aside. "This is my friend, Kieran O'Neill."

The tailor grinned, revealing teeth that had seen too many cups of tea and not enough visits to the dentist. "Congratulations on your victory, Mr. O'Neill. I particularly enjoyed what you did with that crab in the semifinal. My wife had a go the very next day, and it was delicious."

I blinked in surprise. My fan base was mostly millennials who took pictures of their food, but I guess you never knew. "Thank you, I appreciate that very much."

He ambled around the counter. "Now, I suppose a fancy celebrity like you's been fitted for a suit before?"

"Nope, this is new."

"This is truly an honor, then," he said, sounding grand and a little jokey. But his eyes were serious as they zoomed down to my feet, then moved slowly up. My back automatically straightened, and I took my hands out of my pockets.

"Five foot . . . six," he said.

"Seven."

"Six and a half, then. And very lean. What's your sport?"

"Running. Some weight training."

He rubbed his hands together. "Excellent. What sort of suit were you thinking, Mr. O'Neill?"

"Please call me Kieran. I think I'm in trouble when someone uses my last name. And just something basic. Black, I guess?"

He looked over my shoulder. "Are you two going to a funeral?"

"He's going to a party," Ellie said. "And he wants to knock their socks off."

"Indeed? Then we can do better than basic black. It doesn't really suit us gingers, anyway. Too stark." He looked me up and down. "I think a gray blue for you. Definitely slim fit."

"I'll let you work your magic," Ellie said. "I'll be over in that excellent armchair with my book."

"Don't get too caught up," he said, still sizing me up with his eyes. "I'll need you to pick out ties. Do you know what you'll wear for this party?"

"Oh, I'm not going" and "She's not coming" we blurted, our words collapsing in a heap.

Mr. Murphy's eyebrows shot up. "Is she not? All right. Do you trust her, though?"

"Absolutely." The certainty in my chest was solid gold, but a small desperate part of me hoped that Ellie wouldn't be a smartass right now.

She didn't give me any rolling eyes or raised brows. Just a soft smile that made me feel a foot taller.

Mr. Murphy clapped his hands, and I came back down to earth. "Good," he said. "Greens, blues, purples, please, Ellie. Not too much pattern." He swept his arm toward the back of the store. "This way please, Kieran."

He stretched measuring tape down my arms and across my shoulder blades, humming and making notes, then walked around me again.

When he got up close and personal to measure my inseam, I blurted, "Why are you writing so much?"

He looked up, brow furrowed. "I suppose the first time you wore a suit was for your Confirmation, with a polyester tie that felt like it was strangling you?"

I stared at him in surprise, and he chuckled. "Tell me something. When Ellie wears that lovely royal-purple coat, how do you think she feels?"

"Lovely? And royal?"

"Exactly. So, how do you want to feel when you go to this party?"

What I wanted hadn't even been part of the equation for seeing my parents. Getting out of there without shredding my brain into panic confetti would have been a good result. But maybe I could have more than that. I could be the hero of this story. "I want to feel good."

He circled his hand in the air.

I looked at myself in the mirror and wished. "I want to feel strong. Confident. Like they can't touch me."

"That, I can work with." He grunted as he stood up from the floor and ducked behind the curtain. Five minutes later, he returned with sets of pants and jackets on hangers. "I think the subtle plaid will do nicely. You're actually very lucky, being the height you are."

I had thought that zero times in my entire life.

"You can wear suits that would make a taller man look like an absolute clown," he said. "You just need something that's fitted to you properly. No baggy trousers or enormous shoulders, or a tie hanging to your knees. *Can* you stand still?" His voice wasn't angry. It was like he was genuinely curious.

I stopped my fingers on my tattoo. "Sorry. I'm just not used to this," I said cautiously.

Instead of getting grumpy like my parents always had, he laughed. "Fair enough. I imagine that's an asset in your line of work. Try these on and shout when you're ready."

The jacket sleeves were down to my knuckles, and the pants slopped over my insteps. But my hair and eyes looked brighter against the silvery blue, my shoulders broader in the jacket.

"Very promising indeed," Mr. Murphy said when he came back in. "The plaid was the right choice. Plain fabric would be too staid for you."

I cleared my throat. "Speaking of not staid. These pants are *tight*."

"Americans labor under the misconception that their suits should wear them, not the other way around. Paul Smith knows better." He walked behind me and tugged at the waistband. "I could actually take them in a smidge. You're more trim than I thought."

"Can I still have children someday?" I joked.

He snorted. "I won't castrate you. I promise. Let me get my pins, and then you'll have to stay still again."

I could see why Ellie had brought me here. He was so precise, like her. Jacket sleeves adjusted millimeter by millimeter, then each pin slipped in exactly the right place. I understood now how a suit like this could be a second skin. I looked elegant. Put together. "It looks amazing already. Thank you."

"Well, you won't get the full effect without a shirt," Mr. Murphy said as he rolled up the pants.

"Can I buy one from you?"

"Of course. You don't own any?"

"No. I'm not an ironing person." There was plenty of clothing that looked fine fresh out of the dryer, so why would I bother?

He tsked. "You can pay people to do it. If you're buying a suit from me, you can afford that."

After a few more pins, he asked, "How did you meet Ellie? Max was going to be a French professor, not a chef."

I shrunk a little bit. He reminded me that Ellie had run with a brainy crowd, who must have read piles of books like her and spoke other languages like it was breathing. "We work together. She's helping me write my cookbook."

"Straighten up for me?" he asked gently. "And of course, she writes about food, doesn't she? What's she like to work with?"

The laugh jumped out my mouth. "Amazing and terrible at the same time."

He looked up from the floor. "Your smile intrigues me."

I didn't realize I was smiling. "She's so smart. Stubborn as hell. And she cares. She cares so much." When had all of those things stopped making me want to break pens? My fear and frustration felt like they'd happened back in the Stone Age. Instead of running away, I wanted more of her intensity, her certainty.

"That sounds completely horrific," he said, his voice drier than James Bond's martini. "Someone who cares, Jesus Christ. What can you do with a woman like that, except give her every drop of blood and sweat?"

I froze as he stole the thought out of my brain, and then saw him grinning at me. "You're being sarcastic." I exhaled.

"Sort of." He stood up and brushed down my shoulders. "Right. Let's go show Ellie."

Ellie

*I*f Kieran looked any better than he did now, I'd be pounding the table and howling like the horndog in the old cartoons. "Wow. I mean, wow. Mr. Murphy, you've outdone yourself."

I made a show of digging around in my purse to buy myself some time to get it together. The goofy, scruffy puppy dog had disappeared, and in his place was a lethal young fox.

"What are you looking for?" Kieran asked.

"A diamond to cut on your cheekbones." The joke came out high and tight, and I gave in. "Seriously, you look fantastic."

He ran his hands down the silvery blue fabric. "It's not me, it's the suit."

"Tell yourself that, and your family are going to jump all over you. The suit doesn't hurt, though."

"What about shoes?" Mr. Murphy asked.

"I was just going to wear my Converse," Kieran said.

"Do you mean the ones that are more holes than canvas?" I interrupted.

He snorted. "I'm guessing that means *No, Kieran, don't wear the Chucks.*"

"He could wear Chuck Taylors," Mr. Murphy said. "If he'd be more comfortable in them, that's what he should do."

I groaned, and Kieran pumped his fist in the air.

Mr. Murphy raised his finger and said sternly, "I wasn't finished. They must be brand-new."

"You hear that?" I said.

Kieran muttered, "Fine, fine, I'll buy new shoes. But the rest of it works?"

He looked sharp enough to make a *GQ* model weep with envy. "Understatement."

A blush turned his cheeks pink. "Thank you."

And now I was blushing, too. "Don't thank me. He's the genius."

"You're both very welcome," Mr. Murphy said, looking back and forth at us with a little smile on his face. "About my fee . . ."

Ten minutes later, Kieran was four figures poorer, with the suit, a shirt, and an extra charge for Mr. Murphy rushing the alterations. But he looked like it wasn't just his wallet that was lighter. The rest of him was fizzing with energy. Even my insisting on putting his final fitting in my calendar as well as his hadn't punctured his bounce.

"Do you want to go do something?" he asked when we were standing outside.

"You don't need me for buying a pair of Chucks."

He poked me lightly in the arm. "No, I mean, I want to hang out with you. You helped me buy a badass suit. Let's go celebrate."

He was shaken-up champagne, and I couldn't help but feel like

I wanted a sip. "What did you have in mind?" I asked with a smile in my voice.

He bounced in his shoes. "How about bungee jumping? Or skydiving?"

My stomach plummeted in response, and my head started shaking without me thinking about it.

"Or we could go to Ocean Beach and run into the water? I don't know, Ellie, I was dreading the party and now I feel *good*."

I couldn't help but laugh. "How about a cappuccino to start? We can negotiate about the bungee jumping."

CHAPTER THIRTEEN

Kieran

Ellie picked a café she knew on Washington Square, and when we walked in there was the rich smell of fresh espresso, and the dudes behind the counter were yelling in Italian.

"What would you like?" she asked as she took her wallet out.

"Oh, hell no, I'm buying," I said with a laugh. "Celebrating, remember?"

"But you don't have to."

I put my hand on her wrist. "I insist."

Did her mouth just open a little? This kept happening. Every time I was a little bossy with her, like when I'd fed her the blood orange in Sonoma, she went all dreamy-looking. It made me think very bad thoughts.

"All right. Thank you," she said.

I shook my head hard and tapped on the glass counter full of baked goods. "Do you want a croissant or anything?" The pastries were a little pale and flabby, but I'd seen worse.

"No thanks. I'm against sad pastry."

I snorted. "Sad pastry. I like that."

The sun had finally won the fight against the fog, and the light made the grass in the square shine bright green. Older people and a couple with a little black-haired boy took up most of the benches, and I snagged the last one for us.

Ellie put her coffee down beside her, then rested her elbows on the back of the bench and tilted her face toward the sky. A few inches of her coat touched my leg. My fingers twitched with the urge to rub the wool between my fingers.

"Are you not sleeping again?" I said to stop myself.

She shook her head. "Sorry. I like to take a second to really feel the sun on my skin. Something my therapist told me to do. It's the small things, I guess."

I smiled. That was Ellie's whole philosophy in a neat little phrase. She believed in the small nice things that made life better: half-and-half in her coffee, purple coats instead of black, a romance novel always on her nightstand. "If those croissants were sad pastries, what are happy pastries, and where can I get one?" I asked.

"You went to France. I'm sure you ate some good ones there."

"Yeah, but I want to hear what *you* think."

She sipped her drink. "Well, the ones from the bakery around the corner from my apartment in Lyon were awesome, but it was my first time in Europe and basically everything blew my mind. I'd be a little scared to try them now. Maybe they were mediocre."

I said immediately, "I doubt that. You have good taste."

All of a sudden, she looked giddy. "Oh my God, can you say that in front of a witness? No, wait! I should *record* it, so I can play it back when you're questioning me about a recipe!"

"You think you're so smart," I fake-grumbled.

"Anyway. In the States, the best ones I've ever eaten were at Bedford Street Bakery, in Brooklyn."

"I heard the pastry chef at Qui raving about that place. The woman who runs it is Kiwi, right?"

"Yeah. She bakes these beautiful seasonal pastries. I was there around this time four years ago, and there was one with apricots, *crème pâtissière,* and toasted almonds, and it was just gorgeous." Her shoulders dropped, and her mouth went slack remembering the pleasure.

I pressed myself back into the hard bench to hold off the wave of horniness that crashed over me. *Jesus, Kieran, get a grip.* "That was a quality Homer Simpson drooling noise," I said. Jokes were safe. Jokes meant I wasn't turned on.

"Yeah," Ellie said softly, not noticing my struggle. "That was a really good day. Max was running a seminar at NYU, so I just wandered around Williamsburg, went to a bookstore, ate pastry, and read under the trees in the park."

She looked so peaceful, and it quieted down everything that darted around inside me. A crash of piano keys from my phone broke the silence.

"My mom. I should take this," I said.

Ellie nodded, and I hopped up and walked ten yards away. I pressed the green button and heard my mother's cool voice ask, "Kieran?"

"Hi, Mom. How's party prep? I definitely pressed Yes on the Evite last week."

"I saw, and I'm pleased you can make it. But you're really not bringing anyone to the party?"

Well, she'd said she was pleased, so I kept my expectations a little above rock bottom. "That's right," I said carefully.

A deep sigh. "I would have hoped you'd found the right person by now. You can't be a bachelor forever. Goodness knows Brian is trying to be for some reason."

I swallowed a groan of frustration.

"Don't you have anyone in your life you'd be happy for us to meet?" she asked hopefully. "Anyone at all?"

I jammed the heel of my hand into my eye socket, all twisted up inside from not being able to give her what she wanted. Then my eyes found Ellie on the bench, ankles neatly crossed as she studied the paperback in her lap. She was everything my mom would want on the outside: polite, soft-spoken, tidy. But I knew on the inside Ellie would be there for me. An ally. I took a deep breath and said, "You know what? Let me get back to you, Mom."

"I don't have much time for any unreasonable delays, Kieran," she said, all worry. "The caterers need final numbers by tonight."

I gave my best Ellie-style eye roll. "I'll know today. Talk to you later."

As I walked back to the bench, hands jammed in my pockets, Ellie said dryly, "That looked fun."

I laughed a little. "Yeah, Mom's a riot." The snark eased off some of the tension, and I knew it would be exactly what I needed when I faced my parents. "I need to ask you for another massive favor."

She blinked. "Bringing you to Mr. Murphy was my pleasure. Don't worry about it."

I threw myself off the conversational cliff. "Can you come home with me and pretend to be my girlfriend?"

She went still. "Pardon?"

The word was polite, but her voice made it feel like the fog had blocked out the sun again, and I shivered. "I said, can you come home with me and pretend to be my girlfriend."

"And I thought I was having a romance-novel-induced hallucination," she said. "No, Kieran." She hesitated, then said slowly, "I mean, maybe I could come with you. *Maybe.* But I'm *not* going to be your fake girlfriend."

But she'd hesitated. I could work with that. "It could be fun?" I suggested.

"It would be *lying.*"

"It would be *performing.*"

"You're the TV star. Leave me out of this."

I reached for her hand. "Ellie, please. I'll go down on my knees and beg right here in front of all these people."

"Don't bother," she said incredulously.

I'd put one knee on the ground when she grabbed my T-shirt in her fist. Which was absolutely not a hot move at all.

"They'll think you're proposing," she hissed. "Get up here."

Once I was back on the bench, she asked, "Why on earth do you need a fake girlfriend in the first place?"

"My mom's got all fixated on my brother and I being single. I think she wants grandchildren, sooner rather than later. But from that phone call I can tell she's just going to nag me about it all weekend."

"But you know you're OK just the way you are."

I nodded. Years of therapy had laid down that foundation, and Ellie's validation reinforced it. "I do. I know I've moved on. But when my parents really get going, I'm afraid it won't feel like it." The little kid inside me was crying out, and the whole truth came out, sad and plaintive. "I just want someone there who knows me, Ellie. Really knows me."

She rested her elbows in her lap and pressed the bridge of her nose.

Maybe this was a dumb idea. I should have asked someone else. Or not asked anyone at all and been braver. "Ellie?"

"I'm thinking," she said, muffled by her hands.

"I've never met anyone who thinks as loudly as you."

She didn't laugh when she took her hands away from her face. "What am I supposed to do with you, Kieran?"

"Save me," I half-joked. "Pretty please, with whipped cream and a cherry on top?"

The seconds ticked by. She suddenly looked at me, and her face made me think of a mountain lion honing in on a furry little rabbit.

Was it weird that I was OK with being the bunny?

"What will you do for me?" she asked slowly.

"What do you mean?"

"We haven't been friends for super long. This is too big a favor to do out of the goodness of my heart. So what's in it for me?"

I straightened up as Ellie asked the blunt question. There was a little bit of steel mixed in with her softness. I couldn't push her around, and I liked that. I liked that a lot. "I'll buy you happy pastries of your choice every week for a year?" I tried.

"No pastry is so happy that it makes me feel good about lying for twenty-four hours straight."

I rubbed my head. "Money?"

Laughter shot out of her mouth. "Yeah, no. Absolutely not."

"But I've got cash from *Fire on High* and the book deal, and you can't want to live with your in-laws forever."

Her teeth left deep indents in her lower lip. "I'm not planning to. With my fee from Tad I'll have enough to make a down payment on my own apartment. And even if I didn't have savings, I wouldn't take from you like that. Next suggestion?"

Of course she would be careful enough to save, and proud enough not to take money. What else was there? I blinked at the images my libido threw up of Ellie using me for sex. Not that she'd be into that.

Or would she? She was private, and uptight, and a workaholic. But that didn't mean she was frigid. Not with the way she hummed and licked her lips when she bit into a ripe strawberry. Or how she'd stared at my bare stomach that time after my run. Passion flowed under Ellie's surface like a creek under rocks. You couldn't see the water, but if you listened, you would know it was there.

Wait a minute, there was something else. Her book proposal. *Nourish* had honestly made me want to hug her with how much I liked it. It concentrated all the stuff that made Ellie Ellie: food as love and caring and generosity, how making and eating great meals with good people made her happy. It would be a crime to let those beautiful pages sit on her desktop gathering digital dust.

"I'll help you get *Nourish* published," I said.

She shook her head hard. "You don't have that kind of power."

"I kind of do, though. Tad really wants to publish my book, right?"

"Yes?"

"Well, I could speak up for you. Tell him he has to put your book forward, too."

"But I'm not a big enough name. I have only one thousand people following me on Instagram, and I think most of them are bots."

I snorted. "Tell me you remember the two of us yelling at each other in that video that bajillions of people saw? That Tad said got positive publicity for the book?"

She put her face in her hands. "How could I forget? And it was hundreds of thousands, not bajillions."

"But those hundreds of thousands of people know who you are." I nudged her. "Come on, Ellie. Why not give it a shot?"

She put her hands in her lap, and her face got the distant expression that meant she was chewing over a tough problem.

It was kind of amazing that I knew what her different faces meant.

"You could make me your coauthor too," she said. "Something like, Kieran O'Neill with Ellie Wasserman."

"I'll do that, and you'll help me with my family. Deal?"

She exhaled. "Deal." She pulled out her notebook and pen. "But if I'm going to pretend to be your girlfriend, we need ground rules."

I sat back and slung my arm across the back of the bench. "Of course, always the rules and the note-taking with you."

"Number one: no kissing." She wrote and underlined it.

"I like my tongue, so I wouldn't be stupid enough to try to put it in your mouth without your permission. But not even on the cheek?"

She paused, then said, "Cheek is fine. Hand is fine, too . . ."

"Who's kissed anyone on the hand in the past century?" I interrupted.

"But no kissing on the mouth."

That's a shame. I shook my head hard. "What else is allowed?"

"Adoring looks, and laughing at all my jokes."

"You make jokes?" I asked, faking confusion.

Her face was all seriousness. "For your information, I am *hilarious*."

I rubbed my neck. "My family is a tough crowd."

"Just you wait. I am awesome at parents. I can charm the pants off them."

"No pants off, please, for the love of God."

"All right, I will charm to just before the point of pants removal. Another thing: endearments. Do you have a preference?"

"As in, what you call me when you don't use my name? I think as long as you don't call me an arrogant brat, we're good."

Her head dropped back. "That was a bitchy thing to say, and I'm sorry about it."

"Apology accepted, and I'm sorry I provoked the hell out of you."

She smiled. "Apology also accepted." Then she studied me like my name was written on my skin somewhere. "How does 'honey' sound to you?"

All of a sudden, I wanted to be the kind of guy she called "honey." Then I saw that smartass smile flirting across her lips, and I remembered the farmers' market. "Does anyone else know how sneaky and mean you really are?"

She grinned. "All for you, honey."

"That's what I thought. What about you? You look like a 'kitten' to me," I joked.

But Ellie didn't laugh. The little black-haired boy ran across the grass in front of us. As she followed him with her eyes, she finally said, "That's not going to work."

"Why not?"

"Because Max used to call me that."

Ellie

A dead-husband-shaped silence fell. I hadn't felt Max's absence in a while. Maybe all Kieran's light and noise filled the space. I knew I'd definitely found Diane's visits easier for the last few months.

I took a long, deep breath to let missing my husband pass through me, then redirected. "What about you? Is there someone your parents will be comparing me to?"

He shook his head hard. "No. I don't have girlfriends."

This mischievous, playful, gifted man who was dynamite in a suit didn't do relationships? What a shame. What a *waste*. "Ever?"

He shrugged. "I hooked up a lot in my teens and early twenties, and then I got to Qui and I didn't want to be distracted from doing my best. Now I think it's better for everyone if I keep things casual. I won't disappoint somebody by not being around because I'm working super long hours and don't get home until the middle of the night."

Everything hit me at the same time. "Oh, God. I'm going to be the first girl you bring home. And we're going to fake it."

"It's not that big of a deal," he said, sounding less confident than his carefree words.

"Spoken like a man in his late twenties who's never had a real girlfriend." The bells in the church across the square pealed twelve times. "I actually need to head home to take Floyd to the vet. But I have one other request before I go."

"Shoot."

"Get a haircut."

He covered his shaggy head to protect himself from an invisible pair of scissors. "Why? The hair's kind of a trademark."

"I'm not saying buzz it. But you need a style that doesn't cover your eyes."

"I can see fine," he said defensively.

I reached, then hesitated. "Can I touch you?"

"Yeah." His Adam's apple jumped with his surprise. "Go ahead."

His hair was thick and soft when I pushed it away from his face. "See?" I was so close I could see his pupils dilating. "There. Now you're not hiding."

After a long second, he grinned. "Wow, thank you for literally showing me the light."

"Smartass." Smartass with eyes that made me think of a stream hidden deep in the woods. "Sorry," I said as I moved back. "I didn't need to do that."

"Don't be sorry. It's practice for fake-dating, isn't it?" His tone was light, the opposite of his darkened eyes.

"Yeah. Practice." And if I said it enough times, I wouldn't feel an electric shock from touching him.

CHAPTER FOURTEEN

Ellie

I sniffed the air when we got out of the car. "I can't believe I didn't know this place existed. It's magical. It even smells like orange blossoms."

Ojai's red tile and cream stucco buildings sheltered below craggy gray-green mountains, topped with a ceiling of hot June sky the color of a Renaissance painter's heaven. A dusty breeze kicked up more orange blossom perfume, mixed with chaparral.

Kieran slammed the passenger door. "It's fine."

I bit my lip. I supposed if you lived in a place long enough, you'd be immune. But he'd been acting strange for the last hour. Even when my opera playlist came on, he hadn't groaned and muttered. Instead, he'd stared out the window at the ocean, rubbing his thumb back and forth along the knife edge on his forearm.

And I kept looking at him because I was getting more and more worried. I wasn't looking because his haircut suited him way too well. The barber had left his hair longer on top, but shortened the back and sides and parted it to the side in a way that made him even sharper.

No, I could not think about how Kieran looked like an indie rock star, swaggering around on a stage with an electric guitar, singing about how he was going to make somebody love him.

"What's wrong?" I asked tentatively.

"Nothing," he muttered.

"Your nothing doesn't look like that," I said, trying to keep my tone light. "Your nothing is chugging two In-N-Out strawberry milkshakes and making fun of me for having a paper road atlas."

He grunted and grabbed his duffel and garment bag out of the trunk. Before he could charge toward the motel doors, I said, "Wait. Please."

His grumble made his shoulders roll like an earthquake, but he stopped.

"This whole charade is going to go down in flames if you're nonverbal for the whole weekend," I said quietly.

He turned back to me, looking woebegone. "I'm sorry."

"Talk to me. If we're going to lie to everyone else at this party, we need to tell each other the truth." If only so I didn't lose my sense of reality.

"I haven't been back here in five years," he said quietly, kicking at the gravel with his toe.

"Wait a minute. Does that also mean you haven't seen your parents in five years?"

One particular pebble seemed to offend him, and he sent it flying. "I made excuses, and they were just happy I wasn't bumming around."

"But didn't they visit? It's not like you're thousands of miles away."

He shrugged. "They didn't ask, and I wouldn't have wanted them to, anyway. I didn't like who I was around them."

Four-letter words bubbled to my lips, but I blew them out in a long exhale. "Good grief."

"Lots of people have tricky families, Ellie."

Didn't I know it. But saying that aloud would be the opposite of supporting him. I tried to smile and said, "But you're here because you think there's a chance things could be different."

"Yeah. You might need a microscope to see the chance—it's that small. But I'm trying to have a little more faith, I guess." He turned and looked at the doors to the motel lobby. "Look, you don't have to do this. I could say you got sick and couldn't come at the last minute."

My spine straightened. My trepidation didn't matter. I'd promised to help him and that was the end of it. "You think I'm going to abandon you now? Who the hell do you think I am?"

Finally, he smiled. "A stubborn hardass." He paused and his smile turned into an evil grin. "Come to think of it, all the 'ass' words apply to you: hardass, badass, smartass, of course."

I blushed and coughed at what was both the best and most vulgar compliment I'd ever received. "Am I the only one who remembers the whole 'inside voice' thing from kindergarten? Also, you're still incorrigible."

The jerk winked at me. "You're welcome."

We checked in and climbed up an outdoor set of stairs along a balcony to our room. My hopes weren't high because he'd booked the room at the last possible second, but I sighed in relief when the door opened.

"Oh, good, two beds," I said. "Dibs on the far one."

"Fine." He sprawled on his mattress while I swung my little red suitcase onto the luggage rack in the corner. "What is it with you and the worry about there only being one bed? You were talking about it in Sonoma, too."

I shook out my jersey dress. It didn't look like it had wrinkles, but I might steam it a little bit, just in case. "It's a thing that happens in romance novels. If the main characters go on a road trip, odds are very good that they're going to end up in a room where, whoopsie, there's only one bed."

He tilted his head. "They can't change it?"

"Nope. No room at the inn, nowhere else to stay for miles around."

He was nodding thoughtfully, but that puckish gleam in his eyes didn't bode well for me. "Then what happens?"

My mouth dried instantly. What happened was that they woke up tangled in each other, the way they'd both craved deep down. Clinging, desperate, and wanting.

The dress fell off its hanger. "Butterfingers," I said. The AC was blasting in here already, so I couldn't blame it for my blush. "Nothing that concerns you."

Kieran tucked his hands behind his head, smiling. "Sure. Do you want to shower first?"

I held back a sigh of relief. "No, you go ahead. I need to go for a walk."

Kieran

*T*hinking about Ellie and her romance novels had given me a few minutes of peace from the adrenaline racing around my system, but now I couldn't ignore the bitterness in my mouth and the sourness in my stomach. As I paced around the parking lot waiting for her to change, I tried to breathe deeply through the fear and ground myself. Bits of the gravel sparkled like jewelry in the afternoon sun. Mr. Murphy's pale-blue shirt was cool and smooth against my skin, and the weave of the suit made it look like silk. Would it be enough armor for whatever waited for me at my parents' house?

"Hey," Ellie called.

I turned around, relieved. "What's up?"

She made her easy way down the outside steps. "Are you trying to catch flies?" she asked, a laugh in her voice. "You must have seen a woman all made up before."

I closed my mouth. I felt like I'd never seen *her* before. Silky violet fabric hugged her body like it never wanted to let her go, dipping in at her waist and sweeping out at her hip. It ended just above her knees and made her curvy legs look like they went on forever before they got to her gold flats. When her raspberry-pink mouth curled in a warm smile, she *glowed,* and it was like a light bulb suddenly lit up in my head. I wasn't horny and restless because I hadn't gotten any in almost ten months.

It was because I wanted her. Only her.

I wanted to bite her lush lower lip, suck the sweet curve where her shoulder met her neck. I wanted to bury my face where her neckline curved down. I wanted to bury my face in a lot of other places, too.

Her whistle cut through the fantasy. "Mr. Murphy really is a genius," she said as she looked me over. "Good knot on the tie. And I made the right call with the little bit of indigo woven into the silver."

"Thanks to both you and YouTube." I ran my fingers down the silk tie. "I know I look good, but I'll always be short and ginger."

Her eyes narrowed. "What's wrong with being a redhead?"

I shrugged. "I don't know. I just got teased for it." Now I had to know. "Do you like it?" I asked shyly.

She bit her lip, and I thought she'd change the subject when she finally said, "Your hair has so many beautiful colors in it. A person could spend a long time finding them all."

A picture came into my head out of nowhere of Ellie sitting under a tree on a warm day. Me stretched out next to her in the shade, my head in her lap, while she lazily trailed her fingers through my hair. It wasn't sexy, it was sweet. Restful. Like Daydream Me could close my eyes, let go of all my racing thoughts, and just be with her.

"Earth to Kieran?" she asked, lightly snapping her fingers in front of my face.

The picture evaporated, leaving me feeling bewildered. "Yeah?"

"Before we go, what do you need for tonight?" she asked quietly.

"What do you mean?"

She took my hand. "Well, I can be the doting girlfriend who won't leave your side. Or the wildly talented girlfriend who's so awesome that you can just bask in my aura while I charm the room. I can also be the girlfriend who starts feeling nauseated an hour into the party and needs to be taken home."

I stared at our tangled-up fingers. When I took a breath, I got a hit of perfume she'd never worn before, roses and spices and sweet oranges. "Doting girlfriend sounds great."

She leaned up and touched her lips to my cheek, so lightly I might have imagined it. "Then curtains up, honey."

Ellie

"*I*'m not going to fly away if you stop holding my hand," I whispered as we walked up the gravel path to the O'Neills' low-slung 1960s house. A few jacaranda blossoms a little lighter than my dress were scattered around, but the landscaping was otherwise immaculate, with cacti dotted in neat rows across gray pebbles.

"You're not the one I'm worried about," he muttered back. But he loosened his grip just a little.

"Remember, you're a grown man in an excellent suit who's done great things. And for tonight at least, you have a hot, talented girlfriend on your arm."

He gave me a small smile.

"That's better," I said. "I'm available for pep talks whenever you need them."

Kieran stopped all of a sudden, and I noticed the tall, auburn-haired thirtysomething in Buddy Holly glasses. He was leaning against the wall a few feet away from the front door, thumbs flying on his phone screen.

"Bri?" Kieran said.

No response. But that wasn't surprising, because Brian was wearing earbuds with heavy metal leaking out of them. I doubted he'd hear the first shot of World War III exploding next door.

Kieran walked up to him and put his hand in front of the phone.

Brian jumped a foot in the air. "Oh! Oh, it's you. Hi." His arms opened partway when Kieran reached out to shake his hand, then he reached out a hand when Kieran moved his away. Finally, after what felt like a hundred years, they stiffly patted each other on the shoulder.

Brian shoved his phone in his pocket, then put away his headphones. "Totally lost track of time, sorry. You know how it is with work. The boss wants something twenty minutes ago, even when you've booked PTO."

Kieran shook his head. "No, man. My boss isn't a dick."

Brian snorted. "Always so lucky."

We stood there awkwardly. I was beginning to wonder if my dress had given me invisibility powers, when Kieran said, "Do you want to meet my girlfriend?"

I reached out a hand. "Hi, Brian, I'm Ellie."

This time, his handshake connected. "Hi. Wow, you're pretty," he said. He blinked, and his hand froze midshake. "Wait, you're not his girlfriend."

My stomach fell ten stories. How had he found us out already?

"Yes, she is," Kieran said. He tugged me into his side, and his forearm against my back was tense.

"Easy," I said under my breath, and the tension eased the tiniest little bit.

Luckily, Brian didn't notice, just said, "But I saw the way you guys were yelling at each other in that video. It was all over Reddit." His head rapidly turned from side to side. "Wait, is this a stunt? Are we being filmed right now?"

I shook my head. "No cameras. Kieran and I are for real."

"But you *hate* him," he said, like he was saying that the sky was blue.

I couldn't help but smile at how adamant he was. "The opposite." I patted Kieran's lapel. "That was just our chemistry running amok. Right, honey?" I grinned up at him.

Kieran smiled back at me, and all at once our conspiracy wasn't fragile anymore. We were getting away with something, and it was delicious. Sweet and tart like an orange off one of these trees.

"Absolutely," he said, keeping his face straight. "We were fighting because we actually wanted to . . ."

Brian's hands blocked the TMI. "OK! OK, I get it, thank you for not sharing."

We'd gotten away with it for now, but the less Kieran and I talked, the better. "What were you working on just now, Brian?" I asked. "It seemed really important."

Brian immediately launched into a detailed explanation of the code he'd written to automate a machine for packaging a particular chocolate bar. I understood the words "chocolate bar." But it was worth it to see Kieran relax a little, out of the spotlight.

"I guess it's time to go in," Brian finally said.

"I guess," Kieran responded. They both looked like they were approaching the gallows.

"Come on, boys," I said with enthusiasm I didn't really feel. "Let's pull the Band-Aid off."

Brian led the way through the front door, which opened onto a concrete courtyard. There were a few people milling around saying hello, but then another door opened and an older woman called, "Brian! Kieran! What kept you?"

The dark-haired giant coming toward us was Kieran's dad, Joe. He towered over Maureen, who looked like a fairy queen with snow-white hair, ice-green eyes, and razor-sharp cheekbones. She tottered over to us in four-inch heels.

"You must be Ellie! One of my sons finally brings home a girl to meet us. What a happy day this is." Maureen took my hands in hers. She smiled up at me, but the rest of her face didn't move. "Don't you two make a striking couple," she said, sounding pleased. "That is quite the dress. Such a bold color, isn't it, Joe?"

Joe grunted, looking back at the party.

It was a compliment, right? Then why did it make me want to cringe? "Thank you, Mrs. O'Neill," I forced out.

"Oh no, you call me *Maureen*." Like an empress granting a favor to a dumb peasant. She turned to Kieran, dropping my hands and taking one of his. "Your suit looks wonderful, Kieran. It'd be even better if you'd worn dress shoes and shaved, but we can't have everything, can we?"

Joe grunted again. Was he a caveman? Or bored? A bored caveman?

Kieran rubbed his stubble. "Thanks, Mom," he said regretfully.

"Come in, come in," she said, turning toward the screen doors and towing him behind her. "Everyone is so excited to see you again. My son, the champion, returning home."

My fake boyfriend turned and looked at me, the wariness and confusion in his eyes echoing mine. But all I could do was follow.

CHAPTER FIFTEEN

Ellie

To give the O'Neills their due, it was a classy party. White lights dotted the avocado and orange trees in the small backyard. A few college kids dressed in black circulated with prosecco, and one of them poured Sprite into a flute for Kieran. Ella Fitzgerald scatted cheerfully from invisible speakers. And mostly the guests matched the music's mood. Several people came up and congratulated Kieran on winning *Fire on High*, and when he told them who I was, they complimented my dress and asked me about the other books I'd worked on. I asked them lots of questions, smiled big as they told us what a nice-looking couple we were.

But some of the other guests, the ones that introduced themselves as *close* friends of Maureen and Joe's, had sharper smiles.

"You look *very* nice, Kieran," they said. "Who's your lovely friend, *Kieran*," they said.

After one particularly enlightening encounter with one of his mother's fellow librarians who asked if he'd been in any fender benders lately, I took a big swig of prosecco and muttered, "Why are they so surprised that you're doing well? I've never wished for so many people to go jump in a lake. Is there a big one nearby?"

He snorted. "Welcome to years of my life I'll never get back."

The wine and water I'd been drinking took effect and I had to excuse myself. After I found the toilet, I wandered through the O'Neill house. The kitchen was a study in midcentury avocado, with harvest gold and rust paisley curtains over the window, and a sparkling-clean white electric stove with exposed coils. It didn't look like it got used for cooking much.

I turned a corner into a quiet hallway. Through the cracked doors I could see beds neatly made up with white sheets, like this was a hospital, not a home.

But then I found a photo gallery on the walls. Fluffy hair and equally poufy bridesmaids' dresses on the left gave way to one baby picture, then two. I pulled out my phone and captured Kieran's delicious cheeks and wispy carrot hair for future blackmail purposes.

Then a neat line of school portraits. Baby teeth fell out and adult teeth came in, faces lengthened and cheekbones got more defined. Brian's hair turned auburn and he started wearing glasses. But there weren't any more school pictures of Kieran after ninth grade. There weren't any more pictures of him, period. There was teenage Brian wearing protective goggles on his head and holding up a gold-trimmed certificate in a high school lab, Brian shaking hands with an older man in aviator glasses while holding a crystal trophy. I kept moving right, and still there was no sign of Kieran.

I stopped cold at what looked like a college graduation picture. Brian's hair gleamed bronze in the sun. The blue flowers in his lei matched the tropical print of Maureen's dress and the cobalt of Joe's tie. Joe's arm choked tight around someone halfway out of the frame.

Fuck. That wasn't a random punk.

Teenage Kieran's hair stood up in black spikes. Silver piercings studded his right eyebrow and lower lip, exactly where his scars were now. His shiny charcoal button-up shirt turned his skin deathly white and made the purple circles under his eyes and the redness in them stand out even more. Stymied unhappiness radiated from the scrawny teenager in the photograph, and I couldn't imagine him like that now. He'd come so far. Not just that he'd gotten sober and found the help he'd needed. He'd found a purpose, too.

"Are you all right, Ellie?" Maureen asked behind me.

Showtime. "Don't worry, I just needed a moment," I said.

"Are you enjoying yourself?" Her voice was as delicate as the rest of her, but I remembered something important from the fantasy novels I'd loved to read as a teenager. Fairy queens weren't always friendly. They could be real bitches, if they thought someone was a threat to their kingdom.

"I am, thank you, Mrs. O'Neill."

"Oh, gosh, I told you to call me Maureen. No need to be so formal." She tilted her head. "How exactly did you and Kieran meet again?"

"We're working together on his cookbook," I said for the hundredth time today. I sent up a small prayer of thanks that she clearly hadn't seen the video the way Brian had.

"That's right." She chuckled. "Forgive me. It's hard to believe that he's going to have a book with his name on it. Though I don't think it counts if he's not the one writing it."

"It counts. He works just as hard as I do. Harder, even, given that he's got higher barriers to get over."

Her smile was brittle. "Well, I know Kieran's achieving something if someone like you is willing to be in a relationship with him."

"Someone like me?"

She gestured to me from head to toe. "Respectable. Elegantly dressed, if a little flamboyant with color. Beautiful manners, well-spoken. Clearly you listened to your parents when they told you how to behave."

I choked back a snort at the thought of my biological father being Mr. Manners. The sheer *audacity* of it.

"Kieran probably hasn't told you about all the times we had to get him out of trouble," she continued.

I blinked, confused. "No."

She ticked off on her fingers as she spoke. "He skipped classes, he stole money out of my wallet, he crashed our cars more than once. Not to mention the drinking, my God. He couldn't hold his liquor at all. We were so ashamed."

I held back my eye roll. It was like having a conversation with a steamroller. As she continued to list Kieran's crimes, I realized that she relished this monologue, all the ways he'd done them wrong. Like she never wanted him to grow up because then she'd have to stop being a martyr.

"But anyway, that's all in the past. Finally, he's become who we always wanted him to be, and we can hold our heads up."

The thought of being a source of pride to these snobby, plastic people made me want to drink ten flutes of prosecco, climb onto their dining room table, and do Amy Winehouse karaoke, Diane's advice about polish and presentation be damned. But all I needed to shock them was the truth.

"I haven't seen my father in over twenty years," I began. "As far as I know, he's still the lead singer of the second-best hair metal band in Spokane. My mother's salary was for keeping herself in clothes and boyfriends. Sometimes I had to break into my piggy bank so that I could buy Cup O' Noodles at 7-Eleven for my brother and me. I've made a good life in spite of my parents, not because of them. It's one of the reasons I fell in love with your son. I knew he was a survivor, too. But thank you for the compliments. Now, if you'll excuse me."

As I walked away from her aghast sputtering, my gritted-out words resonated through me. Had I fallen for Kieran? I knew he made me smile. I knew he made me laugh. Friends did that, right? But friends didn't also imagine soft kisses and long hours exploring bare skin.

Shit, I was in trouble. I didn't know where fake ended and reality began. All I knew was that I couldn't spend another minute in this house, claustrophobic with fake smiles and bullshit expectations.

Kieran

No, I was not going to be a creeper and follow Ellie to the bathroom. I was going to stay here and look like I could handle being with all these people who didn't know me at all. I leaned back against the courtyard wall and sipped my soda, focused on how good the fake lemon-lime tasted, the hard surface against my back, the smell of orange blossom in the air.

"Still not drinking?" Dad said from two feet away.

So much for relaxing. For a big guy, he could be very stealthy. I'd learned this over and over again as a kid, when I thought I was about to get away with something. He'd magically appear and I'd get punished.

"Five years sober in November," I said, faking a smile.

"But you don't mind if I do?" He waved his whiskey glass in my face.

"Nope." Bourbon had never been my drink of choice. It tasted like anger and disappointment, while vodka had burned me clean.

"Good. It'd be ironic if you became holier than thou after all your teenage antics."

Like a lot of times when Dad talked, he didn't need or want a response. We stood there and watched the crowd. A flash of purple out of the corner of my eye made my heart jump. But one of Mom's librarian friends stopped Ellie, and she smiled and nodded at Mrs. Lange's chatter instead of coming back to me.

Dad followed my eyes. "She seems nice."

"She is," I said. "I'm lucky."

"There's a word for women like her."

Did he mean gorgeous? Hypnotic? Goddess?

He snapped his fingers. "Rubenesque. I hope she watches out for her health."

This from the man who drank whiskey like it was water? "She's fine."

He shook his head mournfully. "For now. You've been seeing each other for long?"

"A few months."

"So still in the honeymoon phase. I remember that with your mother. She was so tiny and delicate back in college. I could pick her up with one arm."

I didn't know what to do with his fond smile. It was such a rare sight.

He took a big sip from his glass and was suddenly all business again. "I want to give you some advice, now that you're on your way up in the world."

I blinked. Advice? From him?

"Make sure Ellie knows your work always comes first," he said like he was handing the knowledge down from on high.

But the words weren't landing. "Ellie knows work is important," I said slowly. "She's really good at what she does, too."

He shook his head. "That's not what I mean. You're more famous than her, and I'm sure you earn more. She's just a writer; she's always going to barely scrape by. She'd be better off giving it up and making things nice for you at home, helping you with whatever you need." A heavy hand fell on my shoulder. "Besides, success is something you have to keep working for. You can't be complacent, and you cannot ever lose focus. Do you understand?"

The Sprite turned bitter in my mouth. All of a sudden, I understood why I only started to see him at night once I was nine or ten—he was constantly working late. Why he'd ignored me on the weekends except to yell at me when I did something he didn't like. I understood how tense and tired my mother had looked whenever she'd heard his key in the lock, how she'd practically run out the door on the days she had a shift at the library or the monthly bridge game with her friends.

What a cold, sad life.

But I would only be a success in their eyes if I lived that same life. Valued working and working, with no time for pleasure or joy or love. Their value system had about as much worth as a steaming pile of trash.

"You don't know anything," I blurted.

My father's face took on a look I'd never seen before. I'd actually stunned him. "About what?"

The novelty made me brave. "About me. About my life. And especially about Ellie. So keep your shitty advice. I don't want it."

Suddenly I smelled roses, and felt a soft hand in mine. "Honey?" Ellie said.

I twined my fingers with hers, and the last chains I'd felt binding me to my family's fucked-up ideals fell off. Instead, something new and strong and golden was growing where our hands touched.

"I was just talking to Dad about you," I said a little loudly. "How lucky I am that you agreed to go out with me."

Ellie glowed with happiness as she looked at my dad. "Oh, I'm the lucky one, Mr. O'Neill. He's incredibly talented."

"I'm glad you think so," he said, raising his eyebrows at me. "He appreciates having you on his arm."

"I'm so happy to hear that." Her voice and expression were sugary sweet, but there it was, the tart twist in the corner of her mouth. My dad would never see that she was brilliant, and driven, and didn't put up with shit. Only I knew that, and I relished the taste of that knowledge.

"I only speak the truth," I said grandly, and lifted her hand to kiss it, just to mess with my dad's head.

I'd watched Ellie's hands a million times in the past three months as she scribbled notes, chopped vegetables, stirred soup. She used them when she argued, gesturing to make detailed points, and when she thought, tapping her fingers on her cheekbone. But now as I brought her hand closer, I could really *see* it. The pale, smooth skin, green-blue veins faint underneath. The tiny cinnamon freckles across her knuckles. A waft of sweet citrus and rose from where she must have dotted her perfume on her wrist.

Then my lips touched the back. She was warmth, and softness, strength and capability underneath.

I'd been a dumbass, making fun of this idea. Of course kissing a woman's hand was hot. I could guess what she looked like right now, silently teasing me. Her eyebrows would be raised, her mouth curled with the snarky comment she'd be holding back.

But then I heard a little sigh, and my eyes jumped up to hers. They weren't sparkling with humor.

They were dreamy. Dazed. Like we'd woken up together and she needed all of my skin against all of hers.

I'd forgotten that hands were *sensitive*.

Ideas bloomed in my head. I could kiss her wrist and feel her pulse flutter. Kiss her fingertips and make her shiver with a flick of my tongue. And finally, finally, when she was squirming a little, gasping for air, kiss her mouth where her raspberry lower lip was the fullest.

Dad coughed. I jerked back just as Ellie pulled her hand away, and I ran my shaking fingers through my hair.

My father grumbled from a mile away, "Your billing and cooing's sweet, but I should go see where Maureen got to."

He stalked off. Ellie's hand came up and smoothed my tie. Was she shaking too? Just a little bit? "Good, keep looking at me like that," she whispered, her voice cracking a little.

I couldn't have looked away from her if I wanted to. "Like how?"

She reached up with her other hand and rubbed her thumb gently over my scarred eyebrow, the ghost of the piercing. "Like you worship me." Her eyes flicked to the side.

I saw my parents staring at us, their arms folded, lips pursed.

I whispered, "Maybe we should kiss? Just to be convincing?" And the instant she said "Yeah," I touched my lips to hers.

Every time I'd kissed someone before, the kiss had said, "You're hot," and "Get naked." A preview of coming attractions, fast and hard.

But Ellie's fingertips brushed over my cheekbone, soft as rose petals. Traced my temple, my jawline.

She touched me like I was precious.

No one in my entire life had been gentle with me.

And her lips said, "I'm here," and "Be mine." But wait. She was *faking it*. We both were. A fake kiss could taste like vanilla milkshakes and prosecco and feel like floating on a cloud.

"Are they gone?" Ellie whispered against my mouth.

I lifted my head, even though something inside me howled to kiss her more. "Yeah, they stormed off."

Ellie said, "They're a match made in heaven. I think they drink vinegar for breakfast. But only champagne vinegar, because otherwise someone might judge them."

I barked out a harsh laugh. She was so mean and it was *amazing*.

"Really, how are you doing?" she asked. "Because I think this is the worst party ever."

The tension came out of me in a big breath. "You're not wrong."

She bit her lip, then said, "I'm not sure the canapés agreed with me. Would you mind if we went back to the hotel?"

Protectiveness surged in my chest. "Oh no, I'm sorry."

She leaned in and whispered. "I'm not sick. But I basically told your mom she won the Lifetime Worst Mom Ever award, so you need to get me out of here before I do worse."

I almost cheered. "Of course we can go," I said loudly. "I'm sorry you're feeling bad, love."

I almost slapped my own face at the strength of that word, how easily it had come out of my mouth, but after a split second, she just said back, "Thanks, honey."

I leaned close and whispered, "Thank you." Her temple was right there, and I leaned forward and brushed my lips over it. I told myself that Mom and Dad might come back any second. I wasn't thinking that she was the perfect height for me to kiss her there, wasn't thinking about how we'd fit in other ways.

I led her to my parents and made our excuses, Ellie suddenly pale and grimacing as she rubbed her stomach. Mom fell for it instantly, but then again, she'd always hated when we were sick.

But then Ellie and I were walking down the street, and I realized that if we went back to the hotel, she would bury herself in her book, and I'd put my headphones on. I wanted more time.

"Can we go somewhere?" I asked.

She laughed. "We can go anywhere that isn't that stuffy party."

"Fresh air sound good?"

"Perfect," she said, grinning hugely. "Race you to the car!" and she suddenly sprinted down the street.

And as I ran after her giddy laughter, I felt like I could fly.

CHAPTER SIXTEEN

Kieran

When we got to Ventura, the fog was stretching thin fingers over the ocean. It had been a long time since I'd been on this beach, longer since I'd been here sober, and as I walked toward the water with Ellie, Converse and socks in my hand, I was aware of everything. The cool grains of sand under my toes, the salt spray in the air. The woman at my side, the lush, generous curves of her against all my jagged edges.

She started speaking quietly, like she was still thinking the words as she said them. "I think you were an asshole as a kid because they wanted to shove you in this ridiculous box. Every time you messed up, they got mad at you for not fitting, instead of asking whether the box was right for you in the first place, and now that you've broken out, now that you're hundreds of miles from that stupid box, they keep running after you with it."

I turned to her. "I can't change it, though. I can't change that I lied, and broke shit, and hurt people." Though suddenly I was desperate to.

"It doesn't matter," she said. "What matters is what you want now."

I wanted her calm. Her gentle thoughtfulness. I wanted to drink her down and feel her warm me from the inside out.

She shivered a little bit, and I put my arm around her.

"No one's looking," she said. But she didn't move away.

"I know."

She nestled into me with a sigh, and I pressed my nose into her hair. Clean laundry and bergamot.

I could stand here and hold her forever. I wouldn't mind that at all. Listen to her dry jokes and excited explanations. Though it would be even better to hold her in bed, discover if the rest of her body was as silky soft as her hands. I wanted to be as close to her as I could get, intertwined, breathing in her strength and her certainty as I breathed out all my loneliness.

"We should have sex," I blurted.

She jerked away. "What?"

I was like Wile E. Coyote sprinting off the cliff without realizing there was nothing under him. "We're hot for each other," I said, trying not to sound as confused as I felt. "We should have sex."

"Yeah, no, still not understanding you."

"We need to get rid of the tension," I said desperately.

She blinked slowly. "What tension?"

"You can't say you didn't feel it." Kissing her hand had been erotic, tender, beyond my wildest dreams. Not to mention her mouth.

"It was fake," she told the waves.

The word was a needle, but I tried to keep my bubble from popping. "If that's how you kiss when you don't mean it, please warn me before you do it for real, because I need to write my will."

She didn't laugh. "That's very flattering, but I'm still stuck on the word *should*. Why *should* we have sex? Because there are several excellent reasons why we *shouldn't*."

I put my head in my hands. "Jesus, you're killing me here. Like, just dig a hole for me and put me in it already."

"I'm sorry you feel that way. But in what universe does having sex make a relationship *less* tense?"

I looked up. "Does that mean you've never had a friend with benefits?"

She stomped away a few steps. "Oh my God, I can't believe this."

"That's a no?"

When she turned back, her face was incredulous. "That's an absolutely not, I would never, what on earth."

I shrank into myself, trying to ignore the chant of *You're not good enough* that played in my head. "You don't need to be all judgy about it. Everyone I've ever done it with has been on the same page."

She shook her head, and her voice softened. "No, that's not it. I don't judge other people for doing what they need to do. But you know what sex does? It makes oxytocin. Bonding hormones. Running around your system willy-nilly and making things all warm and fuzzy. Anyone who thinks that they can have sex more than once without catching at least some kind of feelings is delusional, because catching feelings is *biology*."

I put my hands up. "OK, Einstein, I take your point."

"Einstein wasn't a biologist."

I laughed, all disbelief. "I'm telling you that I want to be naked in your bed, and you're being a smartass?"

She blushed. "Stating facts isn't smartassery. It's pedantry."

She was so fucking smart, and so far out of my league. But right now, she could decide to eat me alive and I'd hand over a knife and fork.

"Look," she said. "We're making good progress with the book. It would mess things up, to sleep together."

I couldn't help myself. "Tell me one thing."

Her eyes closed. "I'm going to regret this. Sure."

"Do you want me, too?"

"That's . . ."

"Irrelevant," we said at the same time.

She half-laughed. "I need to buy more five-dollar words."

"Yes or no, Ellie."

Her hands went to her face. "I shouldn't," she said through her fingers.

"That's a yes, then," I said impatiently.

And there she was. "Oh, for crying out loud. Yes, Kieran, I am sexually attracted to you." My mind snagged on the word "sexually," so I almost didn't hear her say, "But I'm not going to *do* anything about it. So that's that."

Ellie

*O*n the way back to Ojai we barely spoke, and when we did, we were so *polite*. The warm river of complicity that had floated us through that party and out to the beach had dried up. I lost count of the number of times we said, "You go ahead," to each other when we got back to the motel and needed to change out of our party clothes. I'd almost blurted "Rock, paper, scissors?" when Kieran said, "Ladies first, for fuck's sake," and I gave in.

I stripped naked, rinsed grains of sand off my feet, showered off the sweet, spiced perfume Max had given me for our last anniversary. He'd been so excited to give it to me that I hadn't had the heart to remind him that I wouldn't be able to wear it when I worked, which was most of the time.

I rubbed makeup-removal goop all over my face, and as I washed it away, I watched my girlfriend mask eddy in pink-and-black-tinted swirls down the drain. All the while, Kieran's passionate, surprised words echoed in my head.

We should have sex, he'd said. As if it were some kind of biological imperative.

My wide-eyed bare face stared at me, aroused and unsure. The beautiful man on the other side of the door wanted to have sex with me. And it would be so easy. Tad didn't know we were sharing a room. Didn't know we'd kissed, that the kisses had felt like a Fourth of July's worth of fireworks.

But I'd know I'd broken my promise.

"New pajamas?" Kieran asked when I came out of the bathroom.

I looked down at the sleep shirt and pants, with their just-unfolded creases. "Yeah. I don't usually wear them." I turned strawberry red as I muttered the last words. High on the list of things Kieran hadn't needed to know was that I usually slept naked. "Never mind."

I could have sworn I saw Kieran gulp, but maybe that was just a trick of the light. "I'm going to go shower," he said.

When he'd said "shower," he'd really meant it. I'd read a chapter of my book and turned my light out by the time I heard the bathroom door open. I squeezed my eyes shut and willed myself to sleep.

No such luck. The unfamiliar bed felt hard and hot, and the pajama fabric snagged around me every time I turned over. How did people wear clothes to bed? Did they just sleep in their own sweat?

A faint snuffle came from the other side of the room. At least one of us was sleeping. I counted sheep. I even tried burrowing under the sheets and inhaling carbon dioxide.

When I threw the sheets back and flicked my bedside light on, I saw I wasn't the only one who'd overheated. Unconscious Kieran had shoved the sheets and blankets down, leaving them wrapped around his lower legs. The soft gold light illuminated his long, pale, freckled back, cut off by the band of his black boxer briefs. He had his arms wrapped around a pillow, his cheek pressed into it like he was dreaming of having something to hold.

The smile curled my lips before I knew it. He'd been so good at holding me. Kissing me. He kissed like it was the only thing in the world he could imagine doing, like he could explore my mouth for days. Even his lips on my hand had been overwhelming, out of all proportion to the contact.

I told myself to stop staring at him. But another part of my brain was determined to imagine what it would be like to return the favor. Kiss the nape of his neck, lick between his shoulder blades, suck on the base of his spine.

Jesus, I needed to reactivate Hinge when I got home.

I could *not* sleep with Kieran. I could not sacrifice my long-term plans and obligations for short-term pleasure. Even if I wanted that pleasure more than my next breath.

I turned out the light and clamped my pillow over my head.

CHAPTER SEVENTEEN

Ellie

"*H*iya, cowriter," Kieran greeted me on his latest voice note. "Is it sunny in Berkeley? It's freezing here, because summer in San Francisco is a lie. I actually went out and bought a teakettle and breakfast tea so I could make it like my mom does, super strong with lots of milk. The last time I bought milk, I learned that it splits into white gunk and yellow horror-water if you leave it in the fridge for too long. Anyway, enough of my *irrelevant* rambling."

I smiled at my phone. The rambling had become my favorite part of his memos. It was when he got distracted that he actually said the most interesting stuff.

"You made a good point about the onions in the soup for 'Comfort.' They should be sliced thinly like in the second picture you sent, not thick like in the first, otherwise they won't go totally soft. They'll just be floating rubber bands. Is there such a thing as slicing so thin you could read newspaper through them? Translucent, duh, Kieran—that's the word for it."

Floyd hopped up and sniffed the phone, then meowed.

"Love the Floyd cameo in the last video, by the way," Kieran said, and my cat perked up. "It really is all about him, isn't it?" The warmth of his voice wrapped around me like a cashmere blanket.

"Anyway, I have to go. Those weights aren't going to lift themselves. Hope things go all right today. Bye."

Now I was left with the image of him strong and sweaty.

I shook my head hard. I had to ignore it. The same way I had to break the long looks he'd been giving me for weeks, the same way

I had to shift my hand away if it came too close to his during prep for recipe testing. If I acted normal, businesslike and on task, it would be like I'd never thought about sleeping with my coworker. Never thought of throwing away all my plans.

In weak moments, his plea still echoed in my head and in lower-down places, a promise of cool water and sweet breezes. But I'd turned away and kept trudging through the stupid desert, the temperature rising and rising.

Well, there was always more work. There was slicing onions paper thin, then sautéing them in butter until they cooked down into a caramel-sweet tangle. But as I stirred, I wasn't humming Mozart or Puccini. It was a dark, desiring song by the National he'd played for me on the drive home from Ojai. We'd traded albums over the six hours of driving, my classical and jazz for his sad-boy indie rock.

When I'd looked at his hands tapping restlessly on his thighs, I'd thought about what it would be like to have them touch my breasts, stroke between my legs. When his mouth had moved, I'd remembered what it felt like over mine.

Open.

Warm.

Strawberry sweet.

My unconscious wasn't cooperating, either. My dreams undulated with images to make an erotic novelist blush. Extra yoga, daily walks, more sessions with my vibrator—none of them helped.

But could I sleep with him just to scratch an itch, with no guarantee he'd stay? That was without considering the whole my-job-and-future-were-tied-to-his-success thing. And the lying-to-Tad thing.

I could think myself in circles. Or I could do what I always did, when there was something I didn't know.

"Hey, friend." Nicole's voice on the phone sounded like it was coming from a distance, wind rushing around it.

"May I please pick your brain?" I asked, leaning on the counter.

"Sure. I'm on my way to family dinner, but you've got me for the next twenty minutes."

"What's Mama Salazar making?"

"Kare kare. And before you ask, yes, she's making some for you."

"I love her oxtails so much. Please thank her profusely for me, but please also tell her for the hundredth time that what I really want is the recipe *written down*."

She snorted. "Dude, she doesn't even tell her only daughter her cooking secrets. I don't know what you'd have to do to persuade her."

Persuade. I had it bad if even words out of context sounded like double entendres.

"Stop stalling," Nicole said. "What's up?"

I put my phone on speaker and rested my head next to it. "Entirely hypothetically, how does one have a one-night stand?"

I thought the call had dropped, but then I heard her strained voice say, "One? How does one? Hang on a sec." Then a sound like a coyote howling exploded out of the speaker.

"Let me know when you're done laughing at me," I said. "I'm nothing if not patient."

"Uh-huh," she gasped. "God, I needed that, thank you." A few wheezes, then, "So, one-night stands, huh? Why are you calling on my expertise now?"

"I'm curious," I hedged.

"Well, Professor, to commence sexual relations, one would approach the subject and perform the traditional mating rituals of the species."

I pressed my nose into the hard surface. "I hate you."

"I know, I'm being a dick," she said, a smile still in her voice. "But I'm imagining you standing at the back of a bar doing a David Attenborough impression."

I raised my head. "That sounds fun, actually. So, tell me, Doctor, what are the traditional mating rituals of our species?" I asked, half-dry and half-serious.

"Mostly smiling and eye contact, followed by coming close, touching a little."

Like my thumb smoothing Kieran's eyebrow. His mouth brushing my temple.

She continued matter-of-factly: "Hypothetical sex not in a relationship is not that different from hypothetical sex in a relationship, lady."

"They haven't invented new moves in the last three years? Good to know," I joked dryly.

After a moment of quiet, she said, "What are you really asking me, Ellie?"

Note to self: get less perceptive friends.

"Do you think it's possible for *me* to have no-strings sex?" I whispered, even though I was alone.

"Hypothetically?"

"Uh-huh."

"Do *you* think you could have sex without love?"

Stupid Socratic method, making me think. "I don't think I could have sex without feeling safe."

"That's not just you. Consent's important."

What I craved the most pushed its way out of my chest. "I mean, I need to feel like I don't have to do all the thinking. That I can put myself in someone else's hands for a while."

She paused. "Then you're not going to get off in the bathroom of a bar anytime soon. Because what you're talking about requires either trusting someone or genuinely not giving a shit. I don't think you're going to get the first one after thirty minutes, and you can't do the second one. It's one of the things I like the most about you, that you care so much."

I groaned in frustration. "That's what I was afraid of." I'd never thought of my conscience as a burden, but now it felt like a backpack full of boulders.

"But if you met someone you liked, and you felt like you *could* trust them, I don't see a reason why you couldn't try friends with benefits. You have pretty good taste in people. I mean, I *am* your best friend."

The possibility of dropping the weight on my back made me sit up. "I'll keep that in mind." A stab of worry. "But Nicole, what if the sex is terrible?" I had been awkward with Max as we'd learned each other's bodies, but he'd laughed and kissed my embarrassment away. Would someone else be as patient?

Nicole snorted. "Jesus, you definitely need to get laid if you're in this many knots." She continued slowly: "I promise you have not forgotten how to have sex. And even if you had bad sex, you wouldn't have to see this hypothetical person again. Right?" A beat. "Unless he has hypothetical red hair and green eyes and hypothetical sexy forearms from all his hypothetical knife work?"

My entire body cringed. "Oh, is that the time?"

"No, don't hang up," she said. "Talk to me."

"How did you know?" I whispered.

"Well, you're both hot, you're both single, and you've been working together in a tiny kitchen for months; therefore, you want to bang each other. QED."

If only it were as simple as a mathematical proof. "I *shouldn't* sleep with him, though."

She sighed. "How many times have I told you in our friendship what you should or shouldn't do?"

I rubbed my face. "Zero."

"This is *your* life. It's up to you to decide if this is a good idea or not. I mean, what do you *want*?"

I closed my eyes hard, but my mind was blank.

"Yeah." Her sigh sounded a little disappointed. "Maybe don't fuck Kieran unless you know," she said. "I have to go. I love you."

"I love you too, and thanks."

"Don't thank me yet," she said dryly. "Thank me once I don't have to listen to you bitching about the sex desert anymore."

After we hung up, I pressed my fingers into my temples, trying to find some way to release my body's need for touch. I'd been so used to compressing my desires into a manageable ball, easily satisfied with a piece of chocolate, a yoga session, a quick orgasm. But now I felt the tension in my jaw, my locked-up muscles.

I knew it was dangerous to want big, intense things like passion, like connection. What would happen if I asked and didn't get them?

Even worse, what would happen if I did? If I gorged myself on pleasure and closeness like a starving woman at a rich banquet and then they were snatched away? I'd be worse off than I was before. Heartsick and craving.

I exhaled. Responsibility was bland and heavy, but it was filling. Like oatmeal. Speaking of responsibility, my break was over. I got back to work, and if my pan banged on the stove a little harder than usual and my knife bit into an onion with more force, well, it wasn't because I resented eating oatmeal three times a day.

Kieran

"What the fuck are we doing?" Jay panted.

As always, she had a point. It'd been a month since my parents' party, and I saw Ellie naked and smiling every time I closed my eyes. But she hadn't just shut the door that had opened when she'd kissed me. She'd boarded it up and painted DO NOT DISTURB across it.

All I could do was try to outrun wanting her, with wet sand and cold July fog for extra punishment. I ran down Ocean Beach to where the water had packed down the sand and picked up my pace, inhaling salt air in big gulps.

"Jesus, what's the matter with you, slow down!" Jay yelped behind me after a minute.

"Sorry!" I called back so she could hear me over the waves. I dropped to a slow jog, then stopped.

She dragged up beside me. "I hate you so much right now," she gasped.

I said, straight-faced, "I'm your best friend. It's actually illegal for you to hate me."

Her breathless laugh came out bitter. I finally saw the bags under her eyes that looked like she'd gone five rounds with a heavyweight who had a grudge. "You OK?" I asked.

"No. No, I am not OK."

It hit me all at once that I was both freezing and guilty. "I shouldn't have dragged you out. We can forget this and get coffee at Lee's."

"Not just coffee. I want eggs and double bacon and hash browns and a mug of hot chocolate the size of my head." She sighed. "It's not the run." She plunked down on a patch of dry sand, and I joined her. The cold made me think of that night with Ellie, but I had to stop with my bullshit. Jay needed me.

"I'm all messed up," she told her legs.

"What happened?"

"Nicole did."

Her sadness sunk into my skin like the fog. "I thought you were having a good time?" I asked gently.

She grabbed a small piece of driftwood and drew little crosses in the sand. "I want more than a good time. But she's not into that. She won't go out with me. She won't even stay over after we . . ." She hesitated. "I can't even call it making love. After we fuck."

"Wait a second," I said carefully. "Is she not into that stuff ever, or not into it with you?"

"She says it's the first one," she said, her voice dull. "She even gave me the numbers for two of her old fuckbuddies so they could confirm. And my head knows she's right. But my heart," she pressed her hand hard to her chest, "I'm so lonely. I just want to belong to someone, you know?"

I wrapped my arm around her shoulders. "I know." Her mom and stepdad had stopped speaking to her when she came out after college. Her dad had embraced her, but he was retired in Costa Rica with his partner and she saw him once a year, if she could save up the money for a plane ticket. She lived in the Outer Richmond with roommates who were decent people, but not friends. The person she was closest to was me.

"No, you don't," she said. "And that's how you like it. I should have consulted you before I started anything with her, Lord O'Neill of No Strings."

I couldn't hold back a snort.

"What was that for?" She pulled back. "Wait, there was Anjali for a while, but you haven't said her name in months. Greta moved to LA. Taylor met her girlfriend."

"Fiancée now." Was she going to recite the names of all my friends with benefits?

"And you haven't talked about Keisha or Lindsay, either." She dropped the driftwood. "Oh my God, did you sleep with *Ellie*?"

My face burned bright red for no reason. Ellie and I hadn't actually done anything. Wanting a woman so desperately you had to lock yourself in the bathroom at work every damn day wasn't a crime. "No," I forced out.

She stared me down. "Did you think about it?"

"Yes," I told the waves.

At least she was smiling now. "Did you ask her and she turned you down?"

I put my head on my knees. "Ding ding ding."

Jay's beam was like sunlight in the fog. "*Kieran* has a *crush* on a *girl*."

"I do *not* have a crush. I just want to hang out with her all the time, and also make her come."

"You have a crush and you are *adorable*."

"I fucking hate that word."

"So much denial crammed into one cute little carrot-topped package." She rubbed my head, I slapped her hand away, and we flailed at each other until she yelped, "Truce?"

I brushed most of the sand off, but I was sure I'd find it in my underwear later. "Why am I friends with you, again?"

"Because you need someone to be the voice of reason. Though it sounds like she's doing a good job with that."

I rubbed my tattoo. "It would be so much easier not to want her." Both because we worked together, and because she wouldn't want just a few laughs and orgasms. She'd had commitment with Max. She'd had true love. I didn't know how to do either of those. No one had ever told me they loved me, and I hadn't ever said it to anyone.

"Our hearts don't know what's easy," Jay said. She looked out at the water, brow furrowed. "When I met Ellie, she made me think of a swan."

"She doesn't have a long neck."

"Shut up. I mean, she's all neat and tidy on the surface, but you can tell there's a lot of hard work going on underneath. Do you know how you could make her life easier? Because from what Nicole has said, it sounds like she needs someone to lean on."

"That's definitely not me. I'm like this." I grabbed a handful of sand. "I slip through people's fingers and wash out."

"That is poetry, and also total bullshit," she said firmly.

"What?"

"You've been doing your best to be a good friend to me since the first day we met. The same way I try to look out for you as best I can. I know your asshole parents demanded perfection, but the rest of us give points for trying."

Ellie gave me points for trying. She always had.

Jay stood up from the sand with a big grunt. "Nicole told me Ellie's all her in-laws have. She does everything for them. Maybe she needs someone to do for her." She offered her hand, and I let her pull me up. "Come on, you're buying me breakfast."

Ellie

Nine P.M. was early for Diane to knock, but the shadow behind the curtain was taller than my mother-in-law's.

"Let me in, Shrimp," a deep voice said.

I ran to the door and opened it. "Oh my God. Hi, Hank!"

My little brother bent over to put his cheek on my head, and my fingers found the knobs of his spine. I almost didn't notice the furball sneaking past my ankles. "No, Floyd!"

"Why can't he go out again?" my brother asked while I grabbed the cat and closed the door.

"He's sick with cat HIV, remember?" I cuddled Floyd and he headbutted my chin. "He may look big and strong, but if he gets into a fight he might die. He needs more love than most cats."

Hank looked up from his phone. "Oh, yeah," he said vaguely. "I knew that."

I put Floyd down and he fled to the comfort of my bed. "Why didn't you call from the airport?" I said. "I would have picked you up."

Hank slung his duffel bag onto my kitchen table. "I didn't fly. I drove."

I picked up the bag and put it against the wall. "From Pasadena? That's a long day."

He shrugged, shucking his hooded sweatshirt onto a chair. I grabbed it and hung it up on the hooks by the door.

"It wasn't a big deal," he said. "Just got up this morning and hightailed it. You know airplanes suck for me, anyway."

I smiled. "Of course." All of his height was in his legs.

He sprawled on my sofa, and I grabbed a kitchen chair.

"It feels so good to lie flat after sitting for so long," he said with a sigh of relief.

"I'll bet."

He grinned at me. "You're looking really good. Kind of glowy."

At least all the quality time with my vibrator was good for something. "Thanks. What brings you here, Stretch?"

His grin got a little too big. "Can't I hang out with you whenever? I missed you."

"I missed you, too." I hadn't seen him since I went down to Pasadena for Christmas, where Mom had made herself the center of attention by bickering constantly with Don, the boyfriend before Rocky. Hank and I hadn't gotten much one-on-one time.

"And August twenty-sixth is pretty soon, right? This can be an early birthday present. I'll take you out for dinner or something."

I had the same sinking sensation I'd had every time little Hank had come to me with papers from school behind his back. Something he'd forgotten to show me, that he needed a lot of help with in not much time. "Almost two months from now isn't that soon," I said now. "Come on, what's wrong?"

He didn't answer. Sometimes he didn't make eye contact because he was untangling some coding problem in his head. But I had a bad feeling he was doing it for a different reason. "Does Malia know you're here?" I tried.

His shoulders slumped. "Malia doesn't care where I am."

"She broke up with you?"

Hank curled into himself a little. "Kicked me out yesterday when she got home from work. She said she felt more like my housekeeper than my girlfriend. But anytime I tried to help out, she just stepped in after thirty seconds and told me I was doing everything wrong. And she'd been mad a lot recently." He swallowed hard and rubbed his eyes. "I guess she was tired of having me around."

My heart twisted. "I'm so sorry. Where'd you sleep last night?"

"Josh's couch."

No wonder he looked wrinkled and defeated. But something else nagged at me. "What about your research?"

"My professor said I could work remotely for a while. I just needed to get away."

But how long was a while? It was one thing to have Kieran here cooking, but my brother took up a lot of room. "Hank," I started.

"That's OK, right?" he said in a little voice. "I can stay with you?"

"Of course," I said quickly, even as a small part of my brain protested at the invasion of my space. "You always have a home with me."

He perked up and looked around. "It's nice here. You always know how to make things cozy."

"Thanks. I only have one bed, though."

He patted the loveseat. "I'll sleep on this."

I snorted. "Absolutely, I'll just get my handy leg-removal machine out of the closet. I'll sleep on it while you're here."

He smiled warmly. "Thanks, sis. You're good to me."

I reached out and squeezed his hand. "Of course I am. I only have one sibling, I've got to do what it takes to keep you."

"So, got anything to eat?"

My brow furrowed. "Wait, didn't you have dinner?"

He absentmindedly rubbed his nonexistent belly. "Yeah, but you know me. I ate a Double-Double with fries four hours ago and it's like it never happened."

"Hollow leg, hollow arm, hollow pretty much everything." I sighed. "Let me see what I can rustle up."

"Spaghetti?" he asked. "You used to do that tomato-butter-onion thing that was so good."

So good, and so slow to cook. At the rate things were going, who knew when I'd get to sleep.

His hands clasped together as he begged, "Pretty please, Ellie?"

But this was Hank, whom I'd fed brownies and hugs and encouragement every time Mom checked out on us. "Sure."

"You're the best sister ever, and I love you. Can I have a snack, too?"

Kieran

*N*o one answered when I knocked on Ellie's door, which was weird for ten o'clock on a workday. Our first draft was due at the beginning of next month. She'd circled the date on her calendar with red Sharpie and set multiple alerts on her phone.

I turned the knob and the door popped open. "Ellie?" I called.

She was slouched down so low on the couch that all I could see were a few short blond strands.

I checked for jailbreaking cats as I closed the door behind me. "Hey, are you sick? You said we had a lot to get through today."

"Huh?" a definitely-not-Ellie voice said, and that's when I noticed the long legs and huge feet on the coffee table. The guy swiveled and pulled out a pair of earbuds. What looked like lines of computer code scrolled down the laptop screen in front of him.

"You're not Ellie." But he looked like her starving twin.

Big blue eyes blinked. "I'm Hank. Her brother. Who are you?"

"Kieran. I'm working with Ellie right now."

He smiled. "Oh, you're one of her cookbook people. Nice to meet you."

I hung up my backpack on its hook. "Ellie didn't say you were visiting."

He shrugged. "I got here on Saturday." He turned back to his screen.

Why did it suddenly feel so much smaller in here? It wasn't just that he was a big guy. It was because it was *messy*. Dirty dishes were scattered over the coffee table around his feet, and the clean dishes by the sink hadn't been put away. How was Ellie handling it?

And where was Floyd?

Her bed was a mess of quilts and sheets, and when I stretched out on the floor to look underneath, I saw a ball of fur pressed against the wall. "You OK, boy?"

Floyd yowled, but didn't move.

Hank said, "That cat doesn't like me. I don't know why. He won't come out even if I offer him treats."

"How long are you staying?" I asked as I pushed myself off the floor.

"Not sure. As long as Ellie'll let me, I guess." He grinned. "My sister's chill."

If I had to pick a word for Ellie, "chill" would not be it. "Where is she?"

"Out buying groceries." He finished something in a mug. "I'm going to go get breakfast somewhere." He dumped it on top of a stack of plates. "Catch you later, Kieran."

"Wait, Hank."

"What's up?"

"Are those *your* dirty dishes?"

He looked down like they'd appeared by magic. "Oh, yeah. I'll wash them when I get back. See you."

Once he'd left, I grabbed them. Twenty minutes later, when Ellie unlocked the door and knocked it open with her hip, I'd washed everything except the silverware.

"Hi. You didn't have to do those. I was going to take care of it," she said as she juggled two packed bags.

"Let me help you," I said, drying my hands.

"I've got it." Her keys clattered to the floor. "Not."

I took a bag from her and put it on the counter. "You didn't say your brother was coming to stay."

"Thanks. I didn't say because I didn't know until he rocked up. Where'd he go?"

I pulled out bags of potatoes and onions. "To get breakfast."

She opened the fridge and started playing Tetris to make room for two cartons of eggs. "Oh, thank God. I feel like I'm in an arms race, trying to keep ingredients around before he devours them."

I was drying the last fork when I heard her groan. Her elbows were dug into the counter, her head in her hands in front of the empty bags. "I forgot butter. I can't believe I forgot butter."

"I thought it was called I Can't Believe It's Not Butter."

She slumped down more.

"I agree, that was a bad joke."

"I am an idiot. So stupid."

"Hey! Don't talk like that." I'd thought in the beginning that she was cold, but now I knew that the only person she was really cold to was herself. Before I could think about it, I put my hand between her shoulder blades.

She tensed, and I jerked back. "Sorry."

"No, please," she said. "I'm just not used to being touched."

I rubbed soft circles over the cotton, and her head dropped forward, her shoulders relaxing just a little.

But then she sighed, and the sweet noise woke up my body when I needed it to stay asleep. I stepped back fast and said, "Better?"

She turned around, looking a little less haggard. "Yeah. It's been a while since someone rubbed my back."

It took everything I had not to offer to do it anytime. "What's going on?"

She pulled her fingers through her hair. "I didn't sleep super well."

"Did Hank make a lot of noise on the couch? I don't know how he fits on it."

"He doesn't. He's sleeping in my bed. I'm sleeping on the couch."

"But you don't fit on the couch, either."

She shrugged. "I put my feet on a chair for extra room."

Everything in me revolted at the thought of her treating herself so badly. "Ellie, that's awful."

She tried to smile. "I slept on Tad's terrible futon. I can cope. Time to work."

"So what's Hank's deal?" I asked as she started to peel potatoes for the spicy salad we'd sketched together late last week to go with the Korean-inspired grilled short ribs for "Treat."

"He's a good kid who's been both broken up with and kicked out of his apartment in the past week," she said.

I trimmed the bottom of a bunch of scallions. "Ouch. But he's, what, twenty-four? He isn't really a kid anymore." Not that I was any kind of maturity expert.

She cleared potato peels into her compost bin. "Not everyone's like us."

"Like us?" I wouldn't have compared myself to her in a million years.

"We're driven. Ambitious. But Hank kind of floats through life, and sometimes he gets pushed around by it."

A growl climbed up my throat, but I shoved it down. What did I know about other people's families? And I needed to show her I could be helpful. "I'll go buy the butter."

"You don't have to," she said, surprised.

"No, Ellie, I *want* to."

A few seconds went by, and the expression on her face changed into relief. "OK." She grabbed her keys and handed them to me. "But damage my car and I'll damage you."

There was my ferocious woman. "Sure, I won't go faster than ninety on the freeway," I said, and she gave me the perfect amount of blue eye roll back.

CHAPTER EIGHTEEN

Kieran

*H*ank had been right. More than a week had gone by, he was still camped out at Ellie's place, and she hadn't said a word. At least he was going out during the day for longer and longer, and Ellie had stuck Post-its on ingredients in the fridge that said, DO NOT EAT— ELLIE'S JOB, which worked about half the time.

The toughness I'd seen when I'd borrowed Ellie's car was nowhere. Her face was pale, except for the purple under her eyes. She moved stiffly, and she winced every time Diane texted or Hank said her name. She needed a day at a spa and a solid week's sleep on an actual mattress.

My fantasies had changed shape when I was in my own bed. I wasn't thinking about sex with her.

No, that was a lie. But I also thought about tucking her under my comforter and stroking her hair until she slept.

When I got to her place on Friday morning, a white candle flickered on the little wooden table where she normally put her keys. "Vibes," I said.

"It's not for atmosphere," she said, distracted. She pulled a crisp out of the oven, and the warm, sweet smell of cooked peaches and vanilla didn't match her tense face.

The picture of Max and Ellie that normally sat on a shelf in her bookcase was on the table too, like a little shrine.

She yelped, "Butterfingers," and shoved her hand under the faucet. "Don't touch the hot thing after you take off the oven glove, dummy." Her phone beeped, and she sighed.

"What's going on?"

"Today's not a good day." Her phone beeped again.

"Should I go?" I asked when her shoulders slumped and she dried her hands. Though the last thing I wanted right now was to leave her.

"No, I want to keep working." She walked over and put her phone in the nightstand next to mine.

"Are you sure?" I said, trying to keep the worry out of my voice. "You can rest and I'll work."

"Can we start over?" she asked shakily. "Pretend today's normal?"

She looked so weighed down that she might collapse any second. I couldn't, *wouldn't* add to her burden. "Of course we can," I said gently. "What's on the list?"

"Could we try out the leek risotto with scallops for 'Seduce'? I've only cooked scallops once or twice, so I'd like it if you could show me how to do them correctly."

The image of feeding a candlelit Ellie scallops popped into my head and I slapped it down hard. The same way I slapped down thoughts of holding her, soothing her. "OK." I clapped my hands and gave her a big smile. "Cooking scallops, aka less is definitely more."

I'd gotten used to narrating what I was doing so that she could listen back to it. As I trimmed the tough muscle and seasoned them, I described how to pick them at the store so they'd be super fresh and sweet. She stood on a stool and filmed over my shoulder as I seared them just until they were crisp on the outside.

Right after I'd put them on a plate, a tall shadow knocked on the door.

"Ben?" Ellie said when she opened it to the huge white-haired man.

"Hello, sweetheart." He turned to me. "And you must be Kieran."

"That's me," I said, when all I wanted was to ask him why he wasn't looking after Ellie.

He looked me up and down and must have decided I wasn't a threat. "It's good to meet you finally," he said as he reached out his hand and gave me a small smile. "You must be the reason that Ellie's been more cheerful for the past few months."

I stared at him as we shook. Me, making Ellie cheerful?

He turned to her. "I'm sorry to bother you when you're working."

She was already untying her apron. "Diane needs me."

"Can you come? I've tried everything, and she's just lying there."

"Can I do anything to help?" I asked. *Fuck's sake, Kieran, how do you know what's going on? You've only ever seen the woman from a distance.* "Would she like some soup? Or something?" I trailed off.

"Maybe she'll eat some soup," Ben said.

Ellie went to the fridge. "We've got some corn chowder we tested yesterday."

I immediately said, "Go ahead and take it. I wasn't going to eat it."

"Stay here and keep working," she said as she grabbed the container. "Please. Even if you're just recording notes. The schedule's tight, remember?"

"Ellie," Ben called, already halfway across the yard.

She closed her eyes like she hurt, and breathed, "Back soon."

I made the risotto, washed the dishes, ate two of the seared scallops, and she still hadn't come back. I knelt back down in front of the shelf of her notebooks.

Who did I want to hear from? Kid Ellie? Teenage Ellie? But ever since I'd seen that picture of Max and Ellie in love, I knew what I was looking for.

I pulled out the notebook from over a decade ago. Ellie started the year exploring the Asian grocery stores in Stockton and cooking her way through the Martin Yan books she'd found in the library. For her high school graduation, she'd bought herself Claudia Roden's book about Middle Eastern food, and the summer's pages still smelled a little bit like cumin and rosewater. She moved to Berkeley in August, where Nicole was her assigned roommate, and she wrote a little bit about the dining hall food—she hated how everything was greasy and underseasoned and plotted ways to make it taste better. Then, on November seventeenth:

Met Max.

She'd drawn tiny red hearts around his name. From there it appeared every second line.

Max was allergic to a lot of things. Shellfish. Citrus. Nuts. And he didn't like olives, or tomatoes. And the man was obsessed with chocolate. Ellie's homemade cake, brownies, truffles—he'd devour all of them.

I turned to the next notebook. Now Ben and Diane's names appeared too, with recipes for lamb tagine, rich with dried apricots and saffron, cheese blintzes loaded with cherry compote, an intensely boozy tiramisu. The gaunt woman I'd seen loved old-school recipes that dripped with olive oil, butter, and cream? I couldn't imagine it.

What had happened to them?

I grabbed the notebook at the end of the shelf. The back pages were empty, so I flipped and flipped closer to the front until I found the last page with Ellie's handwriting. "Single Lady Pasta," she'd written. She'd loved the shrimp and tomatoes in a buttery sauce, but she'd happily give up the shellfish if it meant that Max was home again. He'd be back from Paris soon.

Paris. Soon.

And there it was in her tidy handwriting: July 15.

Today was July fifteenth.

Fuck. No wonder she looked hollowed out.

Floyd hopped up on the loveseat next to me.

"Hi, pal," I said, feeling a little drained. "Your mom should be back soon."

His meow sounded like a whine.

"I know the feeling. But maybe I can help you out?"

When I went to the kitchen and cut up a scallop, he meowed again and went up on his hind legs, begging.

"Did you just *twirl*?" I said, astonished.

I sat back down on the sofa and put my hand out, and he became a little furry seafood vacuum.

"I didn't know you could purr as you ate. That's kind of amazing."

He headbutted my empty hand, and I took a hint and ran it through his silky fur. I dug my fingertips around his ears and chin, and he closed his eyes and purred even more loudly.

"Such a good boy," I said, feeling a little better. "You like that? Is that, oof!" His big back feet drove the air out of me while he climbed onto my chest. "Jesus, cat, at least buy me a drink first."

He ignored my smartass comment and stretched out from my thighs to my shoulders.

"I guess this is me now. Your throne, forever."

Green-gold eyes blinked slowly.

"Are you *smiling*?"

He rested his head under my chin and sighed.

We hadn't had animals when I was a kid. *Too messy*, Mom said. *Too needy*, Dad said.

But maybe this was the upside of being needed. Quiet, sweet moments like this one. "OK," I told him. "Just for a little bit."

Ellie

*W*as Kieran *crooning*? Maybe the wall of the cottage was distorting his voice?

"That feels so good, doesn't it, bud? Such a big, nice cat. Yes, you are."

Yes, he was. He rubbed Floyd's cheeks and my cat melted for him like fluffy butter.

I stayed as still as I could as I watched them together through the window. Kieran wasn't giving the cat the big toothy grin he gave everyone else. He was smiling like he was content.

Maybe the Tigger-ish bounce was a distraction. This was another side of him he didn't show much. Sweet and gentle, happy with something small to care for.

It was my first time being jealous of an animal. After an hour of holding Diane's hand while she cried, I wished I could curl up on Kieran's chest while he petted me.

"Cat, he's not here to be your mattress," I said as I opened the door.

"No, I like having him there." Kieran ran his hands down Floyd's sides. "It's like I can rev him. See?" I could hear the resonant purr from ten feet away. "But I know we need to work."

"We can talk about what to do next while you serve your new master." I tucked myself in next to him, and he smelled a little like pine, a little like plain white soap.

"Is Diane OK?" he asked softly.

I sighed. "As much as she can be . . ." I spotted the notebook open next to him, where Max's name was written with hearts around it, and the other books scattered on the coffee table.

"I know you said not to touch," Kieran said quickly.

Almost nine years of my life, wide open. "I . . ."

He winced. "I'm sorry, Ellie."

Me, wide open. I waited for anger, but instead I felt almost relieved. No more hiding. "Don't be." I took a deep breath. "Do you want to ask me anything?"

Then he surprised me. "Do you miss him a lot?"

As I considered, I let myself remember Max in pieces. His arm resting easily on my shoulders as he argued an obscure literary point with his mentor Jack. His hand tugging me into a spin as he danced with me in our kitchen to the Ella Fitzgerald I liked to play, singing along off-key to "Night and Day." His mouth whispering *mine* and *always* and *forever* over and over again in my ear as he made love to me in our huge bed. Passionate, determined, so confident in himself, in us.

I settled back into the couch. "I miss how certain he was. I'd just turned nineteen when we met, and he was so far ahead of me in everything. He knew exactly who he was and what he wanted. He talked about running away to Vegas after we'd dated for two weeks." I rubbed my temples. "I felt safe for the first time ever, because I knew exactly what would happen to me. When I was afraid, he'd always hold me tight." I sighed. "But then he was gone, and I didn't have anyone to hold me anymore."

Kieran's head tipped back and he closed his eyes tightly. "I'm so sorry."

"My in-laws put on a memorial dinner every year, invite all his friends over. So I'm working on that for Saturday on top of our stuff, while Hank is staying here. Meanwhile, Diane's so depressed she hasn't left her bed for twenty-four hours."

That was enough venting. Soon enough Kieran would nod, and his eyes would drift away like everyone else's when I talked too much about myself. My preoccupations and fears weren't as vital to other people as they were to me.

But his eyes stayed on my face, like he really wanted to know my worries. Like he wanted to help. "How many people are you feeding?" he finally asked.

"Sixteen." A little of my gratitude snuck into my voice.

"That's no joke," he said thoughtfully. "But these are people you know, right? Maybe they'd help you out."

The automatic "sure" jumped into my mouth, but I didn't let it out. We could be honest with each other. "No. They were Max's friends. I cooked for them, and listened to them moan about job searches, and laughed at their terrible jokes. Then he died, and they were nowhere."

Kieran's hand stopped in Floyd's fur. "What the hell? They didn't bring you food, or call, or just stick around for you? They sound like shitty people."

I appreciated his indignation. "I don't blame them for feeling like if they came near me, their lovers would die young. I felt contagious, too. Like I just radiated doom." So contagious that I hadn't left our apartment for weeks, didn't shower, barely ate. Nicole and

Tad had been the only ones who visited. "But Diane wants them there, so I have to make nice."

Even though smiling would make me feel like the scars on my heart had torn open again.

He reached and tugged lightly on one of my arms. They were twisted around my torso, my hands in my armpits as I rocked myself.

"Give me a second. I'll be OK soon," I said without thinking, even though his touch was gentle and I wanted more of it.

"No, give me your hand."

He wove his fingers through mine. His scars and calluses against my skin, rough and warm and familiar. He squeezed, like he was saying silently, *I see you, I hear you, I'm on your side*. He was so good at touching me.

But I couldn't have that. I shook off the deeply unprofessional thoughts and said, "We need to get back to it."

Floyd buried his head against Kieran's neck, like a small child pretending to be asleep.

"It's like he can understand you," Kieran said.

"Come on, sweet boy." When I slid my hand between them, Kieran's chest was toasty warm, and his T-shirt was the velvet that came with a lot of washes. The cat grunted in protest, reaching his legs back toward his new favorite perch as I put him on the floor. "I know, you were so happy, life is one disappointment after another," I told him. He didn't bother to respond and stalked off in a catty huff.

"Listen," Kieran said quietly. "Can I help you for tomorrow?"

I squinted at him. "But you're going to be at the restaurant."

He nodded. "Yeah, but you have me right now," he said matter-of-factly. "What are you making?"

I listed the dishes on my fingers. "Prime rib, baked potatoes, creamed spinach, Yorkshire puddings. Chocolate cake and vanilla ice cream for dessert. All Max's favorite dishes."

He studied my face. "Which you're not crazy about."

"I like them all fine, and what Diane wants right now, Diane gets."

"Well, I definitely know how to make creamed spinach," he said, cracking his knuckles. "We sold a ton of it at the Pacific, and it's easy to make in advance. You have all the ingredients?"

"Yup, it's all in Ben and Diane's fridge. But you really don't have to."

"Ellie? I *want* to."

He sounded so sure, and all of a sudden I wanted to cry in relief. I hadn't cried in front of anyone in years. "Thank you."

He smiled. "Thank me when I get it done."

I moved for the door, but realized I was missing something.

"What's that?" he asked as I grabbed the rings from the top of my bureau.

I slung the chain around my neck. "A necklace."

"I'm pretty sure I'm not blind," he said dryly. Then more seriously, "But you're always wearing it."

He was too perceptive for my own good, and if I kept dumping my feelings all over him, he wouldn't stay. "You could say that. Let's go."

When we walked into my in-laws' kitchen, patches of purple and green light from the art nouveau stained glass danced across his face. With his red hair and sharp features, he looked like a young David Bowie.

"This is beautiful," he said. "I'd kill for this kind of light in my place."

"Yeah. They kept as many of the old Craftsman features as they could when they renovated, but they tried to open things up, too."

He clapped his hands. "So, how long do I have to make creamed spinach for sixteen?"

I checked my watch. "We've got another hour or so."

"Oh yeah, plenty of time."

I started to pull out chopping boards and he waved me off. "I can find stuff. Your job is to keep me company and answer questions."

"You're the boss." I slung myself into Ben's usual chair.

"For now," he said as he opened the fridge door. "You can order me around again later, if you want."

Images skittered across my vision, thoughts I'd never had with Max. Telling Kieran exactly how to please me, Kieran listening to every word and taking his time, making sure everything felt amazing, worshipping me with his hands and his mouth.

"Penny for your thoughts?" he said as he plunked a sauté pan on the stovetop.

I shoved the involuntary gasp down. "Nothing. Not thinking anything at all."

"OK," he said slowly. "Did you buy frozen or fresh spinach?"

"Frozen." I exhaled in relief. "The boxed kind."

"Smart woman. Less work. And do you like it with béchamel or with cream?"

"I mix heavy cream and crème fraîche. I like a little tang in it, and I think béchamel smothers flavors."

"I get that. I like it with super-bitter things like broccoli rabe, but you're right, it's kind of a blanket. And shallots instead of onions? I'm into it. Very Frenchy."

He hummed to himself as he defrosted and minced and melted butter. I understood a little now why Ben liked to sit here. It was soothing to watch someone be quietly industrious, confident that the end result would be good.

Kieran's "Ellie?" popped my bubble.

"I'm sorry, did you say something?" I said.

He squeezed the spinach like it owed him money. "What's your favorite thing you've ever made?

I closed my eyes and reached for that sense of security and comfort I felt when I chopped and stirred. A carousel of happy faces flipped through my memory, until I stopped on one from decades ago. "It was the first meal I ever made from scratch, start to finish," I finally said. "I was twelve. It was my mom's birthday dinner. She loves fish, so I made salmon teriyaki. Rice, spinach with sesame dressing

I found in an old Japanese cookbook from the library. Lemon bars for dessert."

"That sounds delicious," he said as he poured cream into the pan.

"She was so happy with me. Like she was lit up from inside."

"Did you like it, though?" he asked.

The warm glow of memory fell away, and I was left standing on an edge I didn't want to look over. "Like what?"

He lowered the heat and his voice. "The salmon and the spinach. Did *you* like them?"

I shook my head hard. "Why does that matter? It wasn't my birthday dinner."

"Who's this, Ellie?" Diane asked from the doorway. The bags under her eyes were the color of plums.

I hopped off Ben's seat. "Did you sleep, Ema?"

"Who's your friend?" she said curtly, staring at Kieran.

"I'm Kieran O'Neill. Ellie's helping me with my book. Great to meet you, Diane." He pulled out his biggest Happy Pirate Leprechaun smile, but she just shook her head.

"He's helping me prepare for the dinner tomorrow night," I said.

"But you always cook all the dishes," she said. Was that a little bit of peevishness in her voice? I hadn't heard that before.

"She's delegated this one," Kieran interrupted. "I'm her servant for the next hour." He froze, his skin flushing pink.

I was so busy glaring at him for his double entendre that I didn't notice her hand until it was at my throat. "I never understand why you wear your rings inside your clothes."

Kieran stopped stirring, and I felt his eyes on my chest, on the jewelry where she held it to the light.

Béchamel-thick silence blanketed us.

She rubbed the rose gold ring between two fingers, its miniscule diamond flashing. "I remember when Max asked me for this. My father's family had fled Berlin, lost everything to the Nazis, and when he met my mother, he was scraping by. But he took a job at a shoe factory in Brooklyn, a horrible place, straight out of Dickens, and worked every hour God sent to afford this ring."

Kieran was frozen. I was frozen. Except for my face, which was red-hot. "I know, Ema."

"Max didn't want to give you just any fancy piece of jewelry. He wanted to give you a history. A family. Remember?"

"Yes," I finally said, glad I didn't scream it. "Do you want anything to eat?"

She shrugged. "No. Just came in to see who was here." She dropped the rings and wandered out again. I slumped back into the chair and closed my eyes.

"I'm so sorry," I whispered, the shame clogging up my throat. "I told you today was bad."

"You wear those for her," Kieran said quietly.

"I wore them for me at first. But for the past year, yes. It makes her happy."

"Ellie?"

I opened my eyes, and Kieran was in front of me, arms wide. "I'm all right," I said quickly. "You don't need to hug me."

His arms stayed open. "What if I need *you* to hug *me*?"

I gaped at him. I wanted to be held so badly. His hand on my back last week had already made me want to strip off my shirt so he could stroke bare skin.

"Please, Ellie? Just for a second. All you have to do is stand up."

As if he'd commanded it, my body unfolded, and then I was in his arms. It felt like chicken soup when I had a snotty mess of a cold, like a glass of icy apple juice when my body was on fire with fever. I didn't disappear into his embrace like I had in Max's, but he was still strong and comforting and almost like relief. I buried my face in his shoulder, and he found the sweet spot on my back again, rubbing it until I wanted to purr.

But then my skin prickled, and suddenly I genuinely felt fever-ish. It was only supposed to be a hug with a friend, not me climbing him like a tree. Especially when we were still standing in Ben and Diane's kitchen.

"Is the spinach almost done?" My falsely chirpy words filled the space between us as I pulled away. "Thank you so much for helping me out."

He shook himself awake like he'd been dreaming. "Probably, and you're welcome."

After we both tasted it, he scooped the spinach into a Tupperware box I found for him, then packed up. When he shouldered his backpack and headed slowly for the door, glancing at me as he went, I almost begged him to hug me goodbye, to do more than that, but for the millionth time in my life, I shoved down what I wanted to say.

CHAPTER NINETEEN

Ellie

For a second, I imagined that Max's dinner was a Shabbos meal from five years ago. The dining room table was fit for a king with Diane's mother's china and Ben's mother's crystal. Ben had added every single leaf to the table, and I remembered the raucous voices of their friends and colleagues packed around it, Nicole and Max play-fighting for the last slice of Diane's homemade challah. Diane making sure everyone took seconds of brisket, her cheeks a little red with wine, while Ben and Max's mentor, Jack, dissected the latest Warriors game.

Tonight some of the people were the same. Jack and his wife, Nancy, had come. So had some of Max's old grad school cohort from Berkeley. I waved hello down the table to Dave, his husband, Carlo, and Lila, the toddler they'd adopted. I made small talk with Max's rugby friend Eric and his wife, Scarlett, who was pregnant with their first baby. But we hadn't seen each other since last July, and the conversation didn't have the same flow this time. It tripped and fell, picked back up, stumbled again. People talked over each other, said, "I'm sorry, you go ahead," half-laughed.

Had it always felt this forced? Or was I hearing it differently, now that grief's static wasn't distorting everything? Maybe everyone else had moved forward while I'd stood still.

I'd cooked dozens of meals for these people. Jack had eaten my first-ever coq au vin and said it was better than anything he'd eaten in France. The others I'd fed so many pots of three-bean chili and spicy lamb curry when they came over to watch sports and gossip about the other grad students. Ten years had gone by, and they still weren't spending more than five bucks on a bottle of wine. I took a sip of red that bore more than a passing resemblance to cough syrup.

At least there was Kieran's spinach, which was so delicious I couldn't stop eating it. He'd used less cream than I would have done, but it worked. It was just rich enough. Or maybe it simply tasted good to eat something I hadn't cooked.

Ben and Diane seemed pleased, though. The bags under Diane's eyes were still deep, but she was smiling and asking for story after story about Max. A few people had put their forks down, so I could escape to prep dessert soon.

"Fantastic meal, Ellie," Ben said, smiling at me with his glass raised.

"Max would have loved it," Nancy added.

"That creamed spinach was awesome. I want the recipe," Scarlett said.

"To the cook!" Jack toasted.

"To Ellie!"

I looked at the cluster of raised glasses and realized they weren't the people I wanted to be eating with. I wanted Kieran's playful chatter, not this heavy ritual.

"Are you still living out back, Ellie?" Dave asked once we'd all clinked glasses.

I nodded and tried to smile. "You know what rent is like here, and I wouldn't want to live in a house share." I couldn't handle not having control over my space again.

"We're very lucky to have Ellie," Ben said. "She's such a talented chef."

"Cook," I interjected.

"Yes, yes," Ben said, waving his hand. "And she could be cooking for royalty, but instead she makes the best Shabbos dinner I've ever eaten."

Diane looked up and caught my eye for a moment, then said,

"Ellie's so good at looking after us. But it was even better when she had Max to cook for. He loved her food so much."

Suddenly everyone at the table was staring at their plates, or the wall, or the ceiling. Except Ben. His eyes moved between Diane and me, his brow furrowing like he'd gotten a particularly cryptic crossword clue.

Something was stuck in my throat, even though I hadn't taken a bite. Is that how she saw me? As half a person, incomplete without Max?

Sadness, I was used to. Melancholy, too. But the white-hot, sharp-edged thing trying to tear its way out was something I hadn't ever let myself feel toward her.

Anger.

"I need to cut the cake," I said slowly, unclenching my fists. "Please excuse me."

Ben put his hands on the table. "Do you need help?"

I clung to politeness so I wouldn't scream. "No, thank you." I got up, walked calmly out of the dining room, through the kitchen, past the beautifully frosted cake, and straight out the back door.

Instead of going to my house, I walked to the fire pit and pulled my phone out of my dress pocket. Nicole was on a hot date with someone who wasn't Jay, but her calm matter-of-factness wasn't what I wanted.

Kieran would be in the middle of service. He wouldn't reply for hours, if at all. But I needed to imagine his happy grin, his warm callused hand in mine, his arms around me.

I pressed RECORD. "Hey. So we're in the middle of dinner, but I'm hiding outside. Tell me something. Am I invisible? I thought I was a real person, with flesh and bones, and thoughts and feelings, but apparently not." I looked up, but a thick layer of summer fog hid the stars. "I thought I'd be OK taking care of other people. Being Hank's sister, Max's wife. I'm safe now. No one's going to make me move for no reason or worry about money. But making other people happy isn't the same as *being* happy." I rubbed my eyes. "I want to be happy like you, Kieran. I want to have fun. But I don't know where to begin. Do you know how? Please tell me."

I pressed SEND. Then, groaning, I opened a second memo. "I'm sorry, that was incredibly maudlin and self-pitying. You can just delete both of these messages. I hope you're OK."

"Ellie?" Ben called from the back door.

Had he heard? I pocketed my phone and called back, "Over here, Aba."

His steps across the grass were more careful than they'd been when we'd first met. He still had a standing tennis date with three other doctors, and he worked with a personal trainer every week. But that didn't change the fact that he was almost seventy. I rubbed my chest as I felt my heart twist. "I'm sorry, I'll come back in."

"You don't have anything to apologize for. You've been working hard; you deserve a break." He rested his hands on the chair across from me and looked up at the fog. "The young man who was here with you yesterday."

"Kieran. I'm writing his cookbook," I said carefully.

"Right, Kieran." He paused. "The soup was a smart idea."

"It was." She'd only had a teacupful, but that teacup was full of butter and cream.

"He seems like a kind man," he said, like he was parsing every word. "Caring."

"I know he's not Max," I said to reassure him.

Ben cocked his head. "Of course he's not. But that doesn't mean he can't be special. That he shouldn't be."

I raised my head, surprised. He was right, Kieran *was* special. He was mischievous and fun and he looked at me like he didn't know how he'd gotten so lucky to get to spend time with me. I let myself bask a little in the warmth of that feeling, grateful that Ben had brought it to light.

"Next year," Ben said firmly.

"What about it?" I asked quietly.

He shook his head. "I don't think we should do this next year. The dinner. We need to change how we remember him."

For a moment, all the work, all the emotion, lifted off my shoulders. But then I thought of what Diane would say, and it slammed back down again.

● ' ●

WHEN EVERYONE HAD left, all I wanted to do was put my feet up on my couch and read. But when I got back to the cottage, Hank had beaten me to it. "Hey," I said to my sprawled-out brother as I closed the door on the night.

Hank grunted as he stole a car on *Grand Theft Auto*. "How'd it go?"

"You didn't miss much by not coming. You'd have been bored out of your mind. Have you eaten? I brought back some beef if you want to make a sandwich."

"Mac 'n' cheese," he said.

"I can see that." I held back a grimace at the thought of cleaning dried-up cheese sauce off stainless steel. "You planning on going to bed anytime soon?" I asked, grabbing his dirty pot and running water into it.

"Nah. I'm going to finish this level, then go meet someone."

"This late?"

He blushed. "It's someone from Tinder."

At least someone was getting some. "Will you be back tonight?"

"Don't know."

"Hank, if you come back in the middle of the night . . . " I groaned. He'd wake me up. And then I'd have to listen to him get ready for bed, and then he'd snore, and then I'd have to go to work with Kieran on three hours of sleep, *again*.

"I'll be quiet," Hank said, believing every word.

I couldn't hold back a huge sigh. "OK, well, let me know."

He turned around and his forehead furrowed. "You OK, Shrimp?"

I tried to smile. "Long night."

He finally paused the game. "Do you want a hug? You must miss him a lot."

Bless him, at least he noticed some things. "I do. And sure." For a second I enjoyed his embrace, but I could feel every one of his muscles pulling him back to his game, so I let him go.

Ten minutes of gunfire and gangster rap later, he wandered out the door.

"You want to come out, bud?" I called to Floyd, but he stayed in his hideout. OK, then. Teakettle. Mint tea bag. Romance novel. But I was reading the same page of snarky banter over and over again, and decided to stare at the ceiling instead.

Why was it so fucking easy for everyone else? What would it be like to pick some random guy on Tinder, and damn the consequences? I'd tied myself into so many knots to try to please everyone else that here I was, as bound and gagged as a heroine kidnapped by the villain in one of my books. Except the villain was me, too.

But Kieran wanted to untie me from the railroad tracks. He'd listened, and reassured. He'd stepped up and helped, when I hadn't known I'd needed it.

I listened back to my voice note a few times, cringing at every "um" and "ah," and when I heard how my voice drifted up at the end, my face contorted.

Who'd want to sleep with someone who sounded that desperate?

Kieran

After nine, the kitchen slowed down. The dishwashers were still working, but the stream of tickets had slowed to a drip. I could stop thinking about timings and platings and allergies, and once again Ellie came to center stage in my head.

Was she OK? Were Max's friends nice to her? Or did they just take her sweet, generous Ellieness for granted, the way Hank and Ben and Diane did?

My fingers twitched, wishing for my phone. I did my best to forget it existed when I was working, but it looked like tonight was going to be the exception.

"Chef, I'm taking five," I called to Steve, and he nodded.

Instead of sitting in front of my locker and recentering myself like Dr. Meyer had taught me, I stepped outside, where the air smelled like someone's cigarette break.

Ellie had left me two voice notes. She'd gone back to work after doing this hugely stressful dinner? She was such a workaholic. *Or she doesn't know what else to do with herself.*

"Hey," her voice said, high and tight.

Oh, no. This wasn't about work at all.

When she finished by hoping that *I* was OK, I listened again, and again. She sounded lost and lonely. So, so lonely.

The fog had blown in, and I wished on a star I couldn't see that I could go to her right now, tuck her in on her sofa with Floyd and a cup of tea, and do my best to make her laugh. Yelling at Ben and Diane for hurting her would be a bonus.

"Chef?" Manny called from the doorway. "We need you. Last-minute VIPs, and they want to meet you."

I put her sadness in the back of my mind, but it curled up there as I sorted through the last of the night's tickets, as I wiped down my station, as I said good night to everyone. I could record a voice note for her. But maybe she needed more than that. I sat down in front of my locker and tapped her name on my screen.

"Kieran? Everything OK?" she answered on the third ring. Her voice garbled through the phone as she yawned.

"I'm sorry. I woke you up."

"No, I'm awake. I've just been watching you."

How was she watching me? That was weird.

"On *Fire on High*?" she said. "I don't know what the hell Rainbow was thinking, trying to put cotton candy on a soup."

Oh. "Yeah, that was ridiculous. At one point she was trying to make edible hairspray so it wouldn't dissolve, and she only had ten minutes left. One of the nicest people you'll ever meet, though." I twisted my apron with my free hand. "I got your messages."

I could hear her embarrassed blush. "I'm so sorry I bugged you during service. You can ignore them. It was just me rambling."

"Don't be sorry," I said quickly. "Sounds like you had a rough time tonight."

"It's fine," she said just as fast, then stopped cold. She took a deep breath. "No, it wasn't. It was really hard. But you saying that makes it better."

"How are you doing now?" I asked gently.

A rustle, like she was shifting position. "I'm just keeping on keeping on. If I've learned anything in the past three years, sometimes all I can do is endure."

She deserved so much more than just enduring. "Have you got my boy Floyd there? I know he's selfish, but he wouldn't like you to be so sad."

"I love that he's your boy." Her warm voice stroked down my spine and I shivered. "But I haven't seen him much since Hank came. I can't really blame him. It's been busy." She exhaled. "I don't know why I sent those notes. I have a great job, and a nice place to live. I'm ungrateful."

Baby. Love. Sweet girl. I bit them all back. "Do you feel sad a lot?"

She paused. I thought for a second she would avoid the question, but then she said, "Yeah. But I'm used to it."

"You shouldn't have to be used to it."

"Why not? Millions of people in the world are alone."

I hated that little bit of bleakness in her voice. "I don't think all of them are as sweet as you," shot out of my mouth.

"You think I'm sweet?"

Oh, crap. But she didn't sound mad. Just . . . surprised. And a little amused. "Yeah?"

The low laugh that I'd heard in the back of her voice appeared. "I should have recorded this call for posterity. On the list of adjectives I'd have thought you'd use for me, that's number, like, three thousand and three."

"I know you better now. You are, Ellie. Anyone who gets to spend time with you is lucky."

The air was getting heavier and heavier, and I was about to make a dumb joke about her list of adjectives, when she said, "I'm so tired of being good. But it feels selfish not to help people when I know what they want, and I can give it to them."

Her confession sat between us, raw and delicate. "Ellie?" I said slowly, not wanting to spook her.

"Yeah?"

"You can be bad with me."

A long silence. "What do you mean?"

"Not, like, do crimes. I mean, you can tell me everything you want, and I won't think you're selfish, or ungrateful. You'll just be you."

She exhaled, and I wanted to hold her when she did that, run my hands up and down her back to soothe her. "You make me feel," she started.

My fingers clamped around my phone. "I make you feel what?"

"Free." The way she said it, like it was a revelation. "Can I come over?"

I stood up like I'd touched a live wire. "To my place? Wait, do you mean come over or *come over*?" *Oh, awesome, Kieran. Maybe she just wants you to hug her again. Don't turn it into something dirty.*

"The second one," her husky voice interrupted. "The one where we're naked in your bed."

Pinching myself actually hurt. "Yes. *Yes*. I mean, are you sure?"

I could hear her snarky smile. "There's a saying about gifts and horses and mouths which I'm sure you're familiar with."

Mouths, *fuck*. I'd wanted her smart mouth for what felt like forever.

"Please, Kieran," she said, all her sass gone, and every atom in my body popped champagne at those two begging words.

"Come over now." But my apartment was gross, I smelled gross, and I didn't have condoms. "Wait, no, an hour. Come in an hour. Here's my address." As I recited it, I tried to strip off my chef's jacket one-handed. No dice. I hung up on Ellie saying, "See you soon," and scrambled.

CHAPTER TWENTY

Ellie

Forty-five minutes later, Kieran's block of the Mission was deadly quiet. It felt illicit. Like I'd stepped out of my proper, responsible life and into something that was just for me. Not that I had the right kind of lingerie for a midnight rendezvous. I'd gotten rid of all the lacy, silky stuff Max liked a long time ago. But somehow I didn't think Kieran would mind that I was wearing plain black underwear.

At least, I hoped he wouldn't.

A trash can banged, and a small furry creature skittered away. A cat? Probably not a cat. I shivered. Of course I was shivering. It was cold, because it was almost one in the morning and July fog swirled around the yellow-orange streetlights.

"Stop stalling," I muttered to myself. When I pressed the doorbell with all the force of my impatience, it buzzed harshly.

"Shit, hang on," Kieran's flustered voice said.

A few choice words later, he opened the door. His hair was a wet, spiky auburn mess, and damp patches dotted his blue T-shirt.

He sized me up. "You're early."

I sized him up back. "You're not wearing pants."

He looked down at his Daffy Duck boxers. "Um, yeah. I would be wearing pants if you weren't early."

"Do you want to debate, or do you want to have sex with me?"

He grinned his trickster grin. "I don't know, arguing with you these days is a lot like"—I grabbed a fistful of soft cotton and tugged him to me—"foreplay," he got out before my mouth covered his and sweet mint flooded my senses, like all my Christmases at once.

He pulled me inside, slammed the door shut, and trapped me between the wood and his strong, tense body. It felt so good to give way, to go soft. I opened for him, and we both groaned when our tongues touched. As we devoured each other, my fingers found his damp hair; his, the hem of my dress. One touch of his fingertips to the soft skin at the back of my knee, and I *had* to have him closer. I wrapped my leg around his hips, all the yoga finally paying off, and now I could feel him hard and urgent through his boxers and my underwear. He moaned into my mouth when I rolled against him and clamped his fingers on my thigh.

"Nope, nope, not going to bang you against the door," he grunted.

I leaned over and nipped his earlobe. "But you make me feel so good. Touch me and see."

Kieran's hand was the perfect amount of rough as it coasted over my thigh, tugged fabric aside. He growled, "Fuck. How are you so wet already? I thought you'd be . . ."

"Thought I'd be what?" I slipped a hand under his T-shirt, scored a line across his lower back with my fingernail and his hips jerked against mine. His mouth found my neck, sucked hard, bit. I moaned with how much it felt like his mouth was somewhere else.

"Shy," he finally said. "Never mind. No blood in my brain." He kissed me again. "I can't believe you're here. I can't believe you're this hot for me."

"I want you so much." I ran my hands up his chest, giddy with how good it felt to touch him at last. "I want to see all of this. I want to know what you taste like."

"God, you're fucking wild." He shaped my waist and leaned in. "But I have bad news."

"What's that?" If he ended things now, I'd die of dehydration.

His grin was enormous. "There's only one bed."

My laugh fizzed up and escaped like soda bubbles. I'd forgotten that sex was *fun,* too. "Oh, no. What a disaster. Whatever shall we do?"

He wiggled his eyebrows. "I have some ideas."

What he'd said was a bed was actually a mattress shoved in the corner of the room, but I was the opposite of picky right now. We traded items of clothing for kisses: his shirt for sharp nips along his collarbone, my dress for wet, open-mouthed touches of his mouth to my shoulders. He was especially generous when I threw my bra across the room, mixing licks and sucks with dirty compliments that had me blushing strawberry red.

Finally, we were naked under his scratchy blue sheets, me lying back and him kneeling beside me. He was clearly ready to go, but he wasn't touching me. He was one huge twitch, his eyes darting everywhere.

"Problem?"

He tugged on his hair. "I've fantasized so much about what I'd do if I got you naked that I can't decide. Do I want to start at your toes and kiss my way up? Or do I want to kiss your neck and stroke you between your legs until you're begging for me?"

He was looking at me like I was some kind of goddess. But what if I couldn't come with someone new, after all this time? What if he kept trying, and trying, and I was just lying there writing my grocery list for tomorrow? It'd happened with Max even when we were at our happiest, and I'd had to console him.

"I have a better idea," I said, sitting up.

"What's that . . . oh!" Kieran said as I rolled him onto the mattress. He sighed into my mouth as I directed our kiss.

"I said I wanted to taste you, and I meant it," I whispered.

His lips turned up. "If you're that hungry, I have snacks."

I trailed kisses down his chest, and then he wasn't smiling anymore. He whispered, "You really don't have to do that. I've been so worked up that hugging you almost killed me."

"But I love doing it." I sucked his hip hard and he swore. "You're so sexy and I want to make you feel good."

"Thank you, that's great, but are you . . . *Jesus*, Ellie," he moaned when I swiped my tongue over him.

"Yes, I'm sure." Then I couldn't talk anymore. But he could.

Kieran

*H*ad I thought I wanted to comfort her? That she was fragile and lost? I was completely off base. This was the woman I'd fallen for, strong and stubborn and not afraid to go after what she wanted. She'd come all this way in the middle of the night, and right now all that strength was focused on me.

"Keep doing that, *please* keep doing that." That was my last sentence that made any sense. It all got washed away by wave after wave of hot pleasure that left me with single words like *perfect* and *God* and *fuck* and then her name, over and over again, until she swirled her tongue in exactly the right place and I yelped, "*Stop.*"

She pulled away. "Did I hurt you?"

I laughed, high and desperate. "Nope. I've never been this hard in my entire life."

She gave me a slow smile. Fuck, she looked incredible with her curls wild from my greedy hands and that hot light in her eyes. "And you wanted to stop, why?"

I dragged her up my body and hungrily kissed her swollen mouth. "Because, smartass," I finally said, "I want to be inside you so fucking bad."

"You want me? Really? Are you sure?" she teased.

I groaned. "*Yes,* you. Just you. Please fuck me, I'm dying here."

"OK, OK, I'll fuck you. Where are your condoms?"

I stopped cold. "Did you just say 'fuck'?" I'd literally never heard that word out of her mouth.

She grinned. "You're adorable when I've just blown your mind. Condoms?"

I silently pointed her to the bathroom. When she came back to the bed, she kissed me so hard that I was submerged in her. She was above me, rolling the condom on and making me moan, then against me, then all around me, even more hot and slick than she'd been on my fingers. I ground my teeth into my cheek to force back the urge to come. Instead, I ran my hands up her thighs, and she was so delicious to touch, her skin like a peach.

"Is this good?" she asked, rolling her hips. "Is this what you wanted?"

My body arched under her, totally out of control. "Fuck, you feel incredible. I won't last."

"Then don't." She rocked faster, squeezing around me.

All the ideas I'd had about taking it slow, making it sweet, disappeared like steam. For this perfect moment, she was *mine*, and I wouldn't ever give her up. Not for anyone, or anything. "So good, you're so good," I chanted as she moved.

But wait. She was making all the right noises, but she wasn't getting any tighter. I'd been selfish most of my life, but the thought of Ellie leaving my bed unsatisfied was too horrible to think about. "Come on, love," I begged.

Her eyes opened. "What?"

I ran my hands down her sides, between her legs, and played with her until she gasped. "What do you need to come?"

Her rhythm stuttered for a second. "I don't need to. I love this."

There it was, that shyness. I pulled her down and kissed her hard. "I want you to, Ellie, if you can. I want to feel it."

Wide blue eyes studied my face, and I stared right back at her. I'd never been serious in the middle of sex, but now I silently promised that I was hers. She straightened and put one hand on my stomach while the other slid between her legs, nudging my fingers out of the way. "You feel amazing," she breathed when she rubbed, her eyes squeezed shut. "So big inside me."

She was going to *kill* me. Ellie touching herself and talking dirty with me inside her was beyond anything I'd ever made up alone and horny. "You're the sexiest thing ever," I growled. "Don't stop."

We wound each other tighter, and tighter, until all of a sudden the edge was right there, and I dug my fingers into the mattress to hold myself back, willing her to please, please, please . . .

"Kieran!" My name became a drawn-out cry as she pulsed around me, and I shot up and exploded like a firework.

Ellie

I blinked at the too-bright light bulb in its dingy shade as Kieran panted beside me with his arm slung over his eyes. I wasn't sure if I was seeing stars from the light or from how hard I'd come. Maybe both? I glanced at the digital clock trailing its black cord across the floor. Zero to orgasm in five minutes. I guess we'd both been desperate.

Speaking of desperate, no wonder he made admiring noises when he came to my place. He had a small bathroom behind a pocket door, and a dingy beige carpet, but otherwise it looked like a room where someone would serve time. But it wasn't just that it was dreary. There was nothing of *him* in here. No bookshelves, no posters on the mustard-colored walls, no furniture besides the mattress we lay on and a card table with a single folding chair, a laptop charging on top of it. One wall didn't extend all the way to the door, and I guessed the kitchen was behind it.

When I came back from handling lady business in the bathroom, having valiantly ignored the toothpaste crust in the sink and the black dots of mold on the ceiling, Kieran was sitting up.

"Sorry," he said.

I blinked. "Why? I enjoyed myself, didn't you?"

"Well, yeah," he said sheepishly, "but I can last longer than that." He started at the sight of the clock. "Jesus, definitely longer. I'm twenty-seven, not sixteen."

"No problem." He'd come, I'd come, it was all good.

Who was I kidding? It hadn't been good, it had been fantastic. I'd forgotten how delicious it felt to come with my lover urging me on, his pleasure feeding mine, mine feeding his.

But what happened now? The first time Max and I made love, we'd done it knowing our future was certain. I hadn't realized that was a safety net until I was standing in the middle of this new tight-rope, wondering how far I was about to fall if I stepped wrong.

"Um, I should get rid of this." Kieran held out his hand, latex peeking between his fingers.

"Oh! Of course. Go right ahead." *Smooth, Ellie.* I managed to keep my cringe on the inside.

When he came back from the bathroom, I could only stare. He was exquisite naked. A Greek sculptor would have fallen over himself to capture his torso in marble. In modern terms, if there were thirst accounts for Kieran's forearms, his naked pictures would break the internet.

"So," he said, rubbing his neck.

Was that my cue? His face wasn't giving me any hints. "I guess I should go," I said timidly. I couldn't be hurt if I suggested it myself.

His shyness evaporated. "You don't have to." He knelt on the mattress in front of me. "You could sleep here."

I smoothed a wrinkle in the sheet. "I don't want to mess with your routine."

He cracked up. "You think I have a routine? That's so cute. Anyway, do you really want to sleep on your tiny couch, when you have IKEA's finest mattress available?"

Skepticism sent my eyebrows up. "Finest mattress? Really?"

He blushed. "Nope. I said it because it sounded good. But what do you think?"

I thought that I wanted him to fuck me again. I thought that I wanted him to wake me up with soft kisses and caresses.

"I mean," he interrupted, "you can leave if you want. This isn't me being creepy. Do you want to go?"

He sounded so uncertain. That's when I remembered—he didn't do relationships. Ever. When his parents had called him home, he'd wanted a *fake* girlfriend. If I wanted anything serious, I'd be the one who did all the emotional lifting. He could hurt me badly, without even meaning to.

But maybe there was another way. I asked, "What would a friend with benefits do?"

His face was suddenly all confusion. "I thought you hated that whole idea."

"I thought I did. But I just want to enjoy you, and for you to enjoy me. Not to expect things from each other. Keep things light."

He was going to tear a hole in the comforter if he kept up that thing with his fingers. "No expectations? No plans? Who are you, and what have you done with Ellie?"

"I'm still me, but I want to try something different."

I thought I saw a shadow pass over his face. But then he smiled. "A friend with benefits would stay. Especially if the other option was getting no sleep at home."

I smiled back. "Then do you have an extra toothbrush?"

Of course he didn't, so I brushed my teeth with my finger, washing my mouth out with extra toothpaste to make up for it.

Ten minutes later, we lay in the dark. I was curled up on my side the way I usually slept, but his warmth and breath were a pressure in the air keeping me awake. He was tense again, not like he was aroused, but like he was anxious.

"Friends with benefits would also be exclusive," he suddenly said.

I turned over to see him staring at me. "No one is lining up to sleep with me here," I said, surprised.

He growled something.

"Pardon?" I asked. "Did you just say, *fight them all*?"

"You need to get your ears checked. Anyway, it would make things less complicated if we don't sleep with anyone else."

The thought of him begging someone else made me want to hiss. "Sounds good to me," I said, totally casual.

"Have you been tested for STDs recently?" he asked.

The laugh surged out of me before I could stop it.

"What?" he said, bemused.

"You're the third man I've ever slept with. The last time I had sex with anyone was Max three years ago. I'm boring. I promise."

My laughs petered out in response to his silence. "Have you?" I asked uncertainly.

"Yeah," he said, quietly hurt. "I do it every time I meet a new partner. I want everyone to be happy and safe."

He thought I'd slut-shamed him? "I'm sorry," I blurted. "I'm so sorry. I shouldn't have turned it into a joke." I put my hand gently on his chest. "I'll get tested as soon as I can. And I'll figure out birth control."

"There you are," he said, his voice warm again, and my stomach flipped in relief. "I thought you were going to run out and buy a Harley and get a huge spider tattooed on your butt." He stroked my fingers. "Are you sure about this? I've never met anyone who loves a plan like you do."

"And you don't like being tied down with rules and expectations. But you were the first to say we should be exclusive." I kissed his cheek. "I think we're both out of our comfort zones. So let's—"

"Keep it light," he finished.

But his body was still restless. "I'm so glad I came over here," I said softly.

"Yeah?" he whispered back.

"I was afraid I'd forgotten how to have sex, and you'd be bored and turned off."

He snorted. "You knew exactly what you were doing. I think you were a little too good at it. Do worse next time so I can last longer."

"If I was too good at it, it was because it was with you." I nudged him. "Sex with you is pretty wonderful. It's like when we work together in the kitchen. We fit each other."

Suddenly, he was on top of me, and I squeaked, "Kieran!"

He pressed his nose to mine. "Pretty wonderful, huh? What would it take to make it amazing? Fantastic?"

There was my Puck. Teasing and playful and impossibly sexy.

My kiss on his lips was all affection. "I don't know. But I think I'm going to enjoy figuring that out."

"I have ideas, if you're game." He ran his hand down my chest and made electric little circles with his thumb.

"What kind of ideas?" If he kept doing that, I was going to start slurring my words.

"I want to taste all those sexy little freckles on your back while I fuck you," he growled. The picture he painted made me shiver with sweet possibility.

"You like that," he said.

He was so smug, and I wanted him everywhere. "Can next time be now? Please?"

A finger joined his thumb and tugged gently, and a moan of "more" escaped me.

He tugged a little harder. "Wild thing," he said, a laugh lurking in his voice.

I reached down and stroked him. "I make everything groovy."

He grunted, then said, "Yeah, this is why there's no such thing as poker dick."

I couldn't help the snort that escaped my mouth.

"Oh, you'll pay for laughing at that." When he blew a loud raspberry against my neck, a flicker of something golden and bright shot through me as I scream-laughed.

Joy. I'd missed it.

CHAPTER TWENTY-ONE

Kieran

I woke up warm. Warm and confused.

It seemed like all unconscious me wanted was to keep Ellie from leaving, ever. My mouth kissed her downy shoulder, my arm wrapped around her soft stomach, my leg went over and under hers. Not to mention her butt was tucked against my . . . wow. I had joked about not being sixteen, but my body was a teenager when it came to her. The rest of last night replayed in stereo: Ellie sucking kisses into my skin, banding her legs high on my back and moaning as I drove as deep inside her as I could, trailing her fingers through my hair when I stretched out on top of her afterward.

Now she sighed and snuggled deeper into my pillow. Would waking her up for one more round be wrong?

Yeah, it would. She needed to sleep, and I didn't think waking her up because I was feeling needy counted as keeping it light.

Light, shit. That word was the tiniest little cut. Barely a thing 95 percent of the time, but hit it with a grain of salt or a drop of lemon juice, and it stung like a whole nest of yellow jackets.

I untangled myself from her. I needed the bathroom anyway.

My reflection in the mirror looked like I'd walked through a sex hurricane. My hair stood straight up from her hands, and my lips were dark and swollen. One love bite waved hello from the top of my shoulder, another from my pec. I pressed my thumb against where she'd marked me.

Except I wasn't hers.

I shook my head at my dopey eyes, took my meds, and scooped

water from the tap into my mouth to wash them down. I wasn't going to get excited. This was just fuckbuddy business as usual.

Except I'd never brought anyone back here or slept overnight with anyone, even though I'd told her that friends with benefits stayed over all the time. But who made the rules, anyway? I could totally let a friend sleep in my bed, wake up desperate to bury myself inside her, then feed her donuts afterward.

Wait.

Donuts.

Crap.

I tiptoed as fast as I could out of the bathroom and into my tiny galley kitchen and tried to keep the plastic bag from rustling as I emptied out what I'd bought at the drugstore last night. At least I'd been smart enough to put the condoms in the bathroom first thing.

The tea lights I could save for a power outage or something. And I'd drink the sparkling cider at some point.

But the little bunch of deep-red rosebuds I shoved in the trash under the sink.

"Kieran?" Ellie murmured from the other side of the kitchen wall.

I casually walked around the corner and there she was, stretching her arms over her head and yawning. She looked like she should be lying around in a meadow in the sunshine, with little fat angels bringing her bunches of wildflowers, not in my dank apartment with its mold problem. At least I'd stopped buying stuff I didn't need so that it wasn't messy, too.

"I slept," she sighed, and her smile was like a magnet, putting me on my knees beside her. "I actually slept."

"I must have worn you out. Even if it took a while." I ran my fingers through her mess of curls. "Nice bedhead."

She grinned. "Speak for yourself, Woody."

"Woody?"

"As in Woodpecker. You've got some excellent faux-hawk

action there." The smartass grin softened as she touched my cheek. "Last night really happened?"

I couldn't help myself. I took her hand and kissed her palm. "If that was a dream, I'm about to wake up with the worst morning wood ever. Like, someone could plug me in and use me as a jackhammer."

She giggled, and it was better than any shot of vodka. "Well, we should make sure you're all charged up."

I'd heard enough dumbass jokes about the luck of the Irish during *Fire on High*, but maybe they were a little bit true. "You're magical, you know that?" I said, my voice going quiet with wonder.

My goddess grinned back at me like she knew that already. "Is that a yes?"

"Yes, yes, yes, come here."

Hungry kisses turned to hungry touches, and after what felt like five seconds, I was raring to go. But I'd been desperate to taste her last night before she'd taken over and made me lose my mind.

Now I started to slide down and kiss a trail across her endless soft skin, but when I got below her belly button I felt a gentle tug on my hair.

"Wait," she whispered.

I looked up. "How do you like it?" I could follow directions. I wanted to.

But she shook her head and urged me up to her, wrapped her legs around my hips. "Just fuck me. Please, Kieran."

"Please" was definitely the magic word, and once I had a condom on and pushed inside her, I couldn't hold back a groan of relief. I craved more of her gasps when I rocked into her, more of her soft little moans, more of the pink blush that spread across her chest and cheeks. More of the feeling of her tightening and tightening around me like she'd never let me go.

"Come on, love. I love it when you come," I moaned. Fuck, that wasn't light.

But if she'd heard what I'd said, she didn't give any sign. She just reached between us, and I shifted to give her room. The only thing that felt better than her squeezing around me was the rush of joy when she closed her eyes and called my name.

"It's so good," she said all dreamy as I fell deeper and deeper into her.

I wanted her words. Long, short, whatever. "Tell me."

She pulled me down, whispered in my ear shy and sweet, told me how amazing I felt inside her, how strong and sexy I was. The dirty words echoed in my brain and went straight south, and when I came, I felt dizzy from the pleasure and her clean scent all tangled up together.

Thump. Thumpthumpthump.

Was my heart trying to beat out of my chest?

No, that was a stick hitting a wooden floor. The one above my ceiling.

I buried my face in her neck. "Oh, yeah. I have neighbors."

"Maybe we were a little loud," she whispered, and I shivered at how her soft lips felt on my ear.

"He isn't used to hearing sex noises," I said without thinking.

She shook her head, confused. "What do you mean?"

Great, now I was sending mixed signals. *Get a grip, Kieran.* I kissed the tip of her nose and pulled out to deal with the condom. "Never brought anyone back here," I said as lightly as I could.

Would she let my slip go? Of course not, this was sharp-eyed Ellie. "Really? I'm the first?"

"Yes, you're just that special." A joke, even though it made my insides twist with the truth.

But she just chuckled, and I held back a sigh of relief. "Finally, you noticed," she said.

I'd been noticing for months. Noticing, and wanting, and craving, and now I was on a parallel track to where I wanted to be. So close to her, never close enough. At least I could touch and kiss her now.

When we surfaced from making out, I asked, "Do we have to

go anywhere? I could stay here and"—not make love—"fuck you for days."

"I appreciate that, but we'd starve eventually. Not to mention we need to work."

The book. It had brought her to me, but now that she was in my bed, all I wanted to test were the different ways I could make her sigh and moan.

"What's for breakfast?" she asked, practical as ever.

I went and got the drugstore bag, and underhand tossed the Hostess package to her. "Powdered sugar donuts."

She caught them with a huge smile. "It's been years since I've had these."

I held back the fist pump of success. "Why?"

"Don't know. I used to buy them when I was waiting for Hank to finish math club. I'd eat half the pack and give him the rest." She twisted the plastic, then said, "Wait, are you OK with me making a mess? I can eat at the table like a civilized person."

I squirmed a little at the thought of licking powdered sugar from her fingers and from other places. "It's all good. I can change the sheets tonight."

If I'd told six-months-ago me that, pretty soon, my happy place would be eating donuts with Ellie Wasserman while we were both naked, I'd have thought I was having a nightmare. But here she was, dusted with powdered sugar, breasts jiggling when she laughed, and all I could do was smile. It was like this mattress was our private island, and the outside world was an ocean away.

Halfway through her second donut, her face changed from blissed-out to sober. "We need to talk about something."

"Then you should put your clothes on," I half-joked.

But she grabbed her bra and wrapped the band around her waist. "We need to be discreet."

I mentally waved a sad goodbye to her breasts. "How discreet?"

She let out a long breath once she had the straps over her shoulders. "We can't tell anyone we're sleeping together."

So much for feeling like I was in paradise. "Wait a second. Not even Jay? You can't honestly tell me you'll keep this from Nicole."

When she emerged from pulling her dress over her head, she said, "That's fair. But it wouldn't be great if Tad found out. Or Tobias. It's not a good look for me."

"Why is it a problem for you?"

She blushed. "Sleeping with you wouldn't be considered professional."

I tensed. "Why wouldn't I get into trouble for sleeping with you? Isn't that sexist?"

"Nope, for once, it's not sexist. If I were the celebrity and you were the ghost, you'd be the worried one. There's no book without you, Kieran. But there could be one without me."

I reached out and hugged her tight. "Don't say that. Your name will be on the cover with mine. This book is *ours*."

She was stiff for a second, but then she settled into me. She said, "I know. But other people might disagree."

Suddenly all her talk about lightness made sense. It didn't hurt less, but I could see Ellie's logic. "If we weren't working together," I tried.

"But we are," she interrupted.

"But if we *weren't*. Would you be cool with people knowing we were doing this?"

She grabbed my chin gently. "I'm not ashamed of you," she said. "I would never, ever be that. But right now we can only be like this when we're alone." She brushed her mouth over mine, then pulled away a little and said firmly, "Let's only do this here."

Seriously? My studio was no one's idea of a love nest. "But your place is so much nicer than mine."

"Let's keep it simple. One place for work, one place for fun."

"I guess you're right." I didn't like it, but it was tidy. Ellie was nothing if she wasn't tidy. I leaned in and tasted her sweet lower lip, and as she went soft again, all my thoughts of wanting and longing blew away like powdered sugar.

Her phone buzzed.

"What's up?" I asked when she pushed it away.

"It's probably Diane. She can wait."

But after another round of buzzing, she pulled away from my mouth, groaning. "I'm sorry, if I don't pick up when she's like this, she'll just keep trying . . . huh?"

"What's wrong?

She stared at the screen. "Hank never calls me." She picked up. "Hi, Stretch." She froze. "What? You did *what*? Is he still in the backyard? No? *Fuck*." A silent second. "Yes, I said fuck. I'll be there in thirty minutes. Don't go anywhere." As she hung up, she was already scrambling for her underwear.

"What's wrong?"

"Floyd escaped. And Hank doesn't know where he went."

CHAPTER TWENTY-TWO

Ellie

I was going to kill Floyd when I found him.

Oh, who was I kidding? I'd shower him with kisses and feed him so much he couldn't move.

So much for the delicious rush of oxytocin Kieran had given me. After multiple man-assisted orgasms, I should have been humming with contentment, giggling with joy, even skipping down the street singing a terrible version of the "Hallelujah" chorus. Instead, I was yelling for my idiot cat.

"Floyd!" I called for the thousandth time, shaking his treats.

"Floyd! Come on, pal," Kieran called, bending down to look under the Andersons' hedge.

I'd told him he could stay home and come to work once I'd found the delinquent, but he'd gotten dressed and into the car with me.

"I'm not going to let you deal with this by yourself," he'd said. "You're my friend."

For a second, I'd wished he were more.

"Floyd!" he called again now.

"Why didn't I adopt a dog?" I said. "Cats don't give a shit what name you call them."

"He's a little jerk, but he loves you," he said. "And when he figures out there aren't any snacks where he is, he'll come back."

Ben, Hank, Kieran, and I reconvened in front of the cottage thirty minutes later.

"We'll find him, sweetheart, don't worry," Ben said. "He's so big he'll be hard to miss. And you left out the can of tuna for him—he can't resist that."

"I guess," I said. The neighbors were nice and said they'd keep an eye out, but Floyd could be stealthy.

"Isn't this what cats are supposed to do, Shrimp?" Hank said. "He didn't like being inside."

I rubbed my forehead, pinched my nose, but tears still threatened to break the dam I'd put up. I should have been used to being left, but it hurt more and more every time. "But Floyd is *sick*," I said, my voice tight with the sob I was holding back. "I tried so hard to keep him safe and happy, and now he's *gone*."

My brother suddenly looked ten years younger, shoulders hunched. "Shit, don't cry, Ellie."

I wouldn't cry. I couldn't. The wetness I could feel was just my eyes watering for no reason. But if I stayed here any longer, I'd lose it completely. I grabbed for the cottage door and slammed it behind me.

Kieran

I imagined Ellie crying alone, and my heart bashed against my rib cage.

"But it wasn't my *fault*," Hank said. "Why is she mad at me? She can't be mad at me. I didn't do anything *wrong*."

I didn't realize I'd started toward him until Ben's hand was on my chest. "Wait a minute," he said, his voice oh-so-quiet.

"He *hurt* her," a wolf inside me snarled back. "He made her *cry*."

His hand stayed where it was, but he blinked. Like out of nowhere, he recognized me. "Another young hothead," he said, laughing softly. "Of course she would."

"Ellie?" Hank whined at the door. "Say it's OK, Ellie. I didn't mean to."

Ben shook his head when I pushed against his hand. "Yes, you're furious, that's all well and good. But what would help Ellie right now?"

God damn it, I hated when other people were right. I held my open hands up, and he stepped back, nodding. "Why are you still here?" I growled at Hank.

Ellie's brother turned around and blinked at me, his mouth wide open. "I'm staying here. My stuff is inside."

I stalked over to him and jammed my hands in my pockets so I wouldn't poke him in the chest. "No. Why are you not in Pasadena? You've been making your sister sleep on her tiny couch for almost two weeks. You've been eating her food without paying for groceries and leaving dirty dishes everywhere. You are the worst houseguest ever."

"But she told me I should sleep in her bed," he said, looking confused. "I didn't have anywhere else to go."

"Is that true? You have a job, and friends."

Hank stared at the ground. "Ellie loves me."

What a lucky bastard he was. "Do you love her?"

Hurt blue eyes snapped to mine. "Of course. Who the hell are you, asking me if I love my sister?"

I stopped cold. I was her friend? Who she slept with? The one who thought *mine* when I kissed her and *fix it* when she was sad?

No. I couldn't lie to myself anymore. I'd known who she was to me when her lips touched mine for the first time at my parents' party.

Love.

"He's her champion," Ben said behind me.

The words stopped me in my tracks. That was technically right. I'd won *Fire on High*. But what a weird thing to call me.

"And he's right," he continued. "You need to go home and take responsibility for your own life, Hank."

Hank dragged his toe in the gravel. "I just wanted her to make everything better."

"I know what you wanted. But you're not a child anymore, and Ellie can't fix this for you." He jerked his head toward the house. "Go inside. I'll help you make plans, but I need to talk to Kieran first."

"But Ben," he tried.

Ben's eyebrows snapped together. "*Now,* Hank."

Hank glared at me like he blamed me for his stupid bullshit, and I stared right back. What I felt for his sister must have come through, because even though he was almost a foot taller than me, he shrank back.

When the door to the house finally shut, Ben ran a hand through all his white hair and tugged. "I don't know why she didn't send him to us in the first place. We've got empty guest rooms."

After six months, I knew in my bones Ellie would take care of her own, even if it killed her. "Not her style."

Ben's smile was pained. "You're absolutely right. If I could, I'd go back in time and smash her useless, selfish parents' skulls together, may their names be erased."

Ellie had dropped breadcrumbs that made me think her childhood hadn't been the happiest, but now I felt like I'd opened a door into real darkness. The kind where monsters hung out. "Why?" I asked tentatively.

"She hasn't told you," he groaned. "Of course she hasn't, even though it's not her fault. But it's her story to tell, not mine." His exhale was a long, deep rumble. "You should look after her."

"Me?"

He stared like I'd farted IQ points. "Who else?"

"But she's not my . . ." I hesitated again, unable to name us.

He folded his arms. He had impressive biceps for an old dude. "Before you finish that sentence, remember my daughter is a queen. You shouldn't toy with her feelings."

If anyone's feelings were getting messed with here . . . wait. "*Your* daughter?"

I didn't know a man's eyes could soften and still burn holes in me. "In every way that counts."

I looked for his shotgun and shovel. "But we just work together."

His eye roll was the spitting image of Ellie's. "Sure, that's why you look at her like she's the answer to every question you've ever had."

Embarrassment and shyness and a little bit of relief swirled in my stomach. Like I wasn't carrying a secret by myself anymore. "I don't know how," I said. "And she doesn't want that from me."

Ben sighed. "She just needs someone to *stay*, Kieran. Why not you?"

It was a question as direct as Floyd plonking himself on my chest. Why not me?

"Go on. Take care of her. I need to make sure that feckless boy asks for real help like he should have done in the first place."

I didn't want to say that, not that long ago, I could have been that feckless boy.

"Hank?" Ellie hiccuped from behind the screen when I opened her door.

"No, it's me."

A sad little sigh. "Hey."

I walked around the screen and sat on the end of her mattress. Her body was a curled-up shape facing the wall, and she held on to a pillow like it was a teddy bear. I knotted my fingers together to keep from pulling her into me.

"I'm terrible," she said.

"That's not true."

A wet sniff. "I let everyone down."

"You've never let me down. Ever. And you're not terrible. You're amazing."

She turned over, and her eyes were bloodshot and swollen. A tear leaked, and she rubbed it away. "Sorry. I'll stop crying."

My mouth fell open. "Why the fuck are you sorry? It's Hank's fault that Floyd got out. Of course you're mad and sad."

She gulped a few times. "Bad habit. My parents would get annoyed and walk away whenever I cried." She scoffed at herself. "It's been twenty years. I should be over it."

May their names be erased, Ben had said about Ellie's mom and dad. I silently added, *May their names be blown up with dynamite.* How could anyone be so mean to my sweet girl? I said, "I'm not going anywhere. Tell me how to make you feel better."

She stared at me, and my stomach fell into my shoes when I thought she might ask me to leave her alone. Instead, she whispered, "Hold me tight?"

Oh, thank Christ. I didn't dive for her, but it was close.

She sniffled into my chest. "I know this isn't keeping it light."

I wanted to dropkick those words into the sun. "Just because we're doing that doesn't mean I can ignore it if you're hurting."

She didn't respond, just snuggled closer. It felt so good to have her in my arms again. Even if it was for a shitty reason.

"Do you want a nap?" I asked.

Her wet eyes opened wide. "What about Floyd?"

"We'll go look for him later. But I kept you up too long last night."

After a second, she put her hand gently over my heart. "Last night was fun," she said, giving me a watery smile.

"Life-changing" was what I would have said, but "fun" worked, too. I trailed my hand up and down her arm, then stopped as I remembered Ben's words. "What does the word 'champion' mean? Besides winning something?"

"Keep touching me, please." I started stroking her again. "It means being a supporter or a fighter for someone. It's an old-fashioned way of saying it, like a knight would be a queen's champion in a joust. Why?"

"No reason." I wasn't anyone's idea of a knight in shining armor, but I had to try, for her. I had to know what was really wrong. "Ellie, where are your mom and dad?" I asked gently.

The bleakness that washed across her face made me want to howl. When she didn't answer after a few seconds, I whispered, "I'm sorry, you don't have to tell me."

She swallowed hard. "No, you can ask. I know it's weird with Hank." She focused on her hand on my chest. "My parents dated on and off in college, but when my mom got pregnant, my dad didn't want to keep me. She said she'd raise me on her own, as a 'fuck you' to him. So she and I lived with my grandparents for a few years while she finished her nursing degree. My dad would show up sometimes when he wasn't on the road with his band. Then when I was five, he decided he wanted to be with my mom after all, and they got married and had Hank. Then we moved to LA and it was OK, for a little bit." She sniffled. "They seemed happy. Not so happy when I acted up, so I learned not to. You're tense."

I opened my clenched fists and ran my hands down her back instead. "Sorry. Then what?"

"Then when I was nine, my mom met a hotshot surgeon at the hospital where she worked. They weren't discreet, and when my dad found out, he slept with our next-door neighbor. A lot of shouting, and then he was gone. That last fight was when I found out that neither of them had really wanted me.

"Mom, Hank, and I moved, and then there were a lot of new places, and new men."

My stomach bottomed out. "They didn't hurt you, did they?"

She shook her head hard. "Not that kind of story, thank God. But my mom was either on shifts or out with her flavor of the week, and my grandparents were too frail and sick by then, so Hank only had me. That's how it's been for twenty years."

"You had to be his mother." The hugeness of it hit me. "You grew up way too fast."

Ocean-blue eyes found mine, searching for something. After I held her gaze, silently telling her how brave she was, she nodded slowly. "Yeah, I did. I was the only sixteen-year-old in line at school pickup. But I wanted him to go to basketball practice and math club. I wanted to make him a real dinner and help him with his homework. Give him a stableish childhood."

The one her parents hadn't bothered to give her. I knew I couldn't change what had happened, but I could try my hardest to make things better from here on out.

Her fingertip lightly tapped my forehead. "What's happening in there?"

"You're a lioness," I said firmly.

She blinked. "Lioness?"

"Max thought you were a kitten. But you're so much more. Lionesses do all the hunting and care for the cubs, too. The lions are deadbeats compared to them." I rubbed her head. "It goes with your hair."

Her mouth opened, closed, opened. Just when I was about to backpedal, she kissed me. It was tender and soft, and I tried to tell her all the things I couldn't say out loud: that I adored her, that I would be hers forever if she wanted, that she was sugar and salt and everything good and essential to my existence.

She pulled back from our kiss, pressing her forehead to mine. "Thank you," she whispered, and I told myself that was enough.

Once she was asleep, I got up and checked the list of recipes on the fridge. We had a recipe for eggs poached in a fresh tomato sauce with lots of red onion, cheddar, and fresh cilantro for "Refresh," but it needed fine-tuning. Prepping it wouldn't make too much noise.

A little while later, when I was scooping grated cheese into a bowl, I heard a meow outside. I opened the door, and there was His Majesty Floyd sitting next to his licked-clean can of tuna. He was covered in random pieces of dead plant and glaring at me.

"Where the fuck have you been?" I whispered.

He swaggered in, sat below the treat cabinet, and yowled.

"You think you deserve nice things after that, you little asshole? If you still had your balls, they'd be made of fucking steel."

He trilled and waved his paw at me.

"Fine, you're still disgustingly cute. You can have the treats, but only because I need to clean you up."

While he munched, I picked out grass and untangled burrs from his fur. Once he looked less messy, I tiptoed to Ellie's bed and kissed her softly. "Hey."

"Hey, you," she murmured when her eyes opened, and I wanted her to say that again in exactly the same way the next time we were naked.

"Floyd's back," I said.

She bolted up. "Is he hurt?"

"Nope. Just looks like he rolled in some dry grass, but I cleaned him up a little."

"He's fine." She rubbed her forehead. "I thought he'd get run over, or beaten up, but he's fine. I don't know how I'm this lucky."

She sank into me and I held her up, rubbing her back. "I knew he'd come back. He loves you more than anything."

My heart jumped as I said the words, but she just sighed and burrowed into me. When she finally pulled away, her eyes were so wide and deep, I could have drowned. "Thank you for being amazing today. I know this wasn't what you signed up for."

I couldn't tell her that I'd sign up for everything. We'd agreed. "No worries," I said instead, jamming all my squishy, messy feelings into a way-too-small box. "When do you want to get back to work?"

◦ • ◦

HANK CAME OVER that afternoon and showed Ellie a few Craigslist ads for roommates he'd answered and a confirmation email for an appointment with Caltech's counseling service. When he said sorry and promised he'd do better, she'd hugged him hard, and when he looked at me I'd given him a nod that I hoped said both "good work" and "don't fuck it up." His mouth had tightened, but he'd nodded back.

I'd headed back to my place that night and pressed the magic button to get a pepperoni pizza. My stomach was rumbling in anticipation when Tobias's name showed up on my phone.

"Um, hey. It's late. And the weekend," I said.

"This is how you get to be the best, man." I heard some paper rustling. "I've been planning a New York publicity tour for October.

Just booked you to go on Lamar Wilkinson's YouTube show for *Banquet*."

"Sounds good," I said, a little distracted. "I like New York."

"Who doesn't? I also have some stuff that you need to sign off on. Early promotional materials for the book. I just emailed them over."

"I'll take a look." My doorbell rang and I went hunting for my wallet.

He chuckled. "I like seeing your name in big letters with your grinning face and your bandanna. And it'll make your fans go crazy. The thirst accounts multiply by the day. There's one for your eyebrows now."

I saw my chance to help Ellie even more. "What about Ellie?"

"The ghost? What about her?" He sounded wary.

"She should be in the material. It's her work, too." *Thanks, Al*, I mouthed to my delivery person as I grabbed the warm, spicy-smelling cardboard box and handed them a tip.

"She got plenty of publicity from that little fiasco at your dinner."

I shut the door. "But she's really good at what she does, and she's had some amazing ideas."

"That's what's she's paid to do," Tobias spelled out.

I'd signed with Tobias because he seemed to know what he was talking about, and I'd gone along with every single thing he'd suggested. Until now. I put my pizza down and said, "I want her name on the promotional stuff, too."

I'd never heard him sound mystified before, but now he said, "Where the hell is this coming from? She hasn't done anything to deserve that."

He was wrong. So, so wrong.

"What's really going on, dude?" he said. "Did you sleep with her or something?"

"No." Easier to lie if I just said one word.

"OK. Whatever you do, do not fuck her. This is the Kieran show, remember? Everyone wants *you*. She might start thinking she's entitled to more if she's your fuckbuddy."

But Ellie was special. Even more, she thought *I* was special. Not the fun guy I played on TV, just me. "I'll keep that in mind," I said, digging my fingernails into my leg.

Tobias sighed like I'd loaded him down. "Look, if including her is what you really, really want, I'll see what I can do. But I think it's a bad idea."

"That's what I really, really want."

"Fine. I'll get back to you. But remember what I said. No nookie with the ghost."

"I'll remember you said it." Which was true. "And she's my co-writer," I said. "Not ghost."

CHAPTER TWENTY-THREE

Ellie

*A*fter three years of trudging through the desert, an entire tropical rainforest had bloomed out of nowhere, and Kieran wasn't a mirage. Night after night, it took so little—a word, a smile, a glance, and we'd be kissing again, undressing again. Sometimes we were hungry and just the right amount of rough, and other times we went so slowly that coming together made me want to cry with how good it felt.

Early on, we had an only-in-San-Francisco disaster where I drove in circles for thirty precious minutes looking for a parking space. Now, I'd let Kieran know I was on my way and he'd find an empty spot, send a pin for the map on my phone, and literally stand in the space until I got there. He'd take my hand and walk me back to his apartment. And every time he opened the door, the little studio was different.

"You have a bed now," I said the first time, running my hand over the plain light wood of the frame.

He paused from dotting kisses on my neck. "Did you know it's really bad for you to sleep on just a mattress? The internet told me so. Want to test it with me?"

Another night, after sex that was indeed better with a bed frame, I discovered that the bathroom wasn't moldy anymore.

"Did you know that YouTube has instructions for how to clean a really disgusting bathroom?" he said when I pointed it out.

"Kieran," I said, but his eyes wouldn't settle on my face. "Are you doing this because of me?"

He rubbed his forearm. "It was time," he said. "I'm too old to live in my own dirt."

One particularly foggy night I shivered in his arms from the chill, and two days later he had a fluffy down comforter and the softest flannel sheets.

"I know that down and flannel make beds extra warm," I said when I saw the green-and-blue plaid.

"Good," he said simply. "Means I can make you shiver for a better reason."

After we'd shivered twice, he fell asleep, his forehead pressed to my shoulder and his arm slung across me. In the last seconds before sleep claimed me too, I let myself taste the sweetness of this moment. No explanations, no obligations, no sacrifices.

For these dark, quiet hours, we could just be.

It was getting harder and harder to leave every morning. Harder to ignore Kieran's sighs as I slipped out of his arms, harder to ignore how he sleepily grabbed my pillow and buried his face in it. Somehow, I would sneak out as the sky shifted from black to light gray, driving back to Berkeley to feed Floyd and set up work for the day, but it felt like I was leaving more and more fragments of myself behind.

And when he'd arrive later, bouncy and cheerful, I'd fight so hard to be good. I couldn't throw myself at him, shouldn't tell him to forget about keeping it light, wouldn't ask him for forever. He'd given me what he could, and I was fine with that.

I had to be.

• • •

"I'm so excited," I said to Nicole two weeks later as we literally sped to Milpitas, Bad Bunny blasting from the speakers.

"It's just my mom's cooking," Nicole said as she passed three cars.

"You say this now, when you've been telling me about her lechon for years?"

"OK, fine, she's a crispy-pork-making genius." She flicked off the music. "But now that I have you locked in a car going seventy-five miles an hour, what's happening? I've barely heard from you."

"I've been busy," I said now as she turned up the air-conditioning.

"Busy getting busy. How is the Happy Pirate Leprechaun in bed?"

My hackles shot up on Kieran's behalf. "For the record, he hates that nickname."

"For the record, you're not answering the question. I think you meant to say fantastic, if you're blushing like that. How's the book going?"

"Fine."

"Are you going to make it? August eleventh is next week. The shoot starts on the twenty-fifth."

"We'll make it." I might be borderline hallucinating from too little sleep for too many days in a row, but I needed Kieran's touch more. *Whatever You Want* was almost ready. Just a few more tests and I'd send the complete manuscript to Tad.

"I mean, you deserve some hot action," Nicole said as she passed a Tesla and a BMW. She paused.

"I hear a fat 'but' coming down the pike."

"Do you remember what it was like with Max?"

I rolled my eyes. "No, I totally forgot what it was like when I met the man I married."

"You came home and told me you'd met this hot grad student who'd talked dirty to you in French. The next thing I knew, you'd moved in with him and you were engaged."

That wasn't an approving tone in her voice. "And your point is what, exactly?"

"When you fall, you fall really hard. Is that what's happening here? Because you became the supporting actress for someone else's life."

I cringed. Maybe that was true, but that was because the spotlight found Max. He was the consummate extrovert, the dynamo whose stories everyone wanted to hear, Ben's warmth and Diane's brains wrapped up in a tall, dark, and handsome package. And what was I going to do at age nineteen, tell people about my terrible childhood?

"You would have given Max anything. You went where he went, his friends were your friends."

I bit out, "Also known as *being married*."

"And what did he give you?" she snapped.

"Oh my God, where do I start? Affection, tenderness, care? A sense of purpose?"

"A sense of purpose in giving all of yourself to him. You're a smart, hot, badass woman, and he acted like he'd rescued you from an evil witch's tower."

The outrage shot up my chest like fire. "Why are you telling me now that you thought Max was a dick?"

She put a hand up. "No, I didn't think he was a dick ninety percent of the time. He absolutely adored you. But I think you didn't have much of a life outside him and he liked being your king."

"That's not what's happening now. Kieran and I, we're just enjoying each other. He doesn't have a claim on me, and I don't have a claim on him."

"Oh yeah? How would you feel if he fell for someone else?"

Devastated. "He wouldn't."

"But if he did?"

Desolate. "That's hypothetical. I'm trying to live in the moment."

Nicole burst out laughing. "You, living in the moment? Tell me what you've been smoking because I want some. Unless your drug of choice is Kieran's . . ."

"Stop right there," I said, and she cackled.

Then her phone bleeped with a call. She let it ring out, but then it beeped again.

"I'll silence that." I reached for it.

"Wait, don't," she said.

I looked at the screen. It was Jay. The calls came on top of a dozen missed texts.

"Speaking of someone who's fallen really hard," I said slowly.

She grimaced at the windshield. "I don't want to talk about it."

"So you can dish it out, but you can't take it?"

"Ugh, fine. She's not getting with the program. I told her at the beginning that I like being free and I'm not into romance. But she thought I was playing hard to get, and it got messy last night."

"How messy?"

She took one hand off the wheel and rubbed her face. "After we fucked, she said, 'Please let me love you.'"

"Oh God, poor both of you. But why haven't you let her go yet?"

"Because the sex is the best I've ever had. And when she's not proclaiming her love, she's supersmart and low-key hilarious. Talking to her is almost as good as talking to you."

I sighed. "You know that as long as it's lopsided like this, you're using her, right? You have to stop sleeping with her."

"Jesus, of course I know that. I'm not a fucking sociopath. But my pain tolerance is so much lower than yours, so cut me some slack."

"What do you mean, pain tolerance?"

"You always do what's right for other people, no matter what it costs you." She smacked the wheel. "What about *you*, Ellie? What about finishing *Nourish*, or going back to France like you always wanted?"

"*Enough*. Right now, sleeping with Kieran is just for me. And I'm going to be able to buy my place soon—that's something that's just for me."

"Is it, though? I think you've been saving for an insanely expensive apartment because you won't think about what you want right now. And I'll bet you're planning to have a room for Hank to stay in, and to live close to Ben and Diane."

Nicole's words blew through me like incendiary bombs. They were my family, they needed me. I couldn't abandon them. "Fuck *off*," I exploded.

We whizzed past another Tesla. The curse had blown a hole in the ground between us, one too big to jump across with a joke or a quick apology. I knew there was a fragment of truth in Nicole's harsh words, but keeping Ben and Diane and Hank close was the only way I felt safe, no matter how big the burden got. Sex with Kieran was the one respite I had from all my worries. I couldn't give any of it up, no matter how much of a professional and personal risk it was. Not yet.

"It sounds like you have it all under control," Nicole finally said distantly.

"Thanks," I gritted out. "So do you."

"Thanks," she said back just as curtly.

We found other things to talk about, and the lechon was heavenly, but Nicole had been short with me ever since.

Even though the *Whatever You Want* photoshoot started on the first day of a record heat wave, and the Emeryville studio was flooded with brilliant sunshine, there was a cool edge in the air.

"You and Nicole good?" Cameron asked as I leaned against the test kitchen counter, fanning myself with a page of notes. The food stylist's dark brown hair was in a tidy bun, and as their knife flashed through a pile of heirloom tomatoes, blue and red seahorse tattoos undulated up and down their thickly muscled arms. So different from Kieran's tiny perfect knife, his talisman.

"Earth to Ellie?" they said.

I blinked. "We're fine. Minor disagreement."

Their eyebrows raised. "OK, then. Roci, has Adam texted you?"

Rocío, the prop stylist, was dealing out silverware like playing cards and stacking plates, singing along to Lorde blasting from the stereo. "Nope," she finally said, shaking her long purple hair.

"Fuck, it's like he thinks that there aren't dozens of people who'd love this job."

I walked over to the other end of the room, where Tad was studying the huge whiteboard. Cameron had written the master list of recipes we were cooking and shooting today, and Rocío had studded it with Post-its like "green tablecloth" and "charcoal plate."

"Everything came together beautifully," Tad said. "Excellent work, Ellie. I knew I could rely on you. It must have been difficult, dealing with an attention span as short as his."

I shook my head. "Not at all. He pulled his weight."

He patted my shoulder. "You don't have to be nice about him. You don't even have to see him anymore."

"Morning, gang," Kieran said from the doorway, and every molecule of me woke up.

"Kieran!" Tad said, his voice dripping honey. "We were just talking about you."

Rocío and Cameron glanced at each other. They were in charge of reproducing the recipes from the book, and having Kieran here muddied the waters.

"What brings you here?" I asked.

"I took the day off," he said. "How often do you get to watch your own book being made?"

Behind Tad's back, I raised my eyebrows, but Kieran just beamed back at me.

Almost every second he hadn't been at the restaurant for the past five weeks, we'd been together, either cooking at my place or sleeping at his. It was only with some coaxing that I'd convinced him to give me some introvert time. I'd had four nights alone in my bed with a new Gilded Age romance series.

But it had been quiet, and not in a good way.

I'd missed him. I was allowed to miss a friend with benefits, right?

After Kieran convinced Tad that he just wanted to observe, Tad pointed him to a stool next to the whiteboard. My brain repeated *ignore him* like a life-giving mantra, but the rest of me was attuned to every warm word he said, every flicker of copper in his hair.

"I missed you," he whispered when I went to the board to check something for Cameron.

"Careful," I whispered back.

"When you wear black, I remember the time you chewed me out at Qui."

I couldn't keep the smile off my face, but said, "Behave."

"Cruel woman," he said with a huge grin.

I leaned so close my mouth brushed his ear. It was a risk, but he was just too delicious to resist. "You love it."

Kieran

Ellie's mouth touched my skin for a split second, but that contact and her hot words revved me from zero to sixty. Just as fast she was gone, calling something to Cameron, leaving behind her fresh laundry scent. I'd missed it so much I'd almost gone to the laundromat to huff detergent.

I flapped my T-shirt against my hot skin and imagined dumping a tray of ice cubes down my pants. I was here to watch, not drool. Ellie and Tad's heads were hovering over Nicole's shoulder as he pointed to her laptop screen. Nicole hopped up, adjusted a few pieces of cardboard surrounding a cobalt-blue bowl of corn chowder garnished with bright green chives, and tilted a light. Beep-click went her camera. She went back to her computer, and now Tad nodded.

I couldn't help my smile. I'd been so head-down and single-minded at Qui for so long, but now I felt like I'd made it to the next level of a video game and a whole world of possibilities had opened up. My optimism came with me to work, making me quicker to notice when junior chefs needed help and happier to suggest ideas to Steve instead of waiting for him to tell me what to do.

Now I saw these people working to create a beautiful thing that had come from my head. Mine and Ellie's. When they were done, I'd have the book, Mrs. Hutton might let me have my own restaurant, and I could finally ask Ellie to be with me for real, because I finally believed that I had something to offer on my own and that I could try hard things and succeed.

"Ready for the next one," Tad called to Cameron and Rocío.

"We're not," Cameron said. "Fucking Adam."

"He definitely stood you up?" Nicole asked.

"Yup. So he's totally fired, but we're still short an assistant."

I stood up. "I'll help you."

Cameron's eyes widened. "No disrespect, but I need to reproduce the dishes without your input."

I put my hands up. "I won't say anything. I was a commis once. I can take orders. And Ellie can help too, right?"

Their eyes flicked to her, and she nodded.

"I can't say no." They sighed.

At their command, Ellie and I swung into the dance we'd practiced in her place.

"Where are the . . ." I asked when we were working on the beef stew we'd written for the "Comfort" section.

She pointed at the shallots. "There. Could you pass . . ." She waved a bunch of chives.

"Sure." I handed her the kitchen scissors.

"Behind," she said, handing off a pot to Cameron.

"String?" I asked.

"Here," she answered, giving me the roll.

The flow pushed us through the day, with quick breaks to eat some of the food Nicole shot. We were working on the day's last recipes when she asked Ellie, "What are you doing tomorrow?"

Ellie held up a white plate for Rocío. "You want this one for the duck?"

"Ellie? Did you hear me?"

She gave the duck confit and orange salad one last toss in a metal mixing bowl, and carefully lifted it onto the plate in a pile that was just the right amount of messy. "I'm cooking Shabbos dinner for Ben and Diane. What else would I be doing?"

"Oh, come on!" Nicole yelled.

"What?" I asked from where I was slowly decorating a vanilla cake with strawberry frosting. I should have paid more attention in pastry class.

"Her goddamn birthday's tomorrow," Nicole said.

"Shush," Ellie grumbled.

"You shush." She turned to us. "She doesn't do anything to celebrate, and it's stupid."

"We need to start washing dishes or we'll be here all night," Ellie nonanswered.

Nicole threw up her hands. "Fine, ignore me when I try to make you the center of attention."

Ellie continued to do just that, and Nicole's frustration shifted into something that looked more like sadness. She scared the crap out of me most of the time, but it was reassuring to know that we both hated it when Ellie hurt herself for no reason.

Later on, Cameron was showing Ellie something on the whiteboard, and I grabbed the chance to sidle up to Nicole.

"What's up?" she said, packing a lens into a black foam-lined briefcase. "Besides you making my best friend lose sleep because she's sneaking off late at night?"

Was it ridiculous that I was throwing confetti on the inside, knowing that Ellie was lost in me, too? "You're protective of her. I like that a lot."

She looked up at me. The *skepticism* on her face. "Really?"

"Really. You know how she's your favorite person? She's mine, too." I tried to give off good-guy vibes, and now she looked a lot less wary. "What would you think if we did something to celebrate her birthday tomorrow?" I said quickly.

"Like what?"

"I could cook lunch for everyone, and you and Cameron could pick up some nice wine."

"If you made her a surprise birthday lunch, I would think that you had hidden depths," she said, her voice a little kinder. "Or *a* hidden depth."

I deserved that for all the messing around I'd done. "Do you know what she'd really love? I'd make french fries, but there's no deep fryer."

She tapped her lip. "Something with shellfish. She sneaks off and has lunch at Swan Oyster Depot by herself when she really needs a treat."

"Shellfish, sure. What about dessert?"

"Anything with nuts. She couldn't eat them for years because Max was so allergic. But she loves peanut butter."

"Perfect. I'm gonna be a little late tomorrow. Can you cover for me?"

"Only because I know you're doing something nice for her. And Kieran?"

"Yeah?"

Her eyes narrowed. "Don't make it too over the top. When you're showing off, nothing's safe from being foamed and jellified."

I shook my head hard. "I'm different for her," I said. "What Ellie wants comes first. Always."

I knew my feelings were all over my face, but Nicole still studied me. "Show her that," she said finally, and smiled, like I'd passed her final test.

CHAPTER TWENTY-FOUR

Ellie

*T*he next morning, I woke up to Kieran staring at me like I'd invented both sliced bread and strawberry ice cream. "Happy birthday," he whispered.

"Thanks. What time is it?" I said, reaching for my phone.

He leaned over and grabbed my hand. "Early enough that we have time to celebrate here before you have to go to Berkeley."

"You're not coming to the shoot?"

He shook his head. "Later. Cameron asked me to pick up some special olive oil."

That was strange, and he wasn't making eye contact, but OK. "So, what are we doing to celebrate?"

He grinned, and fuck, he was whatever the male equivalent of a siren was. "Well, I thought you could start the day with an orgasm. Then I was going to make you breakfast, and clean up afterward."

"What did I do to deserve you?" The question flew out of my mouth, and something flashed through his silver-green eyes. Something that couldn't have been yearning, because that wasn't an emotion he experienced.

Then his big smile came back. "Be the sexiest thirty-one-year-old I've ever seen." He brushed a kiss over my lips. "Stay here. Don't touch anything."

• • •

I CAME INTO the studio humming, my mood all sunshine and oxytocin. Part of me was still lying on Kieran's bed, his body stretched out along mine. He'd mouthed greedy kisses across my shoulders and chest while his fingers slipped and slid between my thighs. His praise at how hot and wet I'd been still echoed in my ears, and after I'd come, he'd shoved his fingers in his mouth and moaned, eyes closed. After that exquisitely horny display, what could I do except push him onto his back and return the favor?

At eleven, Nicole insisted on driving me all the way to San Leandro to buy coffee and donuts from her new favorite bakery. When we got back to the shoot, Kieran and Cameron's heads were down in the kitchen, with Kieran clearly in charge. I sniffed the air. Garlic, parsley, and white wine? "Which recipe is this?"

Kieran looked up and winked, and Nicole jumped up and down and waved her arms. "Don't look over there, look over here."

"I call shenanigans," I said.

She handed me a flute of cava that Rocío had poured. "Gold star for you. Now, go sit in the corner like a good birthday girl. Lunch will be ready soon."

I followed her orders, because goodness knows I didn't know how to be a birthday girl. I had some faint memories of a few candles burning on a marbled bundt cake, my Bubbie and Zayde singing. But when my parents moved me to LA, Mom declared, "Big kids don't need birthday parties." After years of my birthday being the day when she would hand me a desultory twenty-dollar bill, it felt silly to make a big deal out of it. Or any deal at all.

But I wasn't making a big deal out of it. Nicole and Kieran were, so maybe the best thing I could do was just be there with them. Maybe, just maybe, let myself enjoy it.

I leaned back in my chair, sipped my sparkling wine, and watched with a little bit of awe as Rocío and Nicole bustled around like the mice in *Cinderella*. A pristine light-blue tablecloth appeared on the table, and Rocío broke out a full set of gold-painted china and what looked like crystal glasses.

We sat down to my dream feast. Fat scarlet-and-white prawns swam in a sea of garlic, butter, and parsley, surrounded by thick slices of crisp sourdough toast. They'd made a huge tomato salad with soft herbs and chunks of avocado, and put out dishes of little green olives. Nicole poured glasses of lemony white wine like it was water.

"I think all the vampires in a ten-mile radius just keeled over," Nicole said after a bite of the scampi. "I hope no one was planning to kiss anyone today."

My eyes found Kieran's, and he wiggled his eyebrows at me. I coughed and said, "It's fantastic. Thank you, everyone."

Warmth filled every part of me, not just from the sunlight outside. As Tad let off a belly laugh at one of Cameron's jokes, and Kieran listened closely as Rocío told him a wild story about a shoot gone horribly wrong, I felt at peace. Good food, good people. What more could I need?

Tad stood up with his glass of sauvignon blanc, his cheeks flushed. "Here's to the most talented ghostwriter."

"Cowriter," Kieran chimed in.

"Hear, hear!" Cameron said.

Nicole got up and grabbed her camera. "I want to record this for posterity."

"But we're tipsy in the middle of the day, at work!" I said. "We shouldn't save evidence of this!"

"Come on, lady. I haven't seen you this relaxed in forever."

She wasn't wrong.

Kieran

I needed to get those photographs from Nicole, because my memory wasn't going to do Ellie justice. She was so pretty it hurt, with her flushed round cheeks and her blue eyes sparkling. And if I didn't find something else to do, I was going to kiss her in front of everyone, then push her out the door so we could repeat this morning.

She was pure fire in my bed, and every time she snuck out before I woke up, winter came.

"Oh my God, there's dessert, too?" she said when I brought out the cake stand and Cameron lined up plates.

"Peanut butter cake with toasted crushed peanuts and salted caramel frosting," Rocío said.

"My favorites! How did you know?" Ellie asked me.

I nodded to Nicole. "People know you better than you think."

When Ellie took her first bite, she moaned softly, and I should just feed her all the time. But instead of getting turned on, I had to say something before Business Ellie came back online. I've been on TV in front of millions of people, and never felt so scared as when I stood up in front of this tiny audience.

I held up my glass of Sprite and said, "I've never done a toast before, so you'll need to bear with me."

Ellie flushed bright red, but Tad said, "Go ahead, Kieran."

"Six months ago, I thought Ellie was a special punishment sent down from whatever power that's up there. So organized. So efficient. I was like Animal from the Muppets in comparison."

My eyes flicked from face to face. Rocío's and Cameron's were open, listening. Nicole had a tiny *Mona Lisa* smile, while Tad's brow creased. Shit, maybe this wasn't such a hot idea, but too late now. "On my worst day," I said, "I thought she was basically a robot. But she's not." Ben's word flickered across my mind. "She's a queen."

Ellie's denim-blue eyes went big. She was fidgeting, but I needed her to know that I *saw* her, that she deserved to be seen.

"She's tough and demanding. But she's also warm, and passionate, and she wants everyone to have their best lives. I've never seen anyone care like that about other people. She makes you want to do the right thing, just to make her happy."

I felt my skin go red to match Ellie's, but I kept going.

"I can't believe I'm lucky enough to have her on my team. So here's to you, Queen Ellie. Thanks for putting up with my shenanigans. Happy birthday."

Ellie

*T*hirty seconds after Kieran finished his speech, my phone buzzed.

Did Kieran just declare his love in front of all of us? Nicole's text said.

He was talking about work, I typed.

Nicole shook her head. That's not the kind of speech you make to a coworker.

We're friends. Not that I knew what that meant anymore. Not when he'd learned everything I liked and made this beautiful meal. Not when I felt drawn to him whenever we were in the same room, seeking his laugh and his smile. Not when I missed his skin when I went to bed alone.

If this was friendship, I needed to rewrite the dictionary definition. Or I had to forget about it entirely, because he didn't do commitment. He'd said so.

"All good?" Kieran said quietly as he sat down next to me.

"Yes." I shoved my phone away. "Thank you for saying all of those nice things."

He smiled. "I wouldn't have said them if they weren't true."

Conversation continued around me, and my head was full of questions, and Nicole was staring at me like I'd just told her the sky was green and she was reconsidering my sanity. I needed to figure this out, now. When Kieran hopped up and excused himself, I counted to sixty and went through the studio doors after him.

The second he came out of the bathroom, I nudged him around the corner until his back was against the wall, out of sight of the studio. His mouth curled up. "Can't wait to have your wicked way with me?" he asked, his voice half-laugh and half-drawl.

"You just came up with that gorgeous meal with all my favorite things," I stated flatly.

The swagger disappeared and left a shy boy behind. He rubbed the back of his neck. "I mean, I had a lot of help. Nicole knows everything about you."

"But it was your idea," I insisted.

"Yup," he said finally.

"I think we can say at this point that making me a birthday lunch doesn't count as keeping it light?" I said in the understatement of the year.

He slumped. "I guess so." He blew out air, head shaking. "I would say I'm sorry for breaking your rule, but it wouldn't be true."

I was trying to solve the equation of Kieran's feelings and ending up with solutions that seemed like nonsense. But maybe I'd done the first step wrong and carried the error forward. "But you were the one who said you didn't do serious when we were talking about going to your parents,'" I said. "You were the one who went from zero to 'We should have sex' on the beach in Ventura." My frustration killed my eloquence. "I don't *get* it," I blurted.

He rubbed a tiny wrinkle in the fabric on my shoulder and smiled a little. "I know you like everything to be tidy."

An urge came out of nowhere to crush my dress in my hands, create a topographic map of creases for him to smooth.

He took my hand. "I didn't get it either. It's messy, how I feel about you." As he spoke, he played with it, tugging gently on my fingers. I resisted the urge to close my eyes. I knew now he liked to do this, to rub my back while he looked at his phone or to trail his fingers up and down my arm when we lay around talking after sex. Touching me focused him, and being touched settled me.

"I wanted you so bad back on the beach," he said carefully. "I wanted to be as close to you as I could. But every other time I've wanted someone, it's just been physical. I couldn't name everything else I was feeling, so I tried to make it just about sex, and of course you shot me down."

"Maybe I was a little harsh."

He half-laughed. "Just a little bit. Only a few flesh wounds. But it gave me a chance to think about it. To sit with the wanting. And

after three months I can finally say what wanting you really means."
He paused. "I love strawberry ice cream."

I blinked, confused. "Yes, I saw you chugging your In-N-Out
milkshakes like you'd spent forty days in the desert. But what does
that have to do with feelings?"

He tugged my hand. "No, *listen*. I mean, I've always ordered it
whenever I go to an ice cream store, because I know I like it, even
the cheap kind that's like the Ghost of Strawberries Past. Until I
met you, I was basically treating my life like strawberry ice cream.
I'd found something that I was good at, that I knew worked for me,
and just did that, day in, day out. I told myself that this was what
it took to be successful, but deep down I was afraid of fucking up,
just the same way my parents are terrified of fucking up. I was
afraid if I got close to someone, I'd make a mess and disappoint
them.

"But now, with you, I want to try the whole ice cream parlor.
I want to order, like, a monster sundae with all the crazy flavors I
can think of. Blueberry cheesecake and mocha almond fudge and
mango sorbet."

It still wasn't adding up. "You want to try new things because
of me?"

"I want to be *brave*," he said earnestly. "To give my all to everything, even though it might not work out." He swallowed hard.
"You're so strong, Ellie, and you believe in me. I want to be worthy
of that. Worthy of your faith and your strength."

He went still, and I studied his face. No mischievous spark in
his green eyes, no playful twist to his mouth. I heard his hard swallow, his breath finding a new, quicker pace.

I didn't know if I could trust myself right now. I'd been so careful for so long, but with those words, it was like he'd put a newborn
chick in my hands.

Romantic love had always meant being the fragile one. That was
the role I'd filled for eight years in the story that my husband and
then Diane told. Shy, gentle, fair Ellie for powerful, charismatic,

dark-eyed Max. I was soft for him and he was strong for me. We completed each other.

Kieran was telling me something different. That I was whole, and so was he, but that together we could create something more than the sum of our parts. A monster sundae, as he'd said in his extremely Kieranish way.

Was I ready for this new kind of love? The kind that demanded more of me?

"Ellie?" Kieran said tentatively from far away. "Is that OK?"

I wouldn't know unless I tried. Unless I took the risk with this sweet man. "Honey," I whispered, and pressed my mouth to his.

He sighed softly into my mouth and all the math I'd been doing disappeared for good. Was that one kiss? Ten? I didn't know anymore—it didn't matter. I pulled him closer until I didn't know where he ended and I began. Something in my chest was cracking open, flowing gold and molten toward him and mixing with his passion for me. "I want you, Kieran," I whispered.

His lips paused on my neck where he'd been tasting me. He put his mouth to my ear. "I want to be yours, Ellie. I want that so bad."

"I'm sorry to interrupt," Tad's not-at-all-sorry, actually-pretty-angry voice said.

Fuck. The flow I'd felt evaporated. There I was, doing exactly what he had told me not to do, like a grade-A sex-drunk idiot. "Tad," I started.

He put his hand up. "Not now. But you know we'll have to discuss this as soon as possible."

I felt myself shrinking to the size of a bug, Tad's admonishing hand about to crush me. "I'm sorry," I said, my voice miniscule.

Kieran looked between us, his face going red. "Don't get mad at her," he snapped at Tad. "Get mad at me. I'm the one who fell first. It was all my idea, right, Ellie?"

Fell first. That was what this felt like, plummeting through the air like I'd chosen to skydive without a parachute because I thought

I could fly for some ridiculous reason, and now I was about to slam into cold, hard dirt.

I shook my head at Kieran. Thank God, he clamped his mouth closed, though his glare could have set Tad on fire.

Tad sighed. "I'm going back to the office now. I'll be in touch, Ellie." His footsteps down the stairs were a Morse code of condemnation, punctuated with the final heavy slam of the metal outside door.

"What the fuck was that?" Kieran exploded. "Who died and made him Darth Vader? We're consenting adults. He doesn't have the right."

My voice was dull rock against his fire. "Except he does."

Kieran's hands were suddenly heavy on my shoulders. "Ellie, I'm so sorry. I'll talk to him with you. I'll explain everything."

I shook my head. "I need to handle this on my own."

He squeezed. "But you don't *have* to. I want to help. I want to be there for you."

I hugged him, and his arms went tight around me. I needed this last little taste of warmth and comfort before going back out into the cold. "Thank you," I said finally. "I mean that. But this is between him and me."

"Are you sure?"

Absolutely not. But I had to pull away anyway, ignore the tenderness and the fear in his expression. "Yes. I'm sure," I said, lying as reassuringly as I could.

CHAPTER TWENTY-FIVE

Ellie

*T*he Berkeley Marina was deserted in the endless heat wave. It was already over eighty degrees at nine o'clock, and a bead of sweat trickled down my spine as I got out of the car. Tad was a dark shape on a bench in the shade of a huge cypress tree, and I was torn between dragging out the seconds until we met and diving out of the early September sun's glare.

When I got close to him, he half-chuckled and put his aviators on his head. "I didn't mean for this to feel like a scene from a spy movie when I suggested we meet here. I honestly thought there would be more people." He held out a dripping plastic cup, a disturbingly cheery pink-and-white striped straw sticking out of the top. "One iced coffee with extra half-and-half. That's your favorite from Milano, right?"

The drink almost slipped out of my hand when the cold condensation met my sweaty palm. "Thanks," I said tentatively as I sat at the other end of the bench. I took a big gulp of bitterness, knowing the caffeine wouldn't help my anxiety, but desperate for something to occupy me.

For a moment we sat silently and looked out at San Francisco, hazy skyscrapers in the heat. This should have been an idyllic scene. Sunshine so bright it shimmered on the black pavement and turned into diamonds on the surface of the Bay, birds chirping sleepily in the trees, seagulls calling on the water.

"You must be angry," I said to get it over with.

He sighed, and my stomach dropped another story. "I'm not angry, Ellie. I'm hurt. Disappointed, too."

I closed my eyes, feeling his pain in my chest, my stomach. Anger I had more experience with. My mother specialized in sudden, quick explosions. I'd developed a protocol: take cover, stay quiet until it was over, and then once she was pretending nothing had happened, do the same.

I didn't have a framework for disappointment. Disappointment was a heavy sludge that got into every corner of me, weighed me down.

Tad turned his iced black coffee in his hands. "*Whatever You Want* looks good," he said thoughtfully, "but we still have the passes to get through, and I need you to bring your A-game to editing. Make the right calls. Can you do that if you're having sex with him?"

It would be so easy to tell him I'd fall in line. But I'd worked my tail off for him for years, and this was how much faith he had in me? "Have you ever had any reason to doubt my commitment?" I said, an edge of anger in my voice.

"No, but then you haven't done something I asked you expressly not to do. This isn't like you, Ellie," he said, sounding exhausted. He looked over at me and his lips curled up a little. "I did some digging in my inbox, and I found the first email you wrote me. Do you remember?"

"Of course," I said, smiling back. In my second semester of freshman year, I'd gotten obsessed with a cookbook by a baker who'd trained in a patisserie in Paris, worked in Michelin-starred kitchens in London and New York, then moved back to her hometown in Down East Maine to open her own shop. The recipes for potato-rosemary sourdough and sticky buns plump with honeyed apples were foolproof and delicious, but what I loved the most was the strong sense of home and joy and community. One day I'd turned to the back of the book and gone through the acknowledgments until I'd found Tad's name, and I'd written him a gushing email, telling him about the recipes I'd tried and asking how I could make a book like that. After a week, he'd written back to offer me a summer internship.

"You know we didn't even have an internship program when I offered the place to you?" he said now. "I had to make one up on the fly. HR was having kittens." He shook his head, laughing a little. "But I had this feeling about you, you know? That you would be brilliant to teach and train, and that if I didn't sign you up now, some other publisher would when you graduated."

He rested his hand on my shoulder. "You've been a dream to work with. You're responsible, and diligent, and you can see what matters the most."

The shame was a rope, tying me up tighter and tighter. "Until Kieran."

"Yes." He sighed and took his hand away. "I know what it's like, to lose your first big love. I remember what it's like to be so lonely it's like you're walking through an endless wasteland. I understand you getting to the point where you want to have a little fun."

The gray sadness I'd been sharing with him turned into something red and bristly. A friend with benefits was the textbook definition of a little fun, but making Kieran sound like fluff was wrong.

"But Ellie, I wouldn't want you to do anything that calls your professional integrity into question. You could have a great career ahead of you. I'd hate to see you wreck it for someone who wasn't serious."

The bristle disappeared, leaving behind fear. What if I became known as the kind of writer who sleeps with the talent? A huge hole opened in front of me, rocks and dust falling into emptiness. No more commissions. No more place of my own. No more possibility of writing my own book someday. Just waiting and waiting for my life to begin, stuck in a swamp of clinging grief.

"I understand," I said to my half-full cup. If I wanted to keep moving forward, I had to stay in my lane. Keep my head down, work hard, get rewarded. Eventually.

Tad nodded. "Good. I know you, Ellie. You'll be back on track in no time. This was a blip, that's all."

I tried not to cringe at the dismissiveness of that word. Tried not to remember the comfort of the haven Kieran had made for me, the whole parlor's worth of ice cream he wanted to try. He wanted to be *worthy* of me. It had been so beautiful, but what if it had been all wrong from the beginning?

He wasn't for me. He couldn't be. "Yes," I said quietly to Tad. "Just a blip."

◦ ◦ ◦

WHEN I PULLED up in front of my cottage, Diane came out the kitchen door and waved to me.

"Wonderful timing," she called cheerily as I got out. "I've just made cookies and the teakettle's boiling."

I didn't know how she could stand to bake in a heat wave, but in the three weeks since the Berkeley semester had started without her, there had been wafts of vanilla and cinnamon and stone fruit drifting from the kitchen windows. Now I could smell a warm, bitter puff of baked chocolate, but unhappiness was making a sour brew with the coffee in my stomach. I wanted to get into bed with Floyd and pull the comforter over us, shut out the world where I couldn't seem to move without disappointing someone. "I'm not super hungry, Ema," I said carefully.

She shook her head, smiling. "You've made me plenty of cups of tea. Let me make you one. Please."

I was too tired to demur. I followed her into the kitchen and took a seat at the kitchen table, where she put a small red-and-white china plate and matching teacup in front of me. "These cookies are held together with powdered sugar and cocoa powder instead of flour. Gluten-free things seem to be everywhere these days. I figured I'd give it a try," she chattered.

I reached for one of the tiny deep-brown cookies on the plate and took a tentative bite. The unprepossessing outside packed a rich, bittersweet punch on my tongue, and then dissolved. Some tiny part of me woke up that had been dormant for three years. Diane hadn't lost her touch. She could still make amazing food, the way she'd taught me to.

"Nothing like a nice cup of English tea," Diane said as she filled my teacup. "Good cookie?"

"Really good," I said, unable to keep the surprise out of my voice. After another minute of Diane's chatter about the vegan chocolate cake she wanted to make next, my confusion overwhelmed me. I put my teacup down and blurted, "Is everything OK, Ema?"

She stopped speaking midthought. Five seconds passed, and I was about to take back the question when she said, turning her teacup in a circle, "It's strange, being retired. I thought things would be better once I wasn't dealing with department politics and students who only wanted recommendations for law school, but they're not better. They're just different."

She put her hand over mine. "I know I haven't been paying you much attention recently. But now that I have so much more time, I'd like to spend it with you. Like we used to. I know you're very busy with your work, though."

It was like my wishes were being granted on a time delay. A year ago, I would have wanted nothing more than that. A year from now, would I suddenly stop wishing for the man I couldn't have if I wanted to keep my career?

"I want to go to the City and pick you out a new dress," Diane said, because she couldn't read my mind. "When was the last time you went shopping there?"

"Not for a long time," I said, dragging myself back into the present. I hadn't gone since I'd started my budget spreadsheet, not to mention that it was easier now to buy plus-sized clothes online than in a store.

She nodded enthusiastically. "That's good. We can have a girls' day out on Union Square. Lunch in the Nordstrom café, too."

From a conversation about the end of my career to ladies' lunches—my poor, overheated brain couldn't cope. I took a deep, shuddering breath.

Diane's brow furrowed. "Ellie? Are you all right? You're so pale under those freckles of yours."

I rubbed my face and let off a strange, high giggle. "Work has been really stressful," I said. "This last project took a lot out of me." True, but not the truth.

But Diane just nodded. "Oh, sweetheart, I'm sorry to hear that. Maybe you need to take a break before you do the next book. Sleep in, go for walks, read for pleasure." She smacked the table lightly. "I know! Maybe we could all go on vacation somewhere! It's been years since we've been down to Monterey. Some sea air would put the color back in your cheeks—I'm sure of it."

I couldn't tell her I wanted to leave her, not when she seemed to be climbing out of the hole she'd fallen into. Maybe I could wait a little longer. Save a little more. Soak in a little bit of her certainty.

So I kept eating the rich cookies, and listening, and when my phone vibrated with Kieran's text, I ignored it.

CHAPTER TWENTY-SIX

Kieran

If this were a normal day, a day where Ellie hadn't ghosted me, you couldn't have paid me to get on BART. It was over ninety degrees outside, and a slick of sweat greased my grip on the train pole. Bleached September light flooded the train car as we surfaced in West Oakland, and the inside air felt hot enough to bake potatoes. But an icy shard of fear kept me from falling asleep on my feet.

It had been over a week since Tad had found me tangled up with Ellie in the hallway, and she hadn't called, hadn't texted, nothing. Maybe I'd cursed myself all those months ago, not answering her messages full of big words and cool politeness.

It wasn't like this hadn't happened to me before. I'd both ghosted and been ghosted. But it hadn't *mattered* before, either. I'd never even been able to think this far ahead before her. But now I could see eating breakfast together, not just protein bars. I could see coming back after service to a home that she'd made all warm and cozy, finding her soft and naked in our bed, arms open for me.

All I could do was hold on to the bits of hope she'd given me. She'd called me "honey," not faking it this time. She'd said she wanted me. A sad little voice in my head suggested that maybe she would have said she loved me, since loving and wanting were so close together, if only she'd heard me say it first.

I'd known it was bad when I'd looked up and seen Tad's stern face. Seen the way her pink cheeks had gone pale, how her blue eyes widened and then found the floor. The wolf that had come out when Hank had lost Floyd had bared its teeth, and I'd just barely pushed that part of me down.

Now Ellie was nowhere, and I was lost. But one night I'd been flipping around between Netflix shows when I'd seen a serious-looking dad resting his hand on his son's shoulder, and all of a sudden I remembered: there was someone else who loved her, who would always look out for her.

So on my next day off, I'd put on the pants from Mr. Murphy's suit and a blue button-up shirt, shaved away my stubble, and made sure my hair looked neat. Now as we crept along the tracks to Berkeley, as I walked from BART up the hill to Ben's house, I silently recited what I'd say to him when he opened the door. He wasn't the kind of guy for fancy words. I could see him now, arms folded across his broad chest, listening intently.

Ben, I love her, and she got hurt because I love her, and I don't know how to make it right. Please tell me what to do.

If he told me to go, I would. Ellie came first, always, even if the thought of never being in her arms again made me want to sob.

But it wasn't over yet, I told myself as I reached the front door. The metal of the round bronze door knocker was hot to my touch as I tapped it three times. A dense pause, then the slip and slide of metal, an opening, then a narrowed eye just above my height looking through it. "Who is it?"

My heartfelt speech collapsed into nonsense. My carefully laid-out plan hadn't included Ellie's mother-in-law opening the door instead.

"Hi, Diane. I'm Kieran. Ellie's . . ." I stumbled. For fuck's sake, I should have nailed down that Ellie was so much more to me. "We met back in July." A nervous cough forced its way out of my throat. "I need to talk to Ben. Is he around?"

She opened the door a little wider. She didn't look like a ghost today, but she still seemed mostly made of frayed edges and cobwebs. "He's at his weekly training," she said. Her voice was soft and cool.

My eyes found my feet before I yanked them back up. "Do you know when he'll be back?" I asked tentatively.

"No," she said in that gray voice. "Why did you need to talk to him?"

I could go home and try again tomorrow. But I couldn't handle the thought of another twenty-four hours of silence. "It's about Ellie."

"What about her?" she said, still monotone.

Maybe she cared enough about Ellie that she could help me instead? "I need to know that she's all right."

She tilted her head. "She's out buying groceries. Why wouldn't she be all right?"

Great, now I sounded paranoid. "She's been quiet. It's not like her."

She folded her arms. "Ellie's been resting. Keeping off her phone." A shrug. "Not that it should matter to you. You're just her coworker, right? The reason she was looking so tired and sick." She sniffed. "Unless you were also the reason that she was gone all hours of the night for weeks? You need to leave her alone. She shouldn't be at your beck and call."

I fidgeted, suddenly guilty. Ellie had promised me that she could cope on not much sleep, but maybe she'd been hiding the toll it was taking. I could fix that. I would stay over in her bed now, be the one to slog back and forth across the Bay. I'd get up to feed Floyd every morning, bring her coffee and toast in bed.

"My son was good for her," Diane interrupted my thoughts. "You should have seen her when he first brought her by for dinner. Shy as anything, wide-eyed, in these battered old clothes. Coming from Nowheresville, with the sorriest excuse for parents I'd ever heard of. But Max saw what she could be, with time and attention. A loving wife, a daughter-in-law we could be proud of." Her dull gaze found mine. "Can you honestly tell me you're as good for her?"

I blinked as the question snuck inside my chest and pricked a hole in my heart. I knew Ellie was good for *me*. My bathroom was cleaner. I was more confident. I knew now that my talent wasn't the only good thing about me.

But what about her? I'd cooked her favorite things. I'd made her laugh and made her come. But was that enough? It suddenly didn't feel like enough. Had I been half-assing it this whole time?

"Max gave her a family, too," Diane continued. "He gave her a home with us."

Her words flipped a switch, and my uncertainty disappeared. Her Ellie was still Max's fragile kitten, not my ferocious lioness. I needed to make her see that. "She doesn't need it anymore," I said firmly. "She's getting her own home."

Diane froze. "What do you mean?"

How could she be so oblivious when she was Ellie's family? "She's been saving up for months to buy her own place! That's why she's been working so hard." I tried to gulp my anger down. "Ellie's so strong now. Definitely stronger than me, maybe stronger than all of us. And I think you should let her go."

Ellie

*B*erkeley Bowl had been full of aging hippies dithering over the produce I needed, and then I'd picked the wrong checkout line and waited behind three different people who wouldn't lift a finger to pack their own grocery bags. By the time I turned onto our street, I was ready to curl up on the sofa with Floyd and swear off the rest of humanity. Muttering to myself, I only noticed at the last second the two people standing in front of the house. Diane in her default black yoga pants and top, flour dusted across her chest, shaking her head. Kieran gesticulating avidly, a copper-haired prince dressed in blue. I pulled over to the curb and jammed my car into park.

"How could you?" Diane called as I got out and made my way to them, at the same time that Kieran asked, "Are you OK?"

I shook my head hard as their words collided. "I don't understand. What's going on?"

"This *man*," Diane said, putting a steaming load of contempt into the word as she pointed at Kieran, "told me you want to leave us."

I immediately turned on him. "You told her that?" I snapped.

He put his hands up, incredulous. "You never said it was a secret!"

Diane's voice wobbled. "It's true, then."

I tried to shake off the shock and make my voice reassuring when I answered her. "I wasn't going to go too far away. I was looking for apartments around here. We can still spend time together."

"But why didn't you tell me?" she cried. "You used to tell me everything. I've always confided in *you*."

I felt myself shrinking, bending, lowering my head. "I didn't want to hurt you. I'm sorry. I'm so sorry, Ema."

"I feel so silly now," she said angrily. "Were you only putting up with us for all this time? I thought you loved us."

"I do. Of course I do. You made my life so much better."

She sniffed. "Not better enough, that you would go off with *him* in secret."

The waves of shame were coming higher and higher up my body. "I'm sorry I didn't tell you."

She suddenly took my hands in hers, squeezed my fingers tight. "It'll be all right if you say you'll stay. Please stay with us. We love you so much."

A car door slammed. "What's going on here?" Ben called. "Why are the three of you outside in this heat?"

Diane's eyes didn't leave mine as he approached. "Ellie was thinking of leaving us. But she's not going to, right, sweetheart?"

I was the main character in this four-person play, Kieran and Ben and Diane looking to me for their cues. All I wanted was to sprint offstage and hide.

An easy truth found its way out of my mouth first. "I'm not leaving yet." I forced out the hard words. "But I don't want to live here forever. I want my own home someday."

Ben paused, then nodded.

"But Ellie," Diane whimpered.

"And I need you to respect my choice when the time comes." My voice broke as I rushed the words out. "Please, Ema."

"No," she immediately answered.

"*Diane*," Ben growled.

She spun on him, dropping my hands. "Why can't she stay with us? Why can't things be how they used to?"

"Because Max is *gone*," he said bluntly. "He died over three years ago. He isn't coming back."

For the first and only time in my Californian life, I wished for an earthquake. Something to split the ground open and drag me down into darkness.

"No, no, no." Diane's moan stabbed into my old scars.

"And Ellie's *alive*."

"But as long as she's here, I can remember Max. If she goes, he'll disappear, too," she said too fast.

"Diane," he said, his voice turning into pity.

She shook her head hard, not hearing him. "We're her family. She needs us. She *owes* us."

I'd loved her son with all my heart, cared for her, made her endless meals, and I *owed* her? "I don't owe you!" exploded out of my mouth. "I love you, but I don't owe you anything."

Suddenly Diane turned to me, unrecognizable, all bitter rage. "How dare you! You were *nothing* before my son picked you."

"Enough!" Ben shouted.

Diane clamped her mouth shut.

Pain and guilt and grief surged in my stomach. I wasn't sure if I was going to vomit, cry, or faint. Maybe all three.

"Ellie?" Kieran whispered next to me. Callused fingers tangled gently with mine. "I'm here. I'm here if you need me."

I couldn't help myself, I turned around, buried my face in his shoulder. He smelled clean, felt safe, secure.

"That's it, love," he said softly, tucking me into him. "I have you."

I heard Ben say, "We'll talk inside. Good to see you again, Kieran." Then two sets of footsteps, the front door closing firmly. Immediately after, Diane's watery soprano, Ben's stony bass.

Kieran and I stood there for a minute, his hand trailing gently up and down my spine, me trying to find air, trying to find the courage to let him go, Tad's words and Diane's pain echoing in my head. Finally, I stepped back.

"Are you OK?" he asked gently. "That was a lot."

I couldn't hold back one wild yelp of a laugh. "Well, I clearly can't live here anymore."

"Come live with me," he blurted, then shook his head. "I mean, not in the studio. It's a shithole. We can rent somewhere together. With my prize money and what you saved up, we can get a really nice place around here."

For a second, I let myself into his vision. Somewhere warm and cozy for just the two of us. Battered pans and soft rugs, laughter and lovemaking. But a home with him would mean losing everything I had outside of it. "Kieran," I said, my voice strained. He was caramel sweet, and I was about to burn him.

He pressed his lips to my forehead, then said, "I love you, Ellie. All I want is to be with you."

I moved away from his warmth, his lips a benediction I didn't deserve. "I can't keep doing this. I'm sorry." The word was a dried-out husk by now, but it was all I had. "I'm so sorry, Kieran."

His mouth suddenly turned down. "Is it because I'm not good enough for you?"

My head jerked up. "*No*. Why would you say that?"

"If I were good enough for you," he said, speaking faster and faster, "like Max was, you'd want to move in with me right this second. Is that why you asked to keep it light? Because you didn't think I could handle more? That I would fuck it up, somehow?"

I couldn't listen to him attack himself. "You're good enough! You're wonderful and funny and sweet. It's me. I just can't."

His mouth opened, closed. Went thin. "You *can't*? Or you *won't*?"

Why was he acting like I had a choice? "Tad said that being with you would mean people would take me less seriously. I need my work, Kieran. I can't get distracted."

A black, bitter laugh. "So I'm a distraction now?"

His words made me feel like I was climbing up a cliff, and every handhold I reached for was crumbling. "Kieran, this thing," I started carefully.

"The thing where I worship you and want to marry you some-day?" he snapped, the love and the anger clashing in his voice.

"It's so new," I blurted. "I had a whole life before you. I can't just rip everything up on a whim."

He pulled at his hair. "Honest to God, I don't know if being a distraction or a whim is worse." The words rushed out of him in a furious cascade. "Sorry to break it to you, Ellie Wasserman, but your life? It fucking sucks. But you like it that way, because at least it means you know what's going to happen. You'll keep writing books for Tad and he'll pat you on the head. Your in-laws will keep clinging to you like you're a fucking life raft. And you'll sit in this cute little place and never, ever leave."

I reached for my throat, like he was strangling me. "That's not true."

"It is. You want to be in control more than you want to be happy." He turned and stomped down the front path toward the sidewalk.

"Wait," I called, suddenly frantic. Neither of us was thinking clearly, and maybe there was a solution I couldn't see. "Can we take a breath? Maybe we can figure out something else?" Anything else that would mean I wouldn't lose sunlight and joy and all the other good things he brought me.

He threw his hands in the air. "Fuck breathing!" he yelled. "I'm not going to wait for you to come up with some kind of complicated solution that ties us both in knots. Either you love me, or you don't."

I gaped, words like stones in my throat, unsayable.

He shook his head and growled, "I'm going. Don't follow me."

I pressed my hand to my chest. "But you said you'd stay." The stones turned jagged, cutting me open, filling my voice with tears.

Kieran's voice was a cold wasteland. "Well, I guess you're not the only one who *can't*."

Then he left me, and I was alone. Totally alone.

CHAPTER TWENTY-SEVEN

Ellie

*W*hen Kieran disappeared around the corner, I made my way on unsteady legs to my place. On autopilot I made tea, patted Floyd's head, stared at the wall.

I'd done the right thing. The responsible thing.

I'd had love that didn't ask anything of me, wanted and adored me for who I was, not what I could do, and I'd denied it, devalued it, thrown it in the trash, because obligation mattered more.

Maybe I was dying. Every breath felt like it was squeezing through a smaller and smaller opening in my throat. The tea mug was hot in my hands, my un-air-conditioned cottage a tiny oven, but I was covered in goosebumps, my teeth chattering.

No. I didn't *want* this. I didn't want to be alone.

"Pick up, pick up, please pick up," I begged as Nicole's phone rang. *Please don't have abandoned me, too.*

"What's up?" Her distant voice laughed over loud reggaeton. "I'm at my cousin's birthday in Fremont."

"Help," I choked out. "Help me."

Her laugh evaporated. "What's wrong?"

I jammed my hand into my eyes, but the tears kept coming. "Everything," I sobbed. "I fucked everything up."

I waited for her to demand answers, but she only asked, "Where are you?" her voice all calm competence.

"Home," I choked out through my tight throat.

She yelled to someone that she was going. "Don't move," she said to me. "I'll be there in twenty."

"Fremont is thirty minutes away," I said, but she'd already hung up.

。 ● 。

I WOKE UP the next morning and took an inventory of my body.

My eyes felt like they'd been buried in salt. My lips and nose were chapped from all the bawling I'd done on Nicole's shoulder. Worst of all was my chest, which felt like a sadistic surgeon had cut it open and hadn't bothered to put it back together again.

"She lives," Nicole said, standing by the screen with a glass of water. Her red Le Tigre T-shirt looked like she'd scrunched it into a ball and then put it on, and her hair was in a haphazard bun on top of her head.

"Maybe," I croaked.

"Take these," she said, coming forward and pressing two ibuprofen into my hand, "and drink this. Do you want food?"

I popped the pills in my mouth, chugged the water she offered, then shook my head. "I want to sleep more." When I was asleep, I wasn't thinking about the mess I'd made. "Wait, where did you sleep?"

She reached for the ceiling and groaned. "The loveseat. You need to take that piece of crap to the dump."

I winced as I watched my friend roll her shoulders and crack her neck. "I'm sorry," I said.

She paused midstretch. "Oh, fuck *that*," she yelled. "You would do the same for me, anytime, anywhere, and you'd do it because you love me."

It was like I'd been wandering in the dark and run smack into a door. I grabbed hold of the hard certainty she offered and said, "I take it back, then. I love you."

She smiled tiredly, reaching out to pat my leg under the covers. "Good. You should."

I dozed for the rest of the morning, occasionally waking up when Nicole spoke softly on the phone. In Tagalog with her mom, then in English with Jay, beginning with Nicole apologizing for being an asshole, and then Kieran's name, anger turning into concern, then sadness.

At one point there was a light knock on the door.

"Is she all right?" I heard Ben ask when it opened. I couldn't see him, but he sounded like he was wringing his hands.

"No," Nicole answered, the single word like a guard dog's growl. "She's sleeping."

"Can I do anything?" he asked tentatively.

"I think you and Diane have done plenty," she said coolly.

A long pause. "This is my fault," he said, sounding twenty years older. "I need to make it up to her."

Another second of silence, then, "She'll tell you how when she's ready."

"I'm glad she has you," he said, and the door closed.

I buried my head under my pillow. I knew it wasn't all Ben's fault. Sure, he'd done a great ostrich impression, burying his head in the sand instead of noticing that Diane's grief had metastasized into something vicious. But why hadn't I said something sooner?

Because I thought love was conditional, that was why. I'd never gotten the enduring, forgiving love that parents are supposed to give, and it had left me without foundations, fragile and insecure. Without those foundations, I'd sacrifice everything to feel valued.

If I wanted to stop hurting, I had to stop hurting myself.

Now I heard more Tagalog, this time in person.

A minute later, Nicole leaned around the screen. "Rise and shine. Nanay delivered leftover arroz caldo for you." She slapped down a crumpled receipt on the quilt, ink scrawled across the back. "She says this is the recipe. Though you should test it, she probably 'forgot' an ingredient."

I felt like the oldest, crappiest dishwashing sponge, raggedy and wrung out. "I'm still not hungry."

"Your sad brain is lying to you." She headed into the kitchen and grabbed a pot from the ceiling hooks.

"I'm not, honest. Leave it in the fridge."

I cringed when she banged the pot onto the stovetop and said, "God, why you do make it so fucking hard to do nice things for you?" She slopped the rice porridge into the pan and turned on the heat. "I want some now, so you can sit and watch me eat it once you're clean."

Clearly there was no reasoning with her.

When I came out after a tepid shower, she was sitting at the kitchen table with a steaming bowl and my first-ever recipe notebook.

"Why are you looking at that?"

She spooned arroz caldo into her mouth and turned the page, sparkling with silver-green ink from my favorite Gelly Roll pen. "I wanted to see where *Nourish* came from. Since you didn't lock them away, I assumed they were fair game."

Don't think of Kieran. Don't think of Kieran.

The rich smells of long-simmered chicken, onion, and garlic curled around us, and Nicole hummed with every mouthful. Ten seconds later, my stomach hissed in protest. "Can I taste it?"

Nicole pulled out a second spoon from under the placemat.

From the first spoonful, the warmth of the rice porridge soaked into my bones. It was care in a bowl, and the tears that surged up almost choked me.

"Ellie?" Her voice was as cozy and comforting as the stew.

No, I was tired of crying. "I like the ginger and the citrus in this," I managed.

She smiled. "Exactly. It's got to have the calamansi lime juice in it to make everything else sing. But Nanay swears it's all about the chicken."

I got my own bowl, and we ate in silence for a little while.

"Now that I've fed you," she said once I'd put my spoon down, "can we talk about what you're going to do?"

"Yeah." I pushed the bowl away. "I need to set boundaries with Tad and Diane."

"Honestly, both of them can fuck themselves. They've been using you as their dress-up doll for years."

I rubbed my eyes. "I don't know why it took me so long to see it."

"Because it started out fine," she said. "They were both mentoring you. But it also meant they were putting you in a little box, and when you tried to leave that box, they shoved you back inside it."

Exactly what Kieran's family had done to him.

"But there's another big thing. I'm sorry I wasn't paying closer attention." She took a deep breath. "Are you in love with Kieran?"

I buried my face in my hands. "I can look back and say yes. But he was so adamant that casual relationships were his thing, so I wouldn't let myself think about him seriously, and I didn't recognize it." The words bubbled up and overflowed as I let myself say everything in my heart. "Love was never about freedom for me. It's always been about taking care of other people. Being what they need. I thought what I had with Kieran was a vacation from reality."

Nicole reached out and rubbed my back. "It shouldn't be a vacation from reality to be genuinely happy, lady." She sighed. "Look, you're my best friend, but you're not the expert on love."

I looked up at her confused and a little offended. "I'm sorry, wasn't I married for years?"

"Yup, to the second man you'd ever dated. I know you and Max had this crazy instant connection, but most relationships, romantic and platonic, aren't just one moment and, bang, you're all the way in. They're a process."

I sat forward in my chair, listening closely. "Like cooking."

Nicole played with her spoon as she thought. "Yeah. Like, you and Max were this perfect peach you found at the farmers' market. It was all sweet and lush and easy."

"Because I was happy to do whatever he wanted," I said, finally seeing it clearly. He'd been so loving, but how easy would it have been to love someone who'd never said no? How easy had I found it to just give in, never voicing my needs, my wants? It had kept me safe.

Kieran had wanted to set me free, and I'd panicked.

"And he was gone before you got to the hard pit in the middle," Nicole said, then held up her spoon. "You and Kieran might be more like arroz caldo. It's all about time and effort, gently bringing everything together."

"But the results are more than what you started with," I said quietly. All those months in the kitchen working together, all the laughing and the debating and the kisses, fake and genuine. We'd been building something, until we'd hammered the foundation at its weakest point and brought everything crashing down.

"Yeah," Nicole said softly.

I rubbed my temples. "He was offering me everything, and I pushed it away because I was a coward. I made him feel like he'd never be good enough. No wonder he lashed out at me."

"Telling you your life sucks was a horrible thing for him to say, though. You hit each other where it'd hurt the most. But you have what it takes to heal each other, too."

I snorted. "Since when did you become Dear Prudence?"

"I don't do romance, but that doesn't mean I can't see what makes people tick. Do things make more sense now?" she asked carefully.

I rubbed my face, trying to drive away the exhaustion I felt. "As much as they ever will." I tried to get in touch with the willpower I'd buried for two decades. "I need to call Tad."

"Do you want me to go outside?"

I was trying to be brave, but I wasn't nearly there yet. "No, stay, please. I need moral support."

I dialed his number and put him on speakerphone. Nicole grabbed my hand and squeezed it.

"Good morning, Ellie," Tad said. "How are you doing?"

"I'm not great." I inhaled a very, very deep breath, as if oxygen would give me courage to do the right thing. "I'm calling because I need to withdraw from *Whatever You Want*."

I could hear his confused blink through the phone. "Wait, you want to withdraw *now*? Gabi just sent me the first pass. We have so much to do."

"I understand." Nicole squeezed my hand hard, and I said less tentatively, "But I thought about what you said, and my priorities have changed. I need to look after myself, which means leaving the project."

Tad paused. "Even though that means your name will be removed from the cover and you'll need to pay back your fee?"

"Correct."

"I'm very disappointed in you, Ellie," he said sternly. "This is a real let-down."

"I'm sorry," Nicole shook her head, but I put my finger up, "you feel that way." Nicole nodded. "But this is my decision. I need to focus on my life outside of work."

"Well, all I can say is that actions have consequences. I may be less quick to think of you for the next great project," Tad said.

How snide. He wasn't used to me refusing, and he didn't like it one bit. "Yes, they do," I said, anger freeing my tongue. "If I stay on this project, I will be the unhappiest I have ever been. It says a lot about our relationship that you care more about my compliance than my well-being."

A moment of silence. "Ellie, that's not true," he said, his voice defensive. "I do care about you as a person."

The words to reassure him that I'd be OK tried to push forward, but I wasn't going to make him feel better to my detriment. "I haven't felt cared for in a long time." I made myself sound businesslike. "I'll set up the payment today. You'll have my money back tomorrow. Goodbye, Tad."

Nicole put her hand up when I ended the call and I slapped it in a resounding high-five. "That was badass," she said. "I'm so proud of you. I wish we had champagne, but I'll have to make you coffee instead."

She hopped up and filled the teakettle with water, then put it on to boil and turned to face me, her arms folded. "Now, tell me again why it's so important that you buy your own place?"

Flippant words came to me first. Because I was a grown-up, because I was tired of living in other people's places. Then the pragmatic words: that I'd have a bigger space, that I could rent out the apartment as a studio. But I pushed all of those aside and said the truth instead. "My life has been so uncertain for so long. Owning my own house would make me feel safe for the first time in forever."

"But safety doesn't have to be about four walls." She smiled. "You can be your own home, Ellie. You can believe in yourself, and go out into the world knowing that whatever happens, you'll stand strong. Life has thrown so much bullshit at you, and you've kept on going."

"I'm the Energizer Bunny?"

"More like the Terminator."

I cracked up, and Nicole said through her laughter, "It's a superpower, babe. You've underestimated yourself."

Or I'd let other people tell me how valuable I was. I needed to stop doing that. "OK, next thing. I need to move. I still don't want to live with strangers, though."

She tilted her head. "You could live with me. My lease is up in January."

I stared at her. "Really?"

She threw up her hands. "Of course. I never asked you before because you were so invested in staying here. Now, I have an idea. How much money have you saved up?"

I opened my budget spreadsheet and showed her the thousands of dollars I'd put into the bank.

She whistled. "You should teach a budgeting class."

For a second, I felt my twelve-year-old self's embarrassment at grocery shopping with a whiny six-year-old and a fistful of coupons. "I wish I didn't know how to do this."

She nudged me. "Survivor. Be proud."

That's right. I knew what I had to do to keep going. "Go me for saving so much money."

"So why don't you spend it on yourself?"

I shook my head hard. "No, I want to save some. I effectively told Tad to screw himself. I'm going to need it."

"Well, save some, spend some." Nicole waggled her fingers in the air, and grinned like she was a mischievous fairy about to grant a wish. "Come on, what does your little heart desire?"

Kieran. The one thing money couldn't buy.

When was the last time I was happy all on my own? Free and light and easy? I closed my eyes and tasted salty frites, buttery pastry. "I want to go back to France for a few weeks," I said after a long pause. Go back to all my old haunts in Lyon and see new places, too. Provence, the Mediterranean, maybe over to the Alps.

She rubbed her hands together. "That's what I like to hear. I can block out some free time in spring."

I blinked. Of course a good life wasn't just about being happy on my own. I could be happy with someone else, partners in crime. "You want to come?" I asked shyly.

She nodded eagerly. "Of course. I want to see Lyon for myself. Who knows, maybe there's a book in it for us. What else?"

I rested my head on my hand. "Not as fun, but necessary. I need to go back to therapy." The apocalyptic meltdown of the last week wasn't going to fix itself. I clearly still had more demons to fight.

"Look at you, doing the work," Nicole said.

Thinking about it made me tired, so I just *hmm*ed in response.

She patted my back and stood up. "Great start." She checked her watch. "I'm going to go meet up with Jay, but my phone will be in my pocket."

"Aren't things still bad with you two?"

She slipped her jacket on and untucked her sheet of black

hair from the collar. "We're figuring it out. It's not easy, but we're talking."

As she stood up and slung her bag over her shoulder, she asked, "When was the last time you looked at *Nourish*, line by line?"

My eyes flicked to my laptop. "I've glanced at it every once in a while, but it's been a year, maybe?"

"You know what I saw when I read through that notebook?"

"What?"

"You've always been so good at doing for other people. Remembering what they like, finding big and little ways to please them. But there's only hints of you."

I sighed. "Kieran said the same thing."

She half-smiled and shook her head. "I knew he wasn't a dummy. You're amazing, Ellie. You should tell *your* story."

She opened the door, and I said, "What you said earlier. That I make it hard for people to do nice things for me."

"Oh, that was bitchy. I'm sorry, lady."

"But it's true."

She came back, tugged me close, and kissed my forehead. "Yeah. You're defensive and stubborn as fuck. I won't stop trying, though. You're worth it. Bye, babe."

That was Nicole, serving up the brutal truth as casually as if it were a Big Mac.

I'd been such a coward with Kieran this whole time, except for that one heady moment back in July when I'd taken the running jump into the unknown and asked to come over.

I needed to make that leap for him now, but from a greater height.

I opened the dossier I'd written about him nine months ago and ran my pen down the screen until a name jumped out at me. After a swift Google for her address and a hunt for my fanciest stationery, I sat down and wrote in my best cursive:

Dear Mrs. Hutton . . .

◦ ◦ ◦

THE NEXT AFTERNOON, after I'd walked to the mailbox and handled my admin, I fired up my printer, pushed all the furniture back against the walls, and rolled up the rug. When Floyd investigated, I bribed him with treats and catnip and he curled up on the bed instead.

One section at a time, I laid out the proposal for *Nourish*. Sheet after sheet in neat rows until it made one huge white rectangle, dotted with smiling faces and plates heaped with food.

I knelt down and studied them. On the surface, all the recipes were good. But a lot of it wasn't me. Or it was me trying to make other people happy, so that they would think I was wonderful.

I started to divide the pages into two piles. I hated hard-boiled eggs, even though I'd made deviled ones for my mom, so that recipe was gone. The fettuccine Alfredo that Hank had asked for five birthday dinners in a row, but that I could only eat doused in hot sauce, gone.

And in all honesty, I wasn't as obsessed with chocolate as Max had been. If the Guittard chips were down, I'd happily never eat a flourless chocolate cake again. Gone.

I put aside some recipes to retest. I was a better cook now than I'd been before Max died. More creative. Not as cautious. Maybe there was a little more chaos in me than I realized.

When I finally looked up at the clock, it was after eight. My knees felt like they'd never straighten again.

I tapped together the rejected pages and carried the stack outside. I stacked logs and kindling in the fire pit the way Ben had taught me, crushed some of the paper, and crammed it into the gaps. When the fire burned strong, I fed it the remaining sheets one by one, words and pictures turning brilliant white, then dark.

When the last page was gone, I sat down on one of the rickety plastic chairs and stared into the roaring flames. I wasn't going to think about how the colors reminded me of Kieran's hair. I was going to think about phoenixes. I was going to think about what could be reborn.

"Can I join you?" Ben hovered outside the firelight, two open bottles of lager in one hand, his box of crackers in the other. He held them out, looking shy. "It's not much, but . . ."

"That's great, Aba. I was thirsty."

He handed me a beer and the crackers, then eased himself down. "Oy. We need to get better chairs. L'chaim."

"L'chaim." We tapped bottles, then sipped and crunched. I saw why he liked this combination so much, the salty-sweet crackers with the bite of lager.

"I don't know why I haven't lit a fire out here in so long," he finally said. "There are so many things I haven't done, since he died." After more silence, he said, "I owe you an apology."

My eyes caught his, huge and black in the firelight. "Aba, it wasn't just you."

He put his hand up. "Let me say this. Please."

I heard Nicole in my head and closed my mouth.

"I didn't understand how hard Diane was leaning on you. It's ridiculous. I know something about mental health, but I was blind. I let you down."

"It's fine," I said too fast. Wait. No. Stop. "No, it was really bad."

He sat forward, hands clasped around his beer bottle. "Can you tell me your side?"

I described the start of the late-night visits a year after Max's death, when everyone else had started to move on. The circular conversations that always, always ended in tears. "She's so unhappy, Ben. She needs real help."

"She will see someone. I promise you." He grabbed a stick and poked at the fire. After a moment, he said, "I want you to know that having you here stopped it from being any worse. I think the three of us would have drowned if we'd been on our own that first year, but together we stayed afloat. But just being afloat isn't good enough anymore. Especially not for you. We need to let you live your own life."

I stared into the fire, the beer bottle dangling from one hand.

"I don't know what my own life would look like." I hadn't realized that the truth could feel so heavy.

"You never will if you stay. The world isn't going to come to you."

Kieran's face, twisted and angry and so, so hurt, wouldn't leave me. "What if no one ever loves me again?" I asked in a small voice, feeling lost in the dark woods. "What if I'm alone?"

He took my hand and squeezed it surprisingly hard. "You know what I thought when Max brought you home for that first dinner?"

My mouth turned up. "'She's so young'?"

He snorted. "OK, some of that. You were just nineteen, for God's sake." His voice became earnest. "But I also thought, 'There you are. My daughter.' That's why I asked you to call me Aba so fast. I saw your sweet face, saw you just as you were, and I *knew*."

My sinuses ached and my eyes closed and I was going to cry. Again.

He reached out and patted my cheek, his eyes wet. "I've never thought differently in the last twelve years. You are magical."

Magical. Kieran had said that, too. I'd only let myself see the desire in his eyes, but there had been amazement there, too. Like I was beyond anything he'd ever wished for, ever dreamed.

"The joy and pride I feel when I watch you create good work, and care for your bandit cat, and laugh with Nicole and Kieran? It's boundless, sweetheart. Boundless. And if you ordered pizza every time we visited you, I would still love you with all my heart."

"I love you, too, Aba." I sniffled.

He leaned over to hug me, and I burrowed into his still-broad chest and his familiar papery smell.

"I'm going to move," I said when he let me go.

His head snapped up. "To where? Kieran's?"

I shook my head hard. "No. I messed that up." I put my hand up when his mouth opened. "I'm not ready to talk about it with you."

"Your life is your own, of course." He sighed. "Then the move?"

"I'll rent somewhere with Nicole. Not until January, though." I turned and looked at him. "I'm sorry I'm leaving."

He grabbed my chin lightly. "Don't be absurd. If you need help with anything, absolutely anything, tell me." His grin was Max's, wide and confident. "I mean, I'll hire movers instead of lifting boxes; a spring chicken I am not. But I'll help you as long as I'm breathing. Let me."

I exhaled in relief, and the concrete that had filled my chest since I'd blown everything up with Kieran cracked open.

CHAPTER TWENTY-EIGHT

Kieran

Enforced vacation. That's what Steve had called it when he sent me home yesterday.

"You've been a fucking zombie for the past two weeks," he said. "I don't want to see you until Saturday."

I didn't answer, just grabbed my stuff and went to my locker.

He followed me, asking quietly, "What the fuck happened? You were on fire, and now what?"

"I guess I'm burned out," I said dully. Or Ellie had put me out, and nothing could light me up again.

I still craved her. Her lush curves, her laugh, her wiseass comments. I hated that I craved something so bad for me. *Once an addict, always an addict,* I thought in my worst moments, counting the cracks in my ceiling in the middle of the night. Ellie hadn't been kidding about what a bitch insomnia could be.

On the third day in my pit of cereal boxes and empty soda cans, someone rang my doorbell. Not once or twice, like a normal person would, but constantly.

"Fuck's sake, I'm coming!" The ringing stopped. I yanked on shorts and a T-shirt and opened the door to Jay's back. Her hands were on her hips as she watched the neighbor's cat hunt a fly. She wore the little backpack she used for longer runs.

When she finally turned around, she raised her eyebrows and gestured to her running clothes. The twenty unread text messages on my phone stopped me from slamming the door. I held my index finger up instead and went hunting for my sneakers.

Five minutes later, she led me on a gentle jog south. After days inside, the Mission woke up my senses. I smelled detergent from the laundromat, saw the bright yellows and deep blues in the murals, inhaled the sizzle of carnitas frying at my favorite taqueria. And now I listened to what was happening inside me.

My stomach, complaining about my Cinnamon Toast Crunch diet.

My heart, sore and cracked but still beating.

We were running at the kind of pace where we could talk at the same time, but Jay was still quiet. Too quiet?

Then she *booked it*. I hauled ass behind her, my quads firing and my arms swinging hard as I attacked the hill, which got steeper and steeper when we got closer to Bernal Heights. She was all legs, but I'd spent more time lifting weights, and those muscles pushed me up and up and up, until we sprinted on a dirt trail, dust exploding under us. No work here, no book, no Ellie, just Jay's flying feet and my body screaming.

She tapped the bench at the top of the slope first, and somehow had enough oxygen to do a silent victory dance. I slumped onto it instead, hands on my head and legs sprawled. The view of the Bay and the mountains was epic, but it was hard to appreciate it when my lungs felt scorched.

"Better?" she finally said as she sat down next to me.

Ellie hadn't been on my mind for a whole thirty seconds. "Ish."

"Damn." She passed me a bottle of water from her pack. "So what's the matter?"

"Everything," I said after I'd chugged half of it.

"OK, drama king. Start at the top."

The top and the bottom and the heart of it all was a soft, curvy woman with a brain the size of a galaxy. "I miss her. She didn't love me, she didn't think I was worth trying for, and I still fucking miss her."

"Sounds like you hurt her just as bad, though."

I blinked at her in surprise, and she shrugged. "I'm trying out this whole 'being friends' thing with Nicole. She tells me stuff. Ellie locked herself away, same as you. Stopped taking care of herself, same as you."

No, heart, I wasn't going to care that Ellie was hurt. "She did it first." I kicked a pebble. "Maybe this was how it was going to work out anyway. I wasn't ever going to be what she needed."

Her eyes narrowed. "Since when are you a pessimist?"

"I'm not."

She wagged a finger. "Don't tell me you're a realist. If you were a realist, if you listened to every single fucking thing your parents ever said about what you couldn't do, you'd still be deep-frying shrimp at Coconut Pete's and pickling your brain in vodka. Every day you've had since you got sober has been an act of optimism. You're the sous chef at one of the best restaurants in the country, and my best friend, and a Chaos Muppet who's acting like no one's had a broken heart before in the history of the universe."

"Chaos Muppet?"

"Yup. And Ellie's an Order Muppet. But that's what makes you two work. You lift her off the ground, and she keeps you from flying into the sun."

"But she doesn't want me," I told my knees sadly. "What do you know about what makes things work, anyway? You and Nicole fell apart."

Jay blew out air, like she was breathing through pain. "We didn't fall apart. We needed different things. I was unhappy because I wanted her to do something she couldn't. That's on me, not her. You have to meet people where they are." Her eyes met mine. "Did you?"

My shields instantly went up. "Of course I did. I made that birthday lunch. I stood up to her mother-in-law."

She raised her eyebrows. "Ellie spent her entire life thinking her needs had to come last. That she had to do what everyone else wanted. Then when she did something to make herself happy for once, that made her feel free, everyone got mad at her. What do you think she would do when everybody who mattered to her was angry?"

I thought of Ellie's high voice, the way she'd shaken and gone pale. "Panic." I put my head in my hands. "She panicked, I yelled at her for panicking, she panicked even more, and I walked out on her."

"Yup."

She'd needed me to listen. To stay. Instead I'd made it about me. "I was an asshole."

"Not going to correct you."

One last wave of hurt hit me. "I said I loved her."

"That's not nothing," she said kindly. "But it's not all about you. It's about where she is, too. She has to want to change her life for herself, not just because you want to carry her off on your white horse and live in a love bubble with her forever." She reached over and rubbed my back. "I don't blame you for being mad that she didn't pick you right away. It's easy to be angry. It's hard to talk to her, it's harder to understand, and it's hardest to forgive. But my friend's never been afraid to do the work when he really wanted something."

She reached into her running backpack. "Steve gave me this. Mrs. Hutton dropped it off last night." She held out an ivory envelope, my name a line of curlicues across the front. When I took it, the fancy paper caught on my calluses.

"The golden ticket?" she asked when I finished mouthing the words on the card inside.

"An invitation to tea at her house on Monday at two o'clock." Four days from now.

She wiggled her eyebrows. "That means your own place, if you get this right."

I dropped the boulder of missing Ellie for a second, and asked quietly, "Can you help me with my pitch?"

"Of course. You're my friend. I will always help you." She took out a notebook and a pen from her bag, and I pinched myself hard at the flash of Ellie.

"What do you think is the most important thing about running a restaurant?" she asked.

I thought of the comforting vibe Ellie had given off when she sliced onions and sauteed mushrooms. She was quiet competence, making something delicious not because she was trying to impress anybody, but because she loved food and loved the people she was cooking for, whether it was her brother, or her in-laws, or the invisible people who'd be making her recipes in kitchens across the country. That wasn't to say that creating something new and exciting and exquisite was bad. But I couldn't just make it because I wanted to look smart. I had to care, and not be afraid to show that.

No gimmicks. No tricks.

• • •

Mrs. Hutton's housekeeper didn't blink when she found me on the brick doorstep on Monday at one fifty-nine, which I thought was a good sign. I looked pretty sharp in Mr. Murphy's suit. No one needed to know that I'd had to belt the pants one notch tighter.

"Mrs. Hutton will be ready shortly," the elegant older woman said, her plain black heels tapping on the honeyed wood of the front hall. "Wait in here, please."

The living room, with its huge piano and fancy Turkish rugs, told me the suit had been the right call. The floor-to-ceiling windows had an excellent view of the gray curve of the Bay Bridge and the gold sweep of the Oakland hills. I wandered over to them, and my eyes tracked north. I recognized the spire of the bell tower on the Berkeley campus. Ellie was in her cottage somewhere near there. I rubbed my chest when I thought of her, exhausted and sad, with just Floyd to keep her company.

"Kieran. Thank you for coming."

I turned to see my boss coming through the doorway. "Hello, Mrs. Hutton."

"Anh, please." She shook my hand firmly. "Have a seat. My

apologies for being late." She tugged my sleeve between two pinched fingers. "That's a lovely suit. Where did you get it?"

"A guy named Mr. Murphy in North Beach."

Surprise flashed on her normally stern face. "Goodness, Fergus Murphy sold you a suit?"

"Is he special?" I asked, confused.

"He has a months-long waiting list. You must know someone important."

I did. Or I had, until I'd abandoned her.

Anh's housekeeper came in with a tray and set it on the polished wood coffee table, next to a folded square of white paper.

"Anyway, enough about fashion," Anh said. "Tea?"

The liquid she poured was rich and dark, even with milk in it, and the pattern on the porcelain cups swirled with deep blue, rust, and gold. Ellie would have liked them. She would have liked the whole room, to be honest. It was like her guesthouse, but with a lot more money behind it. The wall of built-in bookcases packed with hardcovers and paperbacks even matched hers.

"Are you a reader?" Anh asked, following my gaze.

"I'm not, sorry."

She smiled. "My husband wasn't either. But he had those shelves built for me. Otherwise, I would have piled my library on the floor." She linked her hands over her knees. "Now, obviously you're here because it's time to expand the Phoenix Group, and I would like you to become the executive chef of our next restaurant."

I held back a sigh of relief. "I'm honored."

"But there are some things we need to discuss first. As you know, each restaurant in the group has a unique perspective and mission. So tell me. What's your vision?"

If she'd asked me nine months ago, I would have spouted buzzwords. Luxury. Theater. Spectacle. Whatever I thought would impress her.

But that was before Ellie had thought I was great the way I was.

"I want to create a warm and welcoming space," I said, mentally going through the points that Jay had helped me outline. "Where our guests will know that for an hour or two, they can leave their worries at the door and have a nice time."

She took a slow sip from her cup. "You sound like you don't want to chase Michelin stars."

"No. I want it to be a neighborhood place."

Her eyebrows shot up. "Like a diner?"

I took a deep breath and contradicted her. "No, but somewhere that doesn't have as high a barrier to entry as Qui. There's always going to be an audience for fine dining. But there are a lot of people who are scared of the price tag and the unwritten rules. I still want those people to have an amazing night. So no tablecloths or dressed-up waiters, but we'd have candles and a really deep wine list. It would be a place where couples would come for a date night. It'd be where friends could meet up when they hadn't seen each other for a long time, where families could celebrate together. A meal would be an event, but not a once-in-a-lifetime one."

"Your priorities have shifted significantly, then," she said, her voice thoughtful. "Perhaps less ambitious?"

Ellie would be *pissed* with that description. "Planning a local institution *is* ambitious," I said firmly. "I think I can take the color and excitement of what we do at Qui and make it more accessible."

She tilted her head for a second, considering, and I held back a sigh of relief when a small smile curled her mouth. "That's very interesting. I wouldn't have thought of it that way." She asked some more logistical questions, and we spent a few minutes discussing neighborhoods, the kind of premises I'd want, how we would link it to the rest of the Phoenix Group.

Then she said, smiling, "Do you want to know how I made my decision?"

She was giving off strong "I know something you don't know" energy. I raised my eyebrows, smiled back, and said, "I think you're going to tell me anyway."

"The dinner at Qui was certainly a point in your favor. Your culinary talent is undeniable. But I wanted to be confident that you could see a long-term project through. Hence why I challenged you to be serious about your book."

I had the book, but I'd lost Ellie. Thinking that made me want to whimper like an abandoned puppy. "Thank you," I managed to say.

"But what heavily tilted the scales in your favor was a letter that arrived in the mail ten days ago. It turned out to be an extremely pleasant surprise."

No one had ever put on a pair of reading glasses so slowly. Or picked up a piece of paper and unfolded it so carefully. When she cleared her throat, I was ready to scream.

"*Dear Mrs. Hutton.* Such beautiful penmanship. An underrated skill these days."

"Uh-huh," I said, not dying inside.

She beamed. "*I imagine dozens of people are fighting to tell you how wonderful Kieran O'Neill is. You may have already decided his future in the Phoenix Group, but I wanted to write to you anyway. I hope you don't find this letter irrelevant.*"

My brain knew other people used that word. My heart sped up like it'd been slogging through a tunnel and suddenly saw a flicker of Ellie in the darkness.

"Are you all right, Kieran?" Anh asked.

"Fine," trying to keep my professional face on. "Please keep going."

"All right. *Kieran doesn't believe in doing things the way they've always been done. He believes in doing them better. Working with him as your executive chef may be different from what you're used to, but I promise that he'll meet, and exceed, your expectations. Just maybe not how you'd think.*"

I could just see her snarky little smile.

"*At first glance, Kieran might appear frivolous or flighty, but he is neither. He takes the things and the people he cares about very, very seriously. He inspires the people around him to be their best selves, too, and to do the right thing, even when it seems impossible.*"

What right thing? I looked up, confused, and Mrs. Hutton raised her eyebrows. "I called Tad Winthrop and he confirmed that Ellie Wasserman resigned from your book and paid back the money she'd received on September tenth."

The day after I'd stormed away from her. I'd heard on a podcast once about a Japanese technique for fixing broken pottery, where the artist would mix gold with glue, binding the cracks together and making them glow.

I wasn't the distraction, Ellie was saying. The book was, and all the burdens that came with it.

"Shall I continue?" Anh said.

"Please," I said, hope filling me with gold from my heart outward.

"*I'm sure you're aware that Kieran is an exceptionally talented chef. But he's also a good man. The best, even. He is kind, generous with his time and energy, loyal, and, above all, he knows that people matter the most and has no trouble saying so.*"

My head landed in my hands. I'd thought I'd loved her quiet and thoughtfulness, but when she'd begged me to wait, to give her more time, I'd punished her for it.

"*If you put your faith in Kieran and trust him with his own restaurant, he will reward you more than you can imagine. Thank you for reading, and apologies again for being so disruptive the last time we met. Yours sincerely, Ellie Wasserman.*"

She put the paper down. "What do you think?"

The words stuck in my throat and my sinuses ached. Just like when Dr. Meyer told me I wasn't a bad person, just wired differently.

She'd quit the book. She'd sacrificed her spotless reputation and her dream of owning her own place, and I knew she'd done it for me.

"It's a truly excellent letter of recommendation," Anh said. She held out the letter to me and smiled wide. "But I think we both know this wasn't just addressed to me."

I barely heard her goodbye, barely noticed walking to the door. It shut behind me, and there I was, standing on a staircase on Telegraph Hill, totally dazed, a life-changing piece of paper in my hand. I pulled my phone out of my pocket, tapped until I was about to call a car to take me to Berkeley.

I closed the app. I couldn't just throw myself at her feet and tell her I still loved her. My feelings didn't change that I'd left her when she'd needed me to help. She'd made sure that my dream would come true. How could I do that for her?

She had so much talent, so much integrity, so much heart, and the world deserved to know about it. I couldn't write in the elegant, flowing way she did. No one could. But I didn't have a problem *saying* what I thought, how I felt, and I was going to New York soon for the prepublicity tour Tobias had booked. There would be video interviews and a live-streamed cooking demonstration for the *Banquet* YouTube channel.

When I talked about Ellie, millions of people would see.

CHAPTER TWENTY-NINE

Kieran

Banquet's thirty-fifth floor offices near the World Trade Center Memorial had a pretty fantastic view. Downtown Manhattan's office towers shone in the October sunshine, and the trees across the water in New Jersey were turning rich shades of orange, yellow, and red.

A short Afro and horn-rimmed glasses floated high above me in the window. "Stunning, right?" Lamar Wilkinson said over my shoulder. "Nothing like New York in the fall. Sure you don't want to move here, Chef? San Fran's parochial as fuck, you know that."

I turned to the *Banquet* host and shook his hand, plastering on the Happy Pirate Leprechaun grin. "Sure, but I like living where I can't get frostbite."

"A real California boy. Maybe they should have called you the Happy Surfer Leprechaun. Though you'd have needed to lose the bandanna."

I laughed with him. I was more than ready to put it in the trash, but Tobias had insisted. He was hanging out at the back of the room, working on something on his phone.

Banquet-branded blue apron on, mic clipped to the top, some instructions from the director, and then we were live on YouTube.

Lamar clapped his hands and grinned. "'What's up, everyone. I'm here with Kieran O'Neill, who's the sous chef at Qui in San Francisco, but you know him better as the Happy Pirate Leprechaun from *Fire on High*. He's got a new book, *Whatever You Want*, coming out in March, and he's here today to give us a sneak pre-view of one of the recipes. Good to have you, Chef."

"Good to be here," I said, smiling big.

"Word on the street is that you're going to be moving on from Qui pretty soon to bigger and better things."

My smile went down to its real size. "Not bigger, actually," I said, keeping a secret in my voice. "I'm actually going to try a whole new challenge."

Curiosity lit in his eyes. "Tell us about it?"

I shook my head. "I can't yet, I'm afraid. But it's not going to be what people expect from me, that's for sure."

The perfect site for my restaurant had suddenly come up: an old diner on Grand Avenue in Oakland, with original redwood paneling and forest-green booths. The awesome farmers' market by Lake Merritt was a short walk away, a super-chill wine shop called OakVine was a few doors down, and next door to them was a family-owned Ethiopian restaurant that'd been serving the community for years.

I hadn't told Ellie that I planned to set up shop close by. I'd save that for after I'd apologized in a big way.

"That sounds dope," Lamar said. "So, what are you demonstrat-ing today?"

I blasted the full force of Happy Pirate Leprechaun at the cam-era. "It's a beautiful citrus salad with duck confit. I know we think of salad as something we *should* eat, but I wanted to create one that felt like a treat, with a great balance of brightness and richness. Blood oranges are my favorite citrus, so I've put them together with radicchio and homemade duck confit, and dressed it all with a sherry-and-blood-orange vinaigrette."

"That sounds really fancy," Lamar said for the invisible audience.

I imagined Ellie next to me, calm and focused, and took a deep breath. "It's not hard at all. I'll show you."

I walked through the same steps I'd shown her. The salt and the oil and the herbs, massaging the seasoning into the legs.

"You're basically taking the duck to the spa," Lamar said as I put the legs in the oil for their long, slow poach.

"Pretty much! Here's what it looks like once you're done." I traded the pan for one that had been cooked earlier, the duck legs now shiny and golden. "And now, we supreme some oranges."

Lamar said, "Those colors are beautiful. Now, I know you did a duck and blood orange hollandaise dish at your Qui pop-up, but what inspired you to turn it into a salad?"

His question sent me back in time, all the way to a farmers' market in late February, and the first time Ellie had dropped her cool, polite mask in front of me. Her round, freckled face soft with pleasure when I'd fed her the slice of fresh blood orange, the gentle awe in her voice as she'd compared fruit to a sunset. How I'd wanted to be by her side when she discovered other simple joys, other sweet things.

"It's not really my recipe," I said, loving how telling the truth about me and Ellie tasted on my tongue, sweet and refreshing at the same time.

Lamar let off a confused laugh. "Hold up. Do you mean you copied it?"

I resisted the urge to throw my arms up like I was on a rollercoaster. "No, no. I mean, the original idea is mine, but my cowriter took my random thoughts and turned them into a whole recipe. She'd lived in France and thought the duck would work in a recipe like a salade lyonnaise."

"Oh, you had a ghostwriter for the book." Lamar turned to the camera. "A lot of chefs do, folks. We're trained as cooks, not writers. Kieran's not unusual at all."

"Not ghostwriter, cowriter," I corrected firmly. "And her name is Ellie Wasserman. *Whatever You Want* wouldn't exist without her."

"Ellie Wasserman? You mean the woman who yelled at you in that old video?" *What the fuck,* his eyes said, totally confused.

"Yes, that's Ellie. She believed we could make the book happen, and she helped me every step of the way."

Lamar's mouth was wide open. Tobias slashed his throat with his hand again and again.

But I still needed to say the most important part. I kept my voice strong and sure as I said, "Her name should be on the cover with mine. But I messed up, and she didn't get the credit she deserved, because I got angry about something else. And I'm so, so sorry about that."

A small smile appeared on Lamar's face. "Is she more than just your cowriter?"

Her letter hadn't asked me for anything, so I'd do the same. "Ellie's hugely talented and should be a lot more famous. She's the one who wrote the Herat cookbook, and the La Estufa book, and she's worked on a lot of other things that you probably have on your shelves without getting much credit."

"Hear that, Ellie Wasserman?" Lamar said to the camera. "Maybe we should get you on the show. You sound pretty special."

With those words, pride bubbled in my chest like the best champagne.

"Cut!" the director called.

"What the hell, man?" Lamar said to me. But he was laughing as he said it.

My grin could have powered the whole city. "Sorry not sorry I took over your whole show."

He slapped my shoulder. "I was getting so bored with these videos. You turning it into a full-on rom-com apology made my day. Does your girl watch these?"

I took a deep breath. "Not really. But I think someone important will tell her to."

"Man, you're bolder than I thought."

I took off the *Banquet* apron. I knew what was coming. The second I started walking toward the kitchen door, Tobias grabbed my arm and yanked me into a quiet corner.

"That was a mistake," he hissed.

"No, it wasn't."

Tobias pulled on his black curls. "You want to stop being the Happy Pirate Leprechaun, and you just handed half the credit to the fucking ghostwriter! What the fuck is wrong with you?"

"Doing that was about the rest of my life, not just the money," I said calmly.

"What else is there besides the money?" he yelled. "Trust me, someday you're not going to be famous anymore, and you'll spend the so-called rest of your life in some sad house somewhere boring, and Ellie Wasserman will be eating a pack of Oreos a day and nagging you to mow the lawn." He shook his head. "You should have kept her invisible."

I breathed away the wash of red his words painted. "OK. That makes it easy."

"What's easy?"

"You're fired." Wow, the endorphin rush from saying that was *amazing*.

Tobias's mouth fell open in disbelief. "Excuse me?"

I grinned. "You heard me. We're done." And now I needed to call the love of my life.

Ellie

"**Y**es, I know, you're dying without me, it's all so awful and wrong," I crooned.

Floyd yowled again as I walked up to the cottage. He still wasn't used to me being out all day. Despite his outrage, I'd been leaving the house more and more. Instead of tucking myself in at my desk, I'd pack up my stuff and find different places to work around Berkeley. Instead of doing yoga on my own, I went to an evening class near campus, making small talk with other people winding down from their days with slow stretches and hard poses. I'd even gone for coffee with one of them, a freelance web designer, and she'd made me weep with laughter as she told me stories about her two sons.

I'd started another notebook, loving the feeling of sketching new ideas across wide-open pages. I didn't have a title for this book yet, but I had an idea: using recipes to travel. Evoking all the places I'd been, and everywhere I wanted to go. Nicole and I would start work in March, visiting my old haunts in Lyon, then working our way south through Provence, into Spain, and all the way around the northern coast until we'd finish in Lisbon.

It would be even more fun to go with Kieran. But I didn't have the right to get in touch with him. He deserved to be happy, and I'd tried to ensure it with the letter to Mrs. Hutton. If his happiness meant letting our lives split apart after the nine months we'd worked and laughed and made love, I had to accept that, and go looking for joy on my own.

But I still followed him on Instagram, like a complete masochist. The publicity department at Alchemy must have told him to post more often in the lead-up to publication, and he was putting up a new story and post every day. He'd toured the farmers' markets and grocery stores in San Francisco and Oakland, talking about ingredients he was excited about and techniques he liked to use to bring out their best flavors and textures.

His haircut had grown out enough that he had to sweep it out of his eyes, and his stubble had become a short beard. Maybe it was a trick of the light that his cheekbones had gone from sharp to gaunt, and maybe the dark patches under his eyes were just shadows. But the part of me that couldn't remember how everything went so wrong wanted to feed him soup and hold his hand. Give him the chance to turn off and just be.

After I'd spent thirty minutes last night looking at his pictures of Manhattan, I'd shoved my phone in my nightstand when I'd left the house today. I told myself I wanted to work without distractions. But I'd bounced from my favorite café to the library and back, hopped up on way too much caffeine, spending less time writing ideas down and more thinking about him wandering around New York.

If I kept doing this, insomnia was going to bite me again. Not because of Diane's visits, though. Over the last few weeks, we'd started seeing each other in daylight, with Ben mediating. Diane hadn't really gotten to know me without Max between us, and now she listened when I told her about my hopes, about my dreams of a cookbook with my name on it, one that shared everything I knew and loved about good food and good company.

Even better? Ben was cooking Shabbos dinner every week. He'd said that he was perfectly capable of roasting a chicken, and he'd borrowed some of my Barefoot Contessa books for sides inspiration. I couldn't leave him in better hands than Ina Garten's.

"Hi, bud." I greeted Floyd as he capered in front of the opening door. "Anything exciting happen while I was out?"

I bent down to scratch his arched back, but his purr sounded weird. Like he was breathing too fast.

Wait, no. My nightstand drawer was buzzing. It was arrhythmic, but constant. An emergency announcement?

But when I unlocked my phone, alerts flooded my screen, texts and emails and Instagram likes galore. Just as I tapped the screen, Nicole's name appeared.

"Why are you calling instead of texting?" I asked.

"Jesus H. Christ, where have you *been*?"

"Wow, inside voice, please. I was out, like you've encouraged me to be for years. Should I be a hermit instead?" I asked sarcastically.

"You went out without your phone, you weirdo?"

"It's a thing I do now. I turned off Wi-Fi on my laptop, too."

"Today of all the freaking days. Check the *Banquet* YouTube," she ordered.

"What's gone viral now?" Even I'd seen the video where someone made Skittles from scratch.

"Seriously, do it. And fast forward to fifteen minutes in."

I hung up and opened the page on my laptop and Kieran's grinning face was front and center. Of course, that's why he was in New York. He'd be inundated with fans now.

Wait a second. "Kieran O'Neill Makes the Best Salad and Reveals His Secret Weapon"?

I followed Nicole's instructions and pressed PLAY, and there he was. The host, Lamar Wilkinson, towered over him, and Kieran was looking up, all earnestness.

"Ellie's hugely talented," Kieran said, "and should be a lot more famous. She's the one who wrote the Herat cookbook, and the La Estufa book, and she's worked on a lot of other things that you probably have on your shelves without getting much credit."

"Hear that, Ellie Wasserman?" Lamar said. "Maybe we should get you on the show. You sound pretty special."

A squeak escaped me. I clapped my hand over my mouth, then called Nicole back. "Jesus H. Christ."

"I know, right? Hashtag QueenEllie is trending on Twitter. You're the woman of the fucking hour."

That would explain the buzzing. I had ten thousand new Instagram followers, and the visitor count on my website had skyrocketed. Most of my new messages were requests for gossip, wanting me to confirm or deny that Kieran and I were together. But some of them were from chefs and editors, wanting to know if I was free for work. An hour later, I was still sorting through the communication explosion when a text appeared. A brand-new voice note from Kieran.

I knew he'd just handed me the credit for the book, so it couldn't be bad news. Could it?

"Hi, Ellie." A blast of Daft Punk. "Jesus. I'm staying at this ridiculous hotel called the Beacon in Williamsburg and their lobby's like a club. One sec." Shuffling, then relative quiet. "So, yeah, it's Kieran. Of course you know it's me, unless you deleted my number. Or blocked it. I wouldn't blame you if you had."

His anxiety practically radiated from the phone.

"I'm so sorry. I was an asshole, and way too impatient with you, and too stupid to realize that if I hurt you, I'd hurt myself a thousand times worse. Because my heart was yours from the second you told me you had faith in me." He scoffed at himself. "Nice one, Kieran, you should have started with that. But I don't want to take anything from you. I just want you to be happy, and help make your dreams come true, the way you make mine. Because you're magical, and so fucking gifted, and I'm going to love you for the rest of my life." He exhaled. "Thank you for the amazing letter. I don't know if you can forgive me for leaving you. If you think you could, but you need time, you should take it. I think you're worth waiting for." A pause. "I'd wait for you forever, love."

I listened to him again, and again, and again.

I could wait for him to come home. Talk everything out, then have a real first date, dinner and a movie, like normal people did.

But it wasn't his turn to take a chance.

After a few clicks and a sizable hit to my bank account, I was out of my chair, out the door, across the backyard.

"All right, all right, don't break it," Ben called when I pounded on the back door. "Did you want to watch *Holiday* with us after all?"

I took a deep breath. "I'm going out of town for a few days, and I need you to look after Floyd."

He leaned against the doorframe. "Of course. When are you leaving?"

"Um, in thirty minutes."

His eyes went into full-on suspicious-parent mode. "And where exactly are you going in thirty minutes' time?"

"New York."

"Is this to find Kieran?"

I couldn't keep my mouth from curling up. "How'd you know?"

He rolled his eyes. "I, too, can set up a Google Alert."

"Yeah, it's for him." Millions of butterflies darted around my stomach at the thought of the literally incredible thing I was about to do.

"That's my girl," Ben said as he slapped my shoulder, with the biggest grin on his face I'd ever seen. "Need a ride?"

CHAPTER THIRTY

Ellie

*B*oy, I really hadn't thought this through.

I wasn't nearly cool enough to be in this Williamsburg hotel lobby, which looked like Instagram had puked all over it. All the teak with brass fixtures, all the terrazzo, all the millennial pink and eccentrically shaped succulents. I was still in the clothes I'd worn yesterday, three thousand miles away. My jeans were so old the inner thighs were borderline obscene, and my navy Berkeley sweatshirt so worn that the drawstrings were shredded. I didn't have a raincoat, and black clouds loomed outside the windows.

But the name of the game hadn't been "Look Nice," or "Check Weather," or even "Think." It had been "Go."

It had been a kind of flow state, the race in Ben's station wagon to San Francisco Airport, the five hours in a metal tube hurtling across the sleeping country. When I got to JFK, the Lyft driver had been happy to hold up the conversation by himself, and I watched sleepy clapboard suburbs give way to renovated factories, Manhattan's skyscrapers dull silver across the East River.

Now the flow had run out, but it was like regretting the leap when I was falling fast. I was already desperate, already sweaty from hours of transport, already with my imperfect heart in my hands.

"Hi. It's Ellie," I shyly told my phone as it recorded my voice note, but a huge yawn distorted my name. "Sorry. It's Ellie. I'm here. Like, downstairs, in the lobby of your hotel in Brooklyn. But you know where your hotel is! God, I never want to take a red-eye flight ever again. Anyway, it would be nice to see you? If you want to hang?" My cringe tightened my hands on my phone. "Yeah. Let me know."

OK, sent.

One minute passed. Two minutes. Five.

The hotel elevators ascended and descended, and businessmen in skinny dark suits and a few early-bird tourists in tight jeans emerged, drifting toward a room at the far end of the lobby full of the sound of china and silverware and tired conversation. The hazelnutty scent of dark roast mixed with a rich, savory smell like someone was making omelets to order. My stomach gurgled at the thought of spinach and mushrooms and cheese, but exhaustion was winning out over hunger.

He still hadn't come down.

What was I doing? I hadn't even booked a room anywhere. Maybe if I pulled out my laptop and pretended to work, they'd let me take a nap sitting up, and then I could work out what to do.

I'd just rest my head in my hands for a minute. I closed my eyes and the world quieted to just the murmur of the clerks at the front desk and the low thrum of house music.

Then a door slammed, and rubber squeaked against marble.

"Ellie," Kieran said, skidding to a stop in front of me. His hair was slick and auburn with water, his green eyes spring-bright.

He knelt like the champion he was, and I could smell the clean white soap and pine on his skin. Callused fingertips brushed across my cheekbone. "God, it's good to touch you," he whispered. "I thought I'd never get to do it again."

I resisted the urge to close my eyes as yearning opened up inside me. I wanted so much more touch, so much more comfort. I kept my voice light as I said, "Someone told me once I should stop thinking and do something. So here I am."

"They sound really smart." His eyes found my mouth. "Can I kiss you?"

He asked like he thought he was dreaming, and all at once I knew in my heart that he would never, ever take from me without asking, and not without giving all of himself back. "Please," I begged, tugging him to me.

I was so tired, I must have dreamed how soft his mouth was on mine. The way I sighed when I opened my mouth to let him in. How his heart beat fast and strong under my palm.

No. He was real. *We* were real.

When we finally broke apart, he touched his forehead to mine. "Thank you."

"For what?"

"For coming for me, for believing in me." He smiled. "But maybe next time, don't send a life-changing voice note when I'm in the shower? I almost broke my neck jumping down the emergency stairs."

"Why didn't you take the elevator like a normal person?" I teased, tears in my voice.

My Puck grinned at me. "Since when have we ever been normal?"

He was *here*. I hadn't ruined everything. A sob escaped me. "I'm sorry. I love you with all my heart, and I should have trusted you, and I was a coward, and I'm so, so sorry."

He kissed the tears trailing down my cheeks. "Love," he said, voice cracking. "That letter you wrote, that was brave. You being here is brave. I'm sorry I made you sad."

"No, I'm happy. I'm crying because I'm so happy to see you." I scrubbed my face. "Also because I haven't slept in twenty-four hours."

He rubbed my arms gently. "Come upstairs. Let me take care of you."

A flicker of caution in my chest. "We need to talk."

"First you'll sleep, then we'll talk." He tugged me up and grabbed my suitcase with his other hand, and all of a sudden, it was like I had permission to be totally exhausted.

"Hey, Kieran!"

A skinny, smiley dude in a fluorescent pink T-shirt strode over to us from the elevator, a tiny woman with platinum-blond hair trailing him. "Hey, man, I'm a huge fan. Can I get a selfie?"

Did Kieran just glare at him? "Thanks, but I'm kind of busy here, man."

"It's OK," I yawned. "Take a picture with him."

"No, Ellie, you need to rest."

The girlfriend tugged on the too-loud man's arm. "Oh my God, that's *Ellie Wasserman*. The woman from the Qui video. And the one he was talking about on *Banquet*."

I winced and only just resisted the urge to bury my face in Kieran's neck. The last thing I wanted was to be papped while looking like what Floyd dragged in.

She stepped forward eagerly. "I love all the books you've worked on! How did you get such a cool job? Are you going to write your own book someday?"

I opened my mouth to demur, but then I looked up at Kieran. It wasn't just love that shone in his eyes. It was pride. "Thank you," I managed. "I appreciate you saying that. I really hope so." I took a deep breath. "You can follow me on Instagram and I'll keep you posted."

She grinned. "Wicked. We're going to go eat breakfast now. It was nice to meet you."

She dragged her protesting boyfriend away, the elevator dinged, and a giggle escaped me at Kieran's "Thank fuck for smart, self-aware women. Get in."

"I'm not interrupting anything, am I? By being here?" I asked once the doors closed. "Tobias won't be happy if you're distracted."

"Tobias doesn't represent me anymore," he said casually as he watched the elevator numbers tick up.

"Really?" I asked just as casually.

"Yup."

"Why not?"

He turned to me, steadfast and strong. "Because he thought

you should be invisible. And there are thousands of agents, but there's only one Ellie Wasserman."

He chose me. What a sweet rush those words gave me.

The doors opened, and I trailed him down an endless gray hallway lined with black-and-white photographs of industrial Brooklyn. He swiped a card in one of the black doors and opened it. "It's not big, sorry."

"Bed," I said, looking at the king-sized tumble of white sheets and comforter in the middle of the room. I scrubbed my eyes. "No, shower, then bed."

"The important stuff." He nudged me into the bathroom, then knelt down on the black-and-white tiles and unlaced my sneakers.

"This is pretty sexy, you undressing me."

He shook his head, smiling as he stood. "I'm helping you undress because you can barely keep your eyes open. Arms up." He tugged off my clothing piece by piece and tossed it out the bathroom door, softly kissing the skin he revealed.

"I love you so much, Kieran," I whispered.

"I love you, too, Ellie. That means my job is making sure you have everything you want, starting with this." He turned me around and pushed me into the huge, glass-walled shower.

Gallons of hot water and dreamless hours of sleep later, I blinked awake. Rain tapped against the window, and bars of low gray light streaked across the bed and Kieran's chest where he sat in the armchair in the corner. I held perfectly still and just looked at him. His navy hoodie and olive-green T-shirt looked soft and welcoming, and new gray jeans fitted his legs just so. The Chucks were brand-new, too, and he'd traded black for a bright blue that made me think of jay feathers. He watched something on his phone while he rolled a stress ball back and forth along his thigh.

"Hey," I finally said.

He slowly pulled out his earbuds, put his things aside, and came to the foot of the bed. "Hey, love. Sleep well?"

"Yeah." I sat up a little. "Why are you smiling at me like I'm brand-new?"

"You almost always beat me out of bed in the mornings, before. I didn't get to see you soft and dreamy all that often."

What I craved hit me all at once: his warm skin against mine, his open-mouthed kiss on my shoulder, his hands giving tenderness and pleasure, as much of both as I wanted.

"Come here, honey," I said.

God, I loved his huge grin. "I missed being called that." He crawled up the bed, not even taking his shoes off. His kiss was full of sweet, hot promise, his beard rubbed like fur against my cheeks, and the sweatshirt was just as soft as it looked under my fingertips. I traced his shoulders, then tangled my fingers in the silk of his hair.

I nipped his earlobe lightly and he shivered. "Come under the covers," I coaxed.

The tip of his finger trailed along the edge of the sheet, and I shrugged to let it slide down.

"So tempting," he said. "But if I keep touching you, we won't talk." With one last peck, he sprawled out next to me on his stomach, resting his head on his arms. "I want you to go first."

"OK." I sat up and tucked the sheet around me. "My parents were deeply selfish, and I learned fast that I had to take care of myself and of Hank, especially Hank, because he was so much younger. I got really good at doing what I had to, instead of what I wanted. And then I met Max, who knew exactly what *he* wanted, so I didn't have to think at all."

I turned to him, a tear slipping down my cheek. "I thought for so long that wanting things for myself was wrong. I thought what I had with you was a guilty pleasure." I shook my head. "But it wasn't. I'd been starving myself to death, and you brought me back to life. You fed me, you nourished me, and I hurt you."

He reached for my hand. "I hurt you right back, love. I should have told you I'd stay, that we'd figure things out somehow, instead of losing my shit and leaving. I'm sorry I said all those horrible things."

I reached out and stroked his hair. "Thank you. But you helped me see that I needed to stop giving myself away without wanting anything back. That letting you love me"—I shook my head hard—"no, that *enjoying* you wasn't selfish. Because you are a gift, Kieran."

He wiggled his eyebrows. "Oh yeah, I'm a gift. Santa thinks you've been a very good girl this year, ack!"

"And you say I'm such a smartass," I taunted as my tickling fingers reached for him.

He lunged for me, and after some token resistance, I let him pin me under his lean, strong body. His wicked grin became something softer, sweeter, and he rubbed his nose on mine and asked, "So what changed?"

I told him about Nicole, and the trip we'd planned, and the conversation with Ben.

"I knew I liked Ben," Kieran said. "He's scary, but I like him."

"Scary? He's a big teddy bear."

Kieran snorted. "I agree with the 'bear' part." His voice lowered. "What do you want to do? Not, like, now. But the future?"

I ran my thumb over his jaw. "I want to be your lover and your partner. I want to support you when you open your own restaurant."

He smiled warmly. "I'd love that. I'm so excited to show you the plans for the new place, and I want to hear every little thing you think about it. But what about *you*, Ellie?"

I loved him for how he pushed me. "I want you by my side when I'm writing my own books." I took a deep breath. "I want to pick out flowers for us every week, and go on big adventures, and cook whatever we want when we want it. I want us to be free, together."

"Deal." He kissed me, and it tasted clean and fresh, a new beginning. "Now, can we make love, please? I was Ellie-less for weeks and weeks and it almost killed me." His voice was playful, and I couldn't wait to live my life with so much unfettered joy.

"Please," I whispered between kisses. "Please love me." It felt incredible to ask for something so precious and be certain that I'd get it.

He smiled. "Always."

But instead of jumping me the way I thought he would, he went slow. So exquisitely slow. When he kissed me, he memorized every millimeter of my lips, finding all the sweet spots that made me sigh. After a week he moved to my neck, lips and tongue and teeth conspiring to drive me crazy. After a month he got to my breasts, and now I was the fidgety one, my hips rocking and my feet pointing and flexing.

"How do you have any blood left in your brain?" I finally gasped.

After one more long suck, he stretched up and flicked my nose lightly. "How do I turn the smartass off?"

"Orgasms?" I suggested.

"Well, duh. I'm not done playing, though." But he reached down and stroked me a little, and his groan when he found how wet I was said that playtime might be over soon.

Finally, he said, "Lie flat for me?"

But instead of grabbing a condom, he moved off the mattress and knelt on the carpet. When he tugged my hips down the bed, I pushed up on my elbows and said, "Wait a sec."

He sat back on his heels. "Seriously, why won't you let me go down on you?"

His bluntness needed frankness back. "You won't like it. You'll need to go really slow and gentle for a really long time, and you'll get bored and frustrated."

His eyes narrowed. "You have no idea how I'll get." He grabbed my ankles and placed my feet so that my knees were bent, my heels right on the edge of the mattress. "This is my number one fantasy, your legs spread wide just for me." The way he looked at me there was almost feral. "You're soft, and pink, and pretty, and I want to eat you up."

I flushed all over. We'd talked dirty to each other before, but this was a whole other level. "Thanks, but are you sure?"

"Ellie, I want to lick you for hours. Aliens could land on top of the Empire State Building and I'd stay between your thighs. Now lie back."

He kissed his way down, wet and open-mouthed. And then he settled in between my legs, testing me with soft kisses and little licks until I couldn't stop moaning. It was too much and not enough, and I felt like I was going to die of the contrast. "Fuck me."

"Nope."

"*Kieran.*"

"*Ellie,*" he whined back.

He sucked right *there,* and I arched up. "Why *not*? Don't you want to feel good?"

"I feel fucking awesome. You're my queen, and I love being on my knees for you."

He went back to work, and my fingers scrambled for some kind of purchase on the sheets as he ratcheted my need higher and higher. He reached up with one hand and twined his fingers with mine, tugged until my hand was in his hair. The other touched me lightly, and when I raised my hips in invitation, he pushed a finger inside me and curled it, adding a bass note to the pleasure as he stroked in exactly the right place. But it was too soft. "Please, I want . . ."

His eyes flashed green fire. "What do you want? I'll give it to you."

I took a deep breath. "More. And harder."

"*Yes,* my gorgeous, sexy wild thing," he growled.

Then I gave myself up to his thrusting fingers, to his hungry groans, and finally, *finally,* my orgasm crashed through me. He kept his mouth and fingers there, drawing out the sensation with gentle strokes until I tugged him up. "Kieran, Kieran, Kieran," I sighed, boneless and sated.

"Yup, that's my name," he said as he sprawled next to me.

I grinned at him, dopey with endorphins. "I guess you deserve to go outside and beat your chest like Tarzan."

He licked his lips. "You'd be smug too, if the woman you love kept saying your name like you're a legendary sex god. But bare-chested? Fuck that, I'd be an icicle. Or a mancicle."

What could I do with my goofball but kiss him? His mouth was gentle on mine, but when I ran my hands up his back, tension radiated from every muscle. "What about you?"

"What about me?"

"Tell me how to make you feel this good." I rubbed between his legs, and he moaned. "I could use my hands. Or my mouth."

A combination of a hiss and a rumble filled the air.

He sat up. "You're hungry."

"Hungry for you. How are you still wearing all your clothes?" But my stomach protested again.

"I need to feed you before you devour me." A tap on the door. "That's my cue." He pulled the sheets up and kissed me again, then went around the corner. I heard a tap running while he washed his hands, then the door opening and closing.

I waited for a room service cart to roll in, but he reappeared carrying a tray of coffee and orange juice, and a big paper bag.

"What do you have there?"

"It's New York. You can get anything delivered. Close your eyes." Some rustling, then, "OK, you can look."

He'd decanted coffee into mugs and poured juice into glasses. But the centerpiece was a pile of croissants, dark and crisp and so buttery I could smell them.

"Are those from Bedford Street Bakery?"

"Yeah. Best in the country, someone told me once," he said lightly.

I soaked in the sweetness of being genuinely cared for. "You remembered."

His smile could drive the rain away. "You're the love of my life. Of course I remembered."

Before I could respond to those beautiful words, my stomach gurgled. "Give it."

"Oh yeah, I love it when you tell me what you want," he said as he handed me a plate.

After I'd polished off one pastry and was halfway through a second, he asked, "Happy pastry?"

The laugh bubbled up around my mouthful of blackberry jam and vanilla custard. I swallowed and said, "Understatement. Ecstatic pastry. Delighted pastry. I-love-you pastry."

He cracked up. "Wow, strong words. All I had to do was bring you the finest croissants in the land."

I put my plate on the nightstand and crawled to him. "Please don't think you have to buy me fancy pastry all the time so I'll stay in love with you."

"What do I have to do?" He set his plate aside. "Spoil Floyd rotten? Make you shrimp for dinner every day?"

"Be yourself," I said.

His wolfish grin was gorgeous, and when I kissed him, his joy was buttery sweet on my tongue.

CHAPTER THIRTY-ONE

Three Years Later

Kieran

*T*he December sunlight flashed off Lake Merritt like fistfuls of glitter. I still had to dodge a few cars on my bike, but most of my ride to work followed the path beside the lake. I said good morning in my head to the joggers with strollers, the people chilling on the benches, the birds pecking in the grass.

It hadn't taken much to convince Ellie to move to Oakland once we got back from New York, but after three years here, we both loved it more and more. We'd found an apartment to buy on the east side of the lake, with room for a big wooden table for making and eating big dinners, and plenty of sun for Floyd to bathe in. I'd used a chunk of my prize money from *Fire on High* for a wall of custom bookcases, much to my girlfriend's delight. Sexy, sexy delight.

We weren't a perfect match. I'd occasionally forget to do boring but necessary stuff like emptying the dishwasher or buying litter for Floyd, and she'd have to take a deep breath. And she'd never stop trying to plan everything down to the last detail, unless I reminded her that doing stuff on the fly was fun, too. But we'd learned to give each other space to be ourselves, my chaos and her order weaving in and out instead of clashing.

She was still more of a morning person than I was. Sometimes I got woken up by the click of our front door when she headed out to write, other times by soft kisses when she decided she'd rather start the day with slow, sleepy love, like this morning.

It had been so tempting to ask her to marry me when we were catching our breath. She'd nestled into my chest and I'd played with her silky curls, drawing them out and letting them spring back. I'd daydreamed about promising my forever to her in front of all our friends, throwing a massive party celebrating everything I loved about us together. But if I'd learned anything from being with Ellie, it was to trust I'd know when the time was right.

It didn't stop me from looking in jewelry store windows, though. I'd seen a stunning emerald ring two weeks ago and it'd taken everything I'd had to walk by.

I triple-locked my bike in front of Floyd's. I'd insisted on having both her books in the front window of my restaurant—the one we'd written together, reprinted with her name next to mine, and the one she'd done on her own, *Nourish*, that had come out last month. Priya, Ellie's editor, had suggested we write another book based on the weekly menus I created for the restaurant. I was excited to watch Ellie work, her forehead creased with concentration, biting her lip as she thought about how to tell someone to knead brioche dough or to describe how tangerine curd tasted.

I loved arguing with her about those things, too. Three years later, it was still quality foreplay.

But I didn't hear her fingers on her laptop keyboard or see her blond curly head over the back of her favorite corner booth, which Jay had marked with a little plaque that said ELLIE'S OFFICE.

The dining room was empty, and the only sound was the squeak of my Converse on the oak floors.

"Jay?" I called. She should have been here to meet me, with her to-do list and her spreadsheets. She'd happily left Qui behind to manage Floyd's. I called up my texts, but she hadn't said anything about a day off. Maybe her last date with her new woman had been so good that she was running late?

"Hello? Where *is* everyone?"

"Hi, honey." My love pushed open the kitchen door and walked up to me straight-backed and strong, with a smile playing on the lips I loved to kiss. "They'll all be here in a second. Things are running a little late."

I trailed my hands up her bare arms as I kissed her hello. She looked like spring had come early in her poppy-printed dress. "Lunch service starts in two hours, and no one's prepping? As talented as you are, I can't open a restaurant just with you and your lousy knife skills."

She grinned. "It'll be OK, I promise. I have a present for you."

I bounced on my toes. "An early birthday present? I'm already excited."

She reached into the pocket of her dress and pulled out a flash of metal.

My mouth opened, then shut. I'd gotten better about letting Ellie take her time, but that looked a hell of a lot like a ring.

"I love you, Kieran," she said. "You're an amazing partner, and we've built a great life together. I want to marry you. Do you want to marry me?"

A wave of happiness cascaded over me, and I wanted to get down on my knees even though she was the one who'd proposed. "Yes. Yes times a billion." The little rectangle of sapphire embedded in the band caught the light. "I like the blue."

"I thought you would. You've told me how beautiful my eyes are so many times I can't count. But look on the inside."

When I took the ring from her and tilted it, I saw an engraved *E* and *K* with something round in the middle. Not a heart or a plus sign, but a tiny circle with two leaves on top. "Jesus, is that an orange?"

"I thought it was right for us." She blushed. "Is that too weird?"

"No, love, it's perfect. Put it on me."

This was the reverse of how I'd thought this would play out, but it felt so right to have her take my hand and slide the ring on. I'd been so lost, and she'd found me.

We'd found each other.

I held my hand out. "I love it so much, baby. Does this mean I can buy you a ring, too?"

"If you want," she said, a small sweet tease in her voice.

"I definitely want. But you need to come with me to pick it out. I'll buy you something huge and ridiculously shiny if you don't."

She twined her arms around my neck, smiling. "Oh, all right, if only to prevent you buying something as big as a Jolly Rancher."

"Mmm, Jolly Ranchers. It's been years since I've had one of those. Fake watermelon is the best."

She grinned up at me. "How about you forget about them and get the other kind of sugar?"

"What other kind?" Then my fiancée kissed me.

Ellie

"*I* love you, wild thing," Kieran said when I let him go.

"I love you, too." My sweet, big-hearted, loyal Puck, who I'd thought would ruin my life for fun but actually made it infinitely better. Every day now held a lot more laughter, a lot more joy, a lot more delicious food that I didn't have to make myself. Sure, we disagreed and debated and sometimes threw up our hands at each other's stubbornness, but I knew that he'd never walk away if I argued back, and I'd always be on his side, even if he made me slap my forehead sometimes. Every time we worked things out, we added another brick to our foundations, and marrying him would make what we'd built even stronger.

I put my fingers to my mouth and whistled, and a cheer went up from behind the kitchen door. All of the chefs came out, then Jay and her deputy, Isaac, then Diane and Ben, Nicole, and Hank. Even Anh and Steve were here.

"Everyone was hiding?" Kieran said, astonished. "How were you all so quiet?"

Jay grinned. "Ellie threatened us. Your fianceé is a scary, scary woman."

"I know," Kieran said with a huge, proud smile. "Isn't it *great*?"

Anh Hutton elbowed her way to the front and pulled us both down to kiss our cheeks. "Congratulations, both of you. My youngest executive chef getting engaged to the woman helping me write my memoir, what a treat. Now," she said, smoothing her pale-pink Chanel suit, "you must tell me where you'll register so I can get you the best present."

"Register?" we both squeaked.

"And of course you'll have the wedding at one of the restaurants. Steve?"

"Yes, Anh?" he said, ambling up next to her.

She tapped her chin with a neatly manicured finger. "These two should get married in the dining room at Qui. It'll be lovely to have a big celebration on a Monday night."

He raised his eyebrows at us. "A return to the scene of the crime. I like it."

"Thank you, Anh. We'll let you know," I said quickly and graciously.

"Are you cool with her straight-up planning our wedding?" Kieran whispered.

I watched her introduce herself to Ben and Diane, who nodded with dazed smiles. "You know what? I am. I think she'll terrify everyone into making it amazing."

Jay pulled Kieran away so that he could accept congratulations from all the Floyd's people, and Diane came up and hugged me tight. "It gives me such naches, this place. To see you so successful in this restaurant, with a good man who adores you."

I smiled at her. Her color was so much better now that she'd found the right meds for her depression and was genuinely enjoying food and life again. "Well, I adore him, so it all works out."

Despite what she'd said, Floyd's was Kieran's restaurant. He and Anh had asked if I wanted to be involved more closely, but other than making the occasional menu suggestion and befriending the regulars, I let Kieran take the lead. My writing and editing work kept me plenty busy these days. We'd be working together again anyway, if Priya liked our proposal for a Floyd's book.

I smiled as I looked around the lit-up restaurant. We'd made our own family here, people who loved us and whom we loved back.

"Now, is there any chance that I might get a grandchild to spoil?" Ben asked from behind Diane.

"Ben!" Diane smacked his arm.

He put his hands up. "No pressure, Ellie. Honestly."

"I don't know, Aba," I said, giving him honesty in return. "We're going to wait and see." I wanted to savor every day I had with Kieran, not plan the time away. When we decided to try, it would be because I wanted to have a baby with him, not because I had to make up for my childhood.

But I'd caught my new fiancé making heart eyes when Manny brought his baby daughter in to meet everyone, so maybe we wouldn't wait that long.

"Future wife!" Kieran called. "Can I get some more of that sugar?"

He was across the room, hand outstretched.

"Sugar?" Jay said. "Are we low? You need to get after the supplier . . ."

"Not that kind of sugar!" Steve said, and laughter filled every corner of this warm, light-filled place.

"Go get him, Ellie," Ben said. "It's all waiting for you."

I didn't hesitate.

ACKNOWLEDGMENTS

A huge amount of time and effort went into the making of *The Slowest Burn*, and I am beyond privileged to have been able to give them. I support organizations like 826 Valencia in the US and Arts Emergency in the UK because everyone should have the opportunity to make art and get paid for it, no matter their background or circumstances.

Thank you to all the cookbook ghostwriters who have talked openly about their work and planted the seed of the idea that became this book. Thank you as well to Ed Smith, whose excellent cookbook *Crave* was the inspiration for *Whatever You Want*.

Heather Jackson—your Saturday morning email telling me how much you loved Ellie and Kieran changed my life. Thank you so much for your warmth, your sage advice, and your ferocious advocacy for my work. Every author should have a mama bear for their agent.

Alex Sehulster—I knew we would be a good team when we both said how much we loved *The Thin Man*, but your editing took this book into another league. Thank you for bringing me on board at St. Martin's Griffin. Here's hoping we get to line up some cocktails soon!

Thank you as well to the rest of the *Slowest Burn* team at Griffin: Cassidy Graham for your calm steering and responsiveness; Ennis Bashe for a thought-provoking sensitivity read; Angela Gibson for excellent copyediting and Bay Area knowledge; Olga Grlic and Guy Shield for designing and illustrating the gloriously romantic sunset cover; Layla Yuro and everyone else in production; Anne Marie

Tallberg, Marissa Sangiacomo, Brant Janeway, and Kejana Ayala in marketing; and Rebecca Lang in publicity.

Heather Lazare—joining you at the Northern California Writers' Retreat in March 2020 gave me the space and time to take myself seriously as a writer, and your developmental edit transformed Ellie, Kieran, and their love story for the better. Thank you for pushing me to hone my craft.

Katie Greenstreet—thank you for giving me the nudge I needed to switch projects midstream and write this book. Your authors are lucky to have you as their agent.

The 2024 Debut Slack group, particularly the #romance channel—thank you so much for the advice, the commiserations, and the screaming laughter. I'll never think about Chekhov's gun the same way again.

The Ruby—thank you for being such a warm and welcoming community of creators. I am so glad I got to be one of your number.

Robyn Douglas and Rebekah McFarland—my champion beta readers! Thank you for taking the time to read early drafts and cheer me on.

Lucy Hodgman—my brilliant cousin and a thoughtful, considerate editor, thank you for reading the whole manuscript one last time and reassuring me that Kieran rang true to you.

John Stratford—my bad influence and kindred spirit, thank you for driving around San Francisco on your day off to check a vital point of geography when I couldn't do it from six thousand miles away.

Jess Cornwell—thank you for sharing all your writing and publishing knowledge, and for your generous encouragement of my first forays into fiction. I'm so glad our shared tastes in movies and bookstores reunited us after years apart.

Julie Coryell—your yelps of joy when I described Ellie and Kieran to you were a huge boost to my confidence early on. Thank you so much for sharing your enthusiasm and your obsession with all things bookish.

All the friends who called, wrote, and hung out in person during the long pandemic winter of 2020–2021, particularly Ellen Adams, Gwyn Brookes, Felicity Cloake, Kay Collier, Neil Griffiths, Mina Holland, Maddie Ignon, Jazzi Junge, Nupoor Kulkarni, Jordan Meyers, Elyse Oates, Emily Ortmans, Jahnavi Pendharkar, Betsy and John Peretti, Rachel Roddy, Nicola Swift, and Kate Young—I don't think I would have been able to get through the first draft without you keeping my spirits up, so thank you!

Kate Franz and Miranda York—writing the best friendships in this book was easy because I have you two in my life. I am so grateful for more than a decade of late nights talking, all the laughter and just-us vacations and celebrations with gin and champagne, and I'm looking forward to all the decades to come.

Thank you to my amazing family, biological and logical, immediate and extended, for your unstinting love and support. I'd especially like to thank my mom and dad, Joan and Park Chamberlain, and my godfathers Steven Botterill, Craig Davidson, and Marc Rosaaen. (Craig and Steven, I miss you both every single day.)

And most of all, thank you to my husband, Tom Curtis, my best beloved and the only one for me, for sharing your kind heart, your endlessly curious brain, and most of all, your gentle, steadfast soul. I love you AND cake.

ABOUT THE AUTHOR

Andria Lo

Sarah Chamberlain is a writer, editor, and cookbook translator whose articles have appeared in *Vice*, *The Guardian*, and *Food52*. When she's not reading and writing romance novels, she enjoys making cozy dinners for her friends, watching classic movies with witty repartee, and picking up ridiculously heavy things as an amateur competitive powerlifter. Originally from the San Francisco Bay Area, she lives in London.